Zaremba
or
Love and the Rule of Law

Michelle Granas

1

'Then, escorted by five CBA agents, with the siren going, they took me like a mafia boss to Poznań. There I was taken before a court which refused me the right of defense…' – innocent victim of the Anti-Corruption Bureau (CBA)

'But what is happening in Poland is not an exclusively Polish phenomenon. It affects all of post-communist Europe, and the classic example here is Russia…Putin has successfully produced that model of transformation that leads from communism through liberty, disorder and chaos to authoritarian solutions.' – Adam Michnik, Solidarity activist, founder of Gazeta Wyborcza

Sometimes Cordelia wished that she could keep her eyes tight closed for the entire journey. And yet, as her muscles tensed for the thousandth time, she knew it was impossible.

"That truck ahead!"

Cordelia's father didn't turn his head back toward the road; his mind was pursuing some Shakespearian dream out beyond the rows of autumnal lindens and the rolling meadows of the Polish countryside.

"Ah, Cordelia," he said expansively, in his deep, modulated voice, his unidentifiable accent, "the sun is going down and 'kissing with golden face the meadows green.'"

"Yes, but that truck! That truck ahead!" Cordelia's voice rose to a modified shriek.

"Hmm, what? Oh."

Their car, coming up fast, veered a little to the left, swept nearly under the truck's high bumper, rushed headlong between the truck and an oncoming car, and wallowed back into a rut in its own lane.

Cordelia let out her breath and then bit back whatever words she might have uttered. She had known how it would be after all, and there wasn't the tiniest point in saying anything; she would never change him. He was driving now with perfect unconcern, wedged in his seat, the hand on the steering wheel resting on his expanded waistline. His eyes were on the road, but she knew his mind was elsewhere, as he soon made clear, making no effort to avoid the potholes, nor obviously bothered by the resultant jolt.

"It was nice to see Bronka again."

"Yes," said Cordelia.

They had driven two hours from Warsaw to visit an aged relative. Cordelia's father, with that inability to suit his speech to the occasion that so distinguished him, had talked of Herbert's symbolism, folk threnody, and editorial wrangles, and Cousin Bronka had talked of the war, and politics, her long-dead husband and her thyroid problems. At no point during a day which had seen successive courses of tea and cake and soup and sauerkraut had the two conversations ever truly merged into one. Cordelia's task had been to listen in two directions at once and murmur an appropriate response in the appropriate direction. Only once had she grown confused and said to her father "how sad" in response to his "I've got an article on the subject coming out next month." Thereafter they had all talked about food.

"Too bad Antek didn't come. He'd have liked it so much."

4

Cordelia's brother Anthony was reclusive, rather eccentric, and occasionally very perceptive. Cordelia knew that there was nothing he would have liked less than today's outing. But all she said, softly, was "That car. That car ahead is slowing."

They approached it fast, but the oncoming traffic reduced them to a crawl behind its bumper; it seemed to be deciding whether to take a dirt road to the right, but at the last moment it continued straight. Cordelia's father braked sharply and swung the car off the highway and down a bumpy track into a woods.

"Wha-where?" said Cordelia, startled.

"I think I know this road. It's a short cut. It goes through the trees here and meets up with the highway again. We miss all that construction ahead."

"Oh. Well…but it's very muddy." There had been a heavy rainfall the day before, filling depressions with brown water and turning places where the clay showed through the gravel into glue. The station wagon was sliding from side to side in the rutted track. Cordelia's father kept his foot down nonchalantly on the gas pedal and they bounced along, the highway receding into the distance behind them, shut off by overhanging branches and thick-growing underbrush. Occasionally they would pass an opening, there would be a glimpse of green or tawny fields, and then they would disappear back into their own world, where there was no perspective ahead and the only sounds were the splash of water as the tires slid into puddles and the slight metallic whang of twigs whipping the car as it passed.

"We're cutting loads of time off our journey."

Cordelia held her breath as the car slid into a deep rut and the wheels spun as they climbed out the other side. Another hole tossed her nearly up to the ceiling, only to be jerked back by her seat belt. "If we don't get stuck," she murmured nervously, "It seems like a long way."

"Get stuck? Get stuck? Why would we get stuck? The problem with you, Cordelia, is that you have no faith, no sense of adventure." He began to sing the fairy's speech from Midsummer Night's Dream:

'Over hill, over dale
Over park, over pale
Thorough flood…'

The car lurched downwards and muddy spray rose and fell in a wall. Cordelia said nothing, and her father, irritated by her silence, continued his "thorough flood" hum for a while, and then proceeded to direct attack. "Why do you worry so much? The surface is perfectly good. Besides, this car has four-wheel-drive."

I doubt it, thought Cordelia, and if it does you don't know what that is or what its limitations are. But she said nothing, and only raised her good arm to her hair and began to twist a strand, as she did when she was worried.

"I could stop right in the middle of one of these puddles and nothing would happen."

"No, no, no – please don't!" But it was too late.

"See," he said, bringing the car to a stop at the bottom of a pothole, and turning off the engine. The world around them became very still for a moment. "I can now continue again, no problem."

He turned the key, the engine caught, he stepped on the gas, the car moved forward a few inches. "There, see," he exclaimed triumphantly. Then the wheels began to spin and slide. He stamped on the gas – "oh, oh" – and they spun more. The car wasn't moving. "*Cholera!*" he shouted as the engine roared uselessly. Mud splattered in all directions, slashing across the windshield and side windows. The car slid sideways and back and dug itself with an angry whine into a hole. A few more tries, a few more angry curses, and Cordelia's father took his foot off the gas and extinguished the engine. There was silence as the car rocked a little on its springs and subsided into immobility. They were well and truly stuck.

Cordelia's father had exuberance for the smooth parts of life, but no capacity for seeing consequences, and no ability to deal with them when they arrived. He also had a multilingual catalogue of expletives for all occasions, classified according to language and the degree of his perceived guilt. Those in Polish indicated sincere regret. "*Boże, boże kochany!* What have I done? What an idiot I am. God's wounds, *o matko, matko.*"

"*O boże*, what do we do now?" He looked to Cordelia for guidance.

Cordelia swiveled in her seat to look behind them, but could see nothing, only a short stretch of the one lane track and then brushwood closed out the background. The highway, she guessed, was at least several kilometers behind. No one was likely to come along to help them. They had no cell phones. Her father, retired professor and distinguished man of letters, could never remember how to use one, and she never had anyone to call.

She fumbled awkwardly for her crutch. "When we passed those fields a ways back, I think I saw a house on the far side. I'll go there and ask if I can call for a tow truck. I'm afraid you'll have to wait quite a while."

"*Cholera jasna,*" her father swore with a loud sigh, but they both knew there was no question that he would go instead. He had a bad heart.

Cordelia pushed open the car door and stared down for a moment at the beige pool of mud. It was the color of café latte, she thought, but there was nothing to do but to step into it. She put her crutch down first and then swung her two legs to the side and let them drop with a squelch into the sludge. A few awkward hops and she was on more or less firm ground. Behind her, her father took out a cigarette and a book and prepared to pass the time. She spent a moment trying to scrape some of the clinging mire from her shoes with the end of her crutch and then set off at her rather crab-like gait.

The sun was going down indeed, and it was shadowy along the lonely track, but Cordelia was unafraid. She was given to nervous anxieties but there was nothing about the road to set off any of these; some part of her rose to the slight sense of adventure. The last of the sun's rays came in checkered patterns through the turning leaves, birds flitted here and there, settling and calling goodnight to one another. In the grass at her feet there were small rustlings that she knew to be young frogs or toads, scurrying out of her way. Or they might be hedgehogs, little round prickly creatures waddling along the ground, or snakes even – she had seen a large one once in Poland, sunning itself on a brick wall. Neither was dangerous, though.

'*You spotted snakes with double tongue,*
Thorny hedge-hogs, be not seen.'

She owed that to her father, at least; she had good words to fit every occasion, and, in spite of her partially American origins, she had them in several languages, thanks to a life abroad. In fact, if she thought about it, it was chance that she should be walking here. There were so many other lives she might have led. She had memories of the Tuscan landscape, of an American suburb full of cars, of the canals of Amsterdam and an apartment with a sloping floor. She had always found something to regret in moving on, when her father's restlessness or a new job had taken them elsewhere. But now she felt rooted at last. She liked this land, liked the idea that the meadows and plains and woods rolled on and on to the border. There was so much space and yet so many small details of beauty. The goldenrod came high to her shoulders here, and the yellow yarrow too.

She must be coming to the clearing, she thought, from the change in vegetation. The trees had thinned and she was crossing a swampy depression, where cane grew as well as the wild flowers, and the air was colder and damper. But no, the woods reasserted itself, closing in again, drier, and her thoughts became gradually less cheerful.

In fact, the distances were rather long. She began to despair of finding the clearing she remembered. The road seemed to go on and on, and she grew tired and slipped frequently as she sought her way along the uneven surface. Her shoes were wet, her palm on the crutch handle was developing a blister, and even her good leg ached with the unaccustomed exercise.

She came out of the woods at last, with relief, just in time to see the upper parabola of the sun dip downwards beyond a distant cornfield and disappear. Here the air was full of the scent of autumn, of mown hay and ripe vegetation and damp earth. From the rye stubble at her feet came the pulsing chirr of an army of crickets. Before she had crossed half the field a harvest moon, immense and perfectly round and burnished orange had risen over the far edge of the next field, and hung poised there, so close to earth that she might have crossed to it, climbed upon a hay mound, and touched it. She stopped and enjoyed the sight for a moment, resting and feeling that it had been worth the walk. It was so unusual and so seemingly portentous that she hesitated to disturb the moment.

But there was her father still, back in the car, waiting a long time now. She shifted her grip on the crutch again and pushed onwards.

The asbestos roof of a house was just visible in a hollow, where she'd thought she'd seen it, on the far side of two long strips of cultivation. Skirting the rye field she stumbled over the uneven ground towards it.

At first she thought, as she came up to it, that the house was uninhabited. Perhaps it was someone's summerhouse, she thought. It had that air, somehow. It was certainly not a farmhouse, although it might have had outbuildings at one time. Now there was only a woodshed. She stopped some fifty feet from a fence edging a lawn where the grass had not been cut for a month. There was no light inside the house, and she had a sinking feeling that no one was at home. But no, a few steps more revealed that there was car parked, slightly oddly, on the grass behind the house. She had a feeling it was rather a fancy car, but she couldn't have said why, never having been much interested in cars. She hobbled on as briskly as she could to the gate, very much hoping that her journey was nearing its end. Of course, she was going to have to walk back, but she tried not to think about that for the moment.

The gate was unlocked and she pushed it open and stepped through, disliking the task in front of her, and willing the house's owners to be kind-hearted. She knocked on the door and then leaned heavily on her crutch and waited, trying to ease various aches and sore points.

Inside the house a window curtain was jerked back, a face peered out for a second, the curtain resettled, and then the door was pulled open.

The man standing in the doorway was a large man, neither very young nor old, wearing, oddly, dark sunglasses. He wasn't smiling.

"*Pani?*" he said harshly. It sounded like a question – "you?" But he immediately asked again, in polite-enough inflections: "What can I do for you?"

She must not have caught the words the first time, Cordelia thought, as she launched on an explanation: the car, the woods, her father – his heart condition, her walk, a telephone? a tow-truck in the vicinity?

The face before her continued stony, the lips tight compressed, the head slightly bowed as the man listened.

Cordelia had a feeling that there was something familiar about the man, but she quickly dismissed the idea. Lots of Poles looked like other Poles; she was always thinking someone looked like someone else. She was terrible for remembering faces anyway, she so seldom looked at anyone straight on. The impression this man gave was of suppressed anger – of radiating anger – and inner tension. It was unnerving, and Cordelia's explanations faltered; she looked about to see if there were another house near.

"There's no telephone here." A pause. "I'm sorry." But the door didn't close and Cordelia could feel the man staring at her behind the glasses. She dropped her eyes, and began to back away. She knew there was a telephone cable coming to the house.

As if in answer to her thought, the man said "there is a telephone line, but I suppose the subscription hasn't been paid. At least, it appears to be dead."

So he doesn't live here, Cordelia thought. No, he didn't look or speak like a country person. She wondered vaguely what he was doing in the house, whether he even had a right to be there, and began to wish she were elsewhere.

"Where are you going?" The words were sharply spoken.

Cordelia turned back; she was not given to unreasonable fear and yet she had a sudden wild impulse to tell some saving tale…but about what? That she had a cell phone, that she'd already called for help, that someone knew where she was, so if … None of the thoughts that flashed across her mind made any sense.

"To look for another house," she said as steadily as possible, "Or where is the highway? I'll walk to the highway."

"There aren't any houses near. The highway is in that direction," he pointed down a narrow track that looked like the one her father had taken, "it's about two kilometers from here. It'll be dark by the time you get there," he added, as if in afterthought.

"Thank you," she said, "good-bye." She began to hobble towards the gate, feeling somewhat reassured about the man, but quailing at the walk still before her.

The man had come out onto the front step of the house. "I'd help you but…My car wouldn't make it down that track…" A pause. "And I'm rather expecting some people."

"It doesn't matter." Her voice was rather husky and abrupt when she felt unsure. "I'm sorry to have disturbed you. Goodbye."

"Wait!"

She turned back, her face as unsmiling as his, wanting only to get away and get on with her task. But suddenly he gave her a quick and lopsided smile.

"I'm tired of sitting about here. I'll bring a shovel and some boards, and see what I can do. If the lane's as you say it is, you won't find it easy to get a tow truck to go there either. Wait a moment."

"But really," said Cordelia, "if you have someone coming, I didn't mean…"

"They can come and kiss the doorknob," said the man with a look and tone half between anger and wild laughter. "They might not even come, and if they do, it'll teach them to make appointments beforehand."

And without waiting for her answer, the door shut again. Cordelia felt both relieved and uncomfortable. She wouldn't have to walk further, only back, but she didn't like accepting favors from anyone and this man seemed strange. She leaned heavily on her crutch and waited and in a minute the man reappeared from around the side of the house, carrying a small supply of boards and a shovel over one shoulder. She followed him through the gate and set out ahead of him, trying to move as swiftly as possible so as not to delay him; conscious of him behind her, of his unexpected offer and present burden, her indebtedness, and mostly of her three-cornered walk that floundered where the ground was soft.

But she couldn't keep it up. Halfway round the field she was gasping for breath and a pain in her side was bending her nearly double. She had to stop.

"I have to stop for a minute," she said to the man behind her, not looking at him. What was there to look at anyway? She couldn't see his eyes and he made her nervous. She felt more than saw that he put down one end of the boards and the shovel and rested against them as she was resting against her crutch.

They stood without speaking, the only sound being Cordelia's quick intakes of breath. Beyond them the field was darkening at the edges, and the shadows between the blades were blending into one. The harvest moon was still there, glowing, but now it had ceased to be a friendly apparition and had begun to give a touch of something full-moonish and sinister to the scene. Cordelia's existence had been too long encapsulated by her own household. She had no experience of strange men, and this man's physical presence four feet from her was unnerving. Besides there was something odd about him, she was sure. She didn't like to stand there in the dark with him, in the deserted fields. She adjusted her hand on the crutch and prepared to set off again.

"We don't have to hurry," the man said, not moving.

Cordelia hesitated, wondering why he was helping her. He didn't sound kind; he sounded tense and distracted, in spite of the spurt or two of laughter. But what ulterior motive could he have?

And then she guessed, by some flight of intuition – an intuition that had been much honed by her disability, by living in a household of eccentric and impractical persons, where her capacity to sense the future was frequently all that stood between someone and disaster: He was a fugitive from justice and he wanted their car. His car was out of gas or he wanted a different one to disguise his flight. He was going to help them dig out their car and then he would take it and depart. The question was only what he would do with them, with herself and her father? Leave them behind or bury them in shallow graves? He had the shovel.

No, really, it was an absurd idea.

"Let's go," she said to the man.

"You haven't caught your breath."

"My father's waiting."

"The one with the bad heart?" The tone was vaguely ironic.

It irritated Cordelia. Her father really did suffer from angina and arrythmia; he wasn't supposed to exert himself.

"I only have one," she spoke shortly. "Come on, let's go." She turned and stumbled, and would have fallen then, but he dropped the boards and sprang towards her, reaching out and grabbing her above the elbow. She stifled a shriek as he pulled her upright again and held her steady until she found her balance. Then he instantly released her and stepped back.

"Thank you," she muttered in deep embarrassment. *Bože*, she had almost screamed. Her imagination was running wild tonight! She was normally so down-to-earth; she was the only one in the family with her feet on the ground, and tonight she was behaving like a hysterical teenager. She had to get a hold of herself.

"Thank you," she said again over her shoulder to the man, and set off slowly.

"Don't mention it." he replied, and she could hear him shouldering the boards and following.

They continued around the edge of one field, and then another, where Cordelia's crutch tangled frequently in the stems of tall weeds and she struggled and kept going. The man behind said nothing, she could only hear the occasional rustle of his clothing brushing through the same weeds, the slight scrape of the metal shovel on the wood. By the time they reached the track beneath the trees the light was definitely gone from the day, and the slippery road was treacherous. More than once the man put out a hand and prevented Cordelia from falling. She muttered a thank you and moved ahead far enough to be out of reach of his help, with the result that she slid painfully once or twice, before they came unexpectedly in the dark upon the car.

They could see the back of Cordelia's father's head, silhouetted by the overhead car light. He was still smoking and still reading, but he crushed out the cigarette at the sound of their arrival and put the book back in the glove compartment.

"Ah, there you are." He spoke Polish to Cordelia in front of the stranger. "You have brought reinforcements, I see." And to the man, "How very kind of you, sir. I apprehend that you have come to our aid. As you can perceive, we are enmired."

"I perceive nothing. It's too dark. Have you got a flashlight?"

Cordelia's father emerged ponderously from the car before answering. "We have not."

The man propped the boards against the car and knelt in the mud beside the back wheel.

What was that the man muttered? Cordelia wondered. It was almost under his breath, but it sounded like 'bugger.' She must have misheard.

"Do you know where this lane goes?" the man's tone to her father was curt, but he was already working, digging shovelfuls of mud out from before the wheel.

Cordelia's father took his time in answering, taking off his glasses and cleaning them on a cloth as he spoke. "I had a conviction, which has undergone, I admit, some modification and erosion in the matter of its entire certainty, that it connected with the highway to Warsaw again, beyond the construction."

"On the other hand," said the man, as he tossed aside a load of what was probably dark mud into the dark bushes, "for all you know, it may end in a cul-de-sac or in someone's cesspool."

"Eeh," said Cordelia's father, "that is …Don't *you* know?"

"No. I'm not from around here." The man's voice was brusque. "Since I won't be with you to dig you out again – assuming I get you out this time – which isn't sure – I suggest you turn and go back. You can see the road is a little wider just ahead of you there. You should be able to make it around, backing and filling."

Cordelia, standing in front of the car with her father, felt curiously relieved at these words. "I won't be with you…" So he didn't have any macabre designs on them or their car…How silly she had been, and the ridiculous idea had remained in the back of her mind. She noticed he'd taken off his glasses. They couldn't see his features clearly anyway in the dark. He must realize that. But why was he hiding his face? Unless he was in hiding? But nonsense, everyone wore sunglasses. And certainly not everyone who was hiding was a danger to others. Perhaps he was a victim. He didn't have the air of a victim, however. And what, she chided herself, did she know of what a victim looked like, or a criminal either?

"Why don't you both get in and sit down?" The man's words made plain their extraneousness. "No point in just standing there." He paused in his work long enough to pull open the car door for Cordelia.

She was surprised, and relieved again at his gallantry; it was true they were useless and she sank into the car seat with relief; it had seemed improper to sit down while he was working.

A pause, in which they heard nothing but the chonk chonk of the shovel, then another pause, while the man did something with the boards.

"Okay," he called, "It's all in place. You can try now."

Cordelia's father did not wait for the man to retreat to a safe distance. He started the engine instantly and stamped hard on the gas. A shriek of the engine and mud and muddy water rose in all directions. Through the dim illumination of the headlights Cordelia saw a board fly into the air and whack the man in the arm. He was liberally coated with sludge, and his curses of her father were loud, comprehensive, and angry. The car hadn't moved out of its spot.

The man appeared at the window of the car.

"*Idioto*"...he said deliberately and angrily to Cordelia's father.

"Yes," said Cordelia's father, in irritation, "I heard you the first time. I heard you say the same thing three times, in fact. Which, in my opinion, argues a certain limitation in the matter of vocabulary..." He broke off as Cordelia pulled at his sleeve.

"Please, Tato, please – he was trying to get us out."

"Yes," said the man in ire, "you may have heard, but did it really sink in? Did you get it in all its nuances?"

"Leave him alone!" Cordelia snapped indignantly at the man across her father.

The man gave her a look and turned abruptly away.

Cordelia waited with bated breath, twisted in her seat. "I hope he's not going to give up on us," she whispered to her father.

"Good riddance!" snorted her father. "Who does he think he is, to speak to me that way!"

"He was angry," Cordelia said, distraught. "If he leaves, we'll be...we'll be...up a puddle without a shovel."

Her father chuckled, his humor restored. "That's good, Cordelia."

"No, it's not good. None of it's good. We're in a stupid situation – again," but she gave up abruptly. There was no use scolding him. She opened the car door and stepped into the mud. The man was kneeling by the wheel again. He didn't speak. She addressed him softly, so her father wouldn't hear.

"I'm sorry about that. My father doesn't really know how to drive. You have to tell him exactly what to do. We're very grateful for your exertions."

The man just grunted, so she got back in the car. She leaned her head back against the seat and closed her eyes. Everything passed. In a few hours they would be home. At the worst, they would spend the night in this quagmire and be home some time tomorrow. At some point in the near future, they would pull into their own drive, and she could...well, not rest, certainly, but go back to her usual routine. There was her mother to look after. If it was day time, her mother would sleep in front of the television, and then Cordelia could sleep too. If it was night, then she might be up several times. Antek would be having a hard time of it. Since the onset of their mother's dementia some nine, ten years ago, he had withdrawn into himself even further, and it was only rarely that she left him in charge of their mother. It wasn't that he was unwilling to help; only that he seemed so incapable and absentminded. He never kept track of time, so he never got meals punctually; he only spoke when the mood struck him and so had no pleasant small talk to soothe their mother. The sadness of it, the inability of beings that had once been close, to communicate at any level, was one of those things she kept from dwelling on very firmly.

Her thoughts were interrupted by the reappearance of the man at her father's window. He spoke tersely but calmly. "Everything is in place again. I want you to start up very, very slowly. You should feel the wheels move onto the boards and then they'll have traction. I'm going to push – but I promise you, if you stamp on the gas again, I'm going on my way, and you can sit here till you rot." He retreated to the rear of the car.

"Hmpf" muttered Cordelia's father, "'rumble thy bellyful'" – he waved a theatrical arm, "'to a poor, infirm, weak, and despised old man…'"

"Yes," said Cordelia, "but did you hear what he said?"

"I heard his insolence."

"Yes, but you're to start very slowly. Now. I think he's waiting for you to go now. Slowly."

Cordelia's father set the car in motion and Cordelia held her breath. Again there was the spray of mud; she could feel the car being pushed forward by main force, then the tires caught the boards, a moment of sliding and they were propelled forward out of the hole. Cordelia's father stopped the car on the next bit of sound road. "Hallelujah," said Cordelia with heartfelt relief.

She opened the car door, swung her legs out and stood up, with the intention of thanking their benefactor. Her eyes were already sweeping the darkness for him when her attention was caught by the sound of sirens. She stood, holding to the top of the car door, listening. Yes, it sounded like several sirens, coming nearer. Well, an accident on the road, probably. She said a little prayer that no one was seriously injured, and turned to look for the man. But no one was there.

"Hello? *Proszę pana?* Are you there?" she called into the darkness. All around the night was black and still, only the headlights lit a small patch of the road ahead. The sirens seemed to be getting even louder.

"Hello?"

But there was no answer. It was a little eerie. She bent her head to the car. "Tato? Did you see that man leave? I wanted to thank him, but he seems to have disappeared."

"Well, if he didn't want to say goodbye, what is that to us? Get in. We'll no doubt pass him on the road, and then you can say what you like. Personally, I think he was a churl."

There seemed nothing to do but depart. Cordelia got back in the car feeling half relieved and half as if she had left some duty undone. But her father was right, if the man preferred to take off, why should she think her thanks necessary?

"Aren't you going to turn the car and go back, like the man suggested?"

"The problem with you, Cordelia, is that you have no faith, no sense of adventure." He was in fine spirits again and shot the car forward. "Over hill, over dale..." he hummed.

She gave a little moan and subsided again into silence.

The road was still as muddy and as bumpy, but with sufficient propulsion they proceeded without mishap, and after a time it seemed to turn and widen a little, and became almost a civilized drive. Cordelia had a feeling they were moving in a large circle, but they passed a house or two and neither seemed to be the one at which she had found the man.

It was strange how she couldn't stop thinking about him. There was really something rather familiar about him, and it nagged at her mind. Of course, it might easily have happened that she had once passed him on a Warsaw street, stood behind him in a cash register queue in a shop, sat next to him at a café table. She didn't get to town very often; perhaps that made the people she passed stick all the more tenaciously in her subconscious.

They had come into the open, out of the woods, and ahead of them, in a blaze of lights at the edge of a field, they could see four police cars with lights swirling and flashing and two vans with large lights on top, illuminating the whole yard of a house with an asbestos roof.

Cordelia caught her breath. That was the house she'd been to. So he was a criminal!

They were approaching the house now, squeezing past one of the vans. The yard seemed to be over bright and full of faceless men in dark clothing and men with cameras, milling aimlessly amid the pulse of the police lights.

"A murder, I suppose," Cordelia's father said without interest, "some poor woman got tired of her husband's drinking. The film crew seems a bit excessive." Cordelia said nothing.

"Cordelia, my over-compassionate daughter!" said her father rallyingly, "don't worry about it! I know you, you'll get in the dumps about it, and you can be sure it's not at all worth it."

"No," said Cordelia, and for some reason, didn't tell him what she knew. She wondered where the man would run to? He must have heard the sirens, just after he got them out of the hole, and he must have hidden in the woods. She wondered what he had done. How fortunate for him that he had come to help them. Why had he, she wondered? Or maybe his case would be better if he gave himself up? Unless he had done something really bad, something for which he was certain of a very long sentence? That must be it. But then how odd that a person who could commit a very serious crime would have had the goodness to come to their aid. He had really rather suffered for it. Cordelia remembered his splattered clothing and muddy face. Something about that face was definitely familiar.

They were coming to the highway again, turning onto it.

"There, you see, Cordelia, we saved kilometers."

Cordelia didn't point out that they had in fact returned to the highway some half kilometer further from Warsaw than the spot at which they'd left it, and that they would soon be passing the place where they had turned off. Would he notice it? No, he was driving at breakneck speed again through the night.

"Do we have to speed so?" she asked nervously.

"We have to make up for lost time."

"But we saved all those kilometers."

"Cordelia, don't be logical. I hate a logical woman."

Now why was the response that sprang unbidden to her mind 'bugger?' Cordelia blushed at herself. How odd. She didn't swear, and if she did, she wouldn't do it in a British idiom. She lapsed into silence. She had her thoughts after all, and there was nothing ahead of them on the road at the moment.

That's what she'd thought the man had said, as he was kneeling by the car. But a Polish person wouldn't use that word anymore than she would. Strange and often obscene words were said to be spoken by persons coming out of anesthesia. Perhaps driving with her father gave her subconscious the same sort of shake up. She smiled a little to herself and her thoughts turned back to the man. Where had he gone? He had certainly gone quickly. By the time she had stepped out of the car, he was nowhere about. She remembered the feeling of the car being pushed, of its finding traction, sliding sideways a little, hitting firmer ground, a few yards of distance, and the car had stopped. She had emerged to the sound of the sirens and…there had been the sound of a car door shutting to the rear. And then she had called "Hello" and no one had answered.

But she remembered that sound of a car door.

And suddenly, she knew where he was. The thought sent chills up and down her spine. She took a quick intake of breath. Did she dare to look? Was it better to look or not to look? To continue as if nothing were the matter, as if she knew nothing? No she couldn't bear it. She turned her head and looked into the back seat. Nothing. It was empty; she was sure, in spite of the dark, that it was empty. She breathed a sigh of relief, stole a glance at her father, and sat back in her seat.

"Did you lose something?"

"No."

Another man might have found this reply odd, but she knew he wouldn't give it another thought.

Ahead of them the road unfolded, ill lit, dangerous with large trucks and speeding drivers using the middle of the road in whichever direction they were going. There was plenty in the highway before them to make her hair stand on end. She didn't at all need to imagine criminals hiding behind her seat. Logical woman indeed, she chided herself, and this thought was quickly succeeded by the next: he wouldn't have chosen the back seat; he would be behind it, crouched in the baggage area. The car door she had heard would have been the station wagon's hatch. It was an old car; there was plenty of room for him to hide back there. Now she felt hot and cold again.

Even if she turned she wouldn't see him. She sat facing forward, listening as hard as she could for some sound – some slight rustle of clothing, the scrape of a shoe on the worn carpet, breathing – that would give her certainty.

Was he a murderer? Who else but a mass murderer, or a mafia boss, or a politician would rate a television crew? He hadn't looked to her like any of those; although, on second thought, she wasn't sure she would recognize the first: the other two were identifiable enough. He had put out a hand to keep her from falling – she remembered the feel of his fingers on her arm, the solidity of his form beside hers in the dark. She jerked her head as if to rid it of an unwelcome thought. There had been that tiniest bit, that moth's wing, of physical attraction. Had she been attracted, physically, to a murderer? Self-disgust almost overcame fear for a moment. She put up her hand and began to pull on her hair.

"You're very quiet tonight, Cordelia," her father spoke.

It took a moment before the words made sense to her. He had a bad heart and she couldn't tell him that they had a stowaway criminal in the car with them. He might have a heart attack.

Maybe it would be better to prepare him? So it wouldn't come as too much of a surprise when the man appeared – as he must appear sooner or later? Unless, of course, it were all in her imagination. Somehow, she knew it wasn't. Still, perhaps the man intended just quietly to slip away at some stop light in town; perhaps he would just open the hatch and get out and run off into the night and they would never see him again. Then her father need never know. By the time he turned around to the sound of the door the man would be gone.

"Well? You don't answer me? Are you sleeping?"

"No, I was thinking how strange it would be if that man that helped us out of the mud hole had stowed away in the car – if he were really there in the back."

There was a long pause. Then Cordelia's father said: "You know, Cordelia, I've been thinking you don't get out of the house enough lately."

"It was just a funny idea I had," Cordelia returned, abashed.

"Don't *you* start getting funny ideas."

Why not? Didn't she have as much right to funny ideas as the next person – as her father, her mother, her brother? But perhaps, after all, delusions weren't really her province. She was the practical one in the family and she was just in an odd mood tonight; that must be it. There wasn't really a man in the car with them.

There wasn't any exact translation of 'funny ideas' in Polish, she thought, her nerves calming. As a translator she was always considering how to say this or that in another language. Very often it was impossible. One could only say 'strange ideas' or more politely, 'interesting' or 'curious' ideas. She remembered the last time someone had said to her that she had a 'curious idea.'

Funny, now why should she associate that with the word 'bugger'?

And suddenly she remembered. She gasped aloud – so loudly she glanced at her father to see if he had heard. His profile was relaxed, fixed on the road. She sat back in her seat, remembering every detail in fascinated inner turmoil.

2

It had been in the early spring, over a year ago. Yes, that was it; it had been March, because Hal had come from the States, leaving his wife and children to make a flying weekend visit on the last days of his minute annual holiday. It was he who said she should try for the job.

He too had said she didn't get out enough; that it wasn't normal for a person her age to spend all her time within four walls. She had smiled at her older brother and answered: "A person of my age? I feel like a hundred."

"Well, do something about it, before you really are a hundred, and it's too late. Thirty-two is late to start, Cordelia, really late. You're going to end up like Antek."

"But I don't have to 'start' as you put it; I've got my free-lance work at home, and I've certainly got enough here to keep me busy."

"Yes, I know you've got a lot to do here – I don't deny it. And I'm sorry I'm not here to help out more…" He meant that, Cordelia knew, and she knew too that his regret was partial. He had seen that the ship was going to sink and he had jumped off at the first dock. She had stayed to bail.

"But if you were working full time you could get someone to sit with Mom during the day. You'd have a break. Develop yourself. Maybe you'd finally meet someone."

"I don't want to meet anyone."

"That's not healthy. Really, you're going to become a recluse like Antek."

She didn't know now why she had let herself be persuaded. Probably because it had been what she had wanted at some level. She had debated the matter internally for a few days, until slowly it had come to seem to her like it would be her last chance for a broader existence, for more contact with the outside world, for more normality.

It didn't sound like a difficult job from the advertisement. Just translating and interpreting for a development company that sometimes worked with foreign contractors, had foreign clients.

And so one morning she had dressed with particular care – the nylons she so seldom wore, the knee-length skirt and jacket – a suit bought for some distant relative's wedding and never worn again. She looked very crisp and business-like she had thought, surveying herself in the mirror before she set out. What would it be like to set out every day for the office, she had wondered? She looked almost like a career woman, if she didn't let her eyes stray to her withered arm and leg. Perhaps, after all, it would be better to wear trousers. She pushed the waistband of the skirt down, willing it to become longer and hide her leg. No, she had better wear trousers. Only – no, she glanced at her watch, there wasn't time to change.

Her mother was sitting in her chair, staring absently into the garden, and Cordelia knelt in front of her to say good-bye.

"Goodbye, Mom, I'm going out now. I'll be back in a few hours, but Antek will be here, and Tato is in his office."

Her mother smiled at her dimly. "Thank you, Maria, I put the money on the sideboard for you." She took Cordelia for a former cleaning woman.

She stared at her daughter for a moment; then her gaze shifted around the room, coming to rest on a spot by the wall. "They've taken the sideboard away again!" she muttered angrily.

"No, Mom, that was in another house, remember? The house in Florence? We spent two years there, and then we came here. That furniture all stayed."

"I suppose they thought it belonged to them."

"To the owners of the house? Yes, it did."

"That's what they always say. But they let you come with us, at least."

"I'm Cordelia, Mom, not Maria."

"I liked Maria better."

Cordelia straightened to go, uncertain all at once about leaving her mother for so long. She had periods of depression or irritation, when her normal placidity and politeness were overlain with strange worries and resentments.

Her brother Antek came in then; he was holding a camera, his head tilted back to scan the ceiling. He crossed the room from one end to the other, peering into the corners.

"Ah ha," he cried suddenly, as he whipped the camera up to his face and began to twiddle with the lens: "Got you."

Anyone else would have assumed he was deranged, but Cordelia was able to guess that he was photographing a spider.

"So, I'm going out now, Antek," she reminded him.

"Not good, not good," he muttered.

"Your photo, or my going out?"

"It's all...the... same... thing." He drew the words out slowly, as he fiddled some more with his apparatus. "They'll eat you out there just like a fly in this spider web."

"That's not very encouraging, Antek."

"'Know the truth and the truth shall set you free.'" He raised his head from the camera and pondered for a moment. "No, it won't actually, will it? I mean, the fly might know the truth the moment it hits this web, but what good will it do it? So actually, my point was..." He was angling for another shot, twisting his long lean body about. "I forget what my point was." Click, click, click, went the camera. He straightened. "Ah, yes, the point was – don't go flying about. Stay at home. You might end up like poor Hal, after all. Now *there's* a fly in a trap."

Hal had left in the morning, early. He had been relieved, she knew, to leave, even if what he returned to wasn't great either, by her reckoning: his ten-hour-a-day job, his debts, his worries about his children's college education before they were out of preschool; the stress of competition in every sphere of his life. At least, he thought he was 'living a normal life' and that mattered to him.

"Well, I'll remember your words," Cordelia said to Antek. "You'll look after Mom, Anthony?" But Antek was already off in search of more cobwebs. "Antek?"

Antek turned and swept his sister and mother with unseeing eyes. "Yes, yes." His mind was far away already.

And then she had taken the bus and perhaps, if it hadn't been for the dog, everything would have gone normally or, well, differently anyway.

He was there when she got off her last bus. She saw him as soon as she stepped down, a little more slowly than the crowd of quickly dispersing fellow passengers, onto the sidewalk along a busy four-lane highway. The passengers walked along a corridor of sound barriers to staircases and tunnels and the city spreading itself on either side.

The puppy's chances were not great; were, in fact, nil. He was lost, a very little and ratty-looking mongrel, not very steady on his legs yet, wandering from side to side of the road, the wind from the stream of cars buffeting him as they whizzed past, the wheels of the delivery vans way above his head as they bowled down on him as he made a try to cross the street, then flattened to his stomach again, tail clapped down, eyes frightened, as each one passed. It's a terrible thing to see a life crushed out, smashed beneath the wheels of a vehicle, an insensate machine of metal, rubber and destruction – one moment of inattention, of panic, a wrong move: the approach, the split second of disbelief, and then ...Cordelia imagined it all in a split second too.

He couldn't get off the street; he was caught there between the barriers. Beyond there were parking lots, modern office buildings, warehouses, the inhospitable environs of the Warsaw periphery. There was no place for him to go or to have come from; he must have been dumped, thought Cordelia in distress as she stood on the sidewalk uncertainly, watching him. Some dreadful person must have just opened a car door and dropped him out to meet his death.

She glanced at her watch again. She had fifteen minutes until her appointment. She hesitated, closed her eyes and cringed as the puppy started again across the street as another truck came thundering along. The puppy began to run. No, no, no, she wanted to scream at him. Too late. He darted across the road, and she shut her eyes again, waiting for the slight impact of small body and wheel. But when she opened them again the puppy was on the other side of the road, the truck was retreating into the distance. But now the puppy, thoroughly disoriented and distraught, was preparing to cross again.

Oh why hadn't she taken the other bus, the one that would have let her off on the other side of the building, where she would never have known of this poor little dog's fate, but could have gone calmly – well, as calmly as possible – to her job interview. And now, what was she going to do? If she caught the puppy, she would have to take him with her. A fine impression that would make, but really, she couldn't leave him here.

She made up her mind, and began to hurry clumsily down the sidewalk towards the creature, lurching, her bad leg swinging out awkwardly. Really, he was very ugly: a thin blackish puppy with frightened eyes glinting under a mat of wild hair. He was cowering beside the curb.

Stay there, she told him in her mind. I'm coming. I just can't move very fast, you see. I can't really run. But I'll be there in a minute. She was almost level with him; if only there would be a break in the traffic, she would rush over and catch him. Why did people have to drive so fast? Just stay there, puppy.

But he wasn't staying. He was going to run towards her, between that car and another truck coming from the opposite direction. No! She shouted at him, and stepped out into the street, holding up her hand to the approaching car. There was a screech of tires. She was no judge of distance. It had been closer than she thought. It stopped within inches of her as she reached the center line.

There was a whoosh of air as the truck went by on the other side. Out of the corner of her eye she saw that the driver of the car had swung his vehicle up onto the sidewalk, was pushing his door open and surging out of it in anger. He was probably swearing. He was shouting something anyway. But she didn't look at him or stop to listen. The traffic was backing up in both directions, horns were honking, people were shouting. She reached the other side of the street, but as she bent awkwardly to grab the puppy, she dropped her crutch and he bolted again back across the street, and dived under the car of the angry man. She followed.

Behind her in the street, the cars were moving again. She dodged around the driver, who came running across the street towards her. "Good God, I've injured you!" He exclaimed, pulling up short, and stopping a line of cars with an imperious hand so she could pass.

"No," she muttered, without looking at the man, only seeing him as a large shape in the landscape. He was snarling something at her, something about 'was she trying to kill herself?' She wouldn't be able to reach the puppy unless she got down on her stomach. If she got down on her stomach she would dirty her good suit. She would have to lie on her useless arm and it was going to be very awkward.

The driver was still saying unpleasant things in a horrid voice. She was not a tall woman. "Excuse me," she said to his jacket front, "would you mind moving aside? I have to…" She gestured towards the undercarriage of the car. He looked at her as if she were mad, but she didn't see the look.

"You could get killed, stepping into the street like that." The voice was calmer now.

"But there's this puppy you see," she said, her eyes still searching beneath the car. "He was going to get run over."

"Damn the puppy! You nearly dented my bumper."

There was nothing to say to that so she said nothing. She hobbled around the man and crouched on the sidewalk beside the car, trying to see the puppy, but he was hidden behind a wheel. In a moment he was going to run back into the street. It wasn't a warm day, but she felt the perspiration trickling down her back. She lay down on the sidewalk at the man's feet – what nice shoes, she thought with half a thought – and when he moved aside, she grabbed for the puppy. She caught a handful of hair and pulled the creature towards her. The puppy yelped as if she were scalping it and when she pulled again, sank its teeth into her wrist. She gave a cry of pain, but didn't let go, and got him out into daylight. On her knees, she shifted her grasp to the scruff of his neck and held him away from her for a second as he struggled, but he quickly curled into a submissive and terrorized ball. "It's all right, puppy, nice puppy" she coaxed him in a shaky voice, trying to toss strands of hair out of her eyes.

She heard a car door slam and the vehicle beside them moved off with a light squeal of rubber.

She stroked the puppy and it thumped its tail; she gathered it to her, so that it lay tucked between her body and her bad arm and rose. More people had descended at the bus stop and were watching her with interest; that expressionless interest of a Polish crowd. She was aware that she had ripped her nylons and that her pastel suit had not been improved by contact with the pavement. She couldn't retrieve her crutch, and a middle-aged woman from the bus stop came running and picked it up for her.

"Thank you."

"You should keep your dog on a leash; it's very irresponsible of you," said the woman severely and retreated, shaking her head.

Behind her, Cordelia thought, was the building where she was expected in – she bent her head to see her watch around the puppy – ten minutes.

She began to hobble as fast as she could towards the building. There was nothing for it. She'd have to take the creature with her. Well, she certainly wouldn't get the job. But maybe she didn't want it that badly anyway. Probably her chances hadn't been very great in any case. People very rarely wanted employees with disabilities. Or so she imagined; she didn't really know as she'd never applied for a job before. She'd always worked at home. Still, she knew enough to be certain that interviewees weren't supposed to turn up with their pets. It would be too rude not to appear at all, but she could just explain the circumstances and back out.

The puppy was so thin she could feel his ribs through his hair. She guessed he was going to be a smallish dog, and that he was no more than a few months old. He was only about a foot long, and he wasn't heavy. He had decided to trust her or had given himself up for lost, because he lay fairly quiet as she clamped him against her side, only giving a slight struggle now and then. Still it was very tiring, to be hurrying with the dog in one arm and her crutch in the other. Thank goodness she was arriving.

35a: this was the building. She pushed through a set of glass doors into a lobby. A security guard looked her over in curiosity, and she disliked his gaze but she knew he wouldn't stop her in spite of her battered appearance. She headed for the elevator as if she knew where she was going. She pressed the button for the top floor and caught sight of herself in the mirror as she did so. She was beautiful, in a rather exotic and farouche way, but as no one had bothered to tell her so, except a collection of elderly aunts and other such persons of suspect judgment, she did not know it. When people did double-takes in the street, she assumed they were looking at her disability. Now she saw only an assortment of features whose main expression was wariness and distrust; she saw that her heavy dark hair was disarranged and that holding the puppy brought her slightly deformed fingers away from her body, where they were usually hidden. The elevator was already stopping.

She stepped out, crossed a lobby, and found a door with 'Z. Devel.' on it. Zaremba Development Company – that must be it. She paused only a moment before the abbreviated name: was it the result of someone's sense of humor or of a total lack of imagination? She pushed open the door and a cool young woman looked up from a desk.

"Yes?"

Cordelia could feel the woman's eyes sliding over the dog and the crutch and down to her torn stockings. "What can I do for you?"

"Cordelia Fogg. I've come for an interview. But..." She was going to explain that she couldn't go through with it, the puppy, etc., but the telephone rang and the woman answered it, only hesitating long enough to say, with her eyebrows raised and one hand over the receiver. "Take a seat please. It'll be a moment."

Cordelia moved over to the wall and sat in one of a long line of leather chairs. The puppy was asleep in her arms. She realized that she must have dropped her cv when she was grappling with the puppy. She had had it in a folder. Oh well, it didn't matter. She wouldn't have got the job anyway. She looked around the room. The secretary had disappeared. There were two other women sitting along the wall, and one man. They had that vaguely unbusiness-like air of what Polish people call the 'free professions.' Or, more precisely, they had the word 'translators' written all over them. So would she have, she supposed, if it weren't that people tended to take her disability for a sign of mental backwardness. The two women gave her a curious glance each and then looked away. Probably they were nervous about the interview; it wasn't really that she needed to think they were repulsed. She felt herself stiffening. It's all in your mind, she told herself, as she felt her chin rising in pride, her back straightening. She bent over the puppy.

The salary had seemed very high. It was Hal who had seen the advertisement. "Try for it," he had encouraged her, "a real estate developer. You do all that sort of thing for that agency. All that sewage pipe stuff you were telling me about."

"Because I can translate sewer specifications doesn't mean I'd get hired at a development company...Look at me. Who would hire me?"

"Come on, a little courage."

She had been secretly a little offended although of course she hadn't let it show. She had never thought herself lacking in courage, and she suspected that to Hal, who had suffered more than she from their moveable childhood, not living conventionally was a sign of some sort of degeneracy that he couldn't quite name more exactly so he called it cowardice. But these were very slight undercurrents of feeling in the smooth waters of their mutual affection. He was a good brother; he had meant well by his encouragement.

The puppy was beginning to weigh in her arms. She wondered if she could put it down for a while, but she was afraid it would wake if she set in on one of the leather seats. She didn't want to be chasing it under the secretary's desk. She had a fleeting smile of amusement at the thought and the smile changed her face so much that the man sitting next to her dared to speak.

"Are you here for the translating job?" He asked, and then looked embarrassed, as if she might misunderstand him. "I mean, with that dog? I mean, that's a curious idea…bringing a dog…" He looked as if he thought he was putting his foot in it, but couldn't quite stop talking: "Or…is it one of those helping dogs?"

"No, no. He's no help at all. I was coming to this interview and I just found him outside. It wasn't the way I intended to come."

The man was obviously nervous and it inclined him to be talkative. He began to whisper to her, reaching out a hand to scratch the puppy on the head.

"No. Well, I won't get it, that's certain. A woman who already came out said he spoke English to her right off and asked things like 'what's the Polish word for a 'purlin'?' She didn't know what he was talking about. Neither do I, even though I worked in England for ten years." He sighed.

"Yes, that's bad," Cordelia agreed sympathetically. "I think it's a kind of rafter beam. Who's 'he'?"

The man looked at her in surprise. "*Pan* Zaremba? The head of the company. I thought we'd be interviewed by someone lower down. But no." He sank his voice even further, talking with one eye on the door through which one of the women had just disappeared. "Dariusz

Zaremba. He owns the whole firm. I read an article about him not long ago. He's from some tiny place in the countryside, I forget where, but he grew up abroad and came back to make his fortune here…"

"Oh." She'd be seeing Z. Devel himself then.

The secretary returned and motioned to the man. He rose.

"Good luck," Cordelia whispered and he nodded jerkily and walked away.

She was left sitting by herself, and she shifted the sleeping animal to rest her arms. Its fur was dusty and matted. It must have been living outside, and that meant it wouldn't be housebroken. Still, it was alive. Poor little thing, how exhausted it must be. That man in the car had been so rude and uncaring. She hadn't even looked at his face, but she remembered the tone of his voice. "You might have dented my bumper." Really, some people had the most incredible priorities.

To distract herself from these unpleasant thoughts, she turned her head and looked out the window. Beyond a warehouse and a parking lot and another office building going up, half built, with a crane extending its beak over the top, was an ocean of green trees. She supposed they'd all go down soon. Maybe she was glad she wasn't going to work for a developer. How sad it would be to be part of the destruction. That was a good thought. Yes, she really had no desire at all to work for a developer. This one was no doubt responsible for some of those hideously unaesthetic buildings that were destroying the landscape.

She looked around the office. There were photos on the walls, photos of construction sites, of finished buildings. Were these this company's? They were quite nice actually, very nice: A felicitous combination of classical form with modern material.

The door opened and the man who had sat next to her emerged. She raised her eyebrows at him and he gave her a shrug and a 'don't know but maybe okay' gesture. She smiled at him and he disappeared.

But the secretary was speaking to her. "Okay, your turn, *pani*."

"But..." Somehow, she had been intending to say "I can't go in, I've got this dog." And she had never done it. The door was a modern door in smooth wood, large, solid, frightening; she didn't want to go through it. On the other hand, having waited, she couldn't quite turn and run now either.

She rose, walked to the door, turned the handle with the left hand as her right cradled the puppy, and walked through.

A man rose from behind a desk and extended a hand.

"*Dzien dobry, pani.*"

She couldn't shake his hand because she had the dog in her right arm and the crutch in her other, and there was an awkward moment while she hastily tried to shift the impediments, and the man dropped his hand and waved her to a seat.

"I'm afraid, I didn't mean to come with this dog – I found him in the street, and..."

"Yes," he said, speaking English, an unaccented, transatlantic English, "I know all about it. Why don't you put him down and we'll get on with it, shall we?"

He knew all about it? The secretary must have told him she had a dog. Put him down? Well, she could do that here, but he might wake up and run away.

"He might wake up."

She seated herself in the one available chair and the man sat down too.

"Your cv?"

I don't have it with me, I'm afraid, I did have it, but…" She knew she wasn't making a good impression, but what could she do. She wouldn't have made a good impression anyway, she thought bitterly, as she tried to tug her leg back under her. It was just as well that she was seated behind the desk. To give herself courage she made herself take a good look at her interviewer. Hopefully, he'd have a wart on his nose or some other disfigurement that would slightly even their respective positions. Unfortunately though, he didn't seem to have any material defects. He was a man of not vastly more than middle height, but heavy-boned and wide-bodied, so that without being overweight he looked quite large, with coarse light hair cut short and standing at angles, and a very shrewd eye. His age might have been anywhere from thirty-five to fifty. His clothing was of the expensive casual type but he had a look of – well, not the street, exactly – but of lower social origins, or hard times, that was it, she thought, with one part of her mind. He looked tough. But it was all thought in a flash, in the time it took to glance at him, to look down at the dog, and to raise her eyes again.

He wasn't giving her time for contemplation of his background, though, or to put together the myriad nuances of posture and facial expression and tenue that spell a European niche.

"You come with a dog and no cv. It's not a great start, but let's get rolling; let's get our engines in gear and so on." He looked at her to see if she flinched at the phrase.

"No," she said, "that's the wrong idiom for me."

The man regarded her with a slightly puzzled look, but caught her meaning after a moment: "Er, you mean you don't roll?"

"I mean I don't wish to be likened to a vehicle." She regretted the words as soon as they were spoken. Why did she say such things? It was one of the things that made people think her so strange.

The man looked vaguely amused. "Fair enough. It's true – you don't look at all like a vehicle."

Cordelia could feel his eyes look her up and down and blushed, but she felt she'd rather asked for it.

He was continuing, "Well, at least you speak English. I presume you speak Polish as well? Where did you learn?"

"I'm American actually," she said softly, "But I spent years in school here. I graduated from Batory, in fact. My father was teaching at the university. That's why we were here..." Her voice trailed off, her eyes dropped. She almost never spoke about herself to strangers.

"And you've done translating? You must have, or my secretary would have weeded you out."

"Yes. For LMJ Agency, and other places. For years."

"And you know building terminology?"

"Yes." Only as soon as she said 'yes' she had a qualm. Did she know enough? Maybe she didn't know enough.

"Okay. So we'll start with something easy. What's a 'keystone' in Polish?"

"'*Zwornik*'."

"'*Ściąg*' in English?"

"A tiepost."

"I often have foreign contractors working for me. I had an employee once who confused 'waste pipe' with '*kanał scienny*.' Buggered up the building works something fierce."

That, thought Cordelia in the car, was where she'd heard the word. And now the man was back there, a fugitive, hiding in their vehicle.

But at the time, she had only thought – years in Great Britain. Or Australia? And she had looked perhaps embarrassed by the man's vulgarity, because he had excused himself with a wry look at her and had gone on:
"Footing?"
"Um, um, '*Podstawa fundamentowa*'."
"*Zasuwa dławiąca*"? He had fired the questions at her so fast she could hardly draw breath.
"A damper."
"A water main?"
"'*rura wodociągowa*'."
"'*Strefa miejska*'?"
"Urban zone."
"'*Konsortium*'?"
"A syndicate."
"'*Poszycie*'?"
"Sheathing."
"'*Zabląg kompensacyny*'?"
She didn't know. Her heart was pounding. She racked her brain. No ideas. Well, that was that. And she'd been doing so well. Was this how that last fellow had been interviewed? He'd seemed to want the job very badly. With a sinking feeling in her stomach, she admitted, "I don't know."
"Doesn't matter. I made it up. There's no such thing as a '*zabląg*'." He didn't smile; his face remained stony.

She goggled at him and then gave a choke of laughter. The giggle transformed her face. What a strange fellow, she thought.

He didn't say anything for a moment, then he gave her a sudden quick grin. "I didn't want you to get a swelled head," he said and began to play with a pencil.

She hastily revised her opinion of his age. Late-thirties at the most; possibly not much older than she.

They began to speak at the same time. He said: "You can have the job…" Just as she said "You should give the job to that last fellow who came in."

They both stopped.

"I'm offering you the job," he said. And began to describe her duties.

She interrupted him. "No, I really think you should give it to that fellow who came in just before me. He'd been in England for ten years, you know," she continued earnestly, "So he probably speaks English very well, and I think he really wants the job." She'd wished him good luck, so she couldn't just walk in afterwards and take his job away from him.

"Still, it's very kind of you to offer," she smiled warmly at Mr. Zaremba, shifted the puppy in her arms, and prepared to rise.

He rose too, came around the desk, and leaned against it. "You're a very odd lady," he said. "But I think you'll do. Do you want the job?"

"No, I…" She was embarrassed. Here she'd come with very little hope of being hired and she was being solicited. She stroked the puppy.

"No?" he looked surprised. "So…what are you here for?"

"I thought I wanted the job, but I think I was mistaken. I'm sorry to have taken up your time."

There was a pause. "Is it more money you want?"

"No." This was awkward. "It's the competition. I don't like it. Those other people probably wanted the job more than I do."

There was a silence, during which she looked at the floor. She was wasting his time. What nice shoes he had. She'd seen those shoes somewhere recently.

"You!" she exclaimed, suddenly, "It was you in the car! I didn't recognize you."

"So I gathered."

"You were worried about your bumper!" she gasped.

"Yes. It's a Jaguar, you know."

"Well, then, I don't have to feel sorry for you after all! I really couldn't work for you." She spoke calmly but with some heat, and she shifted her crutch under her as she did so, saying good-bye briskly, and heading for the door. There, unfortunately, her exit was somewhat marred by the fact that she couldn't deal with the door knob, and it was only when Mr. Zaremba arrived at her side, reached over and pulled open the door, that she was able to sweep out.

Cordelia, being whisked through the night in the car, was shivering with nerves. She didn't even notice when her father tailgated another car for a quarter of a mile and then passed it on the right. The fugitive, who was perhaps – or perhaps not – in the car with them, was Mr. Zaremba. She was sure of it. When he had reached over and opened the car door, there at the mud hole, there had been that tiniest click of remembrance – it had reminded her of that moment in his office when he had come to open the door for her. What had he done? She couldn't remember reading anything about him in the papers. He had passed out of her existence completely. Although she had to admit she had thought about him for some time: on the way home that day, for instance.

The puppy, at first such a featherweight, had begun to weigh a ton. She had sat at the bus stop between an elderly man with a bottle in a bag and two young women in very tight jeans and she had waited. It was in the middle of the city by the central station. A stream of pedestrians went past. Varsovians were mostly young, good-looking, and well-dressed, but the old tenement buildings on the far side of Jerozolimskie Avenue held the margins of society. A concentration of the homeliest people in Warsaw lived in this area, she thought: she'd noticed it before, and supposed it was the effect of environment on the human physique. Would Mr. Zaremba's buildings contribute to better conditions in the city or worse? They had certainly seemed an improvement on so much of what was being built.

She had one more bus ride to take and a longish walk to get home. She wished she were there already. She'd have to write an email to Hal and let him know how it had gone. He'd be disappointed and so was she; suddenly, she knew how much she'd wanted the job. Why had she refused the way she had? She didn't like to remember it. She could at least have been civil. She remembered the man's quick grin when he had asked her the name of something that didn't exist, and then it struck her that he had been joking about the bumper, too. How stupid she had been to take him seriously. That's what came of not getting out more, of staying home and not seeing other people. She had come to think that only her own people made that kind of jokes. Maybe she could go back and tell him she'd changed her mind? No, of course she couldn't, and there was that other interviewee, the man who had spoken to her in the waiting room – he had wanted the job too. He probably needed it more than she did. Still, she felt hollow and deflated as she sat and waited.

She tried to keep her mind on the day's tasks still to come. She had to stop at the pharmacy for her father's medicine and they were out of milk and she'd better pick up some dog food too. There would be the housework to do and dinner to get in her slow puttering way. It seemed infinitely uninspiring.

And yet, she was aware that she had nothing to complain about. She was extremely fortunate in so many ways, she reminded herself. She had only to look across the street at that group of prostitutes gathered in a doorway, there. They were women in their late fifties, badly overweight, badly over-made-up, badly dressed, drinking surreptitiously as they waited for customers. She'd seen them before and wondered if there were really men that desperate? She didn't think that even with her leg and arm she was as unappealing as they were. But they obviously made a living and as far as she was aware no one had ever looked at her with interest, so maybe she did seem more repulsive. Well, the puppy wasn't repulsed, at least; he was still asleep in her arms. She felt grateful to the little fellow.

This was an ugly spot, though. The wind blew and the odd wavy glass ceilings of the Golden Terraces building seemed to be melting out between the surrounding high rises. Mr. Zaremba's buildings were a big improvement on those. Not that she wanted to think about Mr. Zaremba at the moment. Had he found her repulsive? He had offered her a job at least.

Here was the bus arriving. It was full of people, which meant she'd have to stand. She got on, punched her ticket, and grabbed for a strap to hang from, trying to shift the dog onto her hip so that its legs wouldn't dangle and she had some control when it started to slip.

"Oh, nice doggie" people were turning to look at it, hands extended to pat it – "what a cute puppy" – someone was vacating a seat for her and she was being motioned towards it. Gratefully, she sank down.

A man was standing over her.

"Ticket?"

Oh, one of the ticket inspectors. They rarely got on; half the people rode the bus without a ticket, although it was something she would never do herself. So dishonest. She handed up her ticket.

"Do you have a ticket for the dog?"

"Oh...I...No, I didn't think of it." How extremely embarrassing. She'd never given it a thought. Heads were turning; people were listening and pretending not to.

"I'll have to ask you to get off at the next stop."

The bus stopped and they got off together, the ticket inspector pulling out a pad and a pencil.

"So now, I should give you a fine of 50 zlotys. What do you think of that?"

"What difference does it make what I think of it?" She almost snapped back, offended. He wanted a bribe, she knew.

"Well, perhaps we could arrange something."

"No. Write out the ticket, please."

"*Pani*, such an uncompromising attitude. In this world one has to negotiate. We have to help each other."

"No."

The man sighed noisily. "I.D., please."

She sought for it in her purse, but couldn't reach it because of the dog.

"Here, give me the dog."

She handed the puppy to the ticket inspector, and pulled out her I.D. Another bus pulled up. The man thrust the dog back at her.

"Here, it's your lucky day. Go on." He flipped his pad together and hopped onto the bus.

She had been innocent – at least she hadn't intentionally broken the law – and accused. Maybe Mr. Zaremba was innocent too. Somehow she didn't believe it though. The police surely wouldn't make that much of a fuss and the television crew wouldn't come and such a production wouldn't be made of the matter unless there were a fair amount of proof. Although there had been cases of abuse lately, she knew, cases where the prosecutor's office had received directives of a political nature; quite a number of such cases, in fact, were beginning to come to light and who knew how many more there might be? Still, in a country that had been a democracy since she was a teenager, it was natural to assume that the forces of law and order were generally acting in good faith. The overwhelming probability was that he was guilty – of something.

3

'The rash and premature passing of verdicts by high-ranking state officials responsible for law and order, and the use of preliminary investigation findings for the purpose of propaganda, is not conducive to the observance of binding procedures and may lead to the violation of the principles of the state of law and infringements of human rights' – statement of the Helsinki Committee in Poland, on events in the country, 15/3/2007

'Since the heart surgeon Miroslaw G. was called a murderer without proof of his guilt and a court verdict, why shouldn't an ordinary citizen be called a thief, even without being caught in the act?' – Marek Safjan, head of the Constitutional Tribunal (1998-2006)

'Persons defending Doctor G. are defending the elite and special interest groups.' – Jarosław Kaczyński, Prime Minister

Still, the main thing to know was whether he was really back there or not. It was almost unbearable not to know. She could ask her father to stop the car, and she could go back and look. But what then? She couldn't do it. Besides, it was odd enough that the person she should have found when she went for help was someone she had met before. Or was it odd? The smallness of the world had been noted before. So was he back there, or wasn't he? And if he was, and he didn't just slip out at a stop light in town, what did he intend to do? Would he come with them to their house? And then what? Force them to hide him? Take them all hostage?

But she wasn't keeping her mind on the road; her father was speeding again and they were approaching the stretch of construction; the road was marked only by striped pylons at irregular and confusing intervals.

"Slow down, Tato, please."

"I'm only going 80."

"Yes…but…"

But before she finished there was a flash of red lights in the rear-view mirror. She twisted her head around. There was a police car behind them, signaling them to pull over.

How had they known Mr. Zaremba was hiding in their car? And what would happen now? She waited with bated breath, her compassion all on the side of the hunted, and yet, with a curious sense of relief. They were not going to be taken hostage.

"*Merde*," her father was swearing in French – no sense of compunction. "And double *merde*." He thought he was being stopped for speeding. He would soon find out his error, thought Cordelia, hoping he wouldn't be too startled, hoping there wouldn't be any violence.

A policeman appeared at the car window, the glare of his flashlight throwing the surroundings into utter darkness.

"What's the hurry, sir?"

Cordelia quit holding her breath. So they had been stopped for speeding – only speeding. It wasn't about the man in the back at all. Cordelia felt foolish. There wasn't any man in the back. The policeman had walked right past the end of the station wagon and he hadn't noticed anyone in the back – because, of course, there wasn't anyone.

The policeman was checking the car documents, writing out a ticket in spite of her father's fuming protests. Family feeling put Cordelia's sympathies with her father; but her feelings of justice were stronger; she had to admit to herself that if anyone deserved a ticket it was probably her father. However, she remained very quiet, and she stayed completely silent as the policeman departed and her father turned to her angrily: "you see how this country is run, Cordelia? They can't mark the roads properly and yet they have to harass poor drivers like myself who're only trying to get off this lamentable excuse for a roadway at the earliest possible moment! It's gross injustice! The incompetence with which this country is run defies imagination…"

In spite of having only spent a small portion of his childhood and the later years of his life in Poland, Cordelia's father's attitude to authority was entirely Polish: Authority was always in the wrong and the average citizen was always put upon. Cordelia generally considered this a healthier attitude than too much respect, but at the moment she had other matters on her mind. She couldn't take a proper interest in the evil designs of the traffic police.

"400 zlotys!"

400 zlotys! That did get her attention. She looked at her father in surprise. That would take a chunk out of the housekeeping money. But she said nothing.

"400 zlotys!…" Her father was still fussing angrily as he reached across her to slam open and shut the glove compartment as he tossed in the ticket. The police car had disappeared behind them, leaving them in the dark by the side of the road. Her father threw himself back in his seat and sat there, his arms dropping from the steering wheel. He made no move to restart the car.

"It's too bad," said Cordelia soothingly, "but it can't be helped now. Let's go on."

But her father had become curiously silent.

"Tato?" asked Cordelia, suddenly worried. "Are you all right? Tato?"

Her father's hand had come up to his heart.

"Are you all right?" She asked again urgently.

He turned his head slightly towards her and shook it, ever so slightly.

"Your medicine! Where's your medicine?"

He didn't answer her, but closed his eyes as she sought quickly and awkwardly through the pockets of his blazer, through the glove compartment. No medicine; he must have forgotten it.

"An ambulance, Cordelia," her father murmured.

An ambulance? But how would she call one, here on the deserted highway? Oh, a car was coming, its lights cutting the darkness ahead. The driver would have a cell phone – everyone did. She struggled from the car, the beginnings of panic making her more than usually clumsy, and rushed into the middle of the highway, holding up a shaking hand to the car.

The car slowed, she could see a man and his wife looking her over as the headlights caught her. She was standing in the middle of the lane, waving her crutch. But as the car came to a near standstill and she headed towards the passenger window, the driver suddenly stepped on the gas again and departed at full speed.

"Stop," she cried after it "Stop! Stop! Please! We need an ambulance!" But the car didn't stop. She knew they were afraid of a trap, she knew it was reasonable, and she cursed them from the bottom of her heart, her breath coming in a sob.

What to do now? She looked up and down the highway, but there were no signs of light anywhere – not another car coming or a house light or anything. She turned back to her father.

The door on her father's side was open and a dark shape was kneeling there; it rose. She stifled a scream. It was the man.

"Help us!" she cried to him, "help us!"

The man made as if to step away, but Cordelia dropped her crutch and caught at his clothing. "I can't drive. He needs to get to a hospital. Do you have a cell phone?"

The man reached up a hand, removed her hold from his shirt, and brusquely moved away. No! thought Cordelia, he too would leave them there.

But he skirted her rapidly and went to the other side of the car. "It'll be faster," he said crisply, "if I drive, then if we wait for an ambulance."

He was reaching across, dragging her heavy father by the exertion of superhuman force into the passenger seat, buckling the belt around him.

Cordelia had already climbed into the back, relief at something being done struggling with continued fear for her father. The man ran around the car, jumped in the driver's seat and they were off.

If they had gone fast with her father, it was nothing compared to their speed now. And all Cordelia thought was – hurry, hurry, hurry.

There was a period during which they had the highway to themselves. And then more and more taillights began to show ahead; these were soon overtaken and dropped rapidly behind, one after another.

Her father sat slumped against the window. She had her good hand over the back of the seat to feel the pulse in his throat, with a vague idea of attempting resuscitation if it stopped – but it continued, slight and erratic. Sometimes she would think it was gone, but always, after a moment of panic, she found it again. They were coming to the outskirts of Warsaw.

"There may be a hospital or clinic here," said the man over his shoulder, as the car shot past a line of other cars, and ran, barely checking, through a red light. "But I don't know where it is, and I think we could lose our way if we try to find it. But it's up to you. Say quickly."

How to make such a decision quickly? Yes? No? To make a possibly life-or-death decision in one second? "Go where you know."

"Right."

The traffic was heavier now, but they were making their way through it by the most unorthodox methods. Cordelia didn't flinch as they shot off the street, through a deserted parking lot, and over a sidewalk to avoid an intersection.

And then there was a traffic jam, cars drawn up in a long line because of some unseen obstruction ahead. Their car came willy-nilly to a halt. The man looked over his shoulder at Cordelia.

"Okay?" he asked, "we're a block – half a block away."

Their car inched forward behind the trunk of a gray Subaru. To the right a white delivery van pushed onto the bumper of the car ahead of it. Cordelia could see the driver smoking, flicking ash out the window, unconcerned. She dug her fingernails into her palm, and told herself that a few more minutes wouldn't matter. Details etched themselves into her mind and pulsated there with her nerves: a scratch on the Subaru's light; an edging of rust along the tire-well of the van. She thought her father gave a little moan.

She fumbled again to find a pulse. This time she was sure it was gone: "His heart's stopped!" she shrieked.

The car hit her in the back as it accelerated into a tiny space between two cars, then they were through with millimeters to spare, a turn to the left, over the sidewalk, down an alleyway and diagonally across four lanes of cars – the vehicles scattering in all directions, brakes squealing, horns blasting – and they were pulling up with a screech of rubber before a large building with lights out front, and the man had leapt from the car and was summoning support and a stretcher was arriving and people were pulling her father from his seat and he was being trundled away, into the interior, and disappeared.

It was out of her hands now. She followed more slowly, having lost her crutch and not being able to walk at all well.

By the time she reached the front desk, no one was around.

"My father?" she gasped to an orderly, "He just came in?"

The man shrugged.

"My father?" she queried the desk clerk. The desk clerk didn't know.

Cordelia looked about, wondering which corridor to start down. Far at the end of one, ahead of her, Zaremba emerged from a room and gave her a thumbs-up sign.

She bit back the sob of relief, felt for her crutch for support and remembered again that she'd lost it. At the end of the corridor, Zaremba was making signs to her to sit and wait.

She retreated to a line of plastic chairs and sat down. The lights in the hospital waiting room were dim;

someone was lying asleep on a stretcher behind a curtain there. Were they so short of beds? Cordelia would wonder later, but now she had only her father on her mind. Time passed in a sort of nervous tension where everything seemed unreal. She was hardly aware of the hours following one after the other. The man, she knew, was taking care of everything. She owed her father's life to him. Not only had he traversed that last half block of insuperable obstacles in seconds flat, but also, she had to admit, she herself would never have been able to muster the necessary assistance so authoritatively and effectively.

But in his absence, the man took on an unreal quality. She hardly thought about him. She was worrying about her father, her mother at home – and vaguely, disquietingly, what would happen to them all if her father died.

She had forgotten about the man. After a time, she looked up and found he was walking towards her down a corridor.

"Your father's going to be all right," he said, sitting down beside her. "They managed to reanimate him – I think that's the word. He thinks he may have forgotten to take his medicine in the morning. But the doctors don't seem to think there's been any real damage done."

Cordelia didn't say anything. What was there to say? There was only relief.

The man reached in a pocket and took out his dark glasses, put them on. Cordelia could feel him looking at her through them.

"Thank you," she said, "thank you for everything you did. You saved his life."

The man leaned back in his seat, "Yes, I did, didn't I? But you don't owe me any thanks. It was fun." He stretched his arms behind his head for a moment, one leg out in front, the other bouncing a little, as if in nervousness or restlessness or an excess of energy.

"Fun?" Cordelia looked at the man in offended amazement. "Fun?"

The man shrugged, "I don't usually have a reason to drive like that."

What, not even running away from the police? thought Cordelia, but what business of hers was it after all. She caught hold of the back of the chair and helped herself to rise. To the man she said, "Do you know where my father is? I want to see him."

"He's in intensive care. They're going to keep him overnight for observation. I've already talked to the doctor about him and I can tell you everything. But come this way."

"You talked to the doctor?"

"Yes, I said your father was my father-in-law. It seemed simpler."

Cordelia took this in in silence. The man was all too ready with solutions. And yet she owed him her father's life. They had reached a door. "I'll wait here," the man said, and opened it for her.

She went towards a large form lying on a high bed amongst machinery. She had seen her parents in the hospital before; she was already familiar with the gown, the tubes, the bruises on the wrist from the IV, the plastic identification bracelet – the entire institutionalization of disease which took years from anyone coming in contact with it, and which had made her, indeed, older than her real age.

"Come," said the man as she emerged from the intensive care unit, and found him waiting, "I'll buy you a cup of coffee. You look like you need it. There's a place near here that's open all night."

Cordelia let herself be led down a corridor and out the front door. They emerged from the hospital. There was a slight grayness to the night air. It was the beginning of dawn, Cordelia realized with a start. She hadn't been aware of the hours passing.

"I have to call my brother," she said to the man, "He'll be worried." Actually, he probably wouldn't even have noticed what time it was – but she still had to call. She returned to the hospital, found a pay phone, and called. Antek received the news in near complete silence, which was easy at least, but she didn't at all know what he was thinking. She'd be home soon, she said, and hung up the phone, and as she did so, her eyes were caught by a stack of newspapers that had just been deposited by a magazine stand.

'*Zaremba Flees*,' said the headlines. There was a photo of a car surrounded by men in combat uniform and guns. That must be outside the house with the asbestos roof, she thought: the story must have been sent in just before the paper went to press. She bent her head to read the article, but the owner of the kiosk appeared and picked up the bundle.

"Wait," cried Cordelia, "I'd like to buy one of those."

"Not open yet," snapped the woman.

"But couldn't you just sell me one?"

"No."

"Could I just see it for a moment?"

"No."

Zaremba was waiting for her outside. He'd just saved her father's life. She turned away from the newspapers and went out to him.

"Come, wife," he said as she approached. She gave him a look from under her eyelashes and he grinned at her. He seemed, in fact, to be in quite good spirits, she thought, as she lurched at his side across the street and into a deserted café.

"You seem to be in a very good mood," she said to him in a puzzled tone as they sat at a table and he ordered expensive coffee.

"Life's full of interest."

Is it? She thought. Did he find it so? Her father had nearly died. She would have liked a day with less interest in it. Still – this man….the police were after him and that was his attitude? That she supposed, in some part of her subconscious mind, was what attracted her to him – his pulsing vitality. But, after all, he was a criminal. She was a person of scrupulous and even over-sensitive honesty; she'd never had any truck with criminals; she never even sought loop-holes on her income tax form. And here she was, sitting alone with a man who'd done – well, what, exactly? The silence between them lengthened as she thought these thoughts. 'Zaremba flees, Zaremba flees, Zaremba flees' – but having done what, exactly? Something serious, obviously. A waitress came and set down two cups and disappeared into the kitchen, leaving them alone again.

The man began suddenly to fill her in, with great attention to detail and a grasp of medical terminology, on the doctors' description of her father's condition and treatment.

"Thank you," she said, when she thought she had understood it all. "You explained it all much more clearly than doctors usually do. I think sometimes that anyone with a family has to study medicine."

"Do you have a family? Besides your father, I mean?"

Why was he asking that, she wondered. Just small talk, she supposed. "I live with my mother and one of my brothers, too."

"And they also have medical problems?"

"No, um, rather, mental problems."

He laughed a little as if she were making a joke. "Like your father?"

"No," Cordelia said, rather offended. "He doesn't."

"You're very defensive of him."

"He's my father."

"Just for that reason?"

"I love him."

"Because he's your father? He's a lousy driver and he treats you cavalierly."

"Maybe."

"I couldn't stand mine."

There was a long pause, then:

"What'd you do with the dog?"

The question startled her. So he remembered the interview: What he had said, when she knocked at the door in the countryside, had indeed been "you?"

"I – I kept him." There was no harm in talking to the man. "He digs holes in the garden and chases the neighbor's cat and chews on chair legs. He's a horrible dog."

"Ingrate."

"I love him."

"You like criminal types, do you?"

Cordelia took in her breath.

"No. No, I don't. I – I'm very, very grateful to you for what you did for my father. I don't know how I could ever repay you, but…"

"Yes?" He was watching her in some amusement.

Cordelia didn't know what she had been intending to say. There was a short silence, during which she drank her coffee too hot and felt incredibly tired.

"I didn't remember who you were when you opened the door there in the country," she said.

"So I gathered – but it's come to you, I see."

"Just now I saw the headline of the paper," she said wearily, dropping her voice and looking around to make sure no one was listening, "It says, 'Zaremba flees.' I couldn't read the rest."

"Did it?"

"Yes."

He leaned forward. "Do you think I'm a criminal?"

"I don't know what you've done," she answered uncomfortably. "I'm very sorry for you, whatever it is."

"I like your sympathy, but what if I told you I haven't done anything?"

She didn't answer, but sat staring down at her coffee cup. It was plain she didn't believe him.

"I hope you're not a hypocrite. I hope you're not going to tell me you've never done a dishonest act in your life?"

"In my adult life?" Cordelia paused, considering. "No, I don't think I have," she murmured apologetically. And then she remembered, "Oh, yes – there was one thing – that day I found the puppy – I forgot to buy a ticket for him when I got on the bus. It wasn't intentional though, so I don't know if that counts."

"Hmm. Nothing else?"

"No, I don't think so. Of course," she added, trying to be fair-minded, "I do lead a very sheltered life. I haven't ever been put in the position of having to choose between lesser evils. I imagine there might be very difficult situations at times, if one lived a very full life, engaged with other people…" she trailed off, "but I don't."

"Well, I can't say as much. But my misdeeds have been small. And I've tried very hard to run an honest business. My business is clean. In this case, I can truly say I haven't done a thing wrong. Not one thing."

She still didn't reply and kept her eyes down.

He drank the last of his coffee. "Come on," he said, his tone suddenly bitter, "I'll drive you home."

"Oh," she looked up. "That's all right. You don't have to do that. You've done so much already. I'll take the bus."

"It's no problem. I've nothing else to do. Even we criminals get to have our moments of relaxation."

"But aren't you supposed to be hiding or something?"

"And where better can I hide than with you?"

Cordelia looked at him with wide eyes.

"Ah, I see. You're very, very grateful to me, but I shouldn't ask for any favors?" His tone was ironic. "Come along, I'll drive you home anyway, and then clear off. You can't leave your father's car here – it'll get towed."

With an uncomfortable feeling that she was putting herself more and more in his debt, Cordelia reluctantly acquiesced. This, she told herself, was how people got pulled in to things they should never have touched with a barge pole. And yet she was so tired, and he was right about the car, and she hadn't the money for a taxi, and she would have such a long wait for the bus…And in any case, how could she possibly be more in debt than she already was?

They were driving slowly through Warsaw. How rarely it was, thought Cordelia, only on Hal's occasional visits, that she ever had the luxury of being carried so easily and quietly through the city. Even in her state of nervous exhaustion, she was aware of it. They had been traveling for awhile in silence. His question took her by surprise:

"Why wouldn't you work for me? It wasn't really because of what I said about the car's bumper, was it?"

She smiled slightly. "You know, after I left, I rather regretted it." This was untrue. She had regretted it deeply for a long time. "But there were lots of reasons. The other people who wanted the job; the difficulties of finding someone to stay with my mother. Lots of things." She shrugged in the dark of the car. "Did you hire that man who came in before me?"

"I don't remember any man. I hired a woman. She's okay. You'd have been better though."

"I doubt it. I've never worked for anyone before. Only free-lance. Here, we turn left here."

"You like to stay at home?"

"Yes." This was also not entirely true, but Cordelia was tired, and tired of talking. She just wanted to sit quietly. And, as if sensing her wish, the man refrained from asking any more questions. They drove in silence, turned into the quiet leafy lanes of a suburb on the outskirts of Warsaw, where the fallen leaves made patterns on the pavement beneath the street lamps, and pulled up, at Cordelia's direction, in the street before a large, dilapidated white-stuccoed villa, with a tile roof and a pillared porch and a white crumbling balustrade just visible through the night.

"Here," said Cordelia, "this is it." She prepared to get out of the car. "I want to thank you again, for everything you did. Really, I'm tremendously grateful. Thank you for driving me home too. And, um, I hope, um…" She wanted to say something about his difficulties but it didn't seem tactful, really, to mention the subject.

"What? Do you hope they catch me or do you hope they don't?"

So the man was a mind-reader, then.

"I hope you can prove that you're innocent and that you give yourself up and do so."

"I see you're an idealist," said the man dryly.

"Thank you again," she said, "goodbye." She added softly, "Good luck."

She was standing on the pavement, and she turned away, fumbling with her key to the gate in the high fence surrounding the house. Behind her, the car continued to idle, and she wondered why he didn't drive away.

"Oh," she said, realizing and turning back to the man and the car. "The car."

The man grinned at her through the windshield, then stepped out of the car, leaving it running.

"It was a temptation to make off with it, I assure you! Where do you want me to put it? Do you have a garage?"

"It's that shed at the back. I'll open the gate for you," returned Cordelia, embarrassed, and already turning away to deal with the lock.

He drove through the gate, along the short grassy drive by the side of the house, and parked the car in the garage. The lights went out and left them in semi-darkness as she approached. The man came out of the garage and held out the keys to her. She could just see him in the half light of dawn. Above them, the windows of the house were black.

"Thank you."

He nodded and made as if to walk past her. "Well, it's a cold lonely world out there, but I'm off to it…"

"Where will you go?" she spoke as if the words were forced out of her. She didn't want to know – and she very much wanted to know.

"I don't know. I daresay by the time I've walked a ways, I'll think of something."

"Oh yes. That's true. I didn't think of that. There aren't even any buses at this hour, are there?"

"No buses. But I suppose it's only – what – ten, fifteen kilometers back to the city center?"

"Twelve actually," said Cordelia, who was exact, and who suspected her feelings were being played on, but who couldn't help having sympathy for the man.

"I can walk that far. Although I do have a blister on one foot. It's really rubbing me. I must have got it helping you people out of the ditch. I wonder if I could just trespass on your time and goodness enough – You wouldn't have a bandage would you? I need to sit down somewhere, take my shoe off…" There was a tremor of laughter under his breath, and she heard it and didn't believe him. He didn't have a blister. But somehow she couldn't say to him, "I don't believe you. Go away now."

She hesitated for a moment. She didn't want to invite him inside. There was her mother, and Antek. Perhaps they would be asleep, but perhaps not.

He noticed her hesitation. "I wonder if you'll call the police when you get inside, tell them you know where Zaremba is?" His voice was suddenly serious.

"Of course not," she flashed back, offended, "what do you take me for? Even if you hadn't just saved my father's life, I'm not the kind to – to – to *squeal* on someone."

"It's your duty under the law in Poland, you know," he was watching her with a grimly ironic look.

"Then," she said with dignity, "I agree with Dickens that 'the law is an ass.' I should certainly not be guided by any injunction so counter to morality."

To her surprise, he laughed. "God, I love the way you people talk," he said irrelevantly.

She found him very puzzling, but she was dropping with weariness and she just wanted to go indoors.

"Come in with me; then you'll know I haven't called anyone. I think we have some band-aids." She headed towards the house. The door on the side was always open; she and her father insisted that Antek leave it open when they left as they had been locked out so many times; the neighbors protested against their hallooing round the house at late hours.

She pushed open the door and stepped into the dark hall, the man following her. She didn't bother to feel for the light switch, as she knew the bulb was out. It had been out for months, and would likely stay that way for a year, maybe for several years, as no one ever replaced a light bulb in that house unless forced by absolute necessity. Wasn't it perfectly possible to feel one's way in the dark? Cordelia was accustomed to it, and never gave it a thought unless an unexpected visitor had to be guided through the gloom.

"This way," she said in a low voice to the man as she shuffled across the entry towards the inner door, "I'm afraid there's no light. Watch the step." She was conscious of him following her. So conscious, perhaps, that she paid no attention to the dog, locked in the room ahead of them, scratching and snuffling at the crack under the door.

He burst upon them almost as soon as she'd turned the doorknob, pushing his way towards them with a shrieking volley of barks. She tried to slam the door on him again and caught him across the midriff, smacking him sharply in the ribs, so that he yelped in pain, but he was already wiggling frantically through, confirmed in his conviction of mortal danger, and although she grabbed for him, she only caught hairs from his tail as he launched himself upon the man and sank his teeth into the man's thigh.

The man gave a howl of pain and followed it up by a series of loud curses as he grabbed at his leg.

Cordelia struggled past the man, caught the dog by his collar, hauled him snarling backwards and thrust him protesting through the outer door and slammed it upon him.

Then they proceeded, both hobbling, into the inner hall and thence into the spacious kitchen. The man limped across the room and flung himself down in a chair. "Aaahh," he groaned, clutching his thigh above the knee. "Damn the little bu…" He subsided into inarticulate curses. "Aaah."

"Don't moan so loud, please," Cordelia urged, "please, you'll wake people."

"Why didn't you let him get run over? That is one dog that would not have been missed. Ow-wa. The world would not have been one whit the worse for his non-existence."

Cordelia thought he was overdoing it. "That could be said for most of us," she answered primly, turning her back on the man and searching through a cupboard. "I thought they were here, behind the oregano, but someone must have moved them. Oh, no, here they are." She removed a box of band-aids and held it out to the man.

"*Kurcze blade*! The damned dog's nearly amputated my leg and you offer me a tiny band-aid? "

"You said you wanted one," Cordelia said defensively, "for your blister."

"Yes, but now I need a wound dressing, dammit."

Cordelia didn't like to be sworn at. "I'm sorry he bit you," she said, beginning to get upset at the man, "but really – he's quite a small dog – it can't be that bad." And then, perhaps it was nerves or the beginnings of hysteria, but she gave a little choke of laughter at an unbidden thought.

"What, you think it's funny?"

"No, I was just remembering something in Shakespeare. It's what Mercutio says after he's received a mortal sword thrust and Romeo doesn't take it seriously: "No, 'tis not so deep as a well, or so wide as a church door, but 'tis enough, 'twill serve'."

"God, woman, I'm bleeding to death and you're making jokes."

"You're not bleeding to death."

"How do I know? I can't even see it unless I take my pants off. Can I take my pants off?"

Cordelia stared at him for a split second and then headed abruptly for the kitchen door.

"I didn't mean you had to leave," he called after her with a laugh, but she shut the door on him and leaned against it from the outside, her moment of humor evaporated. This day was a nightmare, unending. Only it wasn't this day anymore – she could see through the kitchen windows that the dawn was coming, dove-colored. It wasn't anymore the day that had begun so very long ago when she and her father had set out in the morning sunshine for Cousin Bronka's house. It was tomorrow. So much had happened, and it was already

70

getting on for morning, and soon she would have to start the tasks of a new day, and look after her mother, and go to visit her father in the hospital.

She straightened from the door. Maybe the man really was hurt. Maybe he should go to the hospital and have stitches. Only, of course, he couldn't do that if the police were after him. It had been her fault that he'd got bit, it was her wretched dog, and she hadn't been very sympathetic. But she was too tired to care about anything anymore. She didn't hear any sound from the kitchen. She would just go into the salon and sit down for one minute. The man would undoubtedly be able to take care of the damage himself. He seemed very competent.

She pushed open one of the double doors and made her way into the salon. Antek had not closed the shutters or the curtains and even as she sat down on a sofa the first rays of day were sifting through the housetops and the tree branches, casting rectangles of light upon the parquet floor, dispersing the last remnants of lingering night. The room, with its heaps of books, its clutter of papers and journals, its small upright piano, its threadbare tribal rugs, its dim oil paintings from the thirties, began to take on clearer contours. It was too familiar a room to impinge quite on her consciousness; and yet she had the vaguely-formed notion that the man in the kitchen had brought an entirely new element into the house. Somewhere a magpie was squawking. One leg still on the floor, she leaned back against a cushion. Instantly a sort of blanket of darkness fell over her and she was asleep.

She didn't know how long she had been asleep. It might have been hours or only a few minutes, but she became aware, even through her sleep, even with her eyes closed, that someone was in the room, standing over her.

She came to with a painful start, but it was only Antek. She made an effort and focused on his long form.

He waited until he saw she was looking at him and then observed, in his lugubrious manner, "There's a man in the kitchen."

She closed her eyes again. "Yes, I know."

"He, uh...he's not wearing his pants."

"That's okay." So it must only have been a few minutes then.

There was a long pause. "No. Because I want a cup of tea."

"I don't think his state of dress should deter you," she observed wryly, closing her eyes resolutely and trying to go back to sleep, but it was impossible now. Antek remained standing.

"His pants, on or off, are neither here nor there," he murmured, "it's his 'presence that disturbs me.'"

"Oh, all right," she said, giving in and rising. "I'll try to move him. Though where I'm going to put him, I don't know." She realized she was speaking about the man as if he were a stray animal. And also, that she had made the decision not to put him out and tell him to go away.

Antek sat down on the sofa to wait, and she was halfway to the door before he asked, "Who is he?"

"His name's Zaremba. The police are after him, I don't know why, but he helped get Tata to the hospital when he was having a heart attack, so we have to be nice to him, okay?"

Antek took all this in without a blink and addressed himself to the latter part of her sentence. "I haven't been nice to anyone for years." He laid himself on the sofa and put his foot up on the arm. "I doubt whether I am constitutionally capable of exerting myself to that degree."

"Yes, I know it would be a mortal wrench. I didn't mean you had to be friendly, just…" What she meant to say was 'just don't be too weird, okay?', but she couldn't say that, even though she knew he'd take it in stride.

"I'll just stay out of the way, shall I?"

"Good idea." It was certainly what he would do anyway. She crossed the room but was stopped by the sound of Antek clearing his throat slightly.

"He said," said Antek thoughtfully, staring out the window, "God-awful and rape. At least, I think that's what he said. Although it may have been…'unlawful tape.'"

"I don't have any cotton wool and tape," returned Cordelia with a little moan.

"Oh. Well, um…I do…for my cameras, you know."

"In your room?"

"Maybe."

"Thank you." She was already out the salon doors and had her foot on the first step of the stairs.

"You'll bring me that tea?" Antek called. He could be annoyingly vague and curiously persistent.

"Yes."

Cordelia, returning to the kitchen with the bandaging material, walked in without ceremony and found Zaremba still sitting on a chair with his pants across his lap, examining a rather nasty gouge a few inches above his knee. She stopped, uncertain whether to back out with an apology, or to hand over the material.

"Took you long enough," he said, the amusement in his voice belying the harshness of the words.

She handed him the cotton and tape. "It's electrician's tape, I think. It's all we've got."

"It'll do. At least it's stopped bleeding now."

"Here's some alcohol too."

"Why do you keep such a vicious beast?"

"Antek? He's my brother."

He laughed aloud at that, even as she realized her mistake. "I meant the dog."

"I'm sorry, I'm really sorry, he doesn't usually bite people."

"Doesn't usually? You mean only on special occasions?"

"Well, it's only happened once – twice – before. And he's never drawn blood like this. He didn't expect you to come in with me. It probably took him by surprise and that's why he behaved the way he did."

"I took your brother by surprise too. He didn't bite me, I'm happy to say, although he did back out without a word, looking like he'd seen a ghost."

"Yes. I didn't have time to tell him you were here. I'm sorry." She watched as the man began to wrap the tape around his leg, still uncertain whether she should retreat or offer help.

"I was afraid he was going to raise the neighborhood."

"No, you didn't. You didn't have any such fears," she corrected him.

"How do you know?"

"You didn't get dressed. If you were going to run you'd have wanted your clothes on."

"True." The man looked up at her as he wound the tape around his leg. "Now, why didn't that occur to me? I'm not a very practiced criminal, you see."

"You said you weren't a criminal at all, before. Have you changed your mind?"

"I haven't done anything wrong, I assure you." The man spoke seriously, looking directly at her, but she refused to meet his gaze. She didn't know why she continued to talk to him. She realized that talking to him, even in a ridiculous sparring sort of way, had somehow drawn them together. She wanted to retreat, so she didn't answer the man, but shrugged and turned away to make the tea for Antek.

"He's not really vicious? Your brother?"

"No, he's quite harmless. It's just that I'm so tired, and I was thinking of him – that's why I made such a mistake. It was stupid of me."

"You do look exhausted, I must say." Behind her back he pulled on his pants, rose, and came towards her, "You should go to bed."

She had started to put the water on, but she forgot what she was doing.

"Yes. You should too. Come, I'll show you to your room."

He stared at her. "You aren't going to put me out and tell me to walk to town?"

"No," she admitted candidly, "I find I can't. Come along." She put down the kettle and left the kitchen, the man following her. She took him upstairs at her slow gait, one step up, pulling the other leg after; she wanted nothing so much as to be rid of him, to be in her own room, to lie down on her bed and find oblivion again. They reached the landing, crossed in front of her mother's room, went up another floor. Here there were two small rooms under the eaves. Cordelia pushed open a door: she hadn't been up here for a long time to clean; the room emitted an odor of dust and old wood, but the large casement windows looked out onto fir branches and lawn. It was a pleasant place, she often thought, which she would have taken for her own room, except for the difficulty of the climb.

"It's a *tapczan*," she said pointing to an old sofa of indeterminate color and texture. "It makes into a bed."

"I know," he said, "when I left the country as a boy, all of Poland was sleeping on *tapczany*." He made a wry gesture, "I'm back where I started."

She pointed to a bucket on the floor. "That's in case it rains, so it's better not to move it. But I don't expect it will tonight. I'll bring you some bedding." She wished she had energy to clean things up for the man, but she realized she didn't. Every muscle ached. It had been agony to climb the stairs. She crept downstairs again, selected sheets from a closet, and wondered whether she could really make it back up to the top floor again. She set her teeth. But the man took the bedding from her. "I can do it, thank you. Go to bed."

She nodded, murmured "goodnight" and turned away, even as she remembered that it was already morning. She passed her mother's room: Please, she thought, don't let her wake up. By the time she reached her own door and looked back, the man was gone. She went into her room, crossed the bare wooden floor to the bed and prepared to lie down. There was something she was going to do, she thought, as she sat on the edge of the bed. Oh yes, she was going to check on the computer, the day's news. The article about Zaremba would doubtless be there. The computer was there on the desk, just six feet away, she had only to rise. Instead she lay down on the bed, drew her feet up, rolled over, and just as she was falling down a deep, deep well into sleep, she remembered, "I didn't bring Antek his tea."

4

'…But for Minister Ziobro, lack of evidence was not a sufficient reason to close the case. In his opinion, if the evidence is insufficient, then it should be twisted…' – Janusz Kaczmarek, Minister of Internal Affairs in Jarosław Kaczyński's government

'A politician like myself has to look after two areas: the prison system and the hospital system. Sooner or later he's going to wind up in one of them.' – Andrzej Lepper, Deputy Prime Minister in Jarosław Kaczyński's government

'…They are gangsters, on both sides. We long ago realized that anything could be expected of Lepper, but we didn't realize in time that that balanced politician Jarosław Kaczyński is not at all better. He also clearly considers that in the political struggle no holds are barred. That's terrifying…we are dealing with the destruction of the democratic state.' – Janusz Piechociński, MP, on whether the CBA's action was a political provocation

When she awoke again it was full sunlight and late, she realized, even before she came to consciousness. She rarely overslept and she had a moment of confusion: where was she and what time was it? The light creeping along the white plaster walls could be an Italian light, but the broad walnut leaves outside the window were Polish. She was in Warsaw. She drifted for a moment half in and out of sleep, dreaming of an article she was translating and for some reason of swamps; she was wallowing through a sea of words, through a brackish wash of real mud, it was clogging movement and pulling at her limbs, and then these images slid away and were quickly replaced by a sensation that something bad had happened. She opened her eyes and sat up abruptly. The whole of yesterday came back to her. Her father was in the hospital, and that man – that man Zaremba was in the house. She turned to look at the clock on her bedside table. Nine-thirty. What was her mother doing? Her mother was usually up before this. Why hadn't she waked her? She usually made enough noise when she rose in the morning that Cordelia would wake too. Cordelia rose hastily, realizing with a start that she was still in yesterday's clothes and that they were crumpled and dirty, with traces of mud around the bottom of her trouser legs. She'd lost her crutch too. She had a spare one though, that didn't fit very well, in the closet. She hopped across the room to fetch it, and then hopped to the door. She opened it and stuck her head out. Everything was very quiet. There wasn't a sound from her mother's room. Did she dare take the time for a shower before she went in search of her? The man was doubtless still sleeping upstairs. She decided to risk the shower, gathered up a set of fresh clothes and whisked into the bathroom. How awful she looked, she thought, regarding herself briefly in the bathroom mirror: pale and haggard and very, very old, but she didn't have time to dwell on the fact. She bathed and dressed as quickly as she could, and then, feeling better, made her way across the hall and peeked into her mother's room. The bed was empty, the covers thrown aside. Cordelia was rather startled to find her mother gone, but she supposed she'd find her downstairs. It was unusual, but not unheard of, for her to go downstairs by herself. She would find her sitting in the salon, looking over old music scores or slowly turning the pages of a book, as if she were reading. There would be an unfocused look in her eyes, and when asked if she liked Auerbach's *Mimesis* or Miłosz's *The Captive Mind* or whatever she had in her hand, she would nod and murmur 'very profound, very profound' – which Cordelia thought rather clever of her, given that it was perfectly apparent she couldn't tell one book from another, but only took them up out of the habit instilled by a lifetime of intense reading. But when Cordelia looked in through the double doors of the salon the room was empty. She glanced out the windows, crossed the room and went out onto the sunny porch, scanning the garden with its pool and clumps of tall perennial sunflowers. Her mother wasn't there, or, at least, not on this side of the house. That left the kitchen then. Cordelia pushed open the door and stopped short.

There sat her mother and Zaremba, peacefully eating bread and jam together. Her wicked dog was sitting by his knee, all enmity obviously forgotten. Zaremba looked up as she came in.

"Morning. Did you sleep well?"

"Er," Cordelia said, confused.

"The water's still hot. Shall I get you some tea?" He spoke as if his presence there in the midst of her family were the most natural thing in the world. He turned to Cordelia's mother "More tea, *pani*?"

"Yes, please."

Cordelia stared. She had the greatest difficulty getting her mother to eat anything and here she was eating breakfast quite normally. The man had risen, was preparing another cup of tea, and a plate of bread and cheese. He set these down at the table and motioned Cordelia towards them. She sat down, torn between gratitude and a feeling that he was usurping her role, that he had no business being there at all.

Her dog had given her the briefest of greetings, and then, as if unwilling to be distracted from a very important task, had returned to sitting beside the man, staring up at him with what might, charitably, have been considered adoration, but was more likely, Cordelia knew, calculating expectation.

"Oh, it's fresh," she said in surprise, taking a bite of her bread. Polish bread went stale four hours after baking. Where did you get all this?" she said, gesturing to the bread and jam, "We didn't have any."

"I went out and found a store. I'm resourceful."

"Obviously," she returned warily, and began to eat her breakfast, running her eyes over her mother's clothing to make sure it was all in place. Sometimes she managed to dress herself, and sometimes she had odd ideas about what to do with buttons, and Cordelia normally helped her. But everything was seemly. Cordelia wanted to ask the man how it had been when he met her mother – had she been surprised at his presence, or he at her, well, absence? But she couldn't say anything in front of her mother.

"And you, did you sleep well?" she asked politely.

"I didn't sleep much."

"No?"

"I had such pleasant company." He smiled at Cordelia's mother.

Oh no, thought Cordelia. She could imagine it clearly. Her mother had probably risen early and gone upstairs to his room. She would have walked in without knocking, seated herself in a chair, and doubtless begun to talk, endless, aimless talk in which half of each sentence made sense but appeared to be attached to the

80

latter end of some other sentence on quite a different subject. And the man, instead of waking her to deal with her mother, had listened politely and brought her downstairs, and made her breakfast, and left her, Cordelia, to sleep. Cordelia looked at her mother. She appeared calm and vaguely pleased, her hair, in a thick iron-gray bob, not much mussed. She looked back at Cordelia, her eyes almost but not quite catching hers and for a split second Cordelia thought there might be recognition. But then the moment passed.

The two women drank their tea, and the man drummed his fingers on the table and jiggled his leg under the table. Weren't you afraid of being seen, Cordelia wanted to ask him, when you went to the grocery shop? Had any of the neighbors seen him coming through their gate?

"What did my mother do while you went to the grocery shop?" she asked, not quite accusingly, because after all, her mother wasn't his problem and he couldn't have known that she shouldn't be left.

"Oh, your mother came with me."

"She came with you? But my mother never leaves the house!"

"We had a nice walk, didn't we *pani*?"

"Yes," Cordelia's mother smiled sweetly at him, "but the gondolier is always so loud."

"Just so. Exactly what I was going to say. They really should do something about these gondoliers."

Cordelia dropped her eyes to her plate. She didn't like him laughing at her mother. That was the worst of being in such a mental condition, she had often thought: people who would formerly have treated you with respect now laughed at you, without meaning any harm, of course – but still. And yet, her mother appeared pleased by the

81

answer – as if finally someone understood. In fact, she seemed unusually relaxed and animated. She had lost, for a moment, the slumped, vacant look that was so disturbing. With a strong effort of imagination, one could picture what a handsome woman she must once have been, rather in Cordelia's style only larger, stronger-featured, and more flamboyant perhaps.

"You weren't afraid someone would see you?"

"The man at the grocery store said he'd never seen me around before. I said I was your cousin, just come from the States for a visit. A very plausible story, I thought, given that your mother was on my arm. Other than that – lots of people saw us. But do you really think someone might be able to identify me? Behind the glasses? Even if they'd seen a picture of me somewhere, sometime? Very unlikely. All Poles fall into categories of facial types. I'm your average, big, broad-faced *facet*. There are five million more of me out there."

"Your…" she was going to say, 'your face isn't at all ordinary – it's the least ordinary face I remember seeing,' but then she didn't want to discuss the man's looks with him. She dropped her eyes to the dog. It was a smallish animal with wild black hair that stood on end like the hair of an electrified sheep-dog; it had roguish eyes which it kept glued on the man's face, and a lolling tongue.

"What about Hempseed here? I see you've got round him too."

"Too? Too? Whom else have I got around? I'm inclined to resent these allegations."

"I didn't mean…" she blushed faintly, "you know I didn't mean anything…anything bad." She saw that he was joking.

"Well, I had your mother for protection on the way out. I used her for a shield, I assure you, keeping her always between me and the teeth. You don't believe me – that's kind of you. On the way back I was armed with a sausage. Ergo, as you can see, we are the best of friends. I'm afraid it's not a disinterested friendship, but unfortunately, it's a Polish dog and what can I expect."

"You're cynical."

"I've had some experiences lately." His mood had changed suddenly, and these last words were spoken with a certain bite. Cordelia didn't know what to say. She was wondering when she could get to a newspaper stand to get the paper – or there was her computer upstairs – if she could find a moment to read the news there...Or did she want to know? Very shortly, she hoped, he would get up and leave, walk out of her life forever. She would take the bus and travel downtown to the hospital to visit her father. Perhaps they would let him come home. If so, they would take a taxi. When they got back, the man would surely be gone and life would resume as before.

As if realizing what sort of thoughts she must be having, the man abruptly changed the subject, asking various questions about the neighborhood and the house. Ordinary questions, like any visitor might ask. There was no harm in answering them, no harm in talking with him, she thought. She had only to get through breakfast – just the time to eat this piece of bread and drink a cup of tea.

The man was looking around the kitchen, running his eyes over the bumpy plaster walls, the high, stained ceiling, the barred windows with their rather crooked window frames, the sill that her father had studded like a hedgehog with crooked nails in one of his rare and soon abandoned attempts to improve their living conditions.

"I love these pre-war villas. There aren't many of them left in their original shape. How'd your father find it?"

"Oh, he inherited it from a great-uncle who died childless. I suppose that's why we're here actually. It seemed like fate, I think, that we got the house just at the point when my father would naturally have been looking for someplace else to go. Before that we always moved, every few years." But he wouldn't be interested in their family life, she realized, and returned to the house. "We were lucky the Communists never put tenants in it, like they did with most large houses. If it had had tenants, it would be in even worse shape than it is. Well, you know about that. You're in the construction business."

"How'd your great-uncle manage it?"

"Oh, he had a lot of relatives – his father had eight siblings – and so he had all his cousins and aunts and uncles registered as living here, even though they actually lived elsewhere. Of course, periodically the authorities would get suspicious and word would get out that an inspection committee was coming round and then all the relatives would be summoned and have to drop everything and flock here on the double to present the appearance of a full house. It was touch and go at times, I gather, and the relatives got rather tired of it too. However, their pleasure at foxing the powers-that-were was greater than any other consideration, I think."

"Yes, I can appreciate the sentiment," the man answered, his gaze continuing to travel around the room, coming to rest on the casement window beyond where they sat eating.

"Those must be chilly in winter."

Indeed, all the window frames in the house were warped; the draft around them was strong enough to slam doors at any time of year, and in winter the house was icy cold. However, Cordelia only answered "yes," absently.

"I could fix them for you. It'll be winter soon. It might make the house more comfortable."

"Oh, no, thank you, but we're used to them the way they are." And that, she realized, was a stupid thing to say, but she didn't want him to fix anything, didn't want to be any more in his debt. She finished the last of her tea and rose.

"I must go and visit my father now." She didn't add, but she hoped he'd understand, "so you'll be running along won't you?" She would have to find Antek, or wake Antek, and make sure he looked after their mother.

"The windows are not comfortable," said Cordelia's mother, with unusual aptness, "it's because of the paint. I'd like them fixed, but it's always too late in the day."

There was a brief moment of silence. It was the man who spoke first, "I'll be happy to fix them for you, *pani*, but first I must drive your daughter to town. We won't be long."

Cordelia's mother nodded her acquiescence graciously, while Cordelia stared.

"But…" she started.

"I daresay you want to…do all those things women do before they leave the house, so I'll get the car out."

Cordelia glanced at her mother. She was smiling and happy-looking for the first time in ages. She continued to eat her breakfast placidly. Cordelia couldn't start an argument in front of her, so she watched the man pick up the car keys from where he'd left them the night before and leave the house.

If he went with her, she wouldn't be able to buy a newspaper. Or could she? She debated the matter as she got ready to go, found Antek still in bed – "What, did you get rid of the fellow? Not yet? I'll wait till he's gone," he muttered, pulling the quilt up to his ears – and met the man as he was closing the heavy gates behind the car.

Now was the time to tell him that she was going to take the bus and that she wished he'd just take himself off – only, of course, since he'd saved her father, she couldn't phrase it so bluntly. She would say something like "I'm sure you have things you need to be doing..." She opened her mouth to say it, but the man forestalled her. "Get in," he said, gesturing towards the car. "I need to talk to you."

"But I don't want to talk with you," thought Cordelia. Or did she? Was it curiosity, attraction, or an unwonted desire to flirt with the devil? Z. Devel. – that's who he was. In any case, here she was, seated in the car.

The man made no move to pull the car away from the curb where it was parked. "Here," he said, reaching between the seats and holding out a newspaper to Cordelia. "I bought it when I went to the grocery this morning with your mother. I knew you'd want to see it."

Considerably startled, Cordelia reached for the paper, but he held it back for a moment.

"Bear in mind," he said, "that it's a pro-government paper. I don't read this one myself usually; I haven't been able to stand the tone it's taken in the last year. I don't know why it has blindly supported the government or why it has ignored the government's growing attempts to take over autonomous institutions and the judiciary, its flouting of due process...well, here." He handed the paper over abruptly. "It's not the time for discussing politics, is it?"

'*Zaremba Flees*' said the headlines. She gave the man a glance, but he was staring straight ahead. A woman with a baby carriage was passing, jiggling the handle up and down; she didn't so much as glance into the car. Cordelia

86

skimmed through the article, then read it again more slowly.

'Zaremba flees...yesterday evening , operatives of the CBA, the Anti-Corruption Bureau, were frustrated in their attempts to arrest a man believed to be involved in rigging a call for tenders to build much needed social housing for Warsaw's lower-income citizens. Pursuing their quarry to a small house in the countryside near Zabrzeg, the special agents of the corruption squad drew a blank. It is assumed that Dariusz Zaremba received inside information about the action. The developer's car was found, abandoned, but the developer himself was not apprehended. The authorities are confident, however, that an arrest is imminent and are intending an investigation into the source of the leak.

Euzebiusz Ogórek, spokesperson for the Ministry of Justice, confirms that an investigation has long been underway of Marek Grzegoliński, of the division of planning and development, a close associate of numerous high-ranking opposition politicians. "The blame for not supplying the ordinary citizens of this country with affordable housing should be placed squarely on the shoulders of those who should be held responsible," says Ogórek. "The Ministry of Justice has been diligent in pursuing those members of the elite who feel they can feed off the nation. We are combating corruption wherever it occurs; Pan Zaremba will not be at large for long."

There was a line or two more about Zaremba's age and fortune, implying that he couldn't possibly have made so much money honestly in so few years, and the note that he was a 'foreign investor,' who was 'passing himself off' with an Australian passport to cover his actual origins. Then there was a paragraph about government building contracts, about other investigations of city hall officials, and a paragraph about the housing shortage and the government's attempts to find out why its campaign promise of three million apartments for persons of lower income had not been fulfilled.

It was a political article, full of unsubstantiated assertions, Cordelia knew. It was either very poor writing or despicable journalism, but she also knew that that didn't mean all the allegations were false. When she'd read it several times, she sat playing with the edge of the paper. What did one say in this situation? "So…it isn't true?" Of course, he would say it wasn't true.

"It isn't true."

"It does sound like political bombast," she admitted. "You didn't corrupt this official?"

"No."

"So – I don't understand from the article, did you get the tender or not?"

"Yes, I got it."

"And you're going to build these apartments?"

"Yes. I've built quite a few already; a tender from last year –" He shrugged, "Why not? The money is only average, not great, but I saw it as a worthwhile – a charitable, shall we say – cause. This tender – that is, the one they're talking about – I won just this last month. Work hasn't started on the project yet.

She read the article again. "Yes, it's so vague…But if you didn't 'rig the call for tenders,' or, I suppose, induce someone to rig it, then I presume you can easily prove your innocence."

"Easily? Firstly, I'm guilty in everyone's eyes from the moment that came out. Look at yourself, for instance." She dropped her eyes, uncomfortable.

"And then – can I? It's very hard to prove a negative. Of course, legally, they have to have proof if they want to take me to court. But I doubt that's what they want; I very much doubt it will come to that. Although if it did, whether I were found innocent in court might depend on how determined the government is to make me guilty."

"What do you mean, how determined the government is? So you have done something or you haven't?" she asked sharply.

"I mean, how badly they need a scapegoat, a victim; whether they want me to be guilty badly enough to concoct evidence or not."

"Would they?"

"Haven't they?"

Cordelia put down the newspaper. She didn't know what to think. She didn't know enough about the laws or the courts or politics to have any idea what the man was facing or how likely his statements were to be true. She liked him, and she was in debt to him, but the fact that he was engaging and had saved her father didn't mean he was financially scrupulous.

"Anyway, as I was saying, I don't think it would come to that. I think they want to make a spectacular arrest for their public relations purposes. They want to show the police jumping on me and knocking me to the ground and dragging me away in handcuffs. Then they can say 'Look what we're doing to fight corruption. Look how we're being tough on big business. Vote for us. Look how we're protecting you against foreign capitalists who want to get their hands on Poland' – all that stuff is part of their campaign rhetoric. Who makes up the majority of their electorate? The uneducated from the countryside: such people aren't convinced by arguments but by slogans, by images – like someone, yours-truly for example, in handcuffs. And then Warsaw, you know, is in the hands of the opposition party. That's very uncomfortable for the party in power, not to mention that the opposition may – please God – win in the next elections. So Grzegoliński is an opposition party member. The government can use me to make the opposition look bad and themselves look good. They don't care what I've done or haven't done. I'm not even such a big figure — just someone whose name is seen on billboards around Warsaw — and winning Warsaw matters."

"So, what are you going to do now? Wouldn't it be better to give yourself up?"

"Why? Why should I let them use me this way?" He swore. "Why should I let them make a spectacle out of me on national television? Why should I give up my freedom for their campaign propaganda? You saw how they came to the house in Zabrzeg? All those sirens, the combat gear! Like cowboys. Like little kids with guns. They make me sick. All that has nothing to do with the law. Afterwards I could file for unlawful arrest, but what good would that do? They'll have had their profit from me: none of them will go to jail for it. I, on the other hand, might end up spending a lot of time in jail if it suited them to keep me there. Not to mention the amount of bail if they let me out."

"But if you run, it makes it seem like you're guilty."

"I told you, I'm guilty in everyone's eyes already. I'm going to wait and see what happens next. If they don't catch me, they might go after someone else. That'll take the pressure off. And in any case, if they lose the elections, everything will change. If they don't..." he shrugged and repeated, "I'm thinking what to do and I'm going to wait for the moment to see what happens."

"That's awful."

"As you say." He started the car, and they slid into the street.

"Aren't you afraid of being seen? Wouldn't it be better to stay hidden?"

"Are you going to hide me?"

"Um…I'm not going to turn you in, if that's what you mean. I told you I wouldn't yesterday. And my father won't say a thing either, you can be sure, and not only because of saving his life. He just wouldn't. He has his foibles but he would never fink on someone. Even if he's read this" – she gestured to the article "or seen the news on a television at the hospital, which I doubt. Antek and my mother are no problem. You don't have to worry about that at all."

"No, I mean, are you going to let me stay at your place for a few days?"

So there she was, caught, and she had to come up with an answer at once.

"You don't have any place to go? What was that place in the country?"

"See, that's the thing. You can't know who's a friend and who isn't in this situation. Someone – a decent-seeming fellow, late twenties, nice wife and kid, who works at the Ministry of Justice – something fairly low down, you know, no salary at all – well, I helped this fellow out a bit when he was trying to buy an apartment in one of my buildings, and so you could say he owed me a little, I mean, he might conceivably have felt one good turn deserved another – anyway, yesterday afternoon early, it was maybe two or three, I think, he called me and told me that he'd heard rumors, that he had ideas, that he thought something was going to happen."

"He said that perhaps they wouldn't bother to send such a big production. Maybe a patrol car would just show up, or maybe they'd just send the local policeman round, and he'd say, 'would you mind showing up at the office to fill out some forms'… I mean, you never can tell how these things will happen, can you? I'm really not such a big fish. One thing seemed as likely to me as the other. I was pretty rattled, then, I can tell you – I mean, completely thunderstruck. As far as the business goes I've always done things by the book – which, as you probably know, with all the conflicting laws here, can be extraordinarily difficult – and then this, like a bolt from the blue."

"So the first thing I did was call the lawyers I normally use. It's always been so 'and what can I do for you today, Mr. Zaremba,'" – he mimicked someone bowing and smiling: "Yesterday," he grimaced a little at the recollection "it was very different: it was all very hoity-toity and 'It's not really our subject, we deal in real estate law.' Like I'm some sort of criminal. I'll have to find others."

"And in the meantime, I thought, if the police are coming for me, I'd rather they didn't drag me out of my office, or from my apartment in the middle of town, with all my acquaintances and the street gaping. My first thought was really only that I preferred to be arrested more discretely – that's the prime reason I left town. That, and to buy a little time to think. I ran out and got in my car – and as I was driving I called a fellow I know on my cell phone and I asked him to get some good lawyers for me and I told him where I was going and to get in touch with me there. And he refused point blank, said if I was having those kinds of difficulties he didn't want to be associated with me. This was someone from whom, for various reasons, I should have been able to expect assistance. Also, I must say, a very honest businessman. It was a taste of what to expect, but fortunately, he's not the only person I know, so I made some more calls. Then I thought that the cell phone might be traced so I threw it in the river when I passed. The house in Zabrzeg belongs to a friend, a real one.

After I'd been there at the house for an hour or two though, and had been pacing about and thinking, I became convinced that the police would have had me under surveillance and probably would have been listening in on my phone call. I was right. I had just about got to this point in my reasoning, and was expecting them to come, when you showed up. – You showed up and it seemed like fate so I decided to follow where you led. Then I heard the sirens and had to make a decision fast. By that time I'd decided it would be very much better if they didn't find me. Why should I be their propaganda tool? Why should I, who hate everything they're doing to this country, help them win the elections, even in such a small way, by being their sacrificial goat?"

He stopped abruptly and looked at her. "Do you know, after you came to my office last year, I got your number and tried to call you?"

"Really?"

"Yeah. I got some gruff fellow growling 'she's out'. So I thought that's that. A boyfriend or a husband. I suppose it was your brother."

Cordelia didn't know what to say, she was too surprised. Had he thought about her then? Just as she had thought about him? This was something she would have to think over later. Her nervous hands inadvertently rustled the newspaper article, and he instantly reverted to his story.

"When I heard the number of sirens I knew they'd decided to pursue me there and realized I'd made a tactical error. So much easier, you know, to arrest me in the countryside than in an apartment building with tight corridors. It'd make for much better television footage and there wouldn't even be any necessity for crowd control while the police are running about waving their guns."

They were driving along slowly, and the man added "I was going to slide out of the car in Warsaw, and hopefully, you would never have known I was back there...Or did you know?" He looked at her quizzically.

"I suspected. I wasn't sure. It was horrible."

He gave her a rather lopsided grin but didn't apologize. "Then your father had the heart attack, and everything sort of changed for me. I was furious thinking about my misfortune – I was totally wrapped up in my problem and then I was jolted out of it all. Now it's just – another pothole." He steered the car smoothly around a real one in the road before them. "Like when we were kicked out of America and we thought it was the end of the world and actually it was the beginning of everything."

Was the man trying to convince himself? Cordelia wondered. He actually did seem to be in quite good spirits most of the time. Maybe that was having confidence or vitality or energy. Or maybe he just didn't have any particular feelings or sensitivities. She didn't say anything. She realized she very much wanted to believe that the man was innocent, but that she couldn't quite believe that even an authoritarian government, even one that had shown it was willing to overstep legal bounds, would go to the lengths of selecting a victim at random. Poles could be blind and bigoted but they were rarely heartless. Still, there was that saying about power corrupting...

"Cordelia," she was startled by the use of her name. He should say *pani* to her, she thought, the formal you, not use her first name as if they were friends. She was mulling this fact, wondering why the sound of her name should have sent a sort of electric shock through her body, when the insistency of his next words effaced these worries.

"I didn't do it." The words were said individually, distinctly, with appeal and sincerity. She almost believed him.

"You don't believe me, do you?"

She had to be honest with him. "I wish I could. But I don't know." There was a moment of silence, then he said something under his breath; she thought it was probably obscene. "Have you heard of that air force officer who was arrested?" He asked after a little silence.

She shook her head.

"This colonel is the head of an elite flying force – dedicated career officer very conscious of his honor – that type. Naturally, the force has an airfield, and naturally, the grass along the runways needs to be mown. The colonel has for years had an agreement with a local farmer, who mows the land for free in exchange for the right to collect the hay, thus saving the force quite a lot of money that would otherwise be spent on mowing services. The colonel was accused of leasing state 'agricultural land' without a tender and of exposing the state treasury to the loss of hundreds of thousands of dollars. As proof of their anti-corruption efforts the powers-that-be wanted to film him being arrested by a squad of CBA agents and policemen at his base – unfortunately for their scenario, when they arrived, he wasn't there. He showed up at a station when he heard that he was wanted and there he was arrested (without a warrant), lied to, prevented from contacting his lawyer, brought to court and placed under arrest for three months. His rights were transgressed in every possible way; he was unable to get in touch with his family; not to mention the humiliations – stripped naked and searched every time he was taken in and out of his cell. The Supreme Court has ruled he's completely innocent. Everyone knows it was a vile public relations move – which, in his case, was uncovered. It's the same with me – only I might not be so lucky; once such people start to abuse their powers there's no knowing how far they'll go."

"I have to go to the hospital," she said miserably, "to see my father."

"Yes," he agreed, "that's where I'm taking you." They drove for a long way in silence, Cordelia only vaguely aware of the passing of landmarks, of people standing at bus stops, of cars and trucks and trees and the thickening buildings, the high-rises. There had been a moment when she had looked up and seen a sign 'Zaremba Development' in front of a construction site with an enormous crane. Yes, his name was visible, only she, who so seldom left home, had been unaware. And now, she knew, with a vague sense of anger at herself, that she should be thinking about her father, and all her thoughts were centered on the predicament of the man beside her. But it wasn't until they were stopped at a busy intersection, watching a stream of pedestrians pass, that she dared to ask the question that had been on her mind.

"And if they catch you, and you can't prove your innocence, what will happen?"

"You mean, how long will I go to jail for?"

"Yes."

"It's not really a question I've ever had to consider before – but I believe it's up to eight years. The laws are not as draconian here as they are in, say, the States. With parole, I shouldn't think it would be for more than a few years at most – if it came to that. The jail bit itself doesn't matter so much."

"Doesn't matter?" She stared at him in consternation.

"No. What matters is that I'll lose my reputation and then my business. That's the – painful – point. The injustice."

And then when she didn't say anything, he added: "Never mind. Easy come, easy go. I just have to look at it as another challenge. I'll go back to Australia; there no one will ever have heard of little dirty doings in Poland. I've made one fortune. I can make another." The words contained both his suppressed anger and his confidence. The light turned green and the car continued effortlessly across an enormous square and on through traffic.

"Don't you think..." suggested Cordelia, as they stopped in the hospital parking lot and he came round to help her out of the car, "that you'd better keep out of sight? Don't you think you'd better wait here?"

"I think the last place anyone would look for me is with you at the hospital."

And also, thought Cordelia with a flash of disquieting intuition, you are excited by danger – some part of you likes it – but as she couldn't command him to stay in the car, there was nothing to do but follow him across the parking lot and into the building.

They found that her father had been moved to a different ward. They had the routine quarrel with various officious persons about whether they would or would not wear little plastic baggies over their shoes – "to be purchased from the machine on the other side of the hospital – 2 zlotys each." – Only worn by those who allowed themselves to be bullied, said Zaremba, who refused point blank and swept on, rather to Cordelia's admiration, and found the room.

Her father was in the furthest of five beds. "Ah," he greeted Cordelia with a loud moan as they entered the room, "They've been giving me to drink mandragora. Mandragora in its worst form. Get me out of here."

"Breakfast must have been bad," Cordelia explained in a murmured aside to her companion.

"Yes, we've come to take you home," said Cordelia more loudly.

His voice sounded thin and tired but had its usual buoyant timbre.

"I wish to leave," he waved an arm full of tubing at the other four elderly men in the room, "'these fat and greasy citizens'."

"Shh, *Tato!*" Cordelia admonished him in scandalized accents.

But the apostrasized citizens – perfectly slim and trim – watched Cordelia and Zaremba proceed through the room with the curiosity born of utter boredom, and no sign of having understood.

"Hi, Tato," said Cordelia, coming up to his bedside, "how're you feeling?"

He didn't answer. He was staring at Zaremba.

"Who *are* you?" he asked.

Cordelia froze. She hadn't thought of what she was going to tell her father. She opened her mouth and closed it again several times, like a carp out of water she thought later in disgust.

Zaremba answered for her. "Your son-in-law, don't you remember?"

Cordelia's father turned his head and gave his daughter a wild look from under raised brows.

"I have forgotten many things", he murmured, "and will, I hope, live to forget many more, but that I had acquired a son-in-law, I don't think would have passed me quite by."

Cordelia spoke quickly. "I'll explain everything later. They're letting you go home, so I'll collect your clothes, and if you want to get dressed, we can go. Here's the nurse to undo your IV." She bustled about and soon they retreated into the hallway again while he dressed.

"What am I going to tell him?" Cordelia muttered urgently to Zaremba during a break in the stream of visitors filling the aisles. But he wasn't listening. He was staring at something down the end of the hallway. Abruptly he swung in front of her.

"Cordelia," he said swiftly, "that door just behind you, step back and step through it. Quick!"

The urgency in voice was such that she was impelled to obey. She backed a scraping, hasty step, pushed against a heavy door and was about to step through when she was grasped and almost whisked or lifted inside by Zaremba, who pulled the door shut behind him. It was dark.

"What...?" she cried, startled, feeling her back bump against a shelf – a linen closet, she felt instinctively – the man's body against hers. He moved away.

"Shhh."

"What is it?" she whispered, not liking the situation at all, her heart pounding.

"I saw someone I know," he whispered back, "someone who works at city hall in the planning department...Of all the bad luck! I suppose he's visiting someone. *Cholera* take him!"

"But we can't stay here!"

"Just a moment. Shhh."

But at that moment someone grasped the door from the outside and pulled it firmly shut. There was the sound of a key turning in a lock.

"Bugger!"

"I wish you'd stop saying that!" Cordelia whispered fiercely. "We're locked in."

The man laughed under his breath. "Yes. What would you say?"

"This is intolerable!"

"Do you want to scream?"

'Bugger,' thought Cordelia, and then, 'this man is demoralizing me'. And then, this is, this is…she was torn between an impulse to burst into hysterical giggles and another to pound her fists on the door. Her father would be waiting for her, waiting, waiting, and she wouldn't appear.

"If you wanted to hide here, okay," she snapped in an underbreath at the well of darkness in front of her that she knew to contain the man. "But why did you have to take me with you?"

"Misery loves company."

"What if they don't open the door again till tomorrow? It's a linen closet, did you see?"

"We'll have to hope someone dies," he whispered back, his voice sounding uncomfortably close to her ear, "And that they remember to change the sheets for the next patient."

"This isn't funny!" she hissed back, "When they do open the door they'll think we came in here to steal something. How embarrassing." Cordelia felt herself flushing at the thought.

"Of course not. Don't worry. They'll think we came in here for a quick…you know."

"Oh!" it came out as a mortified and disgusted wail.

"It takes people that way sometimes, you always read about it – a catastrophe, an escape from danger, and *hop*, people fall about fornicating like mad. Er, want to try?"

She knew he wasn't remotely serious but she answered furiously, "Stop it! Stop it and get us out of here!" Why she had any hope that he could do so, she couldn't have said.

"Let me think." There was a long pause. Beyond the door they could hear voices, the shuffle of slippers, a jangling tray table being wheeled by.

There was a slight scrape and his lighter lit up the closet: shelves of white starched linen, tightly packed, unidentified cardboard boxes, a broom and mop and some cleaning supplies.

Outside they could hear a young man's voice saying "no Tato, I can't bring you a beer here. I can't." Then an older man growling something indistinct, then the younger one again: "No, Tato, forgive me, no *wino* either, no." The argument moved on down the corridor.

"Light switch is on the outside," whispered Zaremba, running the lighter about the space, "that figures – but, we're in luck. See these hinges," he said, illuminating a few inches of the doorframe with the lighter flame. "They're offset, which means – hopefully – I can pull the door off them." He turned and raised an eyebrow at Cordelia, and let the lighter go out. His voice came out of the darkness. "We have to wait till there's no sound in the corridor. When I tell you, you'll have to move back out of the way, and you'll have to be ready to hop when I've got it open, okay?"

"Okay."

"Here, hold the lighter for me." She felt more than saw him holding it out to her.

"I can't. I can't hold the lighter and my crutch at the same time. And without my crutch I can't move fast," she muttered in embarrassment. She hated having to talk to him about her disability. But the situation was desperate.

He took it in stride. "Can you hold it in your other hand?" he whispered.

"Yes, but I can't put it there; I can't light it."

"Okay, where's your hand?" he flicked the lighter on, found her disabled fingers, and wrapped them around the lighter. "Okay?"

"Okay."

He put his ear to the door and they waited. Footsteps came and went, voices grew loud and died away. He looked at her, waiting scared in the dark, the flame beginning to heat her fingers uncomfortably but she couldn't complain. He shook his head, shrugged his shoulders. "Have to risk it sometime." And then he was pulling at the pin, wiggling his car keys under its head, prying, prying, pulling out one, then another, then a third, grasping the edge of the door with the tips of his fingers, pulling it inwards, there was light from the hall; they caught the back of someone's head passing and continuing on, and if there were other people, if anyone was looking, they didn't know. "Go," said Zaremba behind the door to Cordelia, and she scooted as best she could into the passageway, not looking about, not wanting to see if anyone was watching her, and turning she saw Zaremba's back for a second as he pulled the door to, almost closed, and came to her side, taking her arm as they proceeded down the hallway, and then suddenly reaching over and snatching the lighter out of her fingers. The flame went out.

"Damn. Did it burn you?"

"I don't know; let's go." Her one idea was to put as much space as possible between herself and that closet. The passageway was full of people, but no one seemed to be paying them any attention.

"Here, this is the room. Stop looking so scared. No one's after us. 'Least not yet."

"What do you mean?" she cast him an even more agitated glance.

"Never mind. Let's just hurry, okay? Is your father ready?"

He was, and they were shortly making their way back down the corridor. They were passed by a woman carrying a mop and a set of keys.

"Come on, come on, come on," Zaremba urged. Cordelia was all willingness but her father, who was still holding his peace but was looking more and more puzzled and displeased, was not to be hurried.

"Let's wait for the elevator," he said, as they came to the end of the passageway.

"No, no, no, the stairs are just here," said Zaremba.

Down the stairs...Behind them there was a resounding crash and a startled yell.

"What was that?" asked Cordelia, as they paused on a landing.

"The door," said Zaremba with a glint of unholy amusement, "was off its hinges. I couldn't put it back. Come on, come on."

"I've destroyed hospital property," said Cordelia with a look of horror.

"You?" said Cordelia's father with a look of amazement.

They as nearly trotted to the parking lot as is possible for a heart-attack patient and a polio victim.

But when her father was seated in the car, and Zaremba was holding the passenger door for her, she shook her head. "No. You go on, go on home. I have to go back and pay for the damage."

Zaremba stared at her curiously. "There wasn't any damage. They can put the door back on the hinges, the same as I took it off."

"Really?"

"Cross my heart. Get in."

She got in.

5

'[The authorities...] have the right to extraordinary intervention in various areas – not so that fat guys can bask in their own power, but in order to protect the community and the common good, when they are threatened.' – Artur Zawisza, head of a parliamentary investigative commission

'The Kaczyńskis have what they wanted – they are unrestrainedly building the pillars of absolute power, one expression of which is, for instance, the establishment of the horrendous Central Anti-Corruption Bureau.' – Kazimierz Kutz, film director, senator

'Poland is currently a country in which successive safety mechanisms protecting us against authority are being dismantled.' – Irena Kamińska, judge of the Supreme Administrative Court

It was warm out, one of the last, rare warm late afternoons of September when most of the leaves still held firm on the trees, and birds chirped and called, and the soft yellow radiance thrown over all the vegetation seemed truly to deserve the phrase of 'golden Polish autumn.'

Cordelia sat in a wicker chair on the porch, only vaguely seeing the garden, noting only in some distant corner of her mind that the dahlias needed another stake and that the floss jovis, whose fuzzy gray leaves harmonized with the lavender asters and the light-colored walkways, was spreading so fast it would surely swamp the black-eyed-susans. Now she just wanted to be still. She tried very hard to shut the outer world away and not to think of anything.

Nearly every day from spring until late fall, weather permitting, she came out on the porch and spent some small portion of the day in this chair. The garden was an old garden, predating their coming to the house, and it changed, subtly, with each passing day; her own life had seemed immutable in comparison; her habits, she knew, were already the habits of an elderly person. Having been faced too young with the loss and care of her mother, she had managed to make a life for them both, but the process had left its mark. Every day for the past ten years had been almost identical, there had been the same duties, the same small distresses, the same minor excursions to nowhere very interesting; only the seasons had changed, only she herself had grown from being a young woman tentatively hoping that life was still ahead, to a woman aware that youth had nearly slipped away and that the probabilities of the future being different were slim. There had been small pleasures too, of course. She had her books and her love of nature and the self-respect of knowing she was useful and had nothing to reproach herself with. If she had felt in some respects unfulfilled – well, young people always, she thought, started out with greater expectations than were reasonable. If she had felt, occasionally, trapped – well, now she was being given a look at the broader world and it was doubtless going to make her appreciate her usual cloistered existence.

Here, on three sides, the villa's garden was cut off from the neighbors by strategically placed hedges and trees. The other side of the lot bordered a small orchard; the apples fell to the ground and added their ripe scent to the air but no one came to pick them up. It wasn't quiet here, though. Nowhere in Poland was it ever quiet: someone was always hammering or sawing or mowing the lawn or running a power tool; someone was always involved in a manic and often ill-advised attempt to improve his surroundings: someone was always out walking in the street, the sidewalks were never empty, dogs barked, children called, rounded older women passed on squeaky bicycles, but these sounds were too familiar to disturb her or even to register much. For Cordelia, what mattered was the house behind her and there all was still. Her mother and father were both sleeping and Antek had disappeared. She didn't know what had happened to Zaremba. He had also faded from view for the moment.

She wondered where he was and found that she couldn't, after all, not think about him. She was going to have to weigh and consider and take stock. The subject was before her and the subject was: what was she going to do about this man? Or did she need to do anything? But no, she couldn't think about it, because the porch doors were opening and here was Zaremba himself, handing her a glass of tea, and seating himself on the broad porch balustrade with another.

He gestured towards her glass, "I thought it was time someone brought *you* one for a change."

She was grateful, and both rather touched and surprised that he'd noticed her efforts, but she couldn't leave him with misapprehensions. Of course, things had been rather hectic since they'd got home. Her father had retired to his room and asked that lunch be brought to him there, and Antek had shouted from behind his door – they had heard his footsteps pounding up the stairs as they came into the house, only his voice had come booming down the stairwell, "Cordelia, tea for me too," and her mother had become difficult about the change in routine and had fussed and followed Cordelia about asking impossible questions like "why did you put the cat back?"

"It's not like that usually. Antek only asks me to wait on him at the moment because he's trying to avoid you. Not," she hastened to assure him, "that it's anything personal against *you*."

The man didn't answer, and she had time to wonder if she were glad or not to see him. She couldn't make up her mind; there seemed to be no escaping the man. She sipped the tea. The silence between them hung, full of unsaid things. He broke it with an inconsequential question, toying with his cigarette pack as he put his tea down on the cement balustrade.

"So, are you all Polish or American, or what?"

"Or what, I guess," she answered with relief. They wouldn't talk yet of heavy topics, they would just make small talk and pretend they had no problems, but were just two people, beginning to grow acquainted under quite normal circumstances. "Misfits anyway. My father was born here in Poland, but his parents emigrated when he was ten or so. First to France, then to the States. He's been moving ever since. If it hadn't been for getting this house just about the time he was thinking of retirement we'd probably still be moving. I think we moved every three years all through my childhood. But it's more economical to live here, now."

"And your mother? She's not Polish – at least she seems to have difficulties with the language."

"No, no, she's all American. That is, she's of Italian descent, but she was born in America."

"So your hair's that color naturally. It isn't dyed."

Cordelia was taken aback. Anyone living in Poland was accustomed to blunt comments, but people rarely referred to her hair, even if it was unusual in a country where the national average was dark dishwater.

He continued, "I thought that raven's-wing color had to come out of a bottle."

"No," said Cordelia with a scowl, not sure whether he thought raven's wing was a good thing or a bad. At least he hadn't said 'crow color.'

If he was daunted by her expression he didn't show it, but turned the conversation back to her mother. "Must be hard for an Italian-American to fit in here, learn to speak, and all that."

"Yes, I'm afraid that's what probably did it to her, the final straw," Cordelia murmured reflectively, glad to get away from the uncomfortable topic of her personal appearance.

"What, the Polish language?" the man laughed.

"You laugh, but believe me, the Polish language is no laughing matter to a foreigner. Yes, truly, I think it was that. How could anyone deal with three genders in six different declensions, following I don't know how many not very regular patterns? And don't forget plural and singular as well. In English one says 'dog' wherever it comes in a sentence. In Polish one says 'pies', 'psa', 'psie', 'psem', 'psu', then 'psy', 'psich', 'psami', 'psom' and so on. For every noun, there are something like thirty-six possibilities of getting it wrong. It's enough to drive anyone mad. And then, you know, my father dragged my mother from country to country, every few years a different language. And she learned them all – that was what was admirable. But when we finally came back to Poland and she realized she'd have to come to grips with the language, the spirit failed her, I think. Meaning seemed harder and harder to convey, and the essence of what she had to communicate slid further and further away, until it was gone entirely." Cordelia stopped abruptly.

"I'm sorry. You're not interested in my mother's problems, I don't know why I babbled on. I don't usually talk to anyone." She picked at a loose strand of wicker in the chair. Why did she feel this almost uncontrollable desire to unload a mass of stored-up thoughts onto this stranger? Was it because of what they'd been through together in the last twenty-four hours or was it something about the solidity of his physique that was deceiving her into a belief that he was a reliable recipient?

"And you don't think that not having anyone to talk to is a problem?"

"Well, I suppose it is, but not one that's ever going to get solved, so..." she shrugged. She had confided more in this stranger than in anyone in the past fifteen years. And if anyone had problems it was he.

"I only meant, I think you have enough problems of your own."

"Yes, but I must say that yours rather put mine in perspective."

She looked up into his eyes at that, quite surprised. "I? I don't have any serious problems."

"A curious – I mean, an admirable – point of view." He shook his head slightly and took a sip of his tea.

"So your mother has 'dementia *polskości*' not '*precoce*'. And your brother? What's with him?"

"Oh, poor Antek. He wasn't always like this, you know. I mean, he was always reserved, but he was perfectly functional. When we came back to Poland, he set himself up in a printing business. Printing photos, blueprints, that sort of thing. And it went rather well, he was making some money, he hired a few employees. We were all very pleased and impressed at his abilities. An entrepreneur in our family! It was something extraordinary. Of course, I realize it was all small beer compared to your doings, but we'd never had anything to do with the capitalist spirit. My father's friends are mostly university professors, you know: charming, some of them, but, well, they tend toward compartmentalized intellect and two left thumbs. The ability to make money isn't their leading feature. Anyway, it didn't work out so well for Antek; I guess you could say he wasn't tough enough. One day, when he was out to lunch, an employee accidentally threw out some negatives that should have been kept. Just one little oversight. It turned out they were part of a geological survey of Kamchatka – part of someone's doctoral thesis, and this poor person had flown specially to Russia, hired an airplane, special excursions – you know, had gone to tremendous expense to get this material, and it was supposed to be included in his thesis for his upcoming defense. Only it had all gone into a shredder, past retrieval. Of course, Antek offered to pay for a return trip, to cover the damages – but there wasn't any way, really, to repair the harm. We tried to tell him it wasn't his fault; that things just happen. He wouldn't listen. It shook him so much that he closed down the business, and he's been here in the house ever since. He never goes out, never wants to see anyone. He's enveloped in a kind of lethargy; there are days he can't even seem to talk normally. All he does is take photos.

"Yes, in business you have to roll with the punches," said the man reflectively. "But his photos – they're very good, actually, if those are his hanging in the stairwell. Works of art."

"Yes," she looked up at him in pleased surprise. "Yes, they are, but not many people can see it. When my father shows them to his colleagues they don't know what to say."

"Well, of course, insects aren't a topic to appeal to everyone."

"No. But I think people take them as an expression of his oddity, and they're not. They're compositions – I'm glad you saw that."

"Van Gogh…"

"*Not* a good comparison," she cut him off severely. "Antek's sane, just – different."

"Fair enough," he laughed. There was a moment of silence, and his next question took her by surprise.

"Was it a car accident?" he gestured with his chin towards her arm, as he took a drag of his cigarette, letting out the smoke slowly.

"No," she scowled more deeply than before, taken aback. "Polio."

"What, weren't you vaccinated?" the man asked, with casual tactlessness.

Cordelia hated the idea that anyone was noticing her disability. She shrank into herself and didn't answer at once.

"I shouldn't ask?" the man queried, looking puzzled. "I'm sorry…"

"It doesn't matter," Cordelia got a grip on herself, "yes, I was vaccinated. But they're not 100% effective, you know, the vaccinations, that is, nearly but not quite. You won't get it, though; there hasn't been a polio case in

Europe since 2002. But we're still one of the largest groups of disabled people in the world." She relaxed as she spoke, what did it matter, after all, when he spoke so matter-of-factly, why shouldn't she?

He continued to sit on the balustrade, holding his tea cup by the rim between the thumb and forefinger of his left hand, and smoking a cigarette, which he gripped by the thumb and second finger of his right hand, bringing it up to the center of his lips, his fingers cupped around it as he drew it away. It was the way older workmen smoked, or men from the 'margins' as one said in Poland. Cordelia watched the smoke curl up into the air as he regarded her over a drag.

"You'll end up like my father," she observed mildly, "with heart problems."

"'*Hunde, wollt ihr ewig leben?*'" he barked in a very credibly German voice.

Cordelia stared at him in surprise and question.

He grinned. "It's what Frederick II said to some of his guards when they refused to charge against fearsome odds. 'Dogs, do you want to live forever?' It's stayed with me, ever since I read that."

Cordelia opened her mouth to say, "You read?" and closed it again before the words had time to escape. But the man had caught the meaning of her look.

"Oh yes, don't look so surprised. '*Et in arcadia* – or at least, in university arcades – *ego*.'"

"I didn't mean..." said Cordelia, dropping her eyes, embarrassed.

"Yes, you did."

"Yes," admitted Cordelia with half a laugh, "I did." She was surprised at herself; she didn't trust him, not at all, really, and yet she felt she could say anything to him, felt almost exhilarated by the sense of having an interlocutor, and perhaps he felt the same – or perhaps, she admitted the possibility – he was trying, for whatever reason, to win her over, to assert his innocence by gaining her confidence. And yet, she argued internally, what did he have to gain? She'd already agreed to hide him; her house was open to him; her family had accepted him. Her father had listened to their joint explanation in silence, had read the newspaper article; had put his hand on his heart and murmured that since he was indebted to *pan* for his life, he was naturally inclined to offer him every assistance, but that he had no desire to burden the December of his life with unraveling mysteries of such magnitude, and would *pan* just kindly drive on home and let an old man go to bed.

No, Zaremba had been assured of his welcome, he had no need to strive for more.

"So do you have any other brothers or sisters? Someone to help you?"

"There's my brother Hal. He's quite a bit older – Antek and I were very late children. He lives in the States and doesn't really come into the picture."

The man sitting on the balustrade raised his eyebrows.

"He's very busy." She tried to sum up his life as it appeared to her, "He works for a large corporation. He has three kids. They watch television."

"Only?"

"Sometimes they're taken to play soccer or football – and then they're brought back again."

"That's not bad, is it?"

"No-o," she shrugged, thinking but not saying 'bland as boiled potatoes.' On the other hand, she reminded herself, perhaps they wouldn't grow up to be, like herself and Antek, highly-strung, over-conscious, complicated, and complex-ridden. But she didn't say that either. "It's okay. Sometimes I think that my childhood was richer though – whatever its drawbacks. I can remember sitting by myself – when I was quite small – in front of a cathedral somewhere – I don't even remember in which country by now – there were cobbles and old gray stones and I had a feeling of centuries of history. We had more freedom too, to run around. Not, of course, that I ever ran much with my leg as it is."

"And I ran all the time."

He began to tell her about his life: How it had begun in a crowded room on one of the few remaining state farms, a farm that had been failing for as long as it had been in existence, from the beginning of communism to the fall of communism. A place where the men were angry and hopeless, and drank behind the barns and came home and beat their wives and children, and sometimes, the wives, angry and hopeless, beat their husbands, and less often the children. Until one day his father had climbed on a tractor and driven it through five fences down to the river, and no one knew if it were suicide or a miscalculation. Then he and his mother had made their way by various illegal means to America, where they had stayed for several years, he going to school and doing odd jobs and she working as a cleaning woman, until the immigration authorities had caught up with them. Then a distant relative had arranged their immigration to Australia, and there he had finished high school, and worked his way through half a course in architecture at a small university – "nothing great, you'll never have heard of it" – until his mother's illness forced him to work full time, double time. He had worked as a hospital orderly and a bricklayer and a taxi-driver and at every odd job, gravitating more and more towards construction, until he began to be able to put aside a little money…He took several drags on his cigarette here, and Cordelia could imagine, without his saying, the efforts and the sacrifices that had been involved…until he had his own company and had invested in real estate and then things had begun to roll very fast, money coming in after money. He had found it hard to believe sometimes. He paused for a moment.

He didn't look like a multi-millionaire, Cordelia thought, watching him with her indirect gaze. His clothes were good, of course, but just so men sat on walls and steps outside of *monopolowy* alcohol stores, whiling away the time in districts where there was nothing else to do. But he had left Poland too early ever to have taken part in such gatherings himself, so perhaps it was the effect of early memory, or, a worse thought, of inheritance.

And yet again, she thought, as she watched his knee begin to jiggle up and down a little, as if he couldn't quite sit still, wasn't used to sitting still for long, he wasn't like those men. They were passive. This man was full of energy, this man – she felt instinctively – even while he sat and talked, was revolving plans.

But he was speaking, adding, with a touch of the bitterness again but with pride too, "One thing's good. My mother's secured."

Cordelia felt a surge of pleasure. Somehow whenever anyone spoke of someone having been ill she always assumed they'd died – she was that kind of pessimist.

"She has her own money, and her own house, so they can't get that."

Cordelia didn't know what to say. All sorts of questions came to her mind, but she didn't quite know how to formulate them. 'What do you mean?' would be simplest, and she was just about to say it when he said,

"And another good thing, I don't have a family – that would really be a stone round my neck in such a situation. As is, I don't have to take it lying down; I can work on a countermove."

Again she was just about to ask "What do you mean?" when he changed the subject, and they sat talking on and on, sliding from English into Polish and back again, as one language or another best fitted their thoughts, until it grew dusk and chill and the cigarette smoke that had drifted up through the drying clematis vine began to mingle with the murk of evening.

Cordelia was just opening her mouth to say, 'we must go in,' when her mother's hand rattled the porch door knob, her face peered out, and they both rose and went indoors.

"I must make dinner," said Cordelia as they stepped together into the dark but suddenly warm-seeming salon, "I'm afraid I'm not a very good cook. I hope you're not particular."

"I'll make it, if you like. I used to work in the restaurant business."

"Really?" asked Cordelia disbelievingly. Cooking required training.

"Well, as a cook's helper."

Cordelia kept her eyebrows raised.

"Okay, okay, as a dishwasher, but must you be so precise? – It stifles creativity. Really, I'm a good cook."

Cordelia smiled. "I'm sure you're better than I am."

Cordelia, looking around at her family as they gathered for dinner, had a feeling of protectiveness. Her father was frail and ill-looking in spite of his bulk, her mother was pitiable; Antek, elegant even in unkempt clothing, was vulnerable. Beside the solidity of the stranger he looked ethereal. Zaremba took up an inordinate amount of space, somehow, wherever he appeared. She felt her family grow pale and wan in comparison as he sat down amongst them.

The meal he had prepared was a very Polish one, and not fantastic but better than they were accustomed to. Unfortunately, Cordelia's family was not one given to culinary pleasures. They ate what was before them if it looked familiar and the barest minimum otherwise, and only Cordelia, probably, sometimes wished for more variety in this area of their lives as well.

Conversation took several odd turns. Cordelia's father's contributions were limited, as was his wont at dinner. He preferred to dispatch his food quickly in order to get back to his books. "Have you seen my copy of *Polish Poetry of the Enlightenment*?" and "Did Krzysztof call about the proofs?" were almost his only comments. Zaremba he had obviously relegated to one of those many categories – like his wife – that surpassed his competence and would surely be handled by Cordelia. As a manifestation of his detachment, or maybe out of some lasting resentment at having been sworn at the other night in the lane, he seemed to forget that Zaremba spoke English, and instead of speaking Polish to him normally, would address him in English and then add 'translate, Cordelia.' A proceeding that left her feeling rather drained.

"'Luscious as locusts,'" he complimented the chef as he rose – "translate, Cordelia."

Cordelia's mother, on the other hand, continued to be quite animated, and smiled warmly at the stranger whenever he passed her a dish, answered readily if erratically when he spoke to her, and even started a topic or two of her own. "She's so sweet," she said to Zaremba with a nod towards Cordelia, "her name's Maria and we've had her ever since the postmen had a race to see who could get the packet in first."

"Really," said Zaremba calmly, "how – interesting."

Antek had been persuaded to come to dinner on the grounds that since the man was staying it would be better to meet him under cover of other members of the family than to meet him in a situation where he might actually have to speak to him alone. So he sat rigidly through the first part of the dinner, looking half frozen, picking at his food and not eating, his handsome face with its Italianate locks drooping over his plate. Cordelia felt for him.

"I've been admiring your photos," said Zaremba politely to him.

Don't, thought Cordelia, don't try. You can charm anyone but leave my brother alone, he'll just be in agonies if you try to talk to him. Of course, though, there was nothing to do but concentrate on cutting another bite of dinner. It required some effort to eat without letting the awkwardness of her right hand show too much.

"What camera do you use?"

There was a long pause. Then Antek said woodenly and slowly, "A Sponica 645 xlf. One from the later series. For my close-up work. It has a relatively short flange to film distance, 62 millimeters, which gives it, in addition to smaller dimensions, smaller and, therefore, lighter lenses for a same given focal distance. A shorter flange to film distance allows a given view angle to be obtained with a smaller and lighter lens than would be the case with a large flange to film distance. It also has true mirror lock-up, not the timer-operated type and three light metering modes: spot, average-weighted and 12 point matrix. Other cameras have only 4 point, 6 point or 8 point matrixes. The macro lenses that can be mounted on it are…"

He's talking, he's actually talking to someone, thought Cordelia with pleasure. He was perhaps talking because he didn't quite know how to stop once he'd begun, but still, it was a start. Several long minutes later he was beginning to look desperate, but he kept doggedly on, until he finally wound up with "so it's better than the slf." He hadn't lifted his eyes from his plate the whole time.

"Er…" said Zaremba, obviously at a loss, "Er…can I pass you the potatoes?"

He thinks we're all nuts, realized Cordelia, her momentary sense of having a normal family, of sitting at a normal dinner table, dispelled by doubt. But Zaremba was rallying.

"I've heard that Sponica lenses are better than Kiraxes, is that right?"

He doesn't have a clue, guessed Cordelia, he's making it up. But Antek was not so discerning, and actually began another long answer, crumbling his bread in his hand as he did so.

Cordelia, meeting Antek on the landing later, as she came out of her mother's room, said to him, "Thanks Antek, for making an effort at dinner tonight – that was nice of you."

Antek mumbled something that, with a faint gleam of amusement, merged into "teach him not to speak to me, don't you think? It was hard, but hopefully effective."

"Oh, Antek," Cordelia looked at him in dismay. "You bored him on purpose!"

He gave her a look. "Before, you said I was 'nice' to him."

"Don't you like him?"

He shrugged. "I don't like people much, you know. I just want to be left alone."

"Did you know he cooked dinner?"

Antek shrugged again, what was that to him?

"I thought it was nice," said Cordelia in a dispirited tone as she turned away. "Well, Mom's waiting, I have to get her ready for bed."

Antek didn't reply, but when she was a few feet away, he muttered. "Don't fall for him."

She swung around in surprise. "What?"

"Don't...you know. Maybe you don't realize it, but girls...er, girls do that sometimes...fall in love."

Cordelia stared at him in astonishment. They had never in their lives discussed 'love' or any other personal topic. She would have bet he didn't know the word. She was acutely embarrassed by his starting upon the subject, and he was obviously very uncomfortable as well.

"With, er, people they shouldn't."

"I can't imagine what would put such an idea into your head!"

"Oh well, I didn't mean – it's just..." he cleared his throat, not looking at her, and muttered, "I never saw you look at anybody so much."

But at this moment the opening of the door at the bottom of the stairs made Cordelia bolt away into her mother's room, her face burning.

Cordelia's mother must have been tired from all the day's excitement, because she went rapidly to sleep, and Cordelia went into her own room, undressed, and sat down at her desk in her nightgown. She had a lot of work to do. She was accustomed to doing it late at night, or early in the morning, or in the afternoon, or at any spare moment that could be stolen from her other duties around the house. Let's see, she thought – trying hard to concentrate on her work and not let herself think about Antek's words at all, words that were too utterly ridiculous and embarrassing to require a second thought at all – let's see. She waited impatiently for the computer screen to light up, trying to remember what she had been working on: oh, yes, she was translating an article by a professor of law who couldn't write. Or rather, who wrote in an elaborately Polish fashion:

'The initial start of the impetus toward overcoming the barriers to be surmounted before the original genesis of the idea leading to the eventual initiation of the concept necessary for the fulfillment of the meeting of the essential incongruity in the divergent point of view of the trend of thought behind the ideas of the one group of legislators on the one hand, and on the other hand behind the concepts of the other group of legislators was provided by the…'

It wasn't really the sort of stuff that kept one's mind from wandering. "Don't fall in love, don't fall in love…" the words echoed in Cordelia's mind. She jerked her head to get rid of them and made an effort to concentrate. If she paraphrased this sentence, the professor would probably object that she'd left out the key word. If she didn't paraphrase it, some reader would think it was all a bad translation – hers. Someone would say the article was unreadable and she would be blamed. She began to type again: *'The impetus toward overcoming the difficulties in reconciling the viewpoints of the two groups of legislators…'*

Then she stopped abruptly and clicked her mouse on the internet icon; she didn't know, really, what she was looking for; there wasn't much, in fact: Zaremba's name in connection with various building projects, but no particular information; an interview for the website of a construction journal, in which he predicted (correctly, as it turned out) a sharp increase in real estate prices, and, most informatively, an article from a car magazine in which he was shown test-driving a new Audi, with a little box in the corner with his photo and his profession: real estate developer, and age: 38; and hobbies: reading and rally-car racing (with the mention of two races won in Australia some ten years back). She read his opinions on the car's handling and dashboard design with intense application, as if she might find clues to his character therein. But she wasn't much enlightened. She clicked back to her translation work.

'*To prepare the concept...the premises for interpreting the formula of the programmatic concept...*'

But there was no hope. She couldn't for the space of thirty seconds stop thinking about Zaremba. What if the police caught him, she wondered. Would she visit him in jail? Would he want her to? Or maybe he'd be able to clear himself? What if they found he was staying here? Her poor mother would be terrified if men in masks were to come into the house.

How unnerving it must have been for the hospital staff and patients, she thought, remembering an arrest that year that had received a great deal of publicity, when the men in black had burst into the hospital, seized a top cardiologist, thrown him to the ground, and then marched him away in handcuffs and the glare of cameras. "Never again will anyone be deprived of life by this doctor," said the Minister of Justice at a press conference held immediately thereafter. No evidence that the doctor had done so, the court later ruled. Whether he had taken bribes or not, as he was also accused of having done, should have been for the courts to decide – not for a government agency to declare out of hand for publicity purposes. That's what Zaremba said they wanted to do with him; they wanted to use him to make a big splash in the media, to show they were 'fighting corruption.'

Then there had been the woman politician whom they'd targeted. When the CBA agents had come to her door at an unearthly hour of the morning, she was ready: she had let the agents in, then retreated to the bathroom, taken out a gun that she had presumably prepared for the exigency, and shot herself. She wasn't willing, friends said later, to be dragged before the public, her name besmirched and her person used for a political spectacle.

Cordelia shuddered. No, it wasn't that she had any particular feeling for Zaremba. That would be ridiculous when she'd only known him for twenty-four hours or a little more. She was simply appalled at the powerlessness of the individual before the forces of the state. She closed her computer. She felt chill and small and since she couldn't work, she might as well go to bed. Her small world of old house and odd family had been invaded by the outside and insecurity and anxiety nagged at her mind.

But in bed her thoughts wouldn't stop. She remembered the moments when she had been locked in the closet at the hospital with Zaremba that morning, moments of fleeting physical contact – his joke 'for a quick…' She put the pillow over her head, but the thoughts didn't stop. She remembered him sitting on the balustrade that afternoon, all their talk in all its details.

It was a long time before she fell asleep.

6

When Cordelia rose in the morning, feeling considerably the worse for the wear of the last thirty-six hours, old and haggard and stiff, the first thing she remembered was Antek's 'you might not realize, but girls...' Was she a 'girl'? She was a woman of thirty-four, and her brother had obviously never classified her with other females, did not consider that she might have had feelings like other females of her age. Had she? Well, of course. And Antek's words might have been only an indication of Antek's oddities, or it might be that she really seemed too different to be considered in the ranks of other women. Feeling distinctly prickly, she helped her mother dress then brought her downstairs. Zaremba was nowhere in sight, but there were new groceries in the kitchen. She crossed the salon, straightening a stack of books here, a pile of papers there, laying flat her father's crumpled blazer, folding back a shutter or two, trying hard this morning to concentrate on the homely routine of her everyday life. But it was difficult.

She stepped out onto the porch, to take solace in the beauty of the morning, and found Zaremba there. How would it be, she thought in a flash, if she could walk gracefully to the edge of the stairs and stand there straight and supple and with an inner confidence in her own attractiveness? But her leg was bent and her gait was awkward, and she had no inner confidence at all; the idea that Zaremba might look at her and actually see her was disturbing. She had to speak to him, although she would rather have avoided him.

"You went and got bread again, I see. Thank you."

"It was nothing."

The man was sitting where he had sat the night before, smoking again. It was another fine morning, still and yellow and only faintly chill. Cordelia crossed to the edge of the porch, looking out at the garden pool with the leaves floating in patterns on its dark surface. The man was very close. She pulled her sweater up around her neck, turned to go back into the house and met his eyes watching her.

"Do you know," he said quite seriously, "I think you're the most beautiful woman I've ever met."

Cordelia stood stock still, her hand still at her neck, her heart skipping a beat, several beats. The man continued to smoke, his face quite bland, as if the compliment were the most ordinary thing in the world.

She couldn't look at him for more than a second. "I don't think you should say things like that," she said, turning away.

"Why not?"

"Because it's not true and it makes me think you have an ulterior motive."

"As to ulterior motives – not yet, but I could. As to truth, do you want to argue the matter?"

"No."

"Then just say 'thank you'."

"Thank you," she said at last, in a strangled voice, and turned away and crossed the porch.

"And the kindest," he added, when she had her hand on the door.

She was about to step through, she was really running away, when he stopped her. "Cordelia?"

"Yes?" she answered him with her head turned away.

"It would seem that that kiosk with the newspapers beside the grocery store is closed. I couldn't get a paper – that is, there were one or two I didn't get yesterday. Could I take the car out later?"

"Yes, I suppose, sure." She escaped through the door, as the man descended briskly from the balustrade and came after her into the room, helping her fold back the remaining shutters.

The windows, like the rest of the house, had been scrubbed to the height that Cordelia's left arm would reach. Short people thought the house very clean; taller people had a different view.

"I could wash these upper panes for you," he said, "they must be hard for you to get."

"That's all right," said Cordelia, embarrassed again, "You're our guest. You really don't have to do anything here."

"I like to do things; I don't like to sit about."

After breakfast, Cordelia left her mother in the salon, 'reading' the *Rhubayat of Omar Khayyam*, a book she was fond of, for no reason Cordelia could imagine as the words certainly meant nothing to her, and yet she would sit with it for half-an-hour sometimes or longer. Cordelia escaped – escaped was the right word, she thought – qualifying her flight to herself, to her own room, where she sat down and made a determined effort to carry on with her translating. She had a deadline after all, and her father's pension – given that he had moved so many times as never to have amassed any retirement benefits from a single university – was insufficient to the needs of running the household. The family depended on her financially as well, and she had to get on with her work. She opened the article by the prolix professor and began to type, the fingers of one hand flying over the keyboard.

She wasn't going to let herself be distracted by thoughts of Zaremba, or thoughts about her own confused feelings. But it was a struggle. How could one keep one's mind from wandering when faced with a phrase like: '*priorities in the sphere of the government's foreign policy motives were subject to transformation...*' The priorities of the motives? Could a motive have a priority? What motive did Zaremba have? 'I don't have an ulterior motive yet – but I could.' What did he mean by that? What? Did he really think she was beautiful? Of course he didn't. What nonsense. So why had he said so? She wished he hadn't said it. Last night they had talked so comfortably, it had been, well, great, it had been ages since she'd had anyone to talk to. Today though, she remembered he was someone she couldn't trust. Probably, she reminded herself, he *had* rigged the tender. Not that bribery was really a hideous crime, not an 'evil' crime like murder, nothing like so bad as extortion, but merely a distasteful, dishonest action, destructive for society, and something that put him beyond the pale as an acquaintance, surely. But maybe he hadn't done it. She had to keep an open mind. And not wonder what he really thought about her looks.

'*...the bases for implementing the program were supported by the effects of the framework chosen to introduce the plan...*'

This was hopeless. Cordelia's gargantuan effort to bring her mind to bear on bases and effects was shattered by a knock on the door.

"Come in," she called, struggling to rise. Before she could get her crutch assorted, Zaremba opened the door and came into the room. As she swiveled to look at him, he seated himself on her bed.

"Cordelia."

She didn't let him continue: she had to stop the familiarity that had sprung up between them last night. Let him speak to her formally. "I don't think you should call me by my first name. I think you should say *pani*," she said kindly but, she hoped, firmly.

"I can say *pani* in Polish and then what am I supposed to do in English? Call you Miss Fogg?"

Cordelia couldn't help smiling a bit at that, "Well, no. But I don't think you should sit on my bed."

He came and sat on the desk beside her laptop. "This better?"

"You're the most encroaching man," she said, torn between disapproval and amusement and pushing her chair back to put some distance between herself and his thigh.

He brushed off this last comment with no more than a flick of his eyebrows. "So listen, Cordelia, I've been for the papers and there's nothing in them…"

He bent his head and read her screen upside-down, *'the concept behind the idea of forming multilateral foundations for the future performance of the functions of …'* He broke off. "Who writes this stuff? Not you?"

"Of course not me. The author, I've been told, has a quite high position in a government body. This is how the movers and shakers of the nation write. The men who make the laws."

"That, I suppose, is why they are the way they are."

"The terrible thing is that it's presumably also the way they think."

"Yes, that would explain a lot. Poor you having to deal with it – poor me, if it comes to that."

She noticed that the legs dangling from her desk were differently clad than the last time she'd seen them. "Did you go home?" she asked curiously. "Wherever it is you do live?"

"I have an apartment in one of my own buildings downtown; a building from the thirties I renovated. I don't spend much time there usually and I certainly can't go there now. I stopped at Carrefour for some clothes. Not what I'd normally choose – but buggers in my situation can't be choosers. No, I don't dare go home. Or to my office. Which is going to make running my business damned difficult."

"I wish you'd stop using improper language in my company."

"Don't sit on your bed, don't swear, don't say you're beautiful. You're the most repressive woman I've ever met…"

She didn't answer, but picked at a splinter on the wooden edge of her desk.

"Anyway, Cordelia, can I use your computer for a minute, just to check that there's nothing on the news there? I won't be long, I promise."

This at least was a sentence she could deal with. "Okay." She rose and hopped to her bed and sat there, while he clicked the mouse and clicked and found the news. Hempseed found his way into the room as well, and leapt onto the bed beside Cordelia. He wasn't supposed to be there and he knew it; so he rolled about, his laughing eyes checking for her reaction. She was just about to tell him to get off, but instead, she pulled him to her and hugged him. She watched from behind as the man ran through one site after another.

"Nothing in *Gazeta Wyborcza*...nothing in *Dziennik* ...nothing in *Rzeczpospolita* – those two are very pro-government, if anyone were carrying the story it would be they..."

Cordelia began to relax.

A long silence and a certain rigidity about his back made her ask, "well?"

There was just the slightest movement to hide the screen from her. Then he obviously thought better of it.

"Foreign," he muttered, "they call me 'foreign' and I'm as Polish as *pierogi*, as *kiełbasa* as, as..."

"As *kapusta*?" Cordelia couldn't help suggesting.

"No, as cabbage, no." He was angry, but a corner of his mouth couldn't help jerking up at that.

"What is it?" Cordelia asked again, seeing that it looked serious.

"Come and read. Or no, sit there." He brought the laptop to her and she read.

'*Zaremba Still in Hiding*,' said the headline above a photo in *Śmiećpospolity*. She glanced at it quickly. It showed Zaremba clearly, sitting beside a man at what appeared to be a restaurant table, their heads close together as if in confidential speech. She ran her eyes quickly down to the text.

'*New clues have emerged in the case concerning a foreign developer whom the CBA wishes to question in connection with the alleged rigging of a call for tenders to build social housing. Dariusz Zaremba, multi-millionaire developer, has been missing since Friday night, when the police found his abandoned Jaguar behind a house near Zabrzeg. At the moment the police claim that no foul play is suspected, but there have been conjectures they may move to have swamps in the vicinity dragged. Of particular interest to the CBA are the ties linking Zaremba to Marek Grzegoliński. By a curious coincidence, at the time of the call for tenders, both Zaremba and*

Grzegolinski were enjoying vacations at the posh resort of Wirata on the Polish coast. Our reporter has discovered that Zaremba was staying at the ritzy Łabędz Hotel between 10 and 16 August, while Grzegoliński was well accommodated at a pension three blocks away between 13 and 17 August. What were they doing at the same time in Wirata? Presumably more than just swimming and sun-bathing. Our reporter shot the two in close confabulation during that summer month when a multi-million dollar bid was in the balance. What were they discussing? It's not hard to imagine."

Cordelia, feeling considerably shaken, didn't know where to look. She studied the photo. It was blurry, but the man holding the laptop for her was clearly identifiable.

"Yes," she said, "I see." She had a sinking feeling in her stomach. So he was guilty. Well, that was that. She didn't define to herself what 'that' was.

He took the laptop away.

"It's a photo montage. It's not real."

"You weren't in Wirata then?" her voice came out very small.

"Yes, I was. My mother came from Australia and we went there for a holiday. I suppose the dates are correct. I don't remember exactly: it was in mid-August though."

"August is high season in the construction business, isn't it?" she couldn't help asking.

"Yes," he said evenly, knowing she was wondering why he would leave his business at such a time, "it is. But it's a good time of the year in Poland, and I wanted my mother to enjoy herself. I probably was in the restaurant; this background looks familiar. But I never met Grzegolinski there. I never even saw him."

"But if it's a faked photo...I mean, would a newspaper risk using a faked photo? I'm sorry." She hung her head. Since she didn't believe him she couldn't discuss the matter with him.

"No, possibly not. But a reporter might. The editor might not check."

"But then, in court, you could ask them to show the negatives, or no, it isn't negatives anymore, is it, the originals, and they would..." Would what...?

"I don't believe it ever would or will get to court. It doesn't have to. They're getting their publicity; they're showing that they're fighting corruption. The fact that my name is smeared forever is immaterial to them."

"You're sure you never saw this fellow? Maybe he could prove that he wasn't there."

"On the other hand, it's very likely that he was. It's very likely that everything in the article is true except that photo. I recognize this place; I was at that restaurant. Grzegoliński may take bribes regularly for all I know. He just didn't take one from me. He probably was in Wirata – a quarter of the Polish population goes to the seaside in the summer. I just didn't happen to see him – and if I had, I'd have taken care to put distance between us, for the very reason that it wouldn't look good if we were seen together before the issue of the tender was decided."

"But maybe you've forgotten that you met him for a minute in a café. A chance meeting – who would remember? – you must meet so many people." Cordelia struggled to prevent the man from lying more than he already had.

"I didn't meet him. I wouldn't have forgotten. And that photo is a fake...You don't believe me, do you?"

Cordelia's hand twisted in Hemp's hair, so that he looked serious and ceased wiggling.

"I don't know what to think."

"You keep up with the news, don't you?"

"Yes. More or less."

"But you know that the present government is using the Central Anti-Corruption Bureau as a political tool? Of course, every government uses its investigative capacities for its own purposes to some extent – but never this blatantly, on this scale. Did you read not long ago that investigations into members of the opposition have recently increased 2-300 fold? That doesn't tell you something?"

"Yes, I'm aware that there are serious problems. There's Michnik, who speaks of a 'creeping coup d'état.' I'm aware that when the government speaks of tampering with the Constitutional Tribunal if it disagrees with it, then things have come to a bad pass. I know that, as you said yesterday, the government has been making efforts to take over as many independent bodies as it can, and that it's striving for control of the courts." She paused to arrange her thoughts, and then continued, speaking slowly: "But if the nation is undiscerning, if it prefers slogans to reason, if it thinks it *wants* an authoritarian government – what can I do but carry on caring for my family? Democracy may suffer –may eventually even fail – but as an individual I don't see any lines of action. I may deplore the course of events, the growing injustices – but I have neither the stamina nor the personality to pursue large ventures of resistance."

"No," said the man, "Fair enough. I can see that's true. But you'd do your bit if you could? Wouldn't you?"

She played with the dog's fur, still not looking at the man.

"Ye-es. But then too," she continued, trying to be fair, "there has been a lot of corruption in government, and perhaps some – perhaps even most – of the people they catch are guilty."

"But the methods they use are wrong. Having corruption is bad but it's better than having a police state. And *I'm* innocent. Maybe many others are too. To take just one small aspect of the whole subject: Even if some persons are guilty, what do you think it does to a society when functionaries are allowed extraordinary powers of interference and surveillance? It's an insidious form of big-brotherhood. And do you think it will stop with functionaries? Such methods are effective; there's no reason they shouldn't be extended to the population at large, not only to catch crimes, large or small, but also for manipulating society in all sorts of ways."

"Yes," she said, "you're right." But she looked so subdued, that he grimaced.

"I have sympathy for wrong-doers, you see. I suppose you'll think that makes me more suspect?"

"No," she said and rose. They had been getting carried away. She didn't want to continue the conversation. "I have to check on my mother." She didn't know how long it had been, actually, since she'd last checked on her. It was odd, she thought, clambering hollowly down the stairs, that a discussion of the government should have made her forget her immediate duties. There was probably a moral there – *'cultiver notre jardin'* or something. And the man? She had no reason to believe him innocent, no reason not to believe the newspaper article – no reason except that she liked him so much and very much wanted him to be innocent. It was, of course, a vague article, full of unsubstantiated allegations – but that might simply be because the journalist and his editor didn't know how to write any more than the author of the article she was translating. It might be that they couldn't distinguish between what was evidence and what hearsay. It didn't mean the evidence wasn't there or the CBA didn't have grounds for its actions.

And after all, she thought, entering the salon, in spite of her attachment to Hempseed, the teeth marks all over the piano leg were still his. Her desires that someone might be different had never produced the slightest permutation, let alone a sea-change, in anyone's character. She had molded herself instead, adapted, tolerated, accepted her brothers, her father, her mother after her illness, her dog – accepted them with all their idiosyncrasies and faults and loved them. But she couldn't accept dishonesty.

Cordelia's mother was not in the salon. The book she had been reading was lying on the floor. Cordelia stooped automatically to restore it to its place then turned to look out the windows. No one was visible. She made a quick tour of the ground floor: the kitchen – not there; she peeked into her father's office – but her mother would never be there; she had never disturbed her husband in the days of her sanity, and she had carried the prohibition, like a few others, into her darkness. Her father sat with a book in one hand and a pen in the other, obviously working, and she did not disturb him either, but passed out into the garden. The lot was not so large that it took more than a few minutes to circle the house, even at Cordelia's slow pace. She passed under the tall trees, around the back, along the side, and here she was back at the garden pool with its floating leaves. Hempseed joined her, looking cheerful, bouncing about and snapping foolishly at distant birds, but Cordelia began to be worried. She listened carefully; it was Sunday and more quiet than on other days; women's shoes clicked briskly along the sidewalk on the way to church; someone, somewhere, was practicing a violin, the sound came thinly through the air. "Mom?" called Cordelia softly, but it was only a sort of reflex, she didn't expect an answer.

Her mother rarely climbed the stairs on her own. Still, since she wasn't outside or downstairs she must be up. But when Cordelia had climbed to the first floor, she found all the rooms empty. There was nothing for it but to go on up to the attics. Antek's room was there. She knocked on the door. "Antek? Have you seen Mom?"

He turned from where he was sitting, at a table strewn with a debris of screws and springs and other inner camera pieces. He gazed at her blankly for a moment then shook his head. That left Zaremba's room. She knocked at the door and he opened it, as if he had just been on the point of leaving. He was standing right in front of her.

"I..." she said, suddenly and curiously forgetting why she was there.

"You've come to sit on my bed?" His arm, above her head, was resting on the architrave.

She didn't bother to answer that. "I'm looking for my mother. I've looked everywhere and she's not here." She turned away as she spoke, adding over her shoulder as she hobbled towards the stairs. "She must be here. She can't get off the property, but I'm too slow. She could come in one door, while I'm going out the other."

It was probably the fact that he took instant action that had made her turn to him instead of to Antek.

"I'll look about," he said, clattering rapidly down the stairs. She followed more slowly, and Antek also came to his bedroom door and said slowly, "so, is it serious?"

"I don't know," she answered over her shoulder. "She must be here."

But by the time she had reached the ground floor again, Zaremba appeared shaking his head and spreading out his hands. She stepped into her father's office.

"Tato, have you seen Mom? We can't find her."

He raised his head slowly from his book, as if trying to make sense of her words. "You've misplaced your mother?"

"It would seem. When did you last see her?"

"You seek her here, you seek her there/Cordelia seeks her everywhere." He smiled a little at this mangling of the pimpernel rhyme and returned his eyes to his book.

"Yes, but when did you last see her?"

"It was," he answered off-hand, "this morning, sometime."

"I left her reading in the salon."

"Then we are in concordance. She was reading in the salon." He looked at Cordelia over his glasses, "Are you really worried? She can't leave the property, you know."

Zaremba appeared behind Cordelia. "I think she must have. I can't find her anywhere and the gate is unlocked. The keys are in it."

"Oh!" cried Cordelia, "she's never gone out before." And then she thought, but how could she get the keys? But her father was always leaving them about.

Cordelia's father rose in consternation.

"No, no, sit down, we'll find her," Zaremba commanded.

Cordelia's father sank gratefully back into his chair but did not resume his reading. Antek appeared and stood uneasily at a small distance from them.

"We'd better split up and go in different directions to look," said Cordelia. "Where could she have gone? She'll be completely lost, she won't have any idea where she is, or who she is. If someone finds her wandering and calls

138

the police, she won't know what to tell them." And then she realized – the police. And Zaremba was here. But the thought only whisked briefly across the upper current of her worries. Her mother was totally unconscious of what she was doing. She might step out into traffic without a glance. They had to find her fast, before anything happened.

"We'd best take the car," said Zaremba, and to Antek – "Do you want to drive, or do you want to look in that direction?" He waved an arm.

Antek looked distraught. It's true, thought Cordelia, he hasn't driven in years; he hasn't left the property for ages. She couldn't remember the last time she'd seen him in the garden even. But she had no time to feel for him.

Antek shook his head slowly and turned to walk uncertainly in the direction of Zaremba's gesture. That left Zaremba to get the car out, and soon they were cruising slowly along the streets, stopping at each crossroads, looking in both directions. Zaremba was grim-looking, and Cordelia knew it had nothing to do with her mother, but she had no time to feel for him either. They drove in silence. There were fenced yards, trees with changing foliage, sidewalks littered with brown and bronze and yellow leaves, empty streets, empty streets, and then suddenly, there would be a figure, perhaps far in the distance, that spring of hope, until Cordelia realized it wasn't her mother, but someone else – an elderly gentleman, a woman with a dog on a leash. They passed a church, a looming construction, where mass was about to begin, with the overspill of the congregation in the churchyard and on the sidewalks; a crowd of well-dressed people, young women with children, old women in berets and calf-length skirts, men in blazers, all with their spruce and satisfied Sunday air, adapting their faces for the coming service. Perhaps her mother was amongst the crowd? The car slowed but she couldn't find her mother amongst the groups of people still talking, still positioning.

"Where could she have gone?" Cordelia cried, "Where? She'll be so confused, so frightened," she murmured in anguish.

"Don't worry, we'll find her."

Easy for you to say, she thought, it's nothing to you.

"If we don't, you'll file a missing-person report with the police and sooner or later you'll be reunited," his voice was calm, "Such people don't just disappear off the face of the earth. You'll get her back."

"Yes," she agreed, not believing, but soothed anyway. He didn't say, "you mustn't go to the police, what about me?" Probably he realized she couldn't allow his predicament to weigh with her in such a situation. She had a vague sense that she was being ungenerous, but she had no time to analyze the feeling. They were coming to the end of the suburb; they had crossed nearly every street, and had not met Cordelia's mother. They had passed Antek twice, who had also been unsuccessful.

"Perhaps she's gone toward the railway lines," said Zaremba.

"But why would she go there?" But even as she spoke the words she knew, with a dart of fear in her heart, that he was right.

"Why not? Why should she go anywhere? I don't suppose she thinks the way we do, only differently. The railway lines are not far."

"Let's go there, quick, quick."

They drove rapidly to the end of a street, where it met the curving expanse of railway lines, four of them. The car was stopped by cement blocks that had been erected for just that purpose. Cordelia opened the car door and stepped out; she wouldn't be able to see down the length of the lines unless she walked forward and looked around the bend. In the not-too-far distance a train hooted, a long drawn blast. It was nothing, thought Cordelia, trains passed continually here, they always whistled, because of the crossing ahead. But she began to hurry, only she was passed by Zaremba, who reached the viewpoint, checked for a moment, and then took off at a dead run.

"No," thought Cordelia, "no." She rushed forward, and looked down the tracks. On the far side, far, far down the tracks a small figure was standing between the rails, just standing, looking apparently at something in the distance.

Zaremba was running, running at full speed, slipping and sliding in the large gravel by the side of the rails, trying then to run on the crossties, trying the gravel again. He was giving it everything he had, every drop of strength and determination, even Cordelia could see that, but he would never make it, it was too far. The train was coming, its blasts continuous, there was a grinding of brakes as it went by. It would never stop in time. Cordelia opened her mouth to scream, was screaming her mother's name, but her mother would never hear. She closed her eyes. She couldn't bear to watch.

She closed her eyes and kept them shut, as the train whistle and the shrieking brakes and her own screams reverberated in her mind with her sobs. And only some time later she realized the whistling had ceased and the train hadn't stopped but was going on, was disappearing. She opened her eyes.

Far down the tracks, two figures were standing, and as she watched they turned and began to walk towards her. Her mother, safe and sound, and Zaremba. Cordelia's knees were shaking so that she sank down on the grass to await them.

By the time they reached her, she had managed to pull herself together somewhat. She reached for her mother, wishing to hug her, to wrap her arms around her, because she was safe, because she was still alive. But her mother, perfectly unruffled by her adventure, drew back a little, as if surprised.

"Hello, Maria, I didn't know it was your day today. How nice."

Cordelia choked down a sob. To Zaremba she said, "You saved her."

He raised his eyebrows; he was still out of breath, in spite of the long walk back. "No. You didn't see? Your mother moved off of her own accord. I wouldn't have reached her in time. She saved herself." He took a deep breath, "She stepped off just before the train got there. She left about fifty feet of safety distance." He gave her a crooked smile, "plenty of time, eh, *pani*?"

She smiled back at him, but Cordelia didn't feel like she'd ever want to smile again.

People had appeared from nowhere, had come out of their houses and were hurrying towards them, forming a half-circle around them, all talking. "What happened?" "I heard the screaming." "Yes, I heard the screaming too." "Who was screaming?" "Did someone get run over?" "Shall I call an ambulance?"

Cordelia saw faces she vaguely recognized from the neighborhood. People she passed every day at the store, or walking their dogs, pushing their baby strollers.

"It's all right," said a voice, "I called the police when I heard the screams."

"No!" said Cordelia.

"Cordelia," said Zaremba, "do you want to take your mother to the car?" His voice was peremptory, and Cordelia hooked her mother's arm in hers and half pulled her towards the vehicle. She came rather unwillingly and by the time Cordelia had coaxed her into the car and had slid into the passenger seat herself, she looked up and found that Zaremba was striding towards them and the gathered people were departing with shakes of their heads.

"I think I pacified them," he said, "let's get out of here, though, before the reinforcements arrive." He started the car, whirled it backwards, turned it around, and sped away from the scene.

7

'The ruling coalition has gone significantly further – it has taken the subjugation of public institutions to pathological perfection. The prosecutor's offices, the secret service, the Institute of National Remembrance, depository of the documents of the communist security forces…They've become instruments in building a state of suspicion and fear.' – Adam Michnik

When they arrived home, Cordelia's father and Antek were standing on the porch. They looked expectantly towards the car, saw that Cordelia's mother was there, and moved off, each to his own pursuits, without waiting for explanations, which Cordelia had no desire to give in any case.

She settled her mother in front of the television, made sure the gate was locked and the keys out of sight, retreated to her room, curled up on her bed, and lay very still. After an hour or two of motionless misery, in which every bad, tragic, unhappy, evil thing in the world swirled through her brain, she said to herself 'enough' and forced herself to sit up and then to rise and go to her computer.

There was still her work. There was always, in fact, something that needed to be done. She turned on her computer and began to type, and later, when she was feeling a little calmer, she took her laptop downstairs and sat beside her mother, blocking out the mindless noise of the television to continue typing.

Perhaps, she thought, looking at her mother, who was unusually happy-looking, quite without the slack and lost air that pained Cordelia so, perhaps her mother needed to get out, needed more stimulation; perhaps she should have taken her on walks, but it had never occurred to her that it was possible until Zaremba had done so. Perhaps just as she was comforted by Hemp's vitality and joie-de-vivre, Zaremba had brought a breath of life into the house for her mother.

She was aware as she typed and mused on her mother that Zaremba was moving about the house. There were banging and grating noises from the kitchen, after which he emerged and said "I've fixed the windows," and at some point he came into the salon and cleaned the upper panes of the windows, which meant that the room acquired a surprisingly larger amount of light, and then he disappeared, and she was dimly aware that he was screwing in light bulbs – purchased, she presumed, during his trip to Carrefour – and repairing the door knob to the porch that always came apart in one's hand, whenever one grasped the handle incautiously, and – "Please stop," she cried, towards the middle of the afternoon, "you don't need to do all these things. We owe you too much as is!"

"If it'll make you feel better," he said curtly, "consider that I'm not doing it for you."

This was unanswerable. Cordelia mulled various replies, "You aren't?" sounded disappointed; "Then for whom?" likewise. Silence seemed the only response.

"I'd go berserk if I didn't have something to occupy myself; and I don't know how long you'll allow me to stay, but wherever I am, I think light is one of the basics."

"Yes," admitted Cordelia, "it's much pleasanter now."

"And I've saved the best for last."

"What's that?"

"Ah." He disappeared up the stairs.

"Tato," said Cordelia sometime later, as she stood in the doorway of his office, "*Pan* Zaremba has fixed the upstairs toilet."

Her father looked up from his reading, "Has he? Was that necessary? That toilet has been leaking since before the war. Do you think it wise to tamper with tradition?"

"He fixed a lot of other things too," added Cordelia slowly, leaning against the doorframe, after casting a quick glance over her shoulder to make sure Zaremba was beyond hearing distance. She could see that he was sitting on the porch balustrade again, smoking. His profile was full of dark thoughts.

"And he was very helpful looking for Mom," Cordelia continued to her father, "She was at the railway tracks. If he hadn't thought of looking there, I don't know what would have happened." She didn't tell her father the whole.

Cordelia's father took off his glasses and began to rub them. "I presume this is tending somewhere?"

"I was just wondering – what you thought…"

"He's your young man – I leave the thinking to you."

"Tato! He's not 'my young man'!"

"Tsk. Don't take me so literally. I only meant that you seemed to have taken him under your wing, as you did that deplorable canine of yours," he held up his finger in admonition " – which was against my advice too, if I may be so callous as to remind you – so I leave your new acquisition to you to deal with."

"But he's not 'my acquisition.' He's not anything to me. I just wondered...Wait a moment." She went for her laptop, placed it on her father's desk, found the article in *Śmiećpospolity* and showed it to her father. He put his glasses back on and read it slowly, ending with a loud 'hmph.'"

"What do you think? He says it's a fake photo."

Her father sat still for a moment, thinking, while she waited for his verdict.

"We are obliged to consider every person," said her father deliberately, in his professorial voice, "who has not been judged guilty by a court of law, to be innocent: that's one of the principles of democracy. It is also the principle of a country under the rule of law. Furthermore, you can tell yourself that this is an article written in the most tendentious of styles. Reflect for a moment upon this sentence," he pointed to the screen, "or this one: 'what were they doing in Wirata at the same time while a multi-million dollar bid hung in the balance.' It's all insinuation, flavored with not very subtle irony. It's a piece of palpably biased journalism, of a kind that is becoming increasingly common, I'm sorry to say. The evidence they produce is flimsy in the extreme and circumstantial at best. This may indeed be a fake photo. The two men may not have met in Wirata or even have been in Wirata. We have no more reason to take the word of this reporter than we do to doubt the word of Mr. Zaremba; on the contrary, the journalist's very style indicates his inability to fulfill properly the position for which he was hired and harms his credibility. I see no reason to trust a journalist who is unable to produce more substance than is contained here on a subject about which he makes such heavy claims. In addition, there have indeed been numerous cases lately of investigations launched and manipulated for political ends. All these factors must be borne in mind and given their proper weight before we come to a decision involving a matter of such importance as a man's reputation."

"So," said Cordelia eagerly, hope springing up in her breast, "you think this may indeed be all a political maneuver, you think he may be telling the truth, you think he's innocent then?"

"No-o, I think he's guilty." Her father swiveled back to his books.

Cordelia reached over and turned off her computer in silence. She gathered the laptop to her chest and hopped to the door. Her father went on with his reading. At the door she turned around. "He saved your life, you know."

"Hitler was doubtless pleasant to Eva Braun."

"Tato!"

Her father raised his hands in a gesture of despair. "I was only attempting an analogy – extreme, granted – to illustrate that the fact does not affect his guilt or innocence. I was under the impression you wanted my opinion."

"Yes," she said with a wry grimace, "yes, I did. What do you think will happen now?"

He looked at her in mild surprise. "And you the one always telling me I don't think of the future! And here you're asking me for a prophecy!" He was silent for a moment, as if thinking hard, but at last he shrugged. "It's your province, Cordelia, my imagination can't encompass it."

"That's okay," she said, turning sadly away.

"Cordelia," he called after her, rallyingly, "something will happen, one way or the other, it'll turn out."

"Yes," she said wearily and not at all comforted, "It'll turn out one way or the other."

The bell for the gate was ringing. Who could that be? They almost never had unexpected visitors; Cordelia spoke casually to various neighbors on the street, but only when she happened to be out in the garden, when they happened to be passing, when they happened to pass in the street. It was rare that anyone rang. A sense of foreboding gripped her; she went quickly through the porch doors. Zaremba was still sitting on the porch. She knew he couldn't be seen there, from the street, but she wondered if she should tell him to run, to hide? Suppose it was the police?

"Someone's at the gate," she said to him as she passed. He didn't move. She reached the heavy iron pedestrian gate and pulled it open. It was *Pani* Nowak standing there, an elderly woman who lived two houses down and had a large garden. They sometimes talked of flowers over one another's fences. She was holding a large bouquet, which she held out to Cordelia.

"Thank you. How lovely," said Cordelia.

"Yes, you don't have any of these big chrysanthemums, only the smaller ones, that aren't so showy; I used to have those too, but they grow a bit weedy, don't they?" *Pani* Nowak always managed to imply that Cordelia's garden, however pretty, was not quite equal to her own. Cordelia was used to this mild horticultural one-upmanship and had never grudged the woman her small victories, particularly as the bouquets with which she heralded them were always very generous: this was a good-sized vaseful of flowers. It soon became apparent, though, that this time the flowers were only a pretext. She wasn't subtle about it but got right to the point.

"I heard about the dreadful thing with your mother this morning. Everyone's talking about it. Everyone in the neighborhood. Dreadful – it was dreadful."

"Yes, it was dreadful, but all's well that end's well."

"Yes, you should keep a closer eye on your mother, because who knows what might happen – a person in that condition doesn't know what she's doing, it's *pani* that has to think for her, look after her." *Pani* Nowak always managed to imply that Cordelia wasn't quite living up to her duties. "Were you so busy that you didn't notice she'd left?"

With her crutch, Cordelia foiled several determined attempts by Hempseed to squeeze through the gate and run off, and was obliged finally to step out onto the sidewalk and pull the gate shut behind her. Across the street, the next neighbor over came out of his house and nodded 'good-day' as he locked his gate. Usually he was a man in a great hurry, but today he seemed to have become suddenly very interested in adjusting the mirror of his car. Cordelia could almost see his ear throbbing, opening wide in their direction to catch their conversation like a satellite dish catching signals. *Pani* Nowak was waiting for an answer.

"I didn't see her go."

"How did she get the keys?"

"I don't know. We're not sure."

"And the train came within inches of her, they say! What a story."

"I think it was more than inches."

"But you screamed, they say. I'd scream too, in such a situation. They say that everyone heard it over the sound of the train, everyone who lives on the street there. Didn't you have the gate locked?"

"I thought it was locked."

"Maybe that relative you have staying with you left the gate open. Sometimes, when people aren't used to living with elderly people in such a condition, they don't realize how careful one needs to be. That's the way tragedies happen."

"No. I don't think it was his fault." Cordelia's answers were short, but *Pani* Nowak didn't seem to mind. She cheered Cordelia with accounts of several horrific tragedies, until Cordelia could bear it no longer:

"Excuse me, but I really have to get back to my mother now."

"Yes, yes, of course – oh, I wanted to ask you," she stopped Cordelia as Cordelia was stepping back through the gate, "because I heard that your relative comes from America, is that right?"

"Yes," said Cordelia unwillingly.

"Where in America?"

Cordelia was taken aback, her mind a blank. She said the first thing that came into her head. "Boise."

"Boise! I have an uncle living in Boise. I thought you were going to say New York, because I have cousins living in New York. But Boise, what a coincidence, I have an uncle there. Maybe he knows your relative. What's his name?"

His name, thought Cordelia, at a total loss. She wasn't accustomed to invention. She left too long a pause. *Pani* Nowak was looking at her oddly. Cordelia muttered the first name that came into her head: "Wawrzyniec."

She knew she'd taken too long. She had to make up for it. "Um, er, he doesn't go by it in America. I was trying to remember what he calls himself there, um, 'Larry' that's it."

"'Lar-ree?'" *Pani* Nowak pronounced the two syllables with delicate distaste. "Strange."

"It's short for Lawrence, the English equivalent of Wawrzyniec." Cordelia shifted the flowers to her bad arm so that she could put up a hand to twist her hair. No one Zaremba's age was likely to be named 'Wawrzyniec'.

"Hm. What's his last name?"

Last name, a last name. "Kowalski." Smith.

"I will write and ask my uncle if he knows Lar-ree Kowalski."

"Yes, it would be, um – interesting – if they knew each other." Cordelia was retreating through the gate, "thank you for the flowers."

Pani Nowak was not turning away; she looked as if she had more questions to ask, but Cordelia turned her back firmly and went on up the grassy drive and onto the porch.

Zaremba was still sitting there, his angry face somewhat lightened by amusement. He mimicked her stuttered answers. "Uh, uh, Wawrzyniec? Uh, uh, Larry? From uh, uh Boise? You're not a very good liar, are you?"

"I've never had any practice."

She had her hand on the porch knob.

"Where are you going?"

"In."

"Do you have to? Yesterday you sat and talked to me."

"And today I've lied to the neighbor. I don't feel like talking." Her tone held a slight trace of bitterness.

"Then sit and be sad with me. I promise to be silent." His tone was bitter too, and more than a trace.

She felt for him, and, knowing she should go in, she sank down into her usual wicker chair. He kept his word, and sat smoking without any attempt to engage her in conversation. She sat and looked out unseeing at the garden and thought with vague discomfort about the dishonesties on which she had just embarked. Why hadn't she just said, "I don't want to answer your questions?" – well, because that would have made *Pani* Nowak very suspicious. But she could have just shouted 'oh, I've left a pan burning on the stove!' and rushed off. Not that that was the truth either, but it wasn't as bald a lie as what she'd just told. She thought too slowly, that was the problem. Of course, if she had said something of the sort it was certain *Pani* Nowak would have come back later; she wasn't one to give up easily. So the question was really whether she had done wrong or not by protecting Zaremba.

And what it really came down to was whether he was guilty or not, because if he was, then she shouldn't have anything to do with it, and if he wasn't, then he deserved her help as much as possible...And her father was right, her own personal feelings for the man, her own sense of his kindness didn't affect his innocence or guilt.

If she had gone indoors, she could have, perhaps, begun to view the man with some feeling of distance; she might slowly have reasoned herself into believing that his problems were none of her affair. Sitting six feet from him, even though they did not speak, made it much harder to find objectivity. She struggled for it. It was still possible, she thought, it was even her Christian duty, to feel for someone who had strayed from the straight path. It didn't mean she approved of his behavior – if he were guilty – after all, hadn't she just strayed herself? Who was she to cast stones? Of course, a fib to a nosy neighbor hardly classified in the same category as corrupting a public official for personal gain – there were even, she knew, perfectly honest upright people – both her brothers and her father, for instance – who might consider such mendacity to be no mendacity at all but a perfectly justified and even amusing defense. She didn't feel that way. She didn't tell lies and she had been induced to do so by the man sitting across from her.

Probably he thought lies were all right, even much bigger ones than these she'd just told. His background was – not a background known for its attachment to probity. She was acquainted with such environments. Everyone in Poland was; the layers of society had been too much mixed during Communist days for any social group to be in much ignorance about the lower layers of society. She was familiar with families where the men went off to steal any odd bit of metal they could find to take to the scrap yard for drink – a metal pipe, a bit of chain link fence snipped quick with the cutters, a tire iron, the electric wiring to someone's house – ripped out for the copper insides – a treasure. She could easily conjure up women who worked at menial jobs to keep the family going, who stood about smoking and waiting, and when some object of use was lying about unattached, unobserved, and didn't belong to a close friend – saw nothing wrong with appropriating it. When people were poor, one couldn't blame them. She imagined their homes: the grafitti-marred entrances, the staircases where the damp furred the walls with mould, the rotting floorboards and the lack of space. It was a wonder they weren't all a great deal worse than they were. Laws ceased to have much meaning. Hadn't he and his mother gone to the States as illegal immigrants? How could she think he might have a different mentality than most people coming from his situation? He just had a thick veneer of education and worldliness and experience that covered the past. She had no reason to trust him. But she could pity him. She pitied him and at the same time, she was surprised to discover in herself a strong undercurrent of resentment towards him, as if he had let her down. She wanted to believe in him – and she couldn't.

As if in answer to her thoughts, Zaremba said suddenly, "if they had any evidence – even the flimsiest – they'd have gone after Grzegoliński. Arrested him. If they haven't, it's because they don't dare to; because they're afraid his party will back him up and the publicity will backfire. It's easier for them to go after me. No one will come to my support. I have to devise my own countermove."

She began to shiver.

"You're getting cold," he said, abandoning the subject abruptly. "And I said I wouldn't talk. Let's go in, it's starting to rain."

Dinner that evening was a trying affair. Antek emerged from nowhere as Cordelia, a stack of plates hugged against her chest, was preparing to set the table for dinner. It was a massive old table, with carved legs and a badly damaged top, occupying one end of the salon. Cordelia had always liked it, but since Zaremba had admired it yesterday, she had to admit to herself, unwillingly, that it had gained in value. She deposited the plates with a bump, and glanced anxiously at Antek, who was standing still in the center of the room, looking with displeasure at a point beyond her head. He did not speak, but his stance was telling.

"Antek, is something wrong?"

"'Ruin on ruin, rout on rout,'" he answered slowly, shaking his head.

"What do you mean?" she gasped in dismay. "Not more bad news!"

"He's swept away my cobwebs!"

"Oh Antek, is that all?" she sighed in relief, "Yes, he cleaned the windows; I thought it was nice – but I'm sorry about your spiders. I forgot to tell him they're your models. I don't think he killed any, so I suppose they've just gone off to sulk or whatever spiders do when they're evicted. They'll recruit their energies and in a few days it will be as rebuilt and gloomy-looking as before."

"It's been problem after problem with that fellow," said Antek, "everything was fine before."

"Not really," murmured Cordelia, laying out the plates.

"Not...?" began Antek, and then suddenly he broke off, and with a look that Cordelia fortunately didn't see – as its mingled compassion and incomprehension would have wounded her – he began to help her lay the table.

Dinner began badly, when Cordelia's mother, for reasons known only to herself, emptied her water glass into the mushroom sauce.

"Who plays the piano?" Zaremba ended the long and uncomfortable silence that followed this incident with a gesture towards the instrument, which was swathed in gloom at the other end of the salon.

Was it, Cordelia wondered, because he had better manners than her own family and knew people shouldn't sit together at table like deaf-mutes, but should converse, or was he just incapable of being still and quiet for long, but must always be thinking, talking, doing...Or was it, she considered, with one of her sudden insights, that he had some motive? But what could that be? Her family seemed unlikely objects for anyone's attempts at captivation.

"My mother," said Cordelia, with a glance at her mother, who looked up almost with recognition, from a plate of food she was eating with unusual appetite – "has always been very musical. She trained as an opera singer before her marriage."

A certain change of expression, a certain fixity about the faces of Antek and Cordelia's father, made Zaremba look between them and Cordelia's mother...Cordelia quickly tried to divert the subject.

"Antek used to play too."

"Really?" said Zaremba politely to him, "what sort of things do you play?"

There was a long pause, while Antek looked successively annoyed and tongue-tied, "Flight of the Arachnids?" he finally stuttered repressively.

Zaremba looked puzzled, and even Cordelia's father seemed to think this called for smoothing over and a change of subject. "We're very impressed by all the tasks you've undertaken around the house," he said to Zaremba, "We don't often get much work done. Once Cordelia hired a man to rectify what she considered to be some of the more glaring deficiencies in and about our abode. The result was a stockpile of plaster in the entry, the dismantling of several light switches, the demolition of a perfectly functional heating stove, and I forget what other damage. Cordelia paid the man extra, paid him – what was it? – twice, three times what he first asked, because he said his wife needed a hip operation." He chuckled in reminiscence: "Her hip, my foot! Cordelia – translate."

"*Tato*, *Pan* Zaremba speaks English as well as I do."

157

But her father went on as if he hadn't heard: "I don't know what became of the plaster. I remember stumbling over the bags for several months. Maybe Cordelia managed to get rid of it, one dustpan at a time. She's like one of those ants you see at picnics – amazingly industrious."

Thank you, Tato, thought Cordelia, regarding her plate. Why did her family have to make themselves and herself ridiculous before *Pan* Zaremba? Not, of course, that his opinion mattered. She lifted her eyes to his for a split second and caught the faintest suggestion of a wink. She quickly dropped them again.

She went early to bed, immediately after her mother, and lay still there, trying not to think, willing herself to sleep at once. In spite of her weariness it didn't work. Was he guilty or not guilty? It's nothing to you, either way, she told herself firmly, go to sleep, go to sleep, go to sleep. But it didn't work.

The even tenor of her life – so lately and rudely disturbed – had been foretold, she supposed, from the moment as an infant that the polio virus had entered her body. She could not expect much and she must hold onto the good things. If there were bitter ashes, there had also been a walk beneath the harvest moon. Life was a mixed bag, certainly.

And the thing to do, she thought, was always to make a conscious choice. It was important to live consciously, not allowing oneself to be swept weakly one way or the other by the current of events.

Perhaps if she had not grown up disabled, with the likelihood that the ordinary pleasures of young existence would not as inevitably be hers – not love, marriage, children, a career, excursions with friends – she would not have been forced to come to grips so early on with how she wanted to live and what really mattered to her: she wanted to feel she had done good. If that meant that she was closed up in this suburb with her odd family, so be it. She mustn't let herself be beguiled, charmed, persuaded into paths she had never wanted to follow. Zaremba was nothing to her. He would go away in a day or two and he would never think of her again. There was no reason why her thoughts should revolve around him like a wheel on its axle.

She had her family, sometime, perhaps, there would be other duties; she hoped there would always be someone who needed her. Zaremba certainly didn't need her. So there was no reason even to worry whether he was really innocent or not.

Hopeless, it was hopeless, she thought, turning over again uncomfortably in bed. She couldn't possibly sleep. She rose, pulled a thin and shabby robe around herself, shoved her feet into slippers, and quietly opened her bedroom door. She listened carefully but there was no sound in the house. Her mother was sleeping peacefully; her father's door was closed. She stepped carefully out onto the landing and edged up the stairs, where each board creaked beneath her weight and her awkwardness magnified every sound. She thought of retreating, but something pushed her on. She reached the top floor landing. To her right was Zaremba's room. She stilled her breathing, took a few steps as quietly as possible and pressed down the handle of Antek's door.

He was not asleep, but was reading in bed, lying to one side of a bucket into which water dripped, one pinging drop at a time, from the ceiling. He looked up in surprise at her entrance. She skirted another tub strategically placed on the floor, and came to his bedside.

"Antek," she said without preamble, "it's possible to fake a photograph, isn't it?"

He didn't answer immediately – why was he so slow when he was so bright, she wondered? Somehow it had never bothered her very much before; tonight she found it incredibly irritating – "It's possible."

"But how could one tell? If a photo in a newspaper article were faked, I mean?" She was whispering so as not to wake Zaremba, sleeping, presumably, quite near.

"In a newspaper article? No." He kept his finger in his book, but let it fall on his chest.

"Shh. Not so loud. What do you mean, no? It couldn't be faked or no one could tell?"

He shook his head, but she refused to be stymied by his unresponsiveness. "Can I turn on your computer?" He nodded eventually and she found the photo. She brought the laptop to him in bed, just, she thought, as Zaremba had shown it to her. Only of course, she hadn't been lying down.

"What do you think? Can you tell anything?"

He looked at the picture for a minute. She thought he was reading the text as well. Finally he answered.

"Any tampering with the photo would only be visible if it were done by an absolute amateur. Someone at a newspaper would know how to do it so it was undetectable. Here, of course." He pointed at the screen. He stopped, but when she stood waiting expectantly he went reluctantly on: "The original photos, naturally, would be different. You'd have to see those. There'd be a time and a date on them too."

"So there's no way of knowing?" she asked sadly.

"Not unless you know someone at the newspaper, someone who could look at the originals."

"Would anyone be able to see them? At the newspaper, I mean. Or would they be the private property of whoever took them?"

"They'd be on file, I think, but I'm not sure. It's not my field." He picked up his book again. It was incredible, she thought, how like their father he often was.

He was muttering something; she thought it was 'cat amongst the pigeons' but she didn't ask for clarification. She hesitated for a moment, because she hadn't mentioned the subject for eight or nine years, but then she plunged in:

"Didn't that fellow who worked with you when you had the business, the one who wrecked the negatives, didn't he go to work for a newspaper? Was it *Śmiećpospolity*? I thought I remember hearing that...long ago."

Antek let the book fall on his chest again, and stared at the other wall.

"Antek?"

"Could be. Maybe."

"Do you remember? I think I remember you telling me that that's what he'd done, way back then. You were surprised that he wanted to work there, but you wrote him a recommendation, I think."

"Could be." He didn't look interested; he looked like he wanted to get back to his book. The title was spread across his chest: *Guide to Discontinued Russian Lenses (1967-1982)*.

"Antek, please..." she felt like shaking him to get a real response, to force him out of his lethargy. "If he works there, maybe you could contact him and ask him about the photo – if he could look at the files. He sort of owes you, don't you think? What do you think?"

Antek shook his head.

"Please?" She had never begged him for anything before. She didn't like to do it now, but it seemed important.

Antek shook his head again. So there was nothing to do but turn away. Behind her back Antek said, "I can't."

She knew he wasn't speaking of an actual impossibility, but of a psychological one.

"Okay," she said sadly, turning her head, "it's okay. I understand."

She stepped onto the landing, closing the door behind her. And jumped back in fright. Zaremba was standing in the door to his room. He was leaning against the doorframe in what looked like a pair of hastily pulled-on pants and no shirt. She stared at him for a second in embarrassment and anger. Why was it that wherever he appeared she wished there was more distance between them?

"Did you hear?" the words slipped out.

"Not on purpose. But I was woken and I have good ears."

"I'm sorry," she said stiffly, "if I woke you. I tried to be quiet, but…" she made a gesture with the crutch.

"I don't sleep much. Four or five hours a night. You didn't wake me. Unfortunately. I heard a scratch at the door, but when I got up it was only your dog."

Cordelia had a hot feeling that it would be better not to analyze this speech or even to notice it.

"I don't see him."

Behind the man there were strange noises of suffocation.

"I think he's stuck under the *tapczan*."

Cordelia took a step closer and looked past Zaremba, where the *tapczan* was heaving and bits of stuffing were flying out from underneath.

"He'll hurt himself."

The dog was beginning to whine piteously. Zaremba stepped back into the room and lifted the *tapczan*, and Hempseed came scooting out, shaking foam rubber from his fur.

"Thank you," said Cordelia, scooting as quickly after the dog down several stairs. It was born in on her that Zaremba had now saved her father, her mother – or almost, and her dog – perhaps. There was a strange symmetry there but it was doubtless meaningless. "Thank you, I'll try not to disturb you again."

"You didn't disturb me, you've interested me very much," he said, standing in the doorway again, "do you mind if I talk to your brother?"

Cordelia stared at him, not knowing what to answer. 'I don't mind, but he will, he'll mind tremendously,' was what she thought, but she couldn't say that, so she said, "No, but…"

"Don't worry," he said, reading her thoughts, and crossed to Antek's room, knocked, and entered without waiting for a reply.

Cordelia shuddered and went on down the stairs. And yet, she thought, there was a sort of inevitability about the man that might work its way even with a scarcely moveable object like her brother. There was nothing she could do for either of them, though, and her only course of action was to seek her bed, however little likely she was to find sleep there.

But there was no need to lie down to struggle, because when she reached the first floor landing again she found that her mother had been woken, probably by Hempseed's noise, and wanted company.

8

It was sometime in the middle of the next morning, after Cordelia and her mother had breakfasted and Zaremba had asked to borrow the car and departed, that Antek appeared in the salon. Cordelia looked at him in surprise. He was wearing a blazer he hadn't worn in ten years and had made some sort of effort to polish his shoes: he had made the mistake of using black polish on dark brown shoes, but the fact that he had done so at all struck Cordelia as extraordinary.

He sat down on the sofa and stared at the wall.

"You look nice," said Cordelia tentatively, "um, are you going out?" It seemed too impossible to imagine, but she could think of no other reason why he would be dressed as he was.

"You wanted me to."

Cordelia waited for an explanation.

"I told him I'd go." He spoke in a voice so slow it seemed to stress his immobility.

But Cordelia began to hope.

"Did *Pan* Zaremba talk to you last night? About the fellow who works for *Śmiećpospolity*?"

"Yes," Antek sighed deeply and looked disturbed.

So Zaremba *was* the irresistible force, thought Cordelia. And also, she thought, with a surge of joy, if he

164

had asked Antek to make enquiries it could only be because he really did think the photo was a montage. He wasn't just lying to save face before her.

"So are you going to the newspaper offices?" she asked eagerly.

"Yes... It's better in person."

She accepted that, knowing that her brother was sufficiently imbued with the ideas of an older generation to think that any matter of importance couldn't and shouldn't be handled over the telephone, but face to face, so that the personal element could play its full part.

"Thank you for doing this Antek, it's really good of you to do this for *Pan* Zaremba."

"I'm doing it for you."

Cordelia was touched, and made a little uncomfortable. "Thank you."

"And also, he said he'd fix the roof." Antek added.

But he didn't move off the sofa, even when she found a bus ticket and gave it to him.

Cordelia waited patiently for half-an-hour, an hour. He still sat there. Go, she thought, go, go, go. But still he sat. She couldn't urge him, because it might result in his bolting back to his room. She tried to ignore him and was rewarded when, around noon, he rose slowly, wandered vaguely towards the door, opened it, and walked slowly down the drive and away. Cordelia let out a breath of relief. Maybe he'd actually get to the newspaper offices.

But she had to wait for the next day for news. Antek came home saying that the fellow had promised to investigate, and nothing more, but Cordelia could imagine the scene: the surprise of the former employee on Antek's appearance, the invitation to a café to talk, the fellow's curiosity both about Antek's motives and his colleague's activities struggling with the possible difficulties, a sense of obligation to Antek perhaps for that error in the printing shop tipping the balance. But Antek told her none of this, it was only imagination, and at that moment Zaremba had appeared as well, and listened to Antek's one-sentence summary.

"I'll be very grateful if your efforts turn up something. I've been making telephone calls from pay phones. One of my contractors stopped work at a site after reading the article on Saturday. I've got a crane standing. Not to mention the other costs of delay. I tried to pacify the fellow – but it's just my word, which he thinks is worth nothing right now. He's afraid I'll end up in jail and he won't get paid."

There was not much anyone could say to this; Cordelia said she was sorry, Antek faded away up the stairs, and Cordelia's mother chose this moment to tip back her head, fill her lungs, and begin to sing.

Cordelia's family was used to their mother's singing. She had had a very good and powerful voice once, which had been a pleasure to listen to, but after the deterioration of her mental condition, she had lost the ability to carry a tune. So now her voice was still powerful, but utterly uncontrolled: she would sing for hours, the words of a Puccini aria sliding from one bar to the next into a German *lied*, and none of it bearing any relation to the original music. The effect on the nerves of any listener, after only a few minutes, was shattering. And there was nothing they'd ever found that would get her to stop.

Zaremba opened his eyes wide. Cordelia made a helpless gesture, and hopped toward him, ushering him out into the hall. "I'm sorry," she said, "she won't stop now for a long time, not until she wears herself out. I know it's agony. If you go upstairs and close your door –

166

I'm afraid you'll still hear it, but it won't be so loud." How someone, whose affairs were in the desperate state that Zaremba's were, could bear it, she couldn't imagine.

"Can't you get her to stop?"

"No."

"Let me try."

He went back into the salon and spoke to Cordelia's mother, but she ignored him. He picked up an old score of music from the top of the piano and brought it to her, gesturing towards the piano. To Cordelia's amazement, her mother left off singing, let herself be guided to the piano, and sat down on the stool. Zaremba put the music down on the stand. He placed it upside-down, but it made no difference to Cordelia's mother. She hadn't played for ten years. And yet now she let Zaremba put her hands on the keys and suddenly she was actually playing a few bars. They weren't the bars on the score, and Cordelia knew that it was only a sort of physical memory of the finger muscles that had produced those bars, but it was so unexpected that she clapped. Cordelia's mother looked around and smiled, pleased and already forgetting what it was all about. But at least she wasn't making that awful noise anymore.

Cordelia's father appeared from his office, and peered into the salon.

"Oh, it's all right," he said to Cordelia, withdrawing. "I thought something had happened to your mother."

Cordelia followed him back to his office. "*Pan* Zaremba made her stop," she said rather challengingly.

"Did he?"

"Yes, he did."

Her father waved a conceding arm. "Granted. Granted. Give credit where it's due. Decidedly less guilty than before."

"Thank you," Cordelia grinned at him and retreated.

The day passed without further incident, only Cordelia's contacts with Zaremba were warmed by her growing hope that he would be proved innocent by Antek's newspaper man.

The next day passed too. Antek waited for a phone call from his former employee, which didn't come. On the evening news on the television – "*Pan* Zaremba, come quick – it's about you!" – called Cordelia, there was a brief and curious story. A reporter stood on a Warsaw street, in front of the doors of what was presumably an apartment building and spoke about how "operatives of the CBA attempted to search the apartment of foreign developer Dariusz Zaremba, wanted for questioning in the matter of a rigged tender for social housing, but were hampered in their duties by the objections of some of his neighbors, who emerged from their own apartments, and, ignoring the orders of the official in charge, behaved, according to reports, 'loudly and obstructively' – the official in charge speaks of having been called, mm, insulting epithets – and who, apparently not believing that the operatives of the CBA were in fact who they claimed to be, summoned officers of other law enforcement bodies to the scene. The confusion, according to witnesses, was considerable, and is a, mm, regrettable incidence of the lack of trust in the authorities engendered by the very activities the CBA is trying to prevent." (The reporter didn't look convinced though.) She ended with, "We will be keeping our viewers up-to-date on the story of Zaremba's pursuit as further details emerge." That was all.

"Goodness," said Cordelia.

"That's the state-owned station," said Zaremba, looking angry, amused and bemused. "I wonder which neighbors? The old lady at the end of the hall is an ex-insurrectionist and a very tough cookie – she'd stand up for me I think; but it said 'neighbors' in the plural. Whoever they are, I never valued them properly before."

On Wednesday, Antek received a telephone call in the morning. Cordelia heard him saying "all right, all right, at eleven," into the phone and then he hung up the receiver.

"Well?" she asked.

"I'm to meet him. He says he has information for me." He was staring at the wall, not moving, his hand still on the receiver.

"Oh," said Cordelia, suddenly thinking of something, "you didn't tell him that you came from Zaremba did you? I don't know how trustworthy he is. But he must wonder why you're interested. What did you tell him?"

"No."

Cordelia waited, but he didn't seem inclined to elaborate. "Antek?"

"I let on that my photographic interests have induced me to take notice of falsifications occurring in the press; that I had a hunch that that photo had been tampered with," he gestured vaguely, "and I was investigating such things."

Cordelia looked at her brother in surprise and admiration, but he was padding towards the door and it was obvious that he would not be interested in her opinion.

Cordelia waited anxiously for him to come back, but it was hours before she saw, from where she was waiting on the porch, his tall figure by the gate. She rose eagerly and waited for him to come near.

"Well?" she couldn't keep the eagerness out of her voice.

Antek came onto the porch and handed her a manila envelope. "There."

She opened the envelope and extracted a number of photo print-outs. There were several shots of a restaurant, a café table, and one man. In two of the pictures the man was Zaremba and in three Grzegoliński. The sixth photo was the one that had appeared in the newspaper.

Cordelia looked at Antek with raised eyebrows. He sighed and said:

"Those are what were on file. If you look at the ones with your friend – the date is August 14, the three others were taken on August 16, at the same table. This one," he pointed, "is a montage of these two. See, how their heads are together here? It's this photo and this one, put together, with a piece of the table removed to bring them closer together. The date is a transfer too. Very neatly done: I won't bore you with the technical details. Adaś supposes that his colleague assumed no one would ever check. If one isn't specifically looking for some post-processing, one wouldn't know. Adaś says he knows his colleague was in Wirata himself at that time in August. It's possible that he happened to be there entirely by coincidence, was in the café on two different days, and recognized both Grzegoliński and your friend. But it's more probable that he was hired by someone to look for dirt on Grzegoliński, and was following him for that purpose. And that he happened to recognize your friend as well and then – not finding, probably, any of the dirt he'd been hired to dig up – he got the idea of putting them together...' Course nobody in Poland trusts anybody, so the rest of what Adaś says doesn't mean much...." He grimaced, "Adaś is decent enough though, he wouldn't make injurious remarks without some reason..."

Cordelia waited for Antek to sort his thoughts out.

"He says he's never known in the past of his colleague doing anything counter to professional ethics in journalism, but he's never liked him and wouldn't trust him."

"Oh, I'm so glad!" exclaimed Cordelia.

"That man is not improving you," said Antek morosely after considering this remark for a few seconds.

Cordelia was taken aback. "But no," she said, "I meant I'm glad he's innocent – not that that other fellow is untrustworthy."

"Someone's guilty."

"But not Zaremba!" She cried gaily; she heard their mother calling and practically pirouetted away on the point of her crutch.

If Zaremba had been in any doubt that Cordelia had his interests at heart, the joyous smile with which she greeted him when he pulled up in the car and she hopped out to meet him must have put any uncertainties to rest.

"Good news!" she cried, as he emerged from the car and closed the garage door. "Antek has talked to his man and the photo is indeed a fake."

"Yes," he said, with a wry smile, "I know."

She was momentarily taken back. "Oh, well, yes, I suppose you did." She grinned at him.

"O ye of little faith."

"But now there's proof. There are print-outs and Antek can tell you all about it."

She looked so pleased that he didn't have the heart to remind her that it didn't solve his problems. "That's great," he said enthusiastically. "Where is Antek? I must thank him."

Cordelia went around the house looking so radiant that even her father noticed a change as they sat at dinner. "You look different," he said to her in a puzzled tone, "have you done something to your hair?"

"No," said Cordelia. She hadn't changed her hair in the last ten years.

"Cordelia looks like 'trout,'" Cordelia's father continued to Zaremba.

"A trout?" Zaremba looked puzzled. "Cordelia?"

Wondering why anyone should think a family meal a worthwhile exercise, and why they didn't all just take their plates to their separate rooms, Cordelia was about to explain that he didn't mean 'a trout' but her long ago misunderstanding of the poem by Gałczynski, but she was distracted by the necessity of guiding her mother's hand towards the silverware. Her father was already intoning:

'Mackerel in tomato sauce, mackerel in tomato sauce,
Mackerel in tomato sauce. Trout!'

"Cordelia looks like 'trout'," concluded her father.

"My father's never lets me forget – " Cordelia glanced at her father, and tried to explain to Zaremba, feeling that this was rather painful, "that I once came across these lines out of context and thought the phrase meant that life goes along unexcitingly in its everyday grooves and then suddenly something good happens."

"Aha," said Zaremba, his eyes on her. "Still, not a comparison that would have sprung to my mind."

"Not," said Cordelia's father, "that anyone knows what Gałczynski did mean...the key to the poem though – you don't know it? – is 'you wanted Poland, well, you've got it...' Maybe 'trout' is a play on 'nothing at all'. And under that interpretation, of course, I would not have said that Cordelia looks like 'nothing at all'."

Antek seemed to feel that his sister deserved a break. He changed the subject abruptly. "Also," he stuttered, "Bach. And Handel. I like Handel."

There was only a second or two of pause, Cordelia noted with admiration, before Zaremba caught on that this was the continuation of a conversation from two days ago, and leapt, metaphorically speaking, to Antek's aid.

"Do you go to concerts much?"

"N-no. We used to though." He began to tell Zaremba about various performances at the Philharmonic and the Grand Theater.

Wow, thought Cordelia, Antek is making such an effort for my sake and Zaremba has drawn him out, set him running about town on difficult errands and now's he's got him talking. Maybe it would continue, maybe it would be the start of life again for Antek. In her warm glow of gratitude to Zaremba she began to look very much like 'trout' again.

"At least they haven't taken him off the school reading list," said Cordelia's father, who seldom deviated from a topic once started, and who had only waited for a pause in the music to jump in.

"Gałczynski," Cordelia was prepared to supply, but happily, she found that Zaremba was acquainted with the facts and began to talk politics with her father readily enough, her father unconscious that some of his pronouncements might well be considered talking of rope in the house of the hanged.

But her contentment was destined to be short-lived. After dinner, as Cordelia and Zaremba were washing the dishes together in a sociable silence – he washing and she drying and putting them away – and the night was drawing in beyond the windows, he suddenly said to her: "Will you come out with me? For a drive? I want to talk to you alone. I have a proposition, a sort of job offer, for you."

Cordelia thought warily that any sort of job offer could be discussed there in the kitchen and, in any case, the answer would be swift because 'no' didn't take long to say. She remembered how she had gone to his office for a job interview and how frightening he had seemed then. Their respective positions as innocent person and probably-guilty person had given her some confidence in her dealings with him over the past few days. But now she was convinced he was innocent; his worth had gone up; and, in spite of the companionship that had sprung up between them, he still frightened her on several levels. She didn't want to work for him. But instead of speaking these thoughts, she meekly answered 'all right,' and went to call Antek to her mother and to get her jacket.

They left the suburb and headed towards town in a long arc that took them through cornfields where the canes grew taller than the car, and through patches of settlement interspersed with cabbage fields – a sea of silver-purple leaves glinting here and there under the moonless sky.

"Aren't you afraid," she said, as they turned onto a city street, its lampposts spot-lighting the cars with what seemed to Cordelia unnecessary glare, "that you'll be stopped and arrested somewhere if you keep running around town like this?"

"Nothing is less likely than that the police should have an arrest warrant for me. The government doesn't just want me in custody – it would spoil the show entirely if some patrol car were to pick me up quietly; they want to arrest me with the maximum amount of fuss and publicity. No, they'll want to find me at my office, at a building site, in my apartment. It takes some time to organize the whole spectacle, you know."

"I suppose," she answered, and then: "If they do arrest you – what do you want me to do?"

"Well, if they jump on me, stay out of the way, of course. I wouldn't want you to get hurt."

Goodness, she thought, shuddering. It seemed unreal.

"But that's not what I meant," she said, "I mean afterwards – would there be anything I could do? Summon your lawyers or contact someone, or anything? I'd like to help."

"Would you? Brilliant. That's what I wanted to talk to you about. But not yet. We're going to the riverbank. There we can talk in peace."

Some slight little instinct told Cordelia that if he wanted to speak to her alone, about a proposition, it was because alone she was more vulnerable, would be more pliable perhaps, away from her home and family and usual surroundings. In the back of her mind, Cordelia knew that she was going to be asked to do something she wouldn't like, but she pushed these thoughts down, did not let them come up, quite, to the surface of consciousness. And yet she grew rather subdued as they drove along, in spite of her pleasure at the outing, the interest of a change of scenery without having to worry about the possible consequences of her father's driving.

They were passing through the town center. "A few blocks over there," he said waving, "there's an office building from the fifties – do you know it? – if you go in you find that there's a large circular well, with arcades of pillars around each floor, and at the top, a cupola with round windows?"

"No," said Cordelia, "I don't get to the center often anymore. I don't know it."

"The architect designed it, so I've read, as a protest against social-realism."

"Really?" said Cordelia, interested.

"Somehow the significance escaped the authorities. There are lots of ways of protesting."

"Yes," said Cordelia rather wondering where this was tending, but he dropped the subject, and it wasn't until they were driving down the escarpment – between the parliamentary gardens and the large expanse of parks that stretched on to the Lazienki Park, where the last king of Poland had once resided – that he suddenly said:

"Over there, so I've read, there was a grotto, with columns, where Stanisław August's brother used to hold illicit entertainments. *Seks-afery* were nothing to it, I gather. But people thought differently about such things then."

"Yes, although Stanisław August was a decent fellow, if not a monogamist."

"I'm glad you don't equate the two. Personally, I am, by nature – monogamous, I mean."

Cordelia didn't know what to answer. She decided on a cautious, "That's good," and wondered why he was saying so.

As if in answer to her thought, he added: "I wouldn't want you to have got any false ideas about me, from anything I might have said."

"It – doesn't concern me," she replied primly.

"I'm sorry to hear it."

She glanced at him and he smiled back so warmly that she instantly looked out the window, where she saw the world revolve, and he reverted to history: "Still, I like old Stanisław too. Poor old king, he's probably turning in his grave to see what's happening in his country. He saw every attempt he made to reform the country foiled by misguided – patriots. Poland often has to deal with misguided patriots."

"Yes," said Cordelia, getting a grip on herself, "There's that diplomat who says he's 85 but that if the party in power is able to govern alone after the elections he's going to emigrate, because he wants to die in a democracy. I'd like to *live* in a democracy...But you – you said you could go back to Australia." If they don't put you in jail, she added to herself, with a sudden constriction of her heart.

"Yes. But I love Poland. This is where I want to live."

They were coming to the river, catching glimpses of the water as they drove along the esplanade. There were bridges and a tunnel, and then above them on the hill, the long front of the Royal Castle, crowding up close to the Old Town with its turrets and spires and tight-clustered houses in shades of pink and ochre and sepia; and then the houses of the New Town, more spread out and less visible, and they were driving under a railway bridge and pulling up opposite trees.

"Here we can get down to the water without too many stairs." Zaremba said, as he turned off the engine.

Or we can walk along the path at the top. There are benches somewhere I seem to remember."

"Yes," she said, and, mortally curious by now, let herself be guided through a band of trees towards the water. She let him help her down a short flight of steps and then she was standing, looking at the river. It was a broad river, full of dancing reflections from the city lights and the multiplying bridges; beyond, the far bank was a dark band of vegetation, and further away, there were the two spires of St. Florian's Church, and a number of box-like modern buildings.

The night was warm for the time of year, and even here by the river the air seemed soft somehow. Cordelia breathed in the autumn scent of damp leaves and river sand.

"The first year I was back here," said Zaremba, "there was flooding in Poland. The water was up to where we're standing."

"Yes," said Cordelia, "My brother Hal was here at the time, and he brought me to look at the water. This whole bank was lined with people watching the river, to see if it would come up those last few inches. Everyone was very cheerful seeming. A man came along and rode his bicycle through a foot of water at the river's edge. Everyone waited to see if he'd fall in."

"Yes," he said, "shall we sit here?" he motioned to one of the cement slabs lining the walkway. "Or is it too cold? You're not very warmly dressed."

"No, it's fine." She seated herself, wondering if he'd noticed that her fleece jacket had worn thin at the elbows, and feeling, generally, a little shabby. She tried not to think about it. "If you were here too, that day, maybe we passed each other."

"No," he said definitely, "I'd have noticed you."

Not in a crowd, she was going to say, and then she remembered that she did stand out in a crowd, and dropped her eyes, and played with her crutch.

"What did you want to talk to me about?" she said rather gruffly.

He took out his cigarettes, began to extract one. "I was going to go about it slowly," he said, rather jokingly, "talk about the beauty of the evening, and, er, any other topic that would put off the moment – but you're so blunt and confrontational."

"I live in Poland."

"Right, so, cut to the chase, hm?" He didn't seem to find it particularly easy to do so, however. After he'd smoked awhile and she'd waited patiently, silently, and in growing consternation, he began.

"You remember how I told you I was glad that my mother's property was secured, so she'd be all right, whatever happened to me?"

"Yes, I remember."

"Good. And you remember how I asked you three days ago – on Sunday – when I showed you the article in *Śmiećpospolity* – if you'd be willing to do your bit if it came to fighting an injustice?"

"Ye-es." Cordelia was following his statements with extreme intentness. He couldn't have wished for a more attentive listener. If a flash flood had brought the water up to their feet, she wouldn't have noticed.

But Zaremba took another drag of his cigarette and abruptly changed tack: "Do you remember reading, some years back, about a man who owned a very large computer concern? A very honest fellow it would seem. Roughly speaking, he was accused of tax evasion for no good reason. Probably, presumably, he had refused, or failed, to funnel some funds towards persons in power who were expecting it. He decided to fight the judgment. The thing is that in the meantime the government had confiscated some 30 million zlotys of his assets. Even his cars were requisitioned while he was in jail. He was only let out on 8 million zlotys bail."

"8 million," repeated Cordelia.

"Yes. And it's very, very hard to get legal services if one doesn't have money. Fortunately, he had friends, they got to work... Eventually he managed to get the decision overturned and justice was done. So to speak. Not that he got any damages that I ever heard. He's been active since on behalf of people who aren't so fortunate and have been the victims of abuses of power, people without the funds to fight back."

"Ye-es," said Cordelia, "I don't remember the details, but I remember reading something about it."

"So I know what sort of things can happen. They've got my car already. The Jaguar. The one I drove to Zabrzeg where we met."

"Really? On what basis?"

He shrugged.

"How did you find out?"

"People I know."

"So you think they'll confiscate all your assets?"

"I know it has happened. And if it did, then I wouldn't even be able to hire a lawyer – and such cases take teams of lawyers. Expensive ones."

Cordelia considered this for a while.

"Could you quickly transfer your assets to your mother? Then when you need legal help, she'll be able to organize it for you – or at least pay for it."

Zaremba looked gratified. "You catch on quick. I like that about you."

She gave him a rather distrustful glance which he didn't see. He was staring out across the river. Then he turned to her.

"I don't want to get my mother involved. She's not in particularly good health. She doesn't have any idea what's happening here. I'm her boy-who-made-good, you know. It would be very hard on her if she knew about all this. If I were going to transfer money that way, I'd need someone else."

"Well, do you have another relative or a friend you trust?"

He said slowly, "according to the law that just came into force in January of this year, a person can give any amount of money, or assets of any kind, to his parents, his children, or his spouse. If a person gives money or assets over some few thousand zlotys to anyone else, then he has to pay tax on it – 7%. That's a lot. Then the person to whom he has given it will have to pay the same in giving it back – in my case, supposing any is left after paying for the legal services or whatever: 14%. That's too much. Not to mention other difficulties."

"I see," she said.

"So, in my case, parents are out, and children would take too long. What I need," he said, "is a wife."

She opened her mouth, but no sound came out. She closed her mouth. What did one say? Good luck? But after all there were lots of women, probably, who would jump at the opportunity. He didn't need good luck. He could advertise: 'youngish man with no deformities and an engaging manner seeks woman to acquire a fortune,' and they'd no doubt be lining up outside his office. He didn't need her good wishes. Why had he brought her here to tell her this? Maybe he wanted her to sort the candidates out? What a weird idea. But after all, she

181

wasn't being fair. Why should anything he'd said make her feel angry? He was in a terrible situation and needed to find a way out. There was nothing immoral in his idea.

She made an effort and lifted her eyes and found that he was watching her intently. She dropped her eyes again. Ah no, she thought, how silly of her. What he meant was that he knew someone he was going to marry. He hadn't mentioned that he had a girlfriend, but why should he have? That would be it of course. She felt her spirits plummeting down, down to some vastly subterranean depth. She felt decidedly cold. The air along the river was quite frigid and there was probably a breeze blowing too, stinging her cheeks.

"You said you had a job offer for me," she said eventually, when it was becoming necessary to say something and she wanted to turn the subject, "I have a lot of work at the moment, but what is it?"

"Well – that."

She looked at him, able now to look directly at him. "What?" she said, completely puzzled, "I don't understand."

He took a deep breath. "What I want, Cordelia, is for you to marry me. Just on paper. A civil ceremony as quickly as possible at a civil records office. Then I would give you my money – not all of it, just a suitable portion; it would be safe from government clutches. If I need legal help, you'd be able to supply it from the funds. If I don't, then eventually you'd give everything back and we'd get divorced. A very amicable divorce. Naturally, I'd remunerate your, er – services – appropriately. It could either be a straight salary or a lump sum, or I could, say, arrange for the complete renovation of the villa – or anything else you might care to suggest. It would be up to you. But naturally, I'd be immensely grateful."

"No," said Cordelia. She started to rise from the slab where they sat; the reflections on the water danced dizzyingly before her eyes. She couldn't find her crutch, was scrabbling for it.

"Please don't go yet," he said very quietly, "Please could we talk about it?"

She couldn't resist such an appeal. She sat down again and he found her crutch and handed it to her.

"Thank you," she said, not looking at him.

"I meant just on paper. Really just on paper. I'm not an ogre, you know."

Fortunately he couldn't see her blush. Realizing, perhaps, that to have talked of a return was the wrong approach, he continued in a voice of appeal: "I can't see that there would be anything wrong in helping someone this way, can you? There's nothing immoral about it, is there?"

Unfortunately, that was just what she'd thought herself, so she couldn't say, 'yes, if I'm involved.'"

"No-o. I don't know. I'd have to think about it carefully – I mean, to decide if it were immoral or not. There might be aspects that don't immediately suggest themselves."

"I don't see how it can be wrong to help another person, save another person. It would be just like entering into any other contract. If it were some other woman in the case, you wouldn't think it wrong."

"Why not another woman, then? You must know lots."

"You're the only one I'd trust with 20 million."

"You have 20 million?" That's what the paper had said, she remembered, a 'multi-millionaire'. She had never stopped to think just how many multi-millions.

"That's about what I was thinking of transferring. That's not the whole of my personal fortune, nor even, to tell you the truth, the half, but it's enough of my disposable assets to cover the costs, I would think – and perhaps leave me something to start over with if I'm cleaned out."

She said nothing, but stared out over the water.

"You're the only unmarried woman I know who I'm absolutely positive would give it all back the instant I asked for it."

She considered this for a minute. It was perfectly true, but – "you've only known me for a few days. Six, to be precise. How do you know?"

"I'm in business," he shrugged, "I'm a good judge of character. Am I wrong?"

"No," she said, playing with her crutch.

"You told me that you don't have 'the stamina or the personality to pursue large ventures of resistance' – I remember your words – but that you'd be willing to do your part."

"Yes." She had said so; she'd thought she'd meant it, but she hadn't expected to be put to the test quite so quickly or in such a manner.

"Did you mean it?"

"Yes." Her voice was very subdued. "But – "

"So you'll do it? It might mean for me the difference between being ruined – I mean, having my character ruined and maybe the business too – and maybe going to jail, and perhaps, just perhaps, being able to win against the government. You could help make a strike for justice, Cordelia."

She rose with sudden decision, "The idea is abhorrent."

"Abhorrent?"

"Yes. Marrying you, I mean. But I can't make such a decision on the spur of the moment. I'll think about it."

She took a large stride on her crutch and was swinging away, head down, running for the car, so that he had almost to jog to catch up with her, and fortunately for her, she never looked up to catch the strange mixture of entertainment and calculation on his face, and possibly, too, the first beginnings of contrition and regret that he hadn't been quite straightforward.

9

The ride home was a misery. Cordelia was upset enough, but when they were seated in the car, and he was already reaching for the ignition, and she was very aware of his presence in the dark car beside her – the man who wanted her to be his wife (on paper) – his arm extended to the keys, his leg on the pedals, the shoulder of his jacket, and she turned her head and looked out the window so as not to see him, he said quietly, "If you don't want to, I'll understand. Please don't think I meant to pressure you. I thought, from a knowledge of your character, that you'd want to help, but if you find you can't do it, it's okay. I'll understand."

Oh, thought Cordelia, make me feel like a worm. She felt like a worm.

He started the car and it slid out from beneath the trees and into traffic. They drove for a ways in silence.

Then he said, as if trying to restore some normalcy to their situation:

"How's the translating going? You said you have a lot of work."

Cordelia made an effort to be normal: "Yes, but I finished that article you saw before, now I'm back to someone's city-planning opinions."

"That should be more straightforward at least."

She could still talk superficially, even if her mind was overflowing with another subject underneath. "Yes, but sometimes there are strange things even in such texts. Once in a complaint about new housing developments blocking the sunlight someone wrote 'the greenery was condemned to vegetate.'"

He smiled at that and they continued to talk in a desultory fashion, but it was clear that both their minds were elsewhere. On the outskirts of town he stopped by a phone booth, on a street with run-down houses, where no one was about but heavy young men with shaven heads, and broken beer bottles were scattered thick under the bus stop benches. Cordelia watched him standing in the phone booth, his face turned away from her. He didn't have a shaven head, but there was something about his figure and posture that was eerily not out of place in the surroundings. Whom was he calling, Cordelia wondered? She waited in the car and rather wished he'd hurry because the setting was affecting her already plunging spirits. He seemed to be talking for a long time. Then he dialed another number and spoke for a long time again.

"I had to call friends," he said, as he got back in the car.

He had friends, she remembered. Somehow she always imagined him being alone.

"One's a notary. If you agree to my proposition – yes, I know," he made a placating gesture, "you haven't thought about it yet – I don't mean to pressure you – it's up to you – but if you agree, then she's the one who will draw up the donation papers."

"Then why doesn't *she* marry you? She could marry you and draw up the papers too." Cordelia hadn't meant to be sharp or to sound desperate.

"Bigamy is illegal in Poland."

"Oh."

"Besides, I like you better." He started the car.

Cordelia was very silent.

What she really wanted, Cordelia thought, was to go to bed, to be in bed, to be quite alone and quite quiet and be able to think. And yet she couldn't. Zaremba went instantly upstairs to his room as soon as they came into the house, and she went into the salon to find that her mother was fussing, talking angrily to no one, and Antek shrugged his shoulders and said she'd been in that state for an hour and that their father was already asleep, and then he too disappeared.

"Mom," thought Cordelia, sitting down beside her. "Let me tell you what has happened." But it was at moments like these that she realized most sharply that her mother was lost to her. It was an old tragedy, though, and now it affected Cordelia not with the intense pain of its first appearance, but only in that it made her feel more friendless, stretched her nerves a little tighter. Since she was alone she wanted to be truly alone. And her mother was talking, she had to answer.

"Why have they gone?"

"Who, Mom?"

"No one tells me anything."

"What shall I tell you? I had a very strange proposal today."

"Did you, dear?" her mother sounded almost as if she were responding, but Cordelia knew it was only coincidental. Her mother began to mutter something to herself. Cordelia made another effort to distract her.

"*Pan* Zaremba wants me to – to enter into a civil contract with him, what do you think? You like him, don't you?"

"He's a dog."

"No, Mom, Hempseed is a dog." Cordelia's head began to hurt. She glanced at her watch: 10:00. Her mother might be up for hours, and she wanted so badly to go to bed.

She reached for a book and handed it to her mother, but her mother took it weakly and before long put it angrily aside. "It's garbage."

"You're probably right," answered Cordelia wearily.

"It's all garbage." She gestured towards the bookshelves, but that might have been only accidental. "It doesn't help at all."

"No." It didn't. That was true. There wasn't a single book there that Cordelia could reach down and that would help in her situation; and yet, there were lines swimming up to consciousness: Milton, was it, about virtue assailed by force and yet unhurt?

If this fail, the pillared firmament is rottenness,
And the earth's base built on stubble.

Cordelia's mother interrupted her thoughts. "You're garbage too." She reached out and patted Cordelia on the shoulder.

Cordelia knew that her mother didn't mean the words, had no idea what she had said, meant, perhaps, something completely different, if anything at all.

"I'll sit with her if you like."

Cordelia looked up and found Zaremba standing in the doorway. "You look tired out."

"I am a bit," she answered quietly, "but I have to help my mother get ready for bed. And I don't think she wants to go yet."

"Oh, I think so," he said, crossing to her mother, and saying to her, in a cheerful voice, "Come, I'll help you up the stairs."

Cordelia's mother rose gracefully and let herself be guided towards the stairs. How did he do it? Cordelia wondered. Her mother would have resisted if she had suggested such a thing, and yet to Zaremba she was responsive. She remembered, as she followed them slowly up the stairs, that he had spoken of working as an orderly in a hospital. Perhaps it had been in a neurological ward. She would have to ask him. And then she remembered that conversation with him, whatever she decided, was not going to be as easy as before.

Cordelia pulled the covers up to her head and lay still. Around her the old house was full of people, four other adults, all, like herself, with their various problems. Her parents were asleep, she supposed, but she could hear Antek's footsteps creaking slightly on the floor above her bed, and she doubted that Zaremba was sleeping either.

What was she going to do? She had only to make up her mind on which course of action she intended to take. She was, she knew, a strong-minded woman, and, although she could be made very unhappy, she could not be pressured into doing anything she did not want to do. But he had not pressured her in any overwhelming way.

The thing that most struck her, that had been ringing in her mind all the way home, was that he hadn't made use of the most telling, pressing, and irresistible argument, namely, that having saved her father's life, she could hardly refuse him anything. He had never so much as hinted at the subject. He'd never mentioned his pursuit of her mother that day at the railroad tracks either. Antek was another reason to be grateful to him. He seemed to have finally induced her brother to step out of the shell that he had been growing thicker and thicker around himself. He might just have saved Antek too.

This was all very painful. Cordelia stifled a moan. But why was she moaning, what was the basis for her deep reluctance to acquiesce?

Well, of course, there might be repercussions – fairly unpleasant ones – of a legal nature, or a financial nature, or of a being-plastered-all-over-the-media-as-a-gangster's-moll-nature. She could guess that such repercussions might be waiting in the wings; she couldn't know exactly what they might be. Was she afraid of them? Yes, no. If he were innocent, then of course, she would be willing to bear whatever might befall. If it turned out that he were guilty – what then? But she didn't believe that he was guilty. Still, he might be innocent and everyone would think he was guilty. He might even be innocent and still be found guilty by the courts. Then she would be associated with his disgrace. That would be mighty unpleasant, and worse yet, very unpleasant for her family. Perhaps people would be less willing to hire her as a translator and they'd have a hard time making ends meet. All that was enough to give one pause, but none of it was really the crux of the matter.

Was there anything unethical about agreeing to be temporarily someone's wife in order to help him in a –

presumably – righteous cause? Would she find it acceptable if everyone in society were to marry for such purposes? Yes, why not? She couldn't see any objections. People married only occasionally – temporarily or not – for true love, and just as often out of habit, or mistaken feelings, or lack of imagination, or for lust, or money, or because of failed birth control methods – all of which were much less noble reasons for entering into a contract with another human being.

And really, if after he had done so many things for her family, she wouldn't make any return when it was within her power, then she was just a cipher, an empty human being; and she had always believed she wanted to do good. Here was her opportunity and her overwhelming impulse was to say 'no' and even: 'no, no, no'.

Why? Well, the crux of the matter was that if her feelings had been neutral towards him, or had inclined towards warm platonic friendship, there would have been no problem. But that was not the way her feelings tended, and she felt, instinctively more than through reason, that a union, however lexical and non-physical, with someone about whom she couldn't stop thinking morning, noon, and night, opened vast possibilities of indelicacy and distastefulness.

Not that any of that mattered, of course. She would have to do it. It was so stupid of her anyway, she thought wearily as she tossed in the bed, to have let her imagination get off the leash and go trotting about looking for trouble.

She moaned again, and pulled the pillow over her head. Perhaps she could suffocate herself, and then she wouldn't have to meet him in the morning.

She knew and had known perfectly well, after all, that he had a number of qualities that made it very unwise for her to let her feelings get involved with him. She knew that while she had become, in the space of six days, totally wrapped up in him, his mind was – naturally enough – elsewhere; he was revolving schemes that concerned her only incidentally, as she might be useful. He would remain essentially indifferent to her, however much he flirted with her and however kind he might be – and however married they might be.

And yet, he had everything she lacked: confidence and vitality and optimism and the self-assurance of his own strength, both mental and physical. He was a vibrant man and she was a lonely woman, so that her attraction to him was perfectly natural. Cordelia was strong, but nature was very much stronger.

Nature, she was aware, was setting her up for a great deal of unhappiness. For starters, it kept her awake until the sun had risen the next morning.

The first thing she thought when she woke was that meeting him – that moment when their eyes would make contact this morning, would be the worst. Maybe she could just stay in bed and not get up and not meet him. She listened carefully, trying to determine who was up in the house. There was a footstep on the landing; the knob of her door was turning.

If anything more was needed to convince Cordelia of the overwrought state of her nerves, it was the slam of her heart as the door opened.

It was her mother, in her nightgown. Cordelia threw back the covers and slid hastily from the bed. She hopped and struggled into her clothing as quickly as possible, then helped her mother. It was late, she saw by her watch, when they came into the kitchen.

Antek was there, pottering at the stove, and Zaremba was seated, reading a newspaper. In company, their meeting passed off normally enough. She didn't quite look at him, and his 'good morning' was addressed to both herself and her mother. There wasn't any question that they would revert to last night's conversation at such a moment. Whenever she thought he might be looking at her, she would become very busy feeding her breakfast to Hempseed, who was quite astonished and pleased by the attention.

And yet there came a time in the morning when she had to leave the protection of her mother, and drag herself up the stairs to fetch her laptop. She heard Zaremba's rapid step behind her as she reached the landing, and her pace quickened. She bolted into her room and sat down quickly at her desk, feeling like some small woodland animal pursued by a predator. But what did it avail her? He knocked on the door; she hesitated to call 'come in' and he opened the door anyway and stepped inside.

"I don't think you should come into my room like that, when I haven't said 'come in.'" She said rather breathlessly. Her tone was too sweet to cause offence, in spite of the words.

"Now I can; later I would have reservations."

She didn't have to analyze this sentence, she knew what he meant.

He stood still, leaning against the frame, his hand behind his back grasping the door handle. "So: Will you marry me?"

She gathered together some papers and her laptop, trying to be casual, to make it seem as if she was going to go on with her work and everything was business as usual. But she couldn't keep it up. She stopped and answered seriously, "Yes."

There was a moment of silence. Perhaps once again, if she had looked at him, she would have noticed a slight trace of regret cross his face.

"I'll make sure it's worth your while," he said, as if to assuage his conscience.

"No!"

"No?"

"I won't do it on that basis."

"On what basis then?"

"Just to help you. For justice. Not for money." She wished her heart would stop beating so fast. She hoped she wasn't blushing.

"You're very generous."

She made an impatient gesture, to stop him from talking. "I have to work," she said, pointing to the laptop.

"Would it be a big problem to put it aside for a while? We have to meet the notary at" he glanced at his watch, "1:00."

"You've already made an appointment?" She asked in astonishment.

"There's no time to be wasted. I'd like to get married as soon as possible, and there are a lot of papers to be collected."

"But how did you know I'd be willing?"

He didn't look at her, but stared out the window for a long time, obviously revolving various answers. He finally decided on:

"I couldn't see any reason why you wouldn't."

"You're very self-assured. One might even say – odiously so. How did you get such a good opinion of yourself?" she asked in some indignation.

"I'm a self-made man. Naturally I'm pleased with my own creation."

They were back to joking, which made it easier to be normal.

What did one wear to go to a notary? Left alone in her room to get ready, Cordelia hesitated. She didn't want to go to town in her old jeans and old sweater. On the other hand, she certainly didn't want her clothing to signal that she thought it was a special occasion, or anything other than a tedious necessity. She settled on a pair of light wool trousers and a blazer. She knew she didn't look fashionable, but she hoped she didn't look like she'd been coerced out of financial despair.

Soon they were driving to town again, traveling along the same roads as last night. It was an overcast day, the sunlight making it through the clouds as a diffused glow throwing the plant life into relief. There were willow trees, each narrow leaf distinct and silvered, like in a renaissance painting; a cornfield with half the stalks left uncut, high over her head, then a portion chopped and stubbly; and a half-way field, the stalks only shoulder high, a mix of somber yellowing colors. Soon they would leave these little bits of tenacious agricultural land and be back amongst the settled territory. How odd, thought Cordelia, that her own inner turmoil left the landscape unchanged. She had noted this strange dichotomy between human consciousness and the external world before. She stole a glance at the man beside her, wondering what he was thinking.

Whatever it was, it made him slow suddenly and pull the car over onto the side of the road. He turned off the engine.

"What is it?" asked Cordelia, startled.

He turned to her, his arm resting on the steering wheel. "Do you realize that there may be…that you might meet with hassles or unpleasantnesses or problems if you do this? I mean both now and later? I think you'll be all right and I'll try to protect you, of course, but I can't make any guarantees."

"Yes, I know." She stared out at the landscape. She had no more awareness of distinct shapes than if she had been looking through a kaleidoscope. There were spots of burgundy foliage and umber shadows amongst the gray-greens and yellows.

"But have you really thought about it?"

"That aspect of the matter doesn't bother me."

"It bothers me…But if not that, then what?"

"Never mind. Let's just go on, shall we?"

He hesitated quite a long time for him, for several seconds at least; then started the car again, and they were once more under way.

They were driving through the city center; circling the giant Stalinist lampposts of Constitution Square, passing the U.S. embassy –

"You are a Polish citizen?" Zaremba asked suddenly.

"Yes, I have dual citizenship," she answered, "because of my father."

"Good, otherwise it would have bug – um – complicated matters a little." He gave her a glance.

She gave him a satisfied smile: "Thank you."

Then they were traveling along lines of nineteenth-century buildings, embassies and government offices, and the edifice where the Gestapo had its headquarters during the war, and turning into a smaller street, and pulling up before an aged building with a series of small bronze plaques announcing offices inside.

The elevator was very small: a rickety wooden box that had probably been toting people up and down since the time of Piłsudski. Zaremba was just reaching around Cordelia for the sixth-floor button, and she was just about to say – for several reasons – 'I think I'll walk' – only, of course, she couldn't, when a rather older man, with the square shape typical of ex-army officers, squeezed in, effectively blocking her escape. "Seventh floor," he barked, and Zaremba obligingly pushed the button for him. The lift began its slow, swaying, creaking journey upwards. Cordelia kept her eyes on the floor, because if she raised them she found herself staring at Zaremba's chest, but their fellow passenger was not so inhibited. He stared at Zaremba. "I've seen *pan* somewhere," he said. "Are you a television presenter?"

Zaremba denied the suggestion.

"Strange. I have the feeling I've seen your face recently."

"It's a common face," said Zaremba. The lift stopped and they got out, the man nodding them a curt and suspicious goodbye as Zaremba closed the inner doors for him again.

"That was a mistake," said Zaremba, "I should have taken the stairs. Never mind. Can't be helped now. Anyway, there will be some people here to meet me. Friends of mine." He opened the door of the notary's office.

The office seemed to be full of people, and Cordelia was introduced to a number – there were handshakes and hand-kissing; and then she was shown by a secretary into a private room, and seated at a large shiny table and left alone.

She looked about. It was a modern room, with line drawings on the walls and certificates of sorts, filing cabinets along the wall, and in the center of the table, unexpectedly, a very beautiful old silver sugar bowl. She kept her eyes on it, trying not to think too much about anything, or to let herself get too nervous.

Zaremba appeared with a woman in her forties; a very good-looking, confident sort of professional woman, who shook Cordelia's hand briskly and looked her over rather as if she were a piece of furniture under consideration, and said 'very nice' with a lift of her brows to Zaremba, and asked for her identity document and disappeared again.

Zaremba gave Cordelia a one-moment sign with his hand, and followed the woman out of the room. In a few minutes he opened the door again, holding someone's cell phone.

"Cordelia, look up please."

He seemed to be taking a picture of her. Why, she wondered? But he was already closing the door again.

Some time passed, and then the woman reappeared alone and handed Cordelia back her document. "Here's a list of what you're going to be given. I'm going to draw up the donation papers as *Pan* Darek has asked me to do," she said to Cordelia. And then, giving her a very direct look: "And now, speaking as *Pan* Darek's friend and not as a notary – you're not going to pull any fast ones on him are you?"

Cordelia stared in amazement.

"Because he's a very decent fellow, and I wouldn't like to see anything happen to him," she said in a threatening voice.

"I assure you, he's safe from me."

"Good." The woman gave a nod and left the room briskly, leaving Cordelia to wonder a little wildly if she'd just escaped a beating with a file folder, and to think that at least the man had friends who seemed to feel strongly about him and that was in his favor.

She looked at the paper: it said 'undeveloped lot no. 14 with an area of 3000 meters....valued at 900,000 zlotys; 'lot no. 27...one hectare valued at 3,000,000 zlotys; three lots, nos. 14, 15, 16 contiguous, located at... 2,000,000....' The numbers and addresses meant nothing to her. 5 million euros cash...(not included on notarial act...) total value of 20 million euros.'

She sat on alone, and finally the door opened and she looked up and found with relief that it was Zaremba, come back to claim her.

"Sorry it took so long. We can go now." He was coming round the table to help her disentangle her crutch from the chair and table legs, when a sudden sound from the outer office made him stop and jerk his head in that direction, listening.

"*Good afternoon, ladies and gentlemen, good afternoon, madam.*" They were heavy, official voices. Even Cordelia recognized them.

Zaremba froze. "Police," he whispered to Cordelia, casting his eyes rapidly around the room. There was no place to hide.

No, thought Cordelia. They would take him away in handcuffs and throw him in prison and humiliate him and keep him beyond reach of help.

Outside they could hear the policemen saying, in their ponderous, polite voices: "We had a telephone call that a certain person who is wanted for investigation was seen in this building, and, to be precise, entering this office. A certain *Pan* Zaremba? Has *pani* seen such an individual? Is he here?"

"No."

"No."

"No, never seen him," voices were saying to the doubtless disbelieving arm of the law, "– don't know who you're talking about."

"Do you have a warrant for his arrest?" snapped the notary, whose position doubtless gave her inhibitions about untruthfulness, but who was obviously not about to be intimidated. Other voices joined in, civilly and righteously heckling.

Half-rising, Cordelia could see through the semi-frosted glass window of the door that the two men were only regular patrolmen, not special agents, no doubt just caught on their beat by some overzealous citizen – the man from the elevator probably.

A sound pulled her eyes away from the door to which they had been glued; behind her, Zaremba was opening a tall window, climbing onto the sill, sliding along it to the end.

"No!" cried Cordelia, imagining the six long floors down, down to the pavement below.

"Shhh!" hissed Zaremba, searching for a grip along the outside wall beyond the window, "There's a cornice. Tell them I've left," and inched himself out of sight.

No, thought Cordelia, no, no, no.

"We'd like to speak to him," one of the policemen was saying in the other room.

"For what reason?" the notary was putting up a good fight, "On what legal basis? This is a private office."

Cordelia crossed rapidly to the door of the room and opened it wide so they could see it was empty. "He's already gone out!" she cried to the two policemen standing there, intensely aware that behind her back Zaremba was standing on a ledge over certain death, clinging by only his fingertips.

"He just went out this moment," she exclaimed again in such a breathless, terrified voice that they were convinced their quarry must be near, that Cordelia was eager to help them. How long could he hold on? she thought.

"Where did he go, *pani*?"

Cordelia jerked her head in helplessness: "Out!" she cried, "just now!"

The policemen looked at one another and hurried from the office.

Cordelia whirled around, afraid to look. There were a few frozen seconds in which she saw nothing, then she saw his leg reappear and his hand was gripping the window frame again, and he was pulling himself back across the sill and climbing into the room. He was breathing heavily, and he looked rather as if he'd seen a ghost, maybe as if he'd seen several ghosts. "Come on," he said, "let's get out of here!"

They charged through the outer office, where someone said, "they've gone," and someone checked the hallway and held the door for them, and then they were in the elevator and it was going down, down, slowly. Zaremba got off at the first floor.

"Go on ahead. If you find they're still there, talk loudly to them, so that I can hear you."

But when she stepped out of the elevator, heart beating, she found that no one was there. Zaremba came rapidly down the stairs; they made a dash for the car; it was reversing into traffic almost the second they were seated, and traversing several blocks with rather more than usual speed. A short stretch of driving and Zaremba pulled the car into an empty parking space, turned off the engine, reached for his cigarettes, and began to smoke, still not saying anything.

Cordelia sat and shivered beside him.

He finished half the cigarette and grinned at her. "Well, learn something new every day."

"What did you learn?" Cordelia asked, amazed that he could smile.

"I'm afraid of heights. Or was it depths?"

"Why did you do that? You could have been killed!" she spoke angrily.

He shrugged. "I didn't want to get caught. It didn't seem to me an impossible feat – to hold on for a few minutes. If you don't think about the drop you can see it's not a problem."

"How can one not think about the drop?"

"As you say. Now I know."

"Well," said Cordelia, in an injured tone, "I think you've probably given me the start of a heart problem, and I think you're a hateful man – but I'm glad to know there's at least one thing to which you aren't impervious."

He smiled at her, "oh, there are at least two things to which I'm not impervious."

She had had enough experience of his smiles not to ask for explanations; she stared at her fingers, and after a minute she added in a small voice: "I'm glad you didn't get killed."

"Thank you," he said, and pretty soon he started the car and they continued on their round of errands: the collection of birth certificates...

"What for?" asked Cordelia.

"It's just one of the things we need to bring with us to the civil records office when we get married."

"You aren't going in there?" she exclaimed, as he drew up to the curb not far from an official-looking building. "It'll be full of security guards – or at least of one security guard."

"In spite of their frequent delusions in that direction, security guards are not policemen. I have to go in; I can't get the certificate otherwise. It'll be all right, don't worry."

"How can you *not worry* all the time?" she asked in genuine puzzlement.

"The trick is to think that whatever happens it's going to be interesting – then you don't mind so much if it's not exactly what you wanted in the first place."

"I don't want to be interested – I want to be safe." But even as she said the words she wondered if they were completely true. Would she have missed knowing him in order to be quite safe in her usual, rather boring, life? "And you like danger," she added disapprovingly, before she could find herself in anyway agreeing with him on such a subject. "It's a kind of sickness."

"And you like worrying. That's a kind of sickness too."

"I don't like it – I just can't help it."

"I'll teach you."

No, she thought, she didn't want him to teach her anything; she already felt as if she were being shaken loose of her old foundations, more would be too much.

They were entering the building, passing an elderly security guard, whose eyes slid over them but whose mind was elsewhere.

"See?" said Zaremba, as they approached the counter, and were just about to make their request, were two feet from the counter, when the clerk rose from a stool without looking at them, snapped down a sign 'closed' on the marble countertop, and walked away without a backward glance. A row of clerks was rising and departing.

"Excuse me," they called to one.

"We're closed. Read the hours," was all the response they got.

They looked at the sign: Opening hours for the civil records office (birth certificate division) Mon., 8-16:00, Wed., 10-18:00; Tues.-Fri: 9:00-15:00; ...

"Well, tomorrow, then," said Zaremba, "we could probably get them to deal with us, but I don't want to call attention to myself."

"How would you get them to deal with us?" she asked, puzzled, "It's past closing time."

"Have a little faith in people, they're human – appeal to them."

"You mean – beg?"

"Tsk, you're so categorical. I mean – induce them to put themselves in my shoes."

"You mean, make them feel sorry for you. You mean – make Bambi eyes."

"Bambi eyes!? That's something *you'd* do better than me."

Cordelia was silent, considering that he really should be a politician, because he could always bring about the non sequitur. She wondered if that was how he negotiated too, in business, and whether his clients and partners simply gave way before him from the fatigued realization that they'd never get the last word.

Hopefully, he said, as they regained the car, there would still be time to visit one more office and change the registration of her address, so no one would be able to trace her to her home from the civil records office. But it was too late, he said, to visit town halls on the hardest part of the business. They would do that tomorrow. That would give them time to think up a good story.

"The hardest part of the business? A good story? What do you mean?" asked Cordelia.

"It's like this," he said, "the waiting period for a civil marriage is one month and one day. Why the 'and one day,' I don't know, probably just a Polish desire to complicate the matter, but so it is."

A month and a day, thought Cordelia with relief, so it wasn't immediate. Perhaps it would never happen – so much could occur in four weeks.

"A month and a day is too long to wait. However, we can ask – apply – to have the time shortened. I think five days is about right."

Five days! thought Cordelia, who had had no idea about a time frame for all this.

"That gives us just time to collect all our papers, for Edzia to draw up the notarial documents and so on. I think next Monday is good."

"Next Monday!"

"Is that…not good?"

She hesitated; it seemed very soon. Next Monday, *Boże*.

"Did you have plans already for Monday?"

No, she never had plans. He had been living in the same house with her for almost a week. He must know that she had only her translating deadlines and her dreary round of household duties. "No, Monday is all right."

Having managed the registration business successfully and uneventfully, they were stuck in traffic, the fuming, aggressive traffic of the Warsaw rush hour, inching along. Suddenly Zaremba edged the car out of the traffic jam and into a side street.

"I want to show you something," he said, as they drove along, in a different direction than before. Ten minutes of driving, and they entered a residential area, and then pulled up before a group of three elegant smallish apartment buildings, nicely landscaped, their air of light and space contrasting favorably with the heavy new tile mushroom roofs of the surrounding houses. "What do you think?" he said, leaning against the wheel of the car, and looking out at the buildings.

"Very nice. Really," she said, and then, looking about to see if there were any policemen, "Is this where you live?"

"No. These are some of the social-housing apartments I built last year. I'm rather proud of them." He set the car in motion again. "The landscaping was a freebie I threw in – *and* I paid taxes on it. They're full now of people who couldn't otherwise afford housing. I think it's a good thing for the government to do, although, speaking from the experience of my early years, I'm not sure it's a wise idea to place a lot of people with severe income problems together in one building. But I have nothing to say about that. I just arrange for the construction."

They were driving again. Cordelia understood why he had brought her there.

"So what about your business? Is it suffering very much at the moment? Or don't you know?"

"Yes, it's suffering. Quite a lot. One of those men you met at Edzia's is my second-in-command, so to speak, and he's trying to keep things going. But I'll lose a bit, that's for certain. I don't care so much about that though."

Cordelia wondered vaguely what 'a bit' was to a multi-millionaire; something vastly beyond her expectations, no doubt. "About what then?"

"It really bothers me that they can drag my name in the mud and there's nothing I can do, nowhere I can go, no forum in which I can stand up and say 'it's not true.' That's what really bothers me, can you understand?"

"Yes." And then, after a moment's reflection, she asked, "what Antek came up with – about the photos – you can't use that somehow? I don't know how."

"Yes, I'm thinking about it all the time, don't worry. That bit of information will come in handy, I think."

"What about going to the courts yourself? Couldn't you sue for libel?"

"Not unless something definite has been said. If they just say they want me for questioning in a matter of corruption, I'm tarnished but it's not libel."

"No."

Then he abruptly changed the subject, and so they drove home.

10

'The CBA should be punished for spying on me naked in my hotel room...' – victim of the CBA

Cordelia had been wondering how to tell her family of her plans, and finally decided just to mention the fact casually at dinner. She waited until they were all seated, all eating, and then she announced quietly:

"By the way, I think you should all know that I'm going to enter into a contract with *Pan* Zaremba for the purpose of furthering his case."

Cordelia's father dropped his knife. "What... kind of contract?"

"A marriage, but not a real one, only on paper, to help secure his assets."

"A marriage? For his assets? For his ducats, O my daughter!" cried Cordelia's father, his parody of the merchant of Venice being entirely unthinking and his astonishment genuine.

"Yes, in a manner of speaking," said Cordelia, wincing a little. "*Pan* Zaremba is going to transfer some money to me – quite a lot; he can only do so if I'm his wife. The point is that then I'll be able to pay his legal fees when he's in jail."

"Let *Pan* Zaremba go to jail – why should that involve you?" exclaimed Cordelia's father. "No offence, sir," he added to Zaremba.

"None at all," returned Zaremba equably, continuing to eat his dinner unperturbed.

Antek glanced between the three of them and then went on with his meal, his head shrinking a little between his shoulders.

"Because I can help – and I want to," said Cordelia.

"But," said Cordelia's father testily, "but – if it's just a matter of paying his fees, why doesn't *Pan* Zaremba marry an accountant?"

"I suppose," Cordelia said, rather annoyed with herself because she had thought that bringing the subject up at dinner would prevent its discussion and instead they were talking rudely, as if Zaremba weren't there. "*Pan* Zaremba doesn't know one."

"Your life is to be ruined because *Pan* Zaremba lacks acquaintance in the world of bookkeeping?"

"Not ruined, Tato; not permanently, only temporarily."

Zaremba looked up at that with an odd look on his face, but he said nothing.

"I should hope so. But have you thought about the consequences? What will your mother and I do while you're off being temporarily married, tell me?"

"Oh," exclaimed Cordelia, not looking at Zaremba and blushing a little, "No. I'll be right here, don't worry."

"Don't worry? Since when have you started saying 'don't worry'? You're starting to change, Cordelia. You worry me."

"It's all settled, I'm afraid," said Cordelia.

"Your mind is made up? You are quite determined?"

"Yes, quite." The Rubicon had been crossed long before; Rome had been entered the moment she had risen to speak to the policemen. Now she stood and began to stack the dishes.

Cordelia's father watched her for a few seconds, and then turned to Zaremba: "'the female of the species is more deadly than the male.'"

"I beg your pardon?"

"It's just a poem," Antek murmured apologetically – "Kipling, you know," as Cordelia's father began to intone:

'*When the Himalayan peasant meets the he-bear in his pride,*
He shouts to scare the monster, who will often turn aside.
But the she-bear thus accosted rends the peasant tooth and nail.
For the female of the species is more deadly than the male…'

He lifted a warning finger at Zaremba, and went on:

'*Man, a bear in most relations – worm and savage otherwise –*
Man propounds negotiations, Man accepts the compromise.
Very rarely will he squarely push the logic of a fact
To its ultimate conclusion in unmitigated act.'

"Cordelia, it would seem, has decided on 'unmitigated act'."

"Tato, please." But Cordelia, carrying the dishes out to the kitchen, made no attempt to argue.

"Very – er, interesting," said Zaremba.

"You might also remember," Cordelia's father leaned confidentially towards Zaremba, as she disappeared, "'That hell hath – '"

But Cordelia cut him off with unusual severity: "Tato, enough, please!"

He raised his hands in a gesture of resignation. But after a moment, when Cordelia was back in the kitchen, he whispered to Zaremba: "You see. It's starting already. Be careful."

Antek rose suddenly and announced that he would play something on the piano. In fact, he played Mendelssohn's *Wedding March* very loudly – a piece doubtless suggested by his subconscious, as he seemed unaware of its extraordinary unsuitableness to the occasion. It did, however, have the effect of reducing his father to silence, thus proving, thought Cordelia as she listened in some distress and surprise, since Antek hadn't played in years, that music had its uses both for communicating and for preventing communication.

"What was that all about?" Zaremba said to Cordelia in the kitchen, as she began to shift the plates from the counter into the sink for washing. "What was your father on about?"

"I'm sorry. It's just that he's concerned about me, and doesn't quite know how to express it. I'm afraid he'll probably get worse. Try not to pay attention."

"I must say I can see his point, although I would prefer my prospective father-in-law not to try to warn me off. At least not with such gruesome poetry."

"Oh well," she said soothingly, as she began to wash the plates, "He could have found much worse." He could, after all, she thought uncomfortably, have used 'your old virginity is like one of our withered French pears; it looks ill, it eats dryly.' She bent her head over the dishes and hoped that Zaremba wasn't looking at her. "His catalogue of misogynist lines is quite extensive. But it's not like he was really going to be your in-law."

There was a brief moment of silence, and then Zaremba said, moving her aside from the sink, "Here let me get those. Why don't you have a dishwasher? It would be so much easier for you."

"Yes, but we can't afford one." And then, guessing his thoughts, she quickly added, "and please don't buy us one."

"Why not?"

"No. Just no. And besides, we couldn't afford to run it."

"That could also be remedied."

"No," she said to him seriously, "I mean it, no."

It was only when she was finally in bed that evening that she remembered. He had said the hardest part was still to come. But she was too exhausted by the day to stay awake and think about it. She fell almost instantly asleep.

"So," he said, leaning on the steering wheel of the car, and looking at the building – an official-looking building, with a multitude of little plaques on the outside – one of which said 'civil records office' – "the hardest part is to convince them that we have a good reason for wanting to get married before the end of the waiting period."

"Here?" said Cordelia, "this is where we get married? In this building?" She felt rather like she imagined a bank robber must feel standing outside the bank, before a heist – if that was the word. She felt a strong reluctance to go in. She was doing all this because he was innocent, she reminded herself: it had nothing to do with crime.

"Maybe. There are 18 district headquarters – town halls, shall we say – with civil records offices in Warsaw. We can choose any of them. So my idea is that we apply in several – say ten – and see where we can get them to agree."

"Ten!"

"Or maybe a few more – it depends. The other point is that if anyone makes the association of my name and the news – and there might be a few – the authorities will get several such reports at once. That should confuse them a little." He looked amused, "They won't know where I'm likely to show up for the ceremony. At the civil records office in Bielany or in Praga. If they turned up too soon it would spoil everything. Although there's one good thing – we know now there isn't a warrant out for my arrest. Those policemen yesterday would have said so at once. Also, Zaremba is not a very uncommon name, so it may happen that no one will catch on. Let's go."

"So what are you going to tell them?" Cordelia asked, but he was already out of the car and coming around to her side. They couldn't stand and talk in the parking lot, there were people about. And there was also a wind and it was cold. Or maybe she just felt cold. It was a good thing she was wearing a heavy sweater and a large jacket. They went in through glass doors, past a security guard, knocked on a door marked 'civil records,' and went in.

And soon came out again. They had found a woman there, a clerk approaching retirement age perhaps, who had either had a very bad day or whose temper was permanently knife-edged.

"We'd like…" began Zaremba.

"Your desires are no concern of mine," snapped the woman, with the impunity of minor officialdom: "There are the forms; fill them out."

"We'd like a shortening of the waiting period," continued Zaremba suppliantly.

"Then you'd better have a documented reason."

"The problem is…"

"*Proszę pana!* Do you think I have time to listen to everyone who comes in here? I'm not interested in your problem! Bring me a documented reason and I'll consider the matter, otherwise don't bother me!" The woman rose abruptly and left the room.

"That," said Zaremba to Cordelia as he held the door for her, "is a very good tactic: leaving the room. That is one tactic I've never figured out how to deal with."

They got back in the car. "17 still to go," said Zaremba cheerfully.

Soon they were parking again, walking back along the street. This office was in an older building, a gray pre-war façade with the war-time bullet damage still visible, sandwiched between two contemporaries, equally pocked. Zaremba stopped before the entrance and looked up and down the street.

"Not much parking here," he said, shaking his head slightly.

"Does it matter?" asked Cordelia. "You aren't going to invite people are you?"

He hesitated just slightly; then answered: "The notary will have to be present because she has to read the donation paper to you. By law, she has to do it out loud, the whole thing, before you sign it. She'll read it very fast, don't worry, it won't take long. And some of my other friends will be there too; we have to have two witnesses, you know. Also, if the CBA or anyone else does show up for me, it will be good to have moral support – there's no reason we should make it easy for them to behave like mobsters. You won't want anyone from your family to come, I don't think?"

"No," she shook her head. Definitely not: it wasn't that sort of affair. "But why does the notary have to read the paper here? Couldn't we go to her office afterwards?"

"We could, but I want to do it this way, is that all right?"

She nodded; of course it didn't matter to her, but she was slightly puzzled. Still, she didn't have long to ponder; they were entering the building, there was another door marked 'civil records.'

There were two women there, seated at desks. One looked up in inquiry, and Zaremba launched on his explanation: they wanted – he and his fiancée – he gestured to Cordelia – to be married, but he was in the construction business and it was possible that a situation would emerge that might take him out of Warsaw before the waiting period was up, before the week was out, in fact, and then, it would be quite impossible to get back to be married, and therefore they were asking to be married on Monday…

"I see," said the woman politely, "But do you have any documentation? I'll need you to feel out this form, and I'll need some sort of proof. A letter from your employer, at the very least… Your I.D. please."

She began to look at his identity document, while he continued to explain, in the most humble and appealing voice, why it was going to be impossible for him to produce any sort of document, and she looked first totally unwilling and explained again, a little more sharply, that she needed some sort of document on which to base such a decision – and then quite unwilling, and then annoyed, and then, as he launched on his story for the fifth time, as if she might be softening.

"Your I.D?" she said to Cordelia, and Cordelia knew that the moment when an official asked for one's identity document was the moment at which an official had decided to give in, however long it might be before the fact was admitted. Officials specialized in keeping petitioners in suspense. She realized she'd been holding her breath. But she didn't have her I.D; she'd given it to

Zaremba earlier, so there wouldn't be any fumbling with it in front of the clerks.

She said to Zaremba, "You have it; I gave it to *panu* earlier."

There was a moment of silence, during which the clerk's astonishment was palpable and Cordelia could sense that Zaremba had stiffened.

"You aren't his fiancée?" the woman asked, puzzled.

"Yes, I am," said Cordelia, ready to sink. She had spoken to Zaremba as she always did when she spoke Polish to him, using the formal address, which no woman would use in speaking to her fiancé. How stupid he must think her, she thought; she had probably ruined everything.

She had certainly spoiled their chances there. The woman handed the two identity documents back smartly. "The waiting period is a month and a day," she said in a tone of finality, and busied herself with some other papers. Zaremba did not insist further, but retreated, ushering Cordelia out before him.

"I'm sorry," she said, when they reached the car. "I'm really sorry. I can't believe I was so stupid."

"It's all right," he said, and then, as she continued to look distraught, "hey, Cordelia, really, it's all right. We still have 16 to try. If we have to, we can get married on Tuesday. You'll get the hang of it. Just remember: my name is Dariusz – Darek. Say it."

"Darek," muttered Cordelia.

"Good, now stop saying '*pan*' to me, okay?" He started the car.

"But, um…Darek?"

"Good," he gave her an approving look as they took to the street again, "yes?"

She switched suddenly into English, so as not to be confronted with the necessity of speaking to him in the informal you, the '*ty*' in Polish; somehow it made them too intimate, and she was fighting an inner battle to preserve some semblance of distance between them, even if only to herself.

"Some of what you said in there…it wasn't exactly true."

"It wasn't exactly false."

"No, but…" she put up a hand and began to jerk on a strand of hair. "I don't like it."

There was a long pause.

"What do you want me to say?" he said finally. His voice was neutral, but she could feel the tension under it.

"Would it hurt to tell the truth?"

"Which is what?"

"That we have to get married quickly because you might be arrested."

"I wouldn't have the face!"

"I would," said Cordelia.

"Ah," said Zaremba after a pause, "that, I suppose, is because you're 'the female of the species.' I'll put myself in your hands."

She wasn't quite sure she'd expected to be taken at her word. Here they were, drawn up in front of another building. This one was almost identical to the previous one, the only difference was that this time she, Cordelia, was going in alone. She felt her pulse beating in her throat. Bank robbing must be nothing to it, she thought.

"Okay?" said Zaremba.

"No," said Cordelia, but she opened the car door and stepped out. All the way across the parking lot she rehearsed her speech to herself.

There was a door marked 'civil records.' She stopped before it. She repeated her lines to herself again. And then again, to make sure she'd got it all down, that it would come rolling out without too much stumbling. She imagined what questions she might be asked, what answers she would make. Her hands were shaking.

She took a deep breath and entered. There were three women seated in the room, each at her own desk; all three looked up at her entrance, and she could feel them taking in her crutch, her leg, her arm, her hair, her clothes, before their eyes dropped politely or indifferently back to their papers.

"*Dzien dobry, pani*," she said to the nearest, a woman in her thirties, whose stylish clothing argued another source of income.

"Yes?"

"I'd like," she stuttered a little, "to apply for a shortening of the waiting period for marriage. I…"

The woman cut her off. "Do you have a doctor's certificate?"

"No," said Cordelia, surprised and thrown. She hadn't expected to be asked *that*. What did a doctor's certificate have to do with it?

"Well, you have to get one then, *pani*." The woman spoke civilly enough, even with some sympathy, but firmly. "We have to have some basis for our decision. Here, fill out this form."

Cordelia took the form, leaning heavily forward on her crutch.

"Bring it back with you. The cost is 5 zloty for the application, 30 zloty for the decision, and an extra 50 groszy for each page of the documentation added."

"But what do I need a doctor's certificate for?"

"For your condition."

"My condition? But you can see my condition," cried Cordelia in bewilderment and considerable indignation, "It's perfectly obvious!"

The woman turned and looked at the other two clerks, who were now all staring at Cordelia.

Cordelia felt herself turning red with embarrassment. "I don't see why I should have to prove what everyone can see," she said resentfully.

"But *pani* isn't showing anything much," said one of the other clerks tentatively, in support of her colleague.

Cordelia didn't know what to say, she was so taken aback she forgot the speech she had rehearsed, and her obvious distress was causing consternation among the three women as well.

"And the settlement? When is that?" asked one.

"I − ," don't know, Cordelia had been on the point of saying, but she stopped. The settlement? They must be talking about the transfer. She remembered vaguely that Zaremba had said the donation papers would be signed after the wedding. But how had these women known anything about that? She was too confused to think straight. "Next week."

"Next week!"

"So we'd like to get married on Monday."

"But *pani* really isn't showing anything!"

"What do you mean, *pani*? If you look at me you can see perfectly well what my problem is."

There was a moment of silence, while the three women looked uncomfortable, compassionate, and indecisive. Then one of the women signaled to the other and they left the room. In a moment she came back.

"Identity document," she said to Cordelia.

Cordelia handed it over.

"The form? That form I just gave you? I'll fill it out for you."

Cordelia handed it over and watched the woman write in her name, in block letters – Cordelia Eleonora Fogg, and Zaremba's name, Dariusz Władysław Zaremba – without a pause or any indication of recognition – and their dates of birth, and places of birth, and their reason for wanting to be married before the waiting period had passed – she was scrawling something illegible, something no one would ever be able to read.

"At what time do you want the ceremony?" asked the woman. "Is four o'clock all right?"

"Yes," said Cordelia.

"Fine, four o'clock on Monday, come to window seven ten minutes before the hour – here's a list of what you need to bring. Pay at the cashier's. Down the hall to the right." She handed Cordelia back her documents.

"Thank you," said Cordelia, and walked out of the building in a daze, and crossed the parking lot in a daze. Zaremba was leaning against the car, waiting, but he leapt to get the car door for Cordelia.

"Go," she said, as soon as she was seated, "go. I want to get away from here."

He obligingly started the car and they drove a few blocks, before he found a parking spot and pulled the car over to the curb again and turned off the engine. He turned to her in concern.

"What is it? What happened?"

"I don't know." She didn't even know how to tell him what had happened. It was really too awful. She hated talking about her condition or thinking about it or thinking that other people were noticing it.

"They didn't agree? It's all right; there are 15 others, and if we have to, we can try beyond the city limits."

"No. They did agree. At four o'clock on Monday."

"Great! Excellent! Good work, Cordelia! If you weren't my fiancée I'd kiss you."

His hand beat a pleased tattoo on the dashboard, and his eyes on her were alight with admiration, but his words passed over her quite; she only gave him a darkling glance and continued to brood. He observed her for a minute in growing puzzlement.

"What is it? What's wrong? Is it something about what you told them? Is it that you told them a – a lie?"

"No," she said to the dashboard, "I didn't tell them anything."

"Nothing?"

"I went in, and I said that I wanted to shorten the waiting period. And they said…" she swallowed, "that I'd need a doctor's certificate. And I said 'why? My condition is perfectly obvious.' I mean, it is, isn't it? Anyone can see it. And they acted upset, and then one said, 'when is the settlement?' and I …"

And then she realized. "Oh!" she exclaimed, dropping her head in her hands. The word she had taken for 'settlement' was the same as for 'delivery.' They had been talking about a pregnancy. She had been thinking about polio and Zaremba's gift. How embarrassing.

"I was told it's the most common reason for shortening the waiting period," said Zaremba, and he was laughing, laughing so the car was shaking.

"It's not funny!" she whimpered, only it was, actually, and his laughter was infectious, and pretty soon she was convulsed as well.

"One thing is certain, though" she said, some time later, after she had dried her eyes, "I'm not doing that again. I don't care if there are 15 more offices. I'm not going into any of them."

11

'Conscious of the rights and responsibilities resulting from the founding of a family, I solemnly declare that I am entering into marital union with (first name and surname) and swear that I will do everything to make our marriage peaceable, happy, and permanent.'

Cordelia, seated on the porch, was reading the vow she would have to swear on Monday from the paper the clerk had given her. After her success at the civil records office, they had stopped at her bank, and for their birth certificates, and, as usual, for Zaremba to make phone calls, and once to meet someone – a friend, he had said – who had given him a laptop and a number of books – Cordelia thought on law – and then they had come home. They had been home for several hours and Zaremba had, with his indefatigable energy, determined to put the disused lawn mower together and after a considerable struggle he had done so and was now mowing the yard. He was, in fact, mowing a bed of daisies, but Cordelia had no intention of telling him so.

He looked up and saw that she was standing on the edge of the porch, watching him, with a paper in her hand. He turned off the lawn mower and looked inquiringly at her.

She wanted to remember him like that, she thought suddenly, when he was gone from her life. She would try to keep that picture of him as he stood in her garden, with the leaves of the big birch tree like gold flakes over his head, and the mown grass about his feet.

She waved the paper slightly, and he left the mower and came towards her, came and sat on the balustrade beside her.

"What's up?"

She moved away from him slightly; away from his arm, his leg, his shoulder, his smile.

"It says 'permanent.' I can't swear to 'permanent.' 'Happy' and 'peaceable' are all right. I should hope that I am always 'peaceable' and I should try to make my friends 'happy,' but when we know that it's a temporary situation, how can we say 'permanent'?"

"Two out of three seems pretty good to me. It's more than a lot of marriages manage, I'm sure." Then, seeing she wasn't in a mood for joking, he continued, more seriously: "I'm glad you want to make me happy. And 'peaceable' means you're not going to argue with me, right?"

She didn't answer and he took the paper from her hand and looked at it before continuing. "Oh, see?" He struck the paper with his fingers, "It doesn't say 'permanent' it says '*trwałe*' – '*trwałe*' could mean 'permanent' or it could mean 'durable' or it could mean 'lasting' or it could mean 'stable.' It's all in the translation. It's an elastic term, just as time is an elastic and variable concept. How would you define '*trwałe*' anyway?

"I don't know," said Cordelia worriedly.

"Well, it doesn't mean, 'till death do us part' because they'd have put that, and not '*trwałe*,' right?"

"Maybe."

"So we can assume it is not a measurement of time, or a grasping after infinity. So let's say it means 'stable.' Our marriage will be entirely harmonious and a model of stability, until we decide, entirely peaceably, that the time has come to allow our mutual civil statuses to evolve. Cordelia, don't worry. The devil's in the details, they say, but this really isn't one of those. It's just a word."

"Sometimes words matter."

"Yes. But don't let that idea make you lose sight of the bigger picture."

"Are you saying the end justifies the means? Because that's precisely what you're objecting to in the behavior of those in power!" she concluded with sudden energy.

He considered her reply with due seriousness. "No. If I thought there was anything immoral about swearing to the word '*trwałe*' in this situation, I wouldn't ask you to do it. I just don't see that there is. No one expects every marriage to last, or expects a marriage vow to prevent it from ending, and that fact is in the consciousness, willy-nilly, of everyone who gets married in our day and age."

"Yes," she said, but she looked unhappy.

"If it will salve your conscience, we can remain married until there is a pressing reason for one of us to get divorced. If you wanted to marry someone else, for instance."

"No!" she cried, "I didn't mean – I don't want you to have to stay married to me. And I don't want to marry anyone else – I mean, I don't want to marry anyone. We can get divorced whenever you want. It's all right."

She took the paper from his hand and hurried into the house, leaving him sitting bemused on the balustrade.

There had been nothing in the papers about Zaremba in the last few days, and there was nothing on the news that evening either; they watched it, all together, before dinner, Cordelia only occasionally returning to the kitchen to keep an eye on various pots.

They watched a round man make vitriolic statements about a conspiracy of post-communist and criminal elements having its tentacles throughout the state.

"Where do these people come from?" said Cordelia's father, listening with half an ear and considerable distaste. "How do they spring up?"

"They climb on their obsessions," answered Zaremba, "it's hard for a man to emerge from obscurity if that's where he belongs. It's the imbalance in their personalities that sets them in motion."

Cordelia, watching the man, felt cold and worried. She would have felt so anyway, but now, with a pressingly personal stake in the rule of law, she was noting the course of its possible demise with extreme attentiveness. Zaremba was right: these people weren't entirely balanced, but the curious and frightening thing was that they had so many followers. There was a very good chance even that having sown chaos in government, compromised relations with a number of other countries, polarized society, made attempts to suborn independent public bodies and the media, openly condoned ignorance, racism and intolerance, and publicly proclaimed that the law could not be allowed to interfere with their conception of the national interest, their party might win the up-coming elections.

The next day was Saturday. Cordelia spent the day trying to catch up on her neglected translation work and was only interrupted by the unusual afternoon appearance of her father in the salon.

"It has occurred to me," he said to Cordelia, as she looked up from her keyboard, "that if your young man really has a problem, then perhaps I should get in touch with someone."

"I don't think he's faking his problems, Tato, but I don't know whom you could contact that might help in his situation."

Cordelia's father belonged to the generation of Poles who thought solving any problem always required connections, required that someone else be involved, appealed to, enlisted, that problems with the authorities were always solved through the back door, by acquaintances, who knew someone, who might be able to help. Unfortunately, Cordelia's father's acquaintances were professors of literature, of language, editors of small specialist journals; and not persons who had ever trod down the corridors of power, or even stuck their toes into its outer sanctums. Cordelia didn't know if her father's attitude was the offspring or the parent of the corruption with which Poland was riddled, but she knew his suggestions were hopelessly unworldly. After she had politely turned down several, he added:

"There's Skalnik, you know, he used to write opposition poetry in the days of Solidarity. He's editor at *Rebus*. I could ask him to come up with some verses."

"I don't think that would help really, but thanks for the thought."

" – not that he's a very good poet," added Cordelia's father consideringly. "But perhaps your young man wouldn't know the difference?"

"He doesn't seem to me like a fitting subject for literature, really, Tato. Thanks anyway."

"Well, don't say I didn't try for you."

With Zaremba, she hardly spoke all day. He had disappeared from her sight, and she supposed that he was busy with his computer or his books.

Perhaps it was the combination of her father's words, the suspicion that she was only marginally more competent and worldly-wise than he, and the knowledge that Zaremba himself was busy with matters of which she knew nothing that had depressed her spirits to an unusually low level by evening.

As she undressed for bed, taking off her shirt and trousers, she caught sight of herself before the mirror, unclad, and she had a vision, superimposed on her figure there, of herself as a very small individual arrayed against the enormous force of the state, a little insect, perhaps, crawling towards one of Antek's spider webs, and as hopeless as it once caught. This vision held her for some time, as she stood in her bare feet on the cold board floor, her nightgown dangling from one hand, until an image of more vital and visceral immediacy pushed it aside: she tried to see herself as a man might see her, as a crippled woman – she let her eyes slide down the image, from head to floor. She had the figure of a Barbie doll that had been played with too roughly. There was no question which image produced the greater hold on her fears.

It was late, but she would never be able to sleep. She thought about trying to distract herself with more work, but made no move to turn on her computer. If only there were anyone she could talk to, she thought – but there was no one really. Antek had shown himself to be sympathetic; and her father hadn't been offensive to Zaremba today, at least not in her presence, and his offer of help might even be considered a softening towards him. They had all talked politely and inconsequentially at the dinner table after watching the news. But she knew he objected to her plans. There was Hal, of course. She could email him and ask for his advice. She smiled a little wryly to think what his reaction might be. She had better not email him. There was only Hempseed, who came and put his head on her knee, as if realizing that she was in need. She stroked his ears and tried to count her blessings, starting with her horrible dog.

There was a knock at the door. "Wait," she called, and hurriedly reached for her robe, and then, "Come in."

It was Zaremba. He leaned his head through the doorway. "Oh, you're ready for bed. Forget it, then." He started to withdraw.

"What is it?" she asked.

"I was going to ask you to come out with me."

"Out? But where?"

"It doesn't matter. Out for a drive, out for a coffee, just out. I haven't seen you all day."

Cordelia's spirits gave a bound. He wanted to be with her. "But wouldn't it be safer to stay in?"

"Cordelia, I'm going out. Tomorrow I'll be busy. Tonight might be my last night of freedom – and I don't mean marriage. I'd like to spend it with you."

How could she resist such an appeal? She was the happiest of mortals. "I'll be ready in five minutes."

Be reasonable, be calm, she said to herself, but she left the house like an escapee leaping the walls of the prison.

"I'm not sure," he said, as they entered the city center again, "what the etiquette is for last nights. I have a feeling we should drink and dance. But I'm not much for alcohol and I don't know how to dance. I suspect it's not your forte either. Will sitting and talking do?"

229

Later she remembered the evening as a series of snapshots: there was the Opera house, with its chariot of horses above the entrance, and a throng of happy music lovers and wearied curiosity seekers pouring out the entrance; the narrow streets behind Krakowskie Przedmieście, with their eighteenth-century houses and arching carriage ways, and then a door somewhere, and a dark café, with comfortable chairs, and a chic young crowd of bon-vivants, who paid no attention to them as they made their way into a discrete corner. But she did not remember if she had had something to eat or drink, or who had sat next to them. She remembered that they had talked on and on, about everything, their pasts and their ideas and their adventures – so much more dramatic on his side, hers very minor but perhaps more intensely experienced, which he had shown no signs of undervaluing. They had talked about everything except the future.

When they returned to the villa some hours later, Zaremba stopped the car in the garage, but made no move to get out. He twisted towards her on the seat.

"Thank you," she said, "I had a lovely time." It was true, it was extremely true, and she searched for the door knob. The only odd thing, she realized suddenly, was that he hadn't made a single gesture or said a single sentence that might be considered flirtatious. He had been extremely pleasant and entertaining, but almost imperceptibly impersonal, as if the future – so consciously avoided – already had its hand on him.

"Wait," he said, as her hand found the knob. She looked inquiringly at him, her eyes traveling up the dark canvas front of his Carrefour jacket to his eyes.

He put the overhead light on so he could see her in the dark.

"I shouldn't keep you out at such hours. You get too tired."

"No, I'm glad you did. I – " she wanted to ask him if she would see him after they were married, but she couldn't. Probably this would be the last time that they would spend hours together. It might be the last time in her life that she would spend hours talking to someone. She dropped her eyes and her hands fidgeted.

"If anything happens," he said seriously, "and I don't get the chance to tell you, later –"

She looked at him.

"I'm…" He stopped. Whatever he wanted to tell her, there seemed to be obstacles.

"I wonder if you could hate me?" he said, as if to himself. "Never mind." He got out of the car abruptly.

What was that supposed to mean? thought Cordelia, as she got ready for bed for the second time, her interval of seized happiness quite at an end. How could she hate him? For what? Even if everything she thought about him turned out to be untrue – if he was not what she thought him, she was too far gone to retreat. He might make her extremely unhappy, but she still wouldn't be able to rip him, by the roots, out of her mind; the largest part would stay to rot and fester.

Now here she was, after an evening of pleasure, sitting on the bed exactly as she had sat four hours before, and just as miserable, if not more. So that, she thought, was what it was like to get involved with a man: the possibilities for being made happy and being made miserable increased exponentially.

Sunday passed very quietly. At breakfast, Zaremba had given his attention mostly to her mother and then had disappeared upstairs and she hardly saw him all day.

She only knew where he was because Antek said, seeing her standing in the salon, rather lost, looking out the window and not seeing anything, that he had noticed 'her friend' was busy with his computer.

"Ah," she said, thinking that if she had changed in the last week, Antek had changed as well. He spoke more briskly, stood up straighter, and took more notice of his surroundings.

"You still want to go through with it?" he said.

"Yes." There was no need for him to specify what 'it' was.

"You don't have to."

"No. I want to."

"You might end up in jail too."

"Yes."

"If anything happens, Tata would be less than no help."

"Yes."

"You'd better call me. I'll be no help – that's a bit better."

Cordelia laughed a little and looked at him in surprise and gratitude. "Thank you, Antek." The funny thing was, that if he put his mind to it, he might actually be of assistance.

Her father also made an effort to speak to her about her upcoming nuptials, in almost the same terms that Antek had used.

"So are you still going through with it? You're going to tie the knot tomorrow?"

"Yes, in a manner of speaking."

"In a manner of speaking, you're going to be united, amalgamated, bound, leg-shackled…"

"Tato, it's just a civil contract."

232

"A contract is a contract. You'll be as tied as a hog. "

"How uncouthly you express it."

"My daughter is to be contracted to a developer."

"Don't say it like that, it sounds unpleasant."

"It is unpleasant. How would you say it?"

"I'm helping someone who needs help."

"'Out of this flower, safety, you pluck this nettle, danger'? Where has all your wisdom gone, Cordelia?"

"No, I think you've got that backward. Anyway, I've been wise all my life and now I want to be like you."

"Oh, touché, Cordelia. *Cholera jasna*." She watched him struggle between amusement and irritation for a few seconds.

"It's what I want to do, Tato," she said gently, "please don't worry."

But however confident she might try to appear before her relatives, she herself was inwardly worrying plenty.

She couldn't settle to anything. She sat beside her mother, and at some point in the morning, Zaremba appeared in the salon and sat down too. He looked preoccupied and since she knew by now that he never sat down just to sit, but only to smoke or plan or talk, she waited rather tensely for him to speak. He did so abruptly.

"Tomorrow, at the civil records office, it's possible that the police or the CBA will come."

"Do you have some new reason to think they'll come?"

"I *think* they won't, but I know it's possible. You could still back out, if you want to. I won't hold it against you. It's what I'd advise you to do if I were your friend." His knee was jiggling slightly as he sat there, but his face was stony and she could feel his tension.

"If you were my friend?" She repeated, looking oddly at him. What did that mean? "But since you're not my friend, what do you advise?"

"I'm not advising, I'm just warning."

"As far as I'm concerned, it's all settled." She answered quietly, trying not to feel rattled.

"Cordelia's getting married," said Cordelia's mother to Zaremba, as Cordelia looked at her in surprise. She hadn't realized her mother was capable of understanding so much.

"Yes," he said.

"To the gondolier."

"Would you rather know ahead of time what will happen?..." Zaremba was continuing to Cordelia, but he was interrupted by Cordelia's mother.

"But it's too cold now for the boats."

Cordelia said, "You've warned me. It's enough."

"We'll go in a car, don't worry," Zaremba said to her mother, and rising, left the room, leaving Cordelia wondering, suddenly, what he could have meant.

She sat beside her mother and thought about all the possibilities. She thought about being caught up in the cogs of the machine, ground into nothingness by forces beyond her calculation. When that air force officer of whom Zaremba had spoken had been arrested, his case had made it to the Supreme Court in three weeks. It was unlikely that anyone she knew could organize her defense at all, let alone that quickly. And who knew what was going on in the government anyway? – lately one minister had just narrowly escaped the clutches of the CBA, another had been arrested for supposedly undermining the agency's work, a parliamentary commission investigating the matter had ceased its activities, and accusations of lying, of wiretapping, of manipulating evidence, of manipulating prosecutors and journalists, were flying right and left between members of the government and the police forces.

She shuddered. She was unaccustomed to force of any sort. She tried to imagine herself in prison. She remembered what Zaremba had told her about the air force officer being stripped every time he was taken in and out of a cell. She would have to remember to wear her better underwear, she decided, in case it happened to her. She shuddered again. What would happen with her mother while she was sitting in jail? Antek would have to step in; he had been doing so a lot lately, in fact. She thought of him with gratitude.

But all these thoughts, although absorbing, were not the central question. The real question was what Zaremba was planning to do after the ceremony. (Supposing, of course, that he was not dragged away in handcuffs to points unknown.) Would he come back here to the villa, or would he go elsewhere? She didn't know why, but somehow she had the idea that he was not intending to come back. And if that was so, then when would she see him again?

But she knew, both deep down and clearly, that what had been for her – in spite of its traumas – an idyll, was coming to an end tomorrow. As she lay in bed that evening, she had very little thought for the possible dangers ahead; her real concern was whether he would ever think of her again, afterwards. Of course, if he were in jail, she would pay his legal fees, and do anything else she could for him and that would create a sort of long-distance bond between them. But only such a bond as he might have with his secretary, or his accountant. But if none of that happened, then on Monday night, she supposed, he would be gone, and her life would revert to its old mackerel-in-tomato-sauce ways. The difference being that it would be inexpressibly difficult to find contentment again; the former routine in his absence would be as dry and tasteless and unpalatable as eating dust.

12

Somehow the night passed, and Cordelia managed to
drag herself through the morning too. She fed the dog,
and did the breakfast dishes and swept the floors,
translated three pages of shampoo advertising, and made
a wan effort already to get back to that pallid routine, to
carry on as if the day were just any other day in her life.
Zaremba stayed out of sight – only some time in the
morning a young man had rung the doorbell and had
handed him a canvas carry-all and some other piece of
draping luggage. That was Mariusz, said Zaremba, and he
would be back at 3:00 to take them to the town hall. That

would leave them an hour to arrive – plenty of time; his witnesses and the notary would meet them there.

At two-thirty Cordelia left her mother with Antek and went upstairs to dress for her wedding. She had decided on the wool trousers and blazer she had worn to the notary's as being, once again, decent without indicating that she thought it a special occasion.

It was not a wedding-like reflection that looked back at her in the mirror, she realized with wistfulness, but then, it wasn't a real wedding, even if it was the only one she would ever have. She remembered to put some money in her purse so she'd have enough if she had to come home alone.

There was a knock at the door.

"Come in," she said.

Zaremba opened the door, and she stared at him. He was quite resplendent: freshly shaven and in a good gray suit and tie and dress shoes.

"Oh!" they both said at once, taking one another in.

"No," he said, "that won't do. What else do you have to wear?" He crossed to her closet.

"I – hardly anything."

"Damn. I should have thought of that."

"But why? I thought…" She didn't know what she'd thought exactly – only that it would be very business-like and not at all formal.

"Don't you have anything – I don't know – sort of fancy? A dress?"

"No." Cordelia looked at him in anxiety; how should she have anything 'fancy'? To wear where?

"What you were wearing, that day you came to my office? That was nice. Can you wear that?"

"No." She hesitated. "It shows my leg."

"Good. That's fine."

Fine? "No!"

"Cordelia, there's no time. Please, just put it on, okay? Mariusz will be here any minute."

"Okay," she muttered, humble before him. She would do whatever he wanted.

"Good, thank you." He was stepping out of the room, pulling the door shut behind him.

She hurried to the closet, seeking the garment. Here it was. Had the moths gotten it? Not visibly. She flung the skirt and jacket of the suit on her bed. She ripped off the trousers, remembered that she needed nylons, hopped to the dresser and found a pair, tried to put them on in haste, but they kept twisting, they would not lie straight. She jerked them down over her toes and started again. Putting on nylons required two good hands. She had one and it was shaking. The time was ticking past. 3:05. The nylons would not go on. She felt like screaming. She calmed herself, and started again.

3:15. She was hurrying down the stairs to Zaremba.

"Great," he said, and they were rushing down the driveway to a waiting car. Cordelia sat in back. "Let's go," Zaremba said, as he took the seat beside his friend.

3:30. They were stuck in traffic.

"It looks like they've stopped the traffic ahead, *Panie Darku*" said Mariusz, "Maybe an accident. We shouldn't be here long. This street is usually clear at this hour."

"We still have twenty minutes."

3:40. They were still standing. There was nothing to do, and nothing for anyone to say. Cordelia felt her insides twisting. Maybe they would miss their appointed time and then everything would be spoiled – and all because she couldn't get dressed quickly enough.

3:41. The traffic was moving, they were going, they were driving, they were almost there. Mariusz was talking into his cell phone, saying to someone that they were arriving, had arrived. They were pulling into a parking lot.

"Two minutes to spare," said Zaremba, "that's enough."

They were being met by quite a number of people, a well-dressed, well-groomed crowd, some of whom Cordelia remembered from the day at the notary's office. There was the notary, *Pani* Edzia, and Zbyś, who Zaremba called his second-in-command, and a woman who was probably his wife, and a middle-aged man with a small moustache who might be a lawyer, and others. There were also, Cordelia saw, two television vans drawn up on the far side of the parking lot, and several men with cameras were walking towards the building. It wasn't the state-owned station, she noticed. Perhaps some function was going on inside.

They were moving as a body into the building, approaching window seven; showing their identity documents, the identity documents of their witnesses, filling in the preliminary forms. "What name will the bride have after the marriage?" A clerk was asking.

"'Zaremba,'" answered Zaremba.

Really? thought Cordelia, but she supposed he wanted to make it seem more real.

"What name will the children have?"

Children? thought Cordelia.

"'Zaremba,'" answered Zaremba.

"Time," someone said, and they were moving into a very large room or hall, where chairs were lined up and at one end there was a table in front of a wall decorated with a cloth hanging of the state emblem. The cameramen were here, Cordelia noted with surprise. Zaremba didn't seem to be paying attention to them. Perhaps they were setting up for something after the wedding ceremony was through. It was only supposed to take a few minutes, she knew. As they approached the table, a middle-aged woman appeared wearing the heavy chain of office around her neck. The director of the civil records office presumably. They came to a stop in front of her, and their companions fell away to the sides. The woman made a slight gesture for attention and everyone fell silent.

This is it, thought Cordelia, I'm getting married. But why were the cameramen coming so close? The director was saying something in greeting, words about a married couple as a unit of the social whole, but Cordelia was hardly listening. She wanted to ask Zaremba what the camera crew was doing, but she couldn't.

Zaremba was already repeating after the director, without noticeable tremors: "Conscious of the rights and obligations resulting from the founding of a family, I solemnly declare that I am entering into marital union with Cordelia Fogg and swear that I will do everything to make our marriage peaceable, happy, and lasting."

And now it was her turn. She stumbled a little over the words, and particularly over his name – D-Dar-Dariusz – and 'founding of a f-family' but not at all on 'lasting.' And the director was congratulating them, and someone had produced two gold rings – from where? – and Zaremba was taking her hand and sliding a ring onto her fourth finger. It was much too large, but she curled her fingers around it to keep it on, and now she had to put one on his finger; she flinched from touching him, but it had to be done. His hand was trembling very slightly too, she realized. Did he expect the CBA to show up? Was that why the cameras were here? There wasn't any doubt anymore, they were being filmed.

And then someone was whispering "You must kiss the bride," and she stiffened as a wave of embarrassed hotness dimmed her eyesight, because how could she refuse in front of the cameras? But Zaremba, half-turning towards her, caught perhaps, with a quarter glance, the panic in her eyes; he moved slightly away and either didn't hear or pretended not to hear, and the moment passed and Cordelia could breath again. The notary was stepping forward, and saying to the cameras that she had in her hand a notarial act, which she had drawn up, of the assets that Zaremba wished to give to his bride, and which she would now read out in whole, so that it could be signed. A reporter had stepped forward with a microphone and the notary was speaking into it.

She was reading, at top speed, the various official formulas by which such documents begin – 'on-this-day-of-September-two-thousand-and-seven', and Cordelia's full name and her parents' names – Wojciech and Sophia, and Zaremba's full name and parents' names – Stanisław and Jadwiga – and their addresses and the basis on which she had established their identity, and then – here her voice slowed – the list of assets Cordelia was to be given: "real estate, located in Warsaw, constituting undeveloped lot no. 14 with an area of 3000 meters, Registry No. SA1M/00412507/9 in the Registry of the Regional Court for Warsaw Mokotów; 'lot no. 27, located in Warsaw, one hectare; three lots, nos. 14, 15, 16 contiguous..."

Cordelia remembered the list from the day at the notary office.

"...Registry No. WB2M 068125787." Then there was a list of legal bases for the act, with their numbers and items in the Journal of Law, and then she was finishing, holding out the papers on a clipboard, and Cordelia was signing, and Zaremba was signing. And the notary was adding, clearly, into the camera, that the total value of the real estate was approximately 15 million euros, and that there would be an additional transfer of 5 million euros in cash, for a total of 20 million euros.

There was a sort of murmur of amazement at the words, and Cordelia, looking up, saw that the room was full of persons who had come into the room out of curiosity at the cameras – clerks perhaps and incidental persons who happened to be in the town hall at the time.

"*Pan* Zaremba is now calling the bank to make the transfer of the euros to his wife's account." And indeed, Zaremba was talking into a cell phone.

A reporter was saying into the cameras: "We are now calling the Ministry of Justice and relaying events as they unfold."

Then Zaremba took another paper from the clipboard and held it up to the cameras, while a reporter, two reporters held microphones out to him.

"This," he was saying into it, as he held up a paper, "is the form – SD-Z1 – for the treasury office in which my wife will declare the gift of 5 million in money. There is no rubric here asking for an explanation of the gift or she could write that I am transferring this money in order to have the means to organize my defense against the authorities' unjustified harassment…And now, having secured myself in this small way, I would like to take this opportunity to ask the authorities, in connection with the false allegations that have recently been made about me in the news media, and in connection with the dishonor to which my reputation has been subjected, that if they have any proof that I have engaged in any sort of illegal activity whatever, that they should come forward now, and arrest me. I am here, at the town hall on Turawska Street, and I will wait here for half an hour."

243

The reporter said into the microphone: "We have a spokesperson for the Ministry of Justice on the line, and this challenge has been relayed as it was spoken."

No, thought Cordelia, her heart pounding so that she wondered if she would faint. Thank goodness she had her crutch to hold her up.

"I would also like to point out," said Zaremba, "while we're waiting – that I have proof here," he was extracting the faked photos from a binder someone had handed him, "that the photo that appeared in *Śmiećpospolity* last weekend, showing me meeting with Marek Grzegoliński, was a montage. Anyone is free to examine the evidence."

"Our news team has examined the photo," said the reporter, "and is in agreement that it is indeed a montage…And we have now only to wait," she added.

The camera men stepped out from behind their cameras for a second, people raised their eyebrows at each other, shifted their feet. Cordelia wondered if she could ask Zaremba a question, a hundred questions, but there was no time, the reporter was stepping to her side, holding out the microphone to her.

"While we're waiting, how does it feel to be given 20 million euros?"

She had to answer. Please don't let me disgrace him, she prayed a fervent little inward prayer.

She swallowed, tried to look up. "It's not about the money."

"Of course not," a woman reporter was saying smoothly, "We've been told that the groom had known you only six days when he asked you to marry him."

"Yes."

"So this isn't a love story."

"No, it's an abuse of power story."

"And where did you meet?"

"In the street." No, she thought in a frightened flash, that didn't sound good. "I was trying to rescue a stray dog – a puppy – from the traffic and he stopped."

"He helped you?"

"He stopped the cars."

"Aww," said the reporter, or a sound to that effect.

Oh please stop, thought Cordelia, please, please stop. She was vaguely aware of Zaremba's look of approval beside her.

A man with a camera on his shoulder was zooming in on her arm, her leg. She couldn't escape. It was a sort of torture. Her twisted leg would be exposed to television viewers all over the country. She couldn't stop it and any minute now too she was going to be asked a question she wouldn't know how to answer.

"So what are you going to do with all this money?"

"It's intended to serve justice."

"Because you think the groom – your husband – has been unjustly accused – I mean, excuse me – implicated?"

"Yes."

And then suddenly, everyone's attention was elsewhere. Heads had jerked towards the entrance and cameras too.

"They're here!" someone exclaimed.

"But they weren't supposed to come!" someone else said in dismay.

"Cordelia get back!" Zaremba said, and moved rapidly away from her.

There was a slamming of doors and a pounding of feet. Half a dozen men in masks rushed into the room. Cordelia had an impression of dark clothing, of guns, of jackboots, but there was no time to think or move. They were pointing guns and shouting but she didn't understand what they were saying; it happened too fast, it was too frightening. The men with cameras were leaping to get out of the way. Two men with masks had grabbed Zaremba, were twisting his arms. He made an instinctive gesture of resistance and then someone was pointing a gun, pointing it at him.

"No!" Cordelia shrieked, panicked. They wouldn't shoot him, would they? and trying to move, to get between them, her crutch took a masked man between the legs. He pitched forward, tried to catch his balance – "oh, I'm sorry," she cried – as he fell sprawling.

He fell full length, on his elbows, still holding the gun, still with his finger on the trigger – there was a split second of petrifaction in the room – then the gun went off with a terrifying explosion of sound, spraying bullets. People shouted and screamed and dove for the floor. An agent on the other side of the room returned fire, a rapid succession of blasts. Zaremba fell. Plaster pelted down from the ceiling and a light fixture crashed to the ground and shattered.

Silence. "Everyone stay where you are!" an authoritative voice shouted. "Stay where you are!" Everyone in the room was lying on the floor. Heads began to be lifted, to look around. Cordelia was the only one still standing. No, she thought, no, no, no. They've killed him. Time stood still. She took a step towards him.

"Don't move!" shouted a masked man, standing up, waving his gun. She ignored him – she wasn't even aware he was speaking to her. She couldn't see Zaremba's face because of the men on top of him. Was he dead or alive?

"You've killed him!" she cried to the man in agony.

"No, lady, no, calm down. I don't think so! Lady, calm down." The officer was obviously in need of calming himself. "Is he hit?" he was shouting at his underlings.

"Don't think so," one of them said, a little breathlessly.

They shifted their positions a little and Zaremba lifted his head, "Cordelia," he said, almost laughing, "they've buggered it up." The man in the mask who was kneeling on him was swearing – the way someone swears who has been seriously frightened. He gave Zaremba's head a brutal shove downwards, but that didn't prevent his shoulders from shaking. "Stop that!" shouted the man, whose grasp of the situation was slower than that of his captive.

"Stop it! You'll hurt him!" Cordelia yelled at him.

A camera man had risen to his knees and was filming again. In spite of being urged to stay still, people were beginning to get up. The officer with the authoritative voice was talking agitatedly into a headset, obviously seeking instructions from higher up. Cordelia caught the words 'a cripple,' 'an accident,' and 'news crews.' The answer must have been in the nature of a bellow of 'get out of there,' because the man jerked the headset away from his ear with a look of increased anguish and at a gesture, the men were jumping away from Zaremba, and the whole team was stampeding through the doors as quickly as they had come. There was a sound of thudding feet, then outside there was a screech of tires, followed by silence. The members of a film crew that had followed them unnoticed through the door lowered their cameras and looked blankly at one another. It had all happened in the space of two minutes.

They were gone, Cordelia thought with a wild surge of relief. They hadn't arrested Zaremba. They were gone.

Inside everyone stood up and began to talk at once. People arrived from other parts of the building. There was anger, exhilaration, the half-hysterical laughter and bubbling wit that is the frequent aftermath of a common scare. The previous camera-men had sprung into action again. People were assuring one another that they were unhurt; were pointing to the bullet holes in the wall; the white eagle of the state emblem had nearly been drilled. Someone had collected the scattered notarial papers.

"Time to go," said Zaremba in Cordelia's ear, taking her by the arm and, followed by a crowd of people all jabbering, all pulling out cell phones and beginning to chatter into them, guided her towards the door. She went numbly. She was being put into the passenger seat of someone's car; Zaremba was sliding in beside her –

"Hey, don't look like that, everything's all right. That wasn't the way I planned it, but it's going to be all right, I think."

– the cavalcade of civilian cars pulled away from the building just as a posse of police cars with sirens blazing and an anti-terrorist van pulled up from another direction.

"How well coordinated they are," mocked the driver of the car, as he twisted in his seat to watch the show. "Did you see, Darek?" he was asking Zaremba, "that was the crew from the state-owned station that came in after the swat team. I wonder if they'll use the footage?" he laughed. "What a story!"

At a stop light, someone in one of the other cars motioned to Zaremba, and he was out of the car before Cordelia fully realized he was leaving her alone. "I have to talk to Zbyś, you'll go with Maciej, okay?" And then he was getting in the other car, and Cordelia was alone.

"*Proszę pana*, where are we going?" Cordelia asked the back of Maciej's neck as they cruised along the boulevard, rather faster than was really necessary.

Maciej fiddled with his rear-view mirror until he had her in sight, "To Zbyś's place. To Mokotów."

And after that, he seemed to feel no need for further conversation and they drove in silence, until they had turned off the main route, were driving through residential streets, pulling up before a row of imposing houses, rather too tightly placed. The crowd that had been at the town hall had gathered or was still pulling up in cars and everyone was going inside. Zaremba was being ushered inside by Zbyś, but he turned and waited for Cordelia. She hobbled towards him, feeling out of place, wishing she could go home, wondering if she really needed to stay.

He was turning away from her to speak to someone. He was drifting rapidly away from her. His arm, his shoulder, his leg, his smile were moving in the other direction. She put out a hand to catch his sleeve – emboldened by the feeling that he was sliding away, that soon he would be a complete stranger.

"*Proszę pana*, do I need to stay?" The formal words slipped out before she could stop them.

A woman who was standing in the gate turned and gave her an odd look. Zaremba also turned his head. Cordelia realized she'd interrupted him in mid-sentence to someone else. She didn't feel he'd really heard what she said.

"Come on. We're going to see what they put on the news." He was stepping away.

"Come in, come in," someone was saying. Cordelia found herself inside, in a large room, an open-plan ground floor announcing slightly too obtrusively the very comfortable circumstances of its owners, standing on the edge of a group of people all talking, chattering, exclaiming at once. There was obviously nothing like being shot at for getting people's adrenalin flowing. Cordelia, however, had been differently affected; she felt none of their wild excitement but rather a strange dullness.

Inside, Zaremba turned his head, and his eyes catching hers from a distance of six meters, he motioned her towards an armchair. She went and sat in it and the noise went on around her. Everyone was extremely polite to her and she was excluded with a complete lack of intention. At intervals, she was asked if she wanted coffee or tea. No, she didn't want anything; she shook her head, no thank you.

Then someone was saying it was time, time, time for the news and the television was being turned on and everyone was gathering around it.

How odd it was, Cordelia thought, to see one's life replayed. Here they were, after a brief introduction by the reporter, saying their vows; Zaremba standing very straight, she standing very bent; here was the camera playing over their faces and then down to her crutch; a shot of her taking an awkward step. It was only now, seeing the scenes on television, after the news room cuts, that she realized how much the filming had concentrated on her disability. It was given star billing. It was a feature all in itself. There was the notary, seen beyond Cordelia leaning on her crutch, reading out the total of the assets; Zaremba, beyond Cordelia's crooked arm, making his challenge into the camera; the reporter's questions to the two of them; then the CBA squad rushing in and the gun going off, the other agent losing his head and shooting back; Cordelia-the-cripple left standing; Cordelia-the-

250

cripple appearing to plead with the head of the CBA squad; Cordelia-the-cripple crying 'you'll hurt him' to the agent kneeling on her newly-wed husband; the squad stampeding out again.

Of course, thought Cordelia, trying to swallow, perhaps it only seemed that way to her, because she was over-sensitive and had a complex about it. Maybe other people didn't notice; maybe they saw only themselves in the camera shots, wondered how they'd never realized that their legs were so short or their hairdos so funny. Maybe. And of course Zaremba hadn't known it would be like that. Her eyes sought his for reassurance across the room but he was concentrated on the television set.

The crowd in the room was listening in complete silence and riveted attention.

A spokesman from the CBA was being asked for a statement on the incident.

Spokesman: "We received information from the Ministry of Justice about suspect activity at the town hall. Upon the arrival of the intervention team – they were – the team was, um, hampered in its duties by the public, and an accident, as you know, occurred. Very regrettably, but when the public gets involved accidents do happen."

Reporter: "The Ministry of Justice – we've spoken to the Ministry of Justice – denies having made any communication to the Anti-Corruption Bureau – the CBA – in the matter of the town hall on Turawska Street. Your comment please?"

Spokesman: "It is not the place of the CBA to make statements about the integrity of members of the government."

Reporter: "Whose place is it?"

Spokesman: "No comment."

Reporter: "Were the weapons used in the, um, incident, the Glock machine pistols about which it has recently been suggested that the CBA fixed a tender?

Spokesman, blanching: "No comment."

Reporter: "The team left without making an arrest. Does that mean that it did not come to arrest *Pan* Zaremba?"

Spokesman: "We know nothing about *Pan* Zaremba."

Reporter: "But all of Poland has been able to read in the press that the CBA pursued *Pan* Zaremba to Zabrzeg…?"

Spokesman: "Poland is a free country with a free press. The CBA can not be held liable for the effects of irresponsible journalism."

Reporter: "Are you saying the CBA was not in Zabrzeg?"

Spokesman: "Yes, but for other reasons, not to arrest *Pan* Zaremba. This is an unfortunate misunderstanding."

Reporter: "Does this mean the CBA is not investigating *Pan* Zaremba?"

Spokesman: "It is not investigating *Pan* Zaremba."

Reporter: "It has no evidence against him?"

Spokesman, woodenly: "No evidence."

Then a spokesman from the Ministry of Justice was being asked for a statement.

Reporter: "Does the fact that after the incident in the town hall on Turawska street the CBA agents were called off, mean that the charges against *Pan* Zaremba are being dropped?"

Spokesman, with an air of its having nothing to do with him or his ministry: "So far as I am aware, there were never any charges against *Pan* Zaremba. I believe the CBA had various questions it wished to ask him – in an entirely positive and cooperative manner – about an investigation. The Ministry of Justice did not make any communication in this matter to the CBA."

Reporter: "But the CBA says it did receive information from the Ministry."

Spokesman: "That will be a matter for investigation."

Reporter: "An investigation into the investigation?"

Spokesman: "Yes."

Reporter: "And who will do the investigating?"

Spokesman: "No comment."

Reporter: "Is *Pan* Zaremba still wanted for questioning?"

Spokesman: "No. We have received notification that the CBA has all the information it needs to proceed with its investigation against Grzegoliński."

Reporter: "So the action at the town hall on Turawska Street was an error?"

Spokesman: "There will be an investigation into its source; the state apparatus is still riddled with enemies of justice."

Reporter: "Another investigation?"

Spokesman: "Yes."

Reporter: "The incident could easily have ended tragically – will any steps be taken to prevent such mishaps in the future?"

Spokesman: "Naturally, the persons responsible will be subject to appropriate disciplinary action. However, in dealing with criminals the necessary precautions need to be taken; accidents of the sort that happened today are highly regrettable but it mustn't obscure the fact of most importance, which is that law enforcement bodies have to have the ability to deal effectively with those elements of big business that are feeding off the nation from within."

And that was all on the story, said the reporter, for the moment.

"'Criminals' – listen to him, the s.o.b.," said someone. "'The elements of big business that are feeding off the nation' – that's you, Darek," commented someone else.

"It was Darek who told the reporter to ask about the guns," said someone.

"Yes," said someone, "but they've decided they don't want you, Darek. It looks like you're clear."

Everyone was cheering.

"Champagne," said someone.

"We've got it recorded," said someone, "we'll run it again." But first there was the news on the other station to watch, a very similar story. Then the recorded newscasts were run again, this time with more commentary at each stage.

And again. Everyone wanted to see himself getting shot at: "Look, that's you, Zbyś, you look like an Olympic diver, the way you hit the floor." Laughter.

"And you? Did you think that chair would protect you?" More laughter. "Look at your face!" Hoots.

The best, they said, was that *pani* – her, they meant – yelling at the agents. They replayed that bit several times.

Zaremba, Cordelia gathered from listening to the conversation, had been betting that the Ministry of Justice would not send the CBA around when it got the phone call with the facts. Whether it had actually done so or not was unclear, but it was thought most likely that there had been a tip-off by someone at the non-governmental television stations whose crews had been organized by Zaremba, or, less likely, from someone at the town hall.

Cordelia revolved the fact in her mind: Zaremba had known that the television crews would be there; he had known because he had arranged for them to be there. Why hadn't he told her? Looking back, she realized that he had probably been on the verge of it several times. But he hadn't done so. That was what he must have meant by 'you could hate me.' She didn't hate him. He couldn't have known it would turn out the way it did, hadn't expected it to turn out that way. She just wished he'd told her. She remembered that he'd had a thought to spare for her at the moment the CBA had arrived, had told her to get back. There had been no time to do so, but he had moved away from her. If he seemed to have forgotten her existence since, that was only normal. Still she wished he would come to her now, if only for a word, or at least that he would look in her direction, so she wouldn't feel so sad and flat and empty and as if all the people in the room saw her as the sum of her disability. Of course, that was just her complex she reminded herself wearily.

And then she looked up and he was there, holding out a flute of champagne. Her hand closed around it and someone was already speaking to him, he was already being drawn away. He didn't hear her inner cry – "Stop! Stay, please!" Perhaps if she had looked up she would have noticed that he glanced back at her; but she was staring down at the glass; she took a sip and put it aside. She didn't really have anything to celebrate. Except that he was safe, of course.

The talk around her had devolved into politics and business and more usual topics. How long did she need to stay, Cordelia wondered? She tried not to let her eyes keep glancing towards Zaremba, tried not to let her eyes follow his back across the room. You should be proud, she told herself: You set out to help him and you did. It hadn't happened quite as expected but he was saved. She tried to be happy. She did feel relieved, very relieved for

255

him and for herself as well. And yet – it was also all over. He didn't need her anymore. They'd go back to their separate lives and some time, presumably, he'd ask her to show up in court and that would be that.

She wasn't surprised. She knew and had known, after all, that she saw the past ten days in a totally different light than he did. Her central concern had been – him. His central concern has been his name, his business, his plans for resistance, etc., her appearance had been only incidental. 'Man's love is of man's life a thing apart, 'tis woman's whole existence.' Maybe that wasn't true of many women any more. It was of her. She felt the full force of it now. The full scope of her being was invested in him; if she was lucky he might want to be casual friends in the future. Relief at his safety, at his success, warred with the dull ache of loss. Mostly she wanted to go home.

Above or below the commotion a man's voice not far from Cordelia was asking someone else: "Where'd Darek find her, did he tell you? A cripple like that, I mean? It was brilliant. Only Darek'd have an idea like that."

"Yes, a beautiful woman."

"I don't know, I'd be turned off by the…" The man made a slight gesture of twistedness.

Cordelia looked around for Zaremba, but he had disappeared for the moment.

"Shh," said the voice, "she's over there behind you. I don't know where he found her, but Edzia says he made her believe something about saving his assets from confiscation. She must have been surprised at the production."

"She didn't know it was for a publicity stunt?"

"Shh." The voices dropped, but, as they had been loud before, not enough. "Seems not. Probably she's not very bright."

"The thing is – he thinks she'll give it all back." Grimaces and head shakes.

"Maybe she will. Darek always knows what he's doing. The important thing is, he's off the hook."

"Off one hook and onto another."

The man turned and saw her watching him. He glanced at the other man, opened his mouth and shut it again. Cordelia turned her eyes away.

It was some seconds before Cordelia realized the full import of this speech. Zaremba had tricked her. He had used her for a media event because she was a cripple. It wasn't true about protecting his assets. It wasn't that he hadn't known how it would be. He had known exactly how it would be. He had used her. Her knees began to shake and knock. It was minutes before she had the strength to rise. She found the man called Zbyś and asked if she could make a telephone call. "Yes, sure," he said, "over there," and went on with his conversation. She pressed a number. The ring that she had kept her fingers curled around fell off her finger and rolled across the floor. She had to crouch to get it, holding onto the kitchen counter where the telephone sat, the cord tangling as she put down the receiver.

"Hello, hello?" the dispatcher was saying.

She put the phone up to her ear again. "I'd like a taxi please."

The address? She didn't know the address, she had to find Zbyś again and ask him, hop back to the phone.

"Five to eight minutes," said the dispatcher.

"Thank you," she said, and hung up the phone.

What should she do with the ring? She didn't want it on her finger anymore. She dropped it into her purse.

Zaremba was nowhere in sight. She found Zbyś' wife and said her goodbyes and her thank-yous in the stilted manner of a small child remembering its manners after a party, and someone was holding the door for her and escorting her to the gate, and she was standing in the street, waiting for the taxi.

She had only two or three minutes to wait alone, but it seemed very long before she saw it turning the corner, its taxi sign lit. Behind her the door to the house opened –her heart slammed in her chest – and Zaremba came running down the steps.

"Cordelia wait! Why are you leaving?"

She was struggling with the taxi door. He was checked by the locked gate of the property. He swore.

"Cordelia wait!"

She shook her head at him and slid into the taxi.

"Where to?" asked the driver.

She started to say the street name, conscious of Zaremba at the gate. Behind him the door of the house opened, and someone pressed a buzzer. The gate opened. He was running around the taxi and had slid in from the other side.

"Why wouldn't you wait? Why are you leaving like this?" he asked rather angrily.

"I realized I belonged at home."

"No you didn't."

She opened her mouth to object, but was interrupted by the driver.

"Where to?"

She started to give her address again. Zaremba said commandingly, 'the riverbank, just beyond the New

Town.' It was no question, of course, which of them the driver would listen to.

Cordelia couldn't, wouldn't speak in front of the taxi driver, and Zaremba presumably felt the same. The air of the taxi was laced with unspoken words. The driver of the taxi checked his rear-view mirror every few moments, and once turned up the collar of his jacket. But they both sat facing forward. Cordelia's lips were clamped and Zaremba looked grim too.

"Where, sir?" asked the driver rather tentatively, as they drove along.

"A little further – here. Stop, here." The taxi pulled briskly over. Zaremba paid. He got out, and came round to Cordelia's door.

"Come on," he said, "get out."

"Why? Are you going to push me into the river now that you're done with me?" She wished the words unspoken the moment they were out of her mouth.

"Dammit, just get out."

"Um, lady," said the driver cautiously, because he was a small man, and Zaremba large and angry-looking, "is this man bothering you? Do you want me to call for help?"

"No," she said, "no, it's all right."

Zaremba put his hand under her elbow and she found herself willy-nilly standing beside him.

"My wife," he said to the taxi driver in explanation.

"Ah," said the taxi driver with a grimace of sudden empathy and understanding, "I have one too," and departed with palpable relief.

Cordelia pulled away from Zaremba but walked with him under the dark trees and out onto the comparative light of the bank.

"Why are we here?" she muttered to the river.

"It was the first place I could think of where we could talk alone. Why did you run away like that? Why did you say that just now?" He spoke with a fair degree of calmness now and she made an effort to behave with dignity.

"I'm sorry. I didn't mean that about pushing me into the river." She took a deep breath. "I heard some of your friends talking. That you set it up as a media event; that you planned it that way from the beginning. A publicity stunt. It was all a publicity stunt, wasn't it?"

"Yes."

They were above the water. A week ago she had been alive to the beauty of the scene, of old Warsaw beyond and the river below. Today the riverbank was a dark, dirty, and uninviting expanse of concrete and she hated it.

"I don't want to be here," she said, still speaking to the river. "I just want to go home."

"I want to explain…" Zaremba answered.

"There's nothing to explain," she interrupted him sharply. "You lied to me. You told me you wanted to marry me to protect your assets. Protecting your assets had nothing to do with it, did it?"

"No."

"So you lied."

"No, I never lied. I said Kluska's assets had been confiscated and that I wanted to give mine to you. You made the assumptions."

"You let me. You made sure I would."

He paused. "Yes, I did."

"But you just wanted to use me. You wanted to marry me so the cameras could catch you giving your money to a cripple. You used me because I'm a cripple."

"No, because you're a *beautiful* cripple. You can see there's lots of human interest there."

"I don't want to be the object of human interest," she snapped back. "Human interest means *their* interest in *my* misfortune."

"You don't like it – but do you think the media would have come for me alone?" he answered with some heat. "I'm just some bugger the police are after. There's no news value there. The television station would've laughed in my face if I said I wanted a news spot to refute the government's claims. But when the poor bugger – me – gives a fortune away in order to challenge the government – yes, that's what got their crews out. That and only that. If it were only about me, they wouldn't have been interested. If I hadn't given you a huge sum they wouldn't have been interested. And if you weren't disabled, the government would have answered my challenge by throwing me in jail and letting me rot there. The fact that I have some proof against a journalist would have been irrelevant. Perhaps eventually the courts would clear me, but in all likelihood the news media wouldn't even bother to report the fact. But the combination of you and the money – Why do you think the government is calling off their so-called case against me? They want spectacular publicity but not spectacularly adverse publicity. How did it look, when they knocked me to the ground in front of my crippled wife? How would it have looked if they'd carried on? They're not that stupid."

"You used my disability," she repeated woodenly.

"Well, has it *ever* been of any use before?" he was growing more vehement in the face of her intransigence. "I should think you'd be glad it's finally served for something. Because of your disability, I had a chance to assert my innocence on national television, because of your disability we managed – in however small a way – to make the government look bad. You may have contributed to stopping the abuses. Who knows, your disability may be the last, tiny infinitesimal straw that tips the scales against the party and causes them to lose the elections."

"Don't be ridiculous," she snapped, wanting to scream that right now she didn't care about the elections.

"You never know. You never know. Sometimes it's just one small thing, one small action, one little individual's small action that's enough. If people – people like myself, who can – don't stand up for themselves against the powers-that-be, then no one is safe."

"I've just been used for a media stunt! I don't feel safe – I feel cheapened!" She was almost shouting at him.

"Cheapened?" He was almost shouting back, "After all I've said? Cheapened? I give you a fortune and you feel cheapened?"

"While it was happening – I thought, you didn't realize it would be like that. It wasn't your fault it was like that. But you did, you knew exactly what you were doing. That picture you took of me at the notary's – it was to convince the television station, wasn't it? You made a show of…" she made a gesture of helplessness, "my arm, my leg. Of me."

He answered angrily, "There are women all over Poland who would kill to be in your place at this moment. They'd love to have your arm and your leg, just to be in your shoes!"

"Then I wish they were! My shoe has a platform in it!"

He made no answer to that, but stood silently, looking at her.

She wished he would answer. She wished she could speak without this lump in her throat. "Why didn't you tell me?" she muttered.

"You'd have said no."

There was nothing to be said to that, because it was perfectly true. There was a long silence. Beyond she could feel the river flowing past, strong and cold and gray and somber. She wished she could throw herself into it.

"You're right. And there's no point talking now." Her voice was constricted, she turned her crutch and took a wobbly step away, then she stopped. "Contact me when you want me to give the money back. Goodbye." She didn't know where she was going. Just away.

"Cordelia, stop! I don't care about the money."

Well, she thought with hatred and hollowness, you didn't care about me. But of course she couldn't say that.

"Wait, please." He was trotting to catch up with her.

"No," she said over her shoulder, "just leave me alone now. You've done enough."

"Done enough?" He slowed. "I've given you a fortune and I've done enough?"

"You haven't given it to me. You know it's still yours."

"Fine," he said, stopping short. "You've got twenty million. You can keep it. Maybe then you'll believe I care about something besides the money."

She stopped running away and turned to look at him. "You know I can't."

"If you don't want it, you can give it all to charity."

There was a long pause.

"All right," said Cordelia slowly, in the one malicious act of her life, "I will. I'll give it all to charity."

If she had desired revenge she got it. He looked as if he'd been pole-axed.

"Fine," he finally managed to say, "fine." He swung around on his heel and walked rapidly away.

She stood looking after him, knowing she'd never see him again on the old terms, feeling as if she were being torn apart.

He went twenty paces and turned back. He was very pale. He's going to say something insulting, thought Cordelia instinctively, and willed him not to say it. Just go away, she thought, go away and leave me alone.

"And when you've given it all away," he shouted to her, "then call me up, and you'll see – it's not about the money. I never wanted to hurt you."

She didn't say anything. They stood and glared at each other for a few long seconds.

He swore, and then he was walking back towards her slowly. She hung her head, not wanting to see him, struggling with her own pain. It wasn't really that he'd used her disability and deceived her – that was bad, but it wasn't the worst part. The worst was that she'd thought he cared for her; not of course, that he felt as she did, or anything like it, but that he'd liked her a little bit at least. The worst was that everything she'd imagined during the past week was false.

He stopped some ways away from her.

"Yes," he said, "I used you. I didn't know the television crew would make such a point of your disability – it's not like that really, you know. They made it look much worse than it is. I'm sorry I couldn't tell you everything from the beginning. But wasn't it better like this? If you could have it all undone would you? You put yourself at risk for me – we both knew that. I've assumed I could make it up to you, but I appreciated your sacrifice, then and now. You were prepared for the possibility of ending up in jail yourself – is what happened worse? I can't believe you didn't really mean to help me."

Cordelia was silent.

She felt more than saw that he was coming nearer.

"Do you really wish it were all undone?" he asked again. "If you could turn back the clock and not go with me to the town hall – knowing that it would leave me in disrepute, or in the clutches of the CBA – would you?"

She thought a moment and reluctantly shook her head. There was a long moment of silence between them.

"Cordelia?"

"What?" she was staring at the pavement.

"If I come any closer are you going to hit me with your crutch?" He was not far away.

"Yes," she said, although it was painful to speak, "probably. I don't know."

"Well," he murmured apprehensively, taking a slow step, "I'm the man who likes danger."

He was standing quite close.

"So it's all right then?"

"No."

He looked at her for a long moment. "It's not about the publicity, is it?"

She gulped. "All your friendliness, the things you said – it wasn't real, was it? You just saw me as a useful disabled person."

He looked genuinely shocked. "Oh God! No, Cordelia!"

She sat down weakly on a concrete step, the same concrete step where they had sat before, and began to cry. He sat beside her.

"Don't. Cordelia, don't."

He waited until she'd stopped and then he said quietly, "When you've given all the money away, and you

265

can't suspect that I have any ulterior motives, then I'll come every day, and you can tell me I'm not fit to clean your shoes, and I'll beg you to give me one more chance. How's that?"

She dried her eyes on her sleeve.

"No you won't. You won't come. You'll have some other scheme on hand by then." She tried not to let the hurt sound in her voice but it came out pitiful, even to her ears.

He leaned back a little, looked off in the distance, took a deep breath. "Hmm. You're wrong, but if that's what you think, then you'd better listen to me now. Carpe diem." He turned to her with energy.

"When you came into my office a year ago I thought you were one of the most intriguing women I'd ever come across. Within twenty-four hours of our meeting in Zabrzeg I suspected you were the one."

"You started planning from the moment you met me there, didn't you?" said Cordelia with insight, flashing him a look from under her lashes and wiping away the tear that spilled, humiliatingly, down her cheek.

He leaned back again. "No. Well, not immediately, not in all the details. I had a hunch though, that you'd be good for something."

"Good for something!" she gulped again, "Good for something! A media event."

He said carefully, "Seeing and seizing the opportunity is how I got where I am. It's the way I am. You can't blame me for it."

"But I never wanted to be an 'opportunity.' It's so degrading." The anger was gone from her voice, and only the hurt remained.

"Why? To me, it's a compliment. You're the greatest opportunity I ever came across. I…" He sounded sincere.

"I suppose," she shrugged wearily, "you did get a lot of use out of me."

"Cordelia, stop trying to sidetrack me and listen!" his voice was kind but firm. "You make me mad and then I can't tell you the things I want to tell you. – As I was saying: I can't pretend that I haven't had other things on my mind as well in the past week, but I can tell you that you have become the number one, most important thing in my life. When I asked you to marry me, it wasn't about marriage but I thought even then that I couldn't do better. Now I've known you for ten days and I know beyond a shadow of a doubt that you're the woman I want to spend my life with."

She could hardly listen for the confusion of her own feelings.

"...And I'm willing to put up with everything – I'm not bothered by your disability, I'm not bothered by your family, I just want you and I'm really serious about it..."

He wasn't 'bothered' by her family? A first impulse to be offended was followed by cold reason: yes, that was saying a lot. Did he care for her then? Could he? Did he? He was trying very hard to convince her, and she couldn't immediately see any reason why he should now unless he was serious. Unless...

"I didn't mean it – about giving the money away. It's yours."

She arrested him in mid-sentence. He paused and answered slowly, "I'd already written it off. It's not about that, you know – but if you like, let's say it's ours?"

She didn't answer, but she was listening. She willed him to say something that would be clinching, that would sweep away all her doubts and make everything all right again.

"Cordelia, when I spoke that vow today I meant every word, including 'lasting.' Did you?"

She didn't want to answer. Of course she'd wished it were true.

"Do you want a church wedding too?" she heard him asking. "I haven't been to church since we left Poland, but whatever you want."

Now that, she thought, was a hefty argument. She weighed it, looking down and playing with her crutch. But she didn't answer, couldn't answer. Hefty, decidedly hefty, was all she could think.

"Side chapel or center aisle and the full to-do, anything you say." He stopped talking. She became very busy poking the end of her crutch at the pavement.

"Words aren't much use anymore, are they?" he murmured, with a hint of returning amusement.

She felt him slide closer. He was too close, much too close, but she refused to look up.

"You've lost your ring," he said, "or did you take it off?"

"It's in my purse," she said to the ground.

He reached around her, picked up her purse from where it lay on the cement, searched through it, found the ring, and held it for a moment. "It's too big, isn't it? We'll have to get it reduced. But put it on for me anyway, now." He reached across and took her hand, was sliding the ring on before she could protest. She closed her fingers around it.

"Cordelia? Could I kiss you now?"

A jolt went through her body. She looked at him then in surprise. "No" she started to say. Too late.

It began, perhaps, as a joke, but ended very tender. When he let her go, she felt her face turning beet red, so red that tears started from eyes again.

He reached out very gently and closed his fingers over her wrist. "It wasn't so bad, was it?" She didn't answer, and after a time, when she had somewhat recovered, he said, "Again?"

"N-No."

"Bad answer. Try again. Come, you know you like me."

Like him? Like him? thought Cordelia. She was madly in love with him. She averted her head.

"No. Yes…Okay." But her answer was really quite unnecessary.

13

The tidal wave having swept her up and deposited her, whole if breathless, on a distant shore, she had now to make a new existence, and hopefully, a new and better world. She was not afraid; having survived so far, she was gaining confidence in her abilities: she could change and grow – who knew how much?

She sat by a window, cuddled in a thick robe, looking out at a bitter November landscape of faded grass pastures, distant black branches on barren trees, and a windswept lake. Everything announced the end of autumn, the approach of the long eastern winter. Some people might have thought it dreary; Cordelia thought it perfect, beautiful, leaving nothing to be desired. They had taken a carriage along the lake a few times, and there had been swans, and a path through the woods that was covered with pine needles, but mostly, they had stayed in. And here, at the window of the palace hotel where, after the side chapel formalities, they had spent a part of their honeymoon, it was warm and comfortable and she had nothing but happy thoughts before her.

They would go back to Warsaw. The elections in October had brought the opposition party into power. Hopefully, there would be investigations into the use of the prosecutor's office and anti-corruption agency for political ends: hopefully, people would be able to see that corruption was bad, but abuse of power was worse; hopefully, they would not make use of the same tactics as their predecessors. Their own problems in that regard seemed to be over.

They had found two nice women who had agreed to be Maria and to spend part of the day with her mother; they had been encouraging Antek to get in touch with various art galleries about his photos, and he hadn't absolutely refused yet; they would fix up the villa to make it more livable; perhaps – who knows? – they might have children: everything was going to be easy and pleasant.

And there was her husband, of course. She turned her head to look at him as he lay among white sheets and newspapers.

As if aware of her regard, he raised his head and said, "It's been great here, hasn't it?"

"I liked it," she smiled and ducked her head shyly.

"This afternoon, we'll be back in Warsaw, though," he continued after a contented moment of silent communion.

"That's okay. Life will be quieter again, I suppose; it'll return to its routines, but it won't be so – immobile – as it was before you came along."

"Well, that's the thing, Cordelia. But I want your opinion…"

"Yes?" she murmured, taking a last look out the window again. She had no real apprehensions.

"I don't think money really means very much to me anymore. We've plenty enough to take care of the family –"

'The family,' she thought, how nice of him, he meant hers.

"Yes," she said, "we've more than enough."

271

"And I think making money is starting to bore me…"

She turned to look at him, paying close attention now.

"You remember how brilliant you were at our civil wedding?"

"No." she shuddered, "What I remember is that I nearly caused a massacre."

"Yes, that was good too," he chuckled a little in reminiscence, "but I was meaning how well you answered the questions. And when you came to interview for a job with me too, you had everything down. You'd be a great help to a politician."

"A politician!" she tried to keep the horror out of her voice.

"I think I'll go into politics – what do you think, Cordelia?"

Cordelia swallowed. She realized in some swift readjustment of the brain, that his mind was already made up. But he had asked her. It was a courtesy and a compliment and an improvement. She made a great effort of self-denial, shoved down all her fears and objections, and, because she loved him, adapted her desires to his, and said:

"I think you could do a lot of good as a politician."

"Yes, but would you mind, Cordelia?" he was asking her rather searchingly.

"No," she tried to put conviction into her voice, "I'll be happy to be Mrs. Politician."

He grinned at her, "You're still a lousy liar though. We'll have to work on that."

"No," she said.

"I'm joking, Mrs. Politician. Come here," he patted the bed. She went to him gladly, happily. The political future was fortunately still distant. She could change, and grow; she might even, in a million years, learn to like it.

PART 2

'And so it's going to be vital for us to use any means at our disposal, basically, to achieve our objective.' – Dick Cheney

14

"Something's wrong," said Darek. "Listen, do you hear that?"

Cordelia listened. The car was running smoothly it seemed to her, hardly disturbed by the unevenness of the pavement, its warmth and clean leather interior still a marvel to her. "No," she answered, "it seems very quiet."

"Mm," he said, and slowed the car and pulled it up along the verge. The highway was empty. They had been climbing for a while and were in the middle of a nearly mountainous no-man's land, where the clear sharp air and a few inches of snow indicated the change in altitude. He opened his door and slid out. "I'll just take a look."

Cordelia sat for a moment and then pushed open the car door on her side and swung her legs out into the snow. Darek already had the hood up. They were stopped on the edge of a meadow, an expanse of white with tawny bent grass stems showing through in occasional clumps, and beyond a line of dark conifers, their branches dusted here and there with the snow still. Closer to the road, where the sun had been striking all day, it was beginning to melt though. Cordelia poked at the snow with her crutch, hopped a few steps and stopped. She should be worried about the car, she thought, but she wasn't. She was only happy. Darek would deal with it, she knew. She balanced on her good leg, shifted her crutch into the crook of her bad arm, bent to scoop up a handful of snow. She rolled it a little in her hand, jiggling and compacting it, feeling its numbing coldness on her skin. A snowball. Her husband was still bent over something in the engine. He was busy and unsuspecting. It would be unfair to throw a snowball at him. She tossed the ball a little in her hand, considering. If she threw it, one thing was certain, his reaction would be swift. She had never seen him throw a snowball, but she had no doubt that his aim would be very accurate. She would doubtless get pasted. So the question was only – would he feel compunction about pounding her because she was crippled? Or not? Somehow, she had an almost irresistible urge to find out. Darek, as if aware of her regard, suddenly looked up and caught her impish look, the snowball – he straightened and one eyebrow shot up in surprise – she was not given to playfulness – and challenge. Cordelia hastily dropped the snowball.

"Chicken," he grinned, catching her and giving her a kiss as he headed for the trunk of the car. He extracted a tool box and returned to his job.

"All the same," he said, as he slid into the car beside her some while later, "I wish you'd thrown it."

"Why? You'd have clobbered me."

"Maybe," he smiled, "but I'd have known you finally trust me."

"I do trust you."

"A little."

She gave him a glance that combined her adoration and her shyness, and he reached out a cold hand and caressed her cheek.

"What's the matter with the car?" she asked.

"I don't know. It's just a slight rattle, but it's a slight rattle that shouldn't be there. It's strange…" He listened to the engine for a moment and then shrugged. "I can't find anything. I'll have to have it looked at when we get back to Warsaw. Nothing to do here." He put the car back on the road and they continued on their way.

"Maybe when the police had it, the officers went joyriding," said Cordelia. Darek had only managed to extract the Jaguar from the police impound a couple of weeks before – just in time for their wedding, in fact.

"Oho. I see the honeymoon's over and you're set on cruelty. Is this the shape of things to come, Mrs. Zaremba?"

Cordelia smiled, she knew he was joking. Although it was true the honeymoon was, strictly speaking, over. Half an hour ago she had taken a final look around the room of their hotel in the highlands, a last glance out the window at the gun-barrel grey lake and the dark November woods and had followed Darek with the luggage – such elegant luggage, nothing like the cardboard and duct-tape contraptions she remembered from the days of her family's many moves – out to the car. It didn't matter really that they were leaving; it didn't matter if they were in Warsaw or here in the foothills of the Bieszczady or anyplace in the world, so long as they were together. She was sure the future was going to be pleasant, even if Darek wanted to go into politics. She didn't need to think about that yet.

They were cresting the top of a steep rise, starting down; below and all about them were high, rounded hills and woods and half-frozen watercourses and cliffs.

"How beautiful," murmured Cordelia.

"Bugger!" said Darek vehemently, his leg shifting, pounding on a pedal.

Cordelia jerked her head around to look at him in surprise, but his eyes were concentrated forward. The road before them wound, in sharp turns, downwards. The curve was coming up and they were going fast, much too fast. Cordelia looked at her husband again, her eyes widening.

"No brakes," he said curtly, "hang on!"

The curve was coming, coming – please let him live – Cordelia breathed a passionate prayer and closed her eyes, her muscles flinching from the roll and crash that would surely come, and then she felt the car skidding sideways and she opened her eyes to see the grey and white world flashing past and she closed them again quickly, unable to breath, only the car had righted itself and was continuing straight. She opened her eyes and found that they were running fast, way too fast, faster even than before, along a straight course, and approaching the next bend. No, she thought, no, this time would be it. The land seemed to drop off after the curve. Oh, Darek, she thought, and closed her eyes again. But the darkness made her feel even more ill, and so she opened them just as they reached the corner and again they were sliding round sideways in one direction, sickeningly, and then, as the curve turned in the other direction, skidding around again, and the shoulder was right there, and they were going to go over it surely, only they didn't, but were once again headed straight, but only for a moment, because another curve was coming. And they made it round that one too, just barely, and then they were approaching another and Cordelia sat in silence and contemplated their approaching end in horror as the car gained momentum.

"This one," said Darek, "we won't make."

Let's just get it over with, thought Cordelia.

"We're going straight," said Darek, "hang on!"

And they were into the turn, shooting over the edge of the pavement, becoming airborne for a moment, landing with a thud, and careering downhill, mud and snow flying past the windows as the wheels sank in the soft earth. Cordelia flung her good arm up to protect her head in the inevitable roll, as the car bounced on the uneven ground. But they were slowing, slowing, they were stopped. They were actually stopped, in a field, on the hillside, and they were alive.

"Well," said Darek, with pleasure, "that was fun."

Cordelia looked at him with loathing, pushed open the car door, and was sick.

Sometime later, when his sufficient concern for her and the realization that, after all, however much he had enjoyed the ride, he hadn't intended it to happen, had mollified her, she sat back weakly in her seat, breathed in the cold air and looked out at the countryside. Before it had been beautiful; now the steep slopes and dark firs looked vaguely savage, as if they had desired victims and been cheated. That was only her imagination, she knew; she shook her head to rid herself of the thought and looked at her husband.

"Okay now?"

She nodded. "I'm sorry," she murmured, "I didn't mean to get sick."

"Yes, it's very disappointing. I had really hoped you were going to be my navigator when I took up rally car racing again. Tsk."

"I can't read maps either."

"No use at all, are you?" he teased. "Better wait here, while I see what I can see." He opened the door with some difficulty because of the terrain, and got out.

Cordelia, calmed by her husband's good humor, looked out at the countryside again and found that it had regained its neutrality. Everything was all right. They were having an adventure, that was all; it would be uncomfortable perhaps, but it would end happily. On an impulse she slid across the seat to the driver's side, opened the door, and got out. The wind struck as soon as she emerged from the car. It was very cold. Darek was lying on the ground, in the half-frozen grass, searching for something under the car. He slid out then, and stood up, brushing dirt and ice particles from his car coat and looking extraordinarily grim. Cordelia was gripped with a sudden foreboding.

"What is it? What happened?"

"A problem with the brake cables."

He looked so strange that Cordelia hesitated to speak, but something prompted her to ask: "Is that usual, on such a new car?"

"No. Not usual." He seemed disinclined to elaborate.

Cordelia shivered. "Do we call for a tow truck?"

"We're out of range here. There's no signal on my phone."

Darek's eyes were searching the horizon, looking with creased forehead toward the road. Cordelia had one more question she had to ask.

"Do you think it was tampered with?" she asked with a sinking feeling of fear.

He jerked his eyes away from the road and looked at her – only Cordelia had the feeling that he wasn't seeing her – sliding his pocketknife and some other object into a pocket, rubbing some grease from his fingers. "Yes."

"But you don't have any enemies, do you?" Cordelia asked, wide-eyed. She couldn't say – someone who'd want to kill you?

He spoke rapidly then, as if making up his mind, without answering her question. "Is there anything you absolutely need from the luggage?"

She shook her head.

"Good, then we're going to leave the car. Where's your hat?" He retrieved it for her from the interior, crammed it on her head, over her dark hair. "We need to get away from here, come on, downhill to the woods, as quick as you can."

He was already pulling her away from the car, almost roughly, his hurry so evident that she asked no more questions, but concentrated her efforts on swinging forward, down the slope. With his tight grip on her damaged arm to give her balance, she could move fairly rapidly in spite of the terrain. But she was no athlete; soon she was panting. Still Darek did not slacken his pace. And once or twice he looked behind, towards the road.

Cordelia was infected by his sense of urgency, by an intense desire to leave the car behind, to put as much distance between the car and themselves as possible. What were they running from? She didn't know, but once started she had the panicked animal's instinct of flight. The dirt and rocks skidded from beneath their feet as they pelted down the hillside – better safe than sorry and the pace was too quick for enquiries. But eventually her breath was coming in jagged sobs and she stumbled repeatedly. She couldn't keep it up. Darek pulled her upright as she nearly fell.

"It will be faster if I carry you," he said.

"No," she said, but he was already suiting the action to the words, even as she protested, and they continued downhill, at a run, into the fir woods and beyond, until the intervening trees and a valley closed off the car from their view. Zaremba slowed to a walk, winded, choosing his path with care now, so that he avoided the patches of snow and stepped on the moss and needles under the trees, where no footprints would show.

"I can walk now," said Cordelia, "can't you put me down?" She weighed not much more than a hundred pounds but she was still a considerable burden to run with. Darek was breathing very heavily.

"Yes, but let's keep going," he put her down and they continued together, on and on, downwards, until it was clear that they were not being pursued, and Cordelia became increasingly aware that her legs and her arm on the crutch were aching. This, she thought, was how they had met when her father got the car stuck and she had walked in search of help. Her muscles had ached then too. But she hadn't been running away from anything. She didn't know what she was running from now.

"We'll rest for a moment," Darek said, and they stopped and panted.

"Are you warm enough?" he asked after a time.

Cordelia nodded. But within moments, as soon as the exercise ceased to heat her blood, she felt the bite of the breeze even through her warm coat. Or maybe it was fear that was chilling her? She looked at her husband, with questions in her eyes, and he responded by taking up the conversation from her last query.

"Do I have enemies? I would have said not. Except, of course, when I pulled off that stunt at the town hall thanks to you – it's obvious I didn't make any friends in certain quarters then. But I shouldn't think any one would have taken it so hard as to want to do me in – much less you…Although it's conceivable that it's not known that you're with me. More likely, I would think, someone is after the car. Ordinary thieves. They'll expect us to be stopped along the road, so before long they'll show up to claim it. Although it's possible they went straight when we made the turn-off for the scenic route. Still, I imagine they'll figure it out before long." He smiled a little grimly. "They're going to be a bit surprised to see how far the car is from the road, but they'll doubtless think of a way around the difficulty. They'll have a tow truck or they'll simply take it in pieces. It seems to me very likely, however, that some unpleasant characters are going to be turning up before long – probably have already turned up. That's why we ran. The car is nothing. I didn't want anyone to get hurt."

Meaning he didn't want her to get hurt, she knew, but she said nothing, and felt cheered. Car thieves, even organized car thieves, were not that sinister seeming. Their motives were clear and their moves easily calculable. It wasn't that anyone wanted to murder Darek. She began to relax.

"Is it such an expensive car?" she asked innocently.

He gave her a look full of mixed emotions: disbelief, amusement, surprise. "No," he answered, with an attempt at a straight face. "I bought it second-hand."

She nodded. She knew his tastes were simple.

"It's last year's. But good enough for many people. After all, it used to be the tiny Fiats that were the hot item on the stolen car market."

"Yes, I suppose…Still," she added after a pause, as they resumed their walk, "don't you think the thieves were taking a big risk of smashing the, um, object of their desire, by nobbling the brakes? It seems so lacking in forethought."

"Yes, I admit that puzzles me. But perhaps they expected the denouement to occur earlier, before we got to the hills. Perhaps there on the plateau, not far from the hotel. At the first intersection, say."

"Because it must have been done – whatever it was – at the hotel last night? When we were driving yesterday there wasn't any problem."

"Yes, it must have been at the hotel. The car was in a locked enclosure but it isn't guarded. Anyone could have jumped the fence in the night to do the business."

"Why didn't they just take it then, I wonder?"

"I don't know."

"Thieves are probably the only people in Poland who ordinarily choose to do things as directly as possible," she added consideringly, her doubts returning.

"It's conceivable they were also hoping for our luggage and whatever else we might have about us – cell phones, credit cards, money."

"True. Rather greedy, but possible." She was quite cheered by the idea and walked for a time with greater ease.

"But they'd better hurry don't you think?" she added, "I mean, if they hadn't shown up by the time we made it down the hill, they must have been quite a ways back. Some one else might come along the road first."

"Cordelia, you're not going to feel sorry for people – I assume there's more than one – who are trying – who are going – to rob us?"

"But I don't like the idea of so much effort going to waste. Such a disappointment, I would think."

"Come, some discretion in your compassion, *kochanie*."

"Well, I hope the spoils go to the most needy, anyway." It was hard to talk and keep up the pace. She fell silent and it was only after they had been walking quite some time that she asked, "And by the way, where are we going?"

Darek stopped again to let her rest. They had been talking quietly, knowing that their voices would carry far in the still air. But here, once the sound of their conversation and their movement stopped, Cordelia was aware how alone they were. They had come a long ways from the slope with the car, far enough so that there was little snow any more, only the dark damp forest about, where patches of ice clung to branches and drops of water fell occasionally from black limbs. The leaves and needles underfoot were that odd layered texture between freezing and thaw. There was nothing to be seen between the trunks of the trees, only the forest stretching on, seemingly endless and quite silent. Cordelia tried to find a position in which to rest various aching muscles; she wished she could sit down but there was no possibility. The ground was far too wet. The first of what she knew to be a host of unwelcome thoughts began to crowd for attention. Perhaps they would walk here until night fell and they dropped from weariness; perhaps they would freeze to death and all winter the snow would cover and uncover their decaying bodies. She shivered. If Darek left her he could easily walk back to the highway, at some point distant from the car; uphill was no problem for him; someone would come along eventually and he could hitchhike to civilization. Even if it was the car thieves who came along he could claim to have just come from a nearby farm. She mulled this thought.

"I've always read," said Darek, "that if one is lost in the wilderness one has only to walk downhill or follow a watercourse downstream to find civilization – well, let's call it that anyway – I'm not sure how civilized we'll find the inhabitants around here. I've always wanted to find out if the theory's true. Other than that, I have a lighter, and if we get too cold we can build a fire. Missing a meal or two will be painful but we'll probably survive. Okay?"

"Okay." She was glad to have her moral dilemma put off for the moment.

"You know," he said, as they started off again. "One of the things I've always liked about you is your stoicism."

"That's not a very appealing attribute."

"Useful, though. Shall I tell you what else I like?"

"No," she shook her head, because his compliments embarrassed her, they seemed so unconnected to her own dim image of herself. "Anyway," she said, to change the subject, "I've read that one can eat the inner bark of pine trees if one's starving. Unfortunately," she looked about, "these seem to be fir. I don't know about fir bark."

"I think I'd have to be a lot hungrier than I am to try it."

"Yes, and I'm not sure whether one eats it raw or cooks it." She misquoted gaily:

"One can live without music, and loving, and books
But where is the man who can live without cooks?"

"Hm. Personally, I don't think I could live without loving," said Darek with a slight smile, his eyes sweeping the forest.

"No!" said Cordelia, definitely, reading his mind, "it's much too cold."

But they had hardly gone another hundred yards before it became clear that her stoicism would not be tried too high. The forest dropped abruptly onto a lane; a short and – in Cordelia's case, awkward – scramble down a bank and they were standing in it, a brief walk and the forest ended and they could see across a field to a house, one of several in a hamlet, and barns. Already two nondescript dogs were rushing towards them, circling and barking. They ignored the dogs and continued on towards the house, Cordelia limping badly by now. A man, an elderly man with a weather-beaten face and soiled clothing, emerged from a barn and stood staring at them as they approached.

"*Dzien dobry, panu,*" Darek greeted him genially.

"*Dzien dobry,*" the man grunted in reply, unsmiling and continuing to regard them with suspicion.

Cordelia was made aware of how out-of-place, how rich and citified in spite of Darek's casual clothing, they must look; the man's gaze swept them from head to foot and back again.

"How d'ye get 'ere, hey?" the man asked. His tone implied that he thought them disreputable and his regional accent made him almost incomprehensible. Only a small number of people in Poland still spoke this way.

"Our car broke down on the highway above," said Darek, with a wave of the hand.

"Fra the highway, hey?" The man looked towards the upland as if Darek had said they'd dropped from the sky.

"Have you a telephone?"

"A telephone? Na, na."

"Is there a towing garage nearby? A mechanic?"

"Na, na," the man shook his head, "there's nothing."

"Is there anyone in the neighborhood who could drive us to the nearest town? I would pay well, of course."

The man's eyes became thoughtful. But after a moment he shook his head, "na, na, there's no one 'ere, 'sept me and m'wife." He jerked his head towards the other houses, "they're all gone, gone ta the town."

They looked towards the other houses, which did have a look of emptiness and decay about them. There didn't seem to be anything to do, Cordelia thought wearily, trying to rest her aching leg and shivering uncontrollably in the cold wind. She tried to warm her face by ducking it into the thick plush of her collar. The yard was littered with bits of machinery, with a plow, a decomposing tractor, and various other unidentifiable bits of refuse. The dogs strutted back and forth at a distance of ten feet and barked low growling barks, their hackles up, and the man made no effort to quell them. Cordelia turned away, her wariness and distrust matching the man's own; she would have walked away into nowhere rather than beg help from this unfriendly hill-dweller.

"My wife needs a place to rest, out of the weather," said Darek, reaching for his wallet, when the man made no move to invite them in on his own. Something passed between them, and the man grunted again and gestured for them to follow him towards one of the houses.

They stepped through a windtrap into a dark, low-beamed kitchen redolent of grease and sausage and smoke, where a heavy elderly woman, in skirt and apron, rose at their entry, shuffled her feet into rubber slippers, straightened her kerchief, and regarded them with the twin of the man's faintly hostile stare.

"Make tea!" said the man roughly. He pointed Cordelia to a bench behind a small table. Cordelia arranged herself in the narrow space with some difficulty, as there were too many table corners and chair legs to be navigated easily with a twisted foot and a crutch. When she looked up, she found that Darek and the man had come to some agreement, and were leaving the kitchen together. She kept her eyes down so as not to cast a pleading, 'don't leave me here alone' look at her husband.

"Were'dyeca'fra, *pani?*" said the woman, staring at Cordelia after the men had left.

"I beg your pardon?"

"Were'dye ca'fra?" The woman repeated herself loudly.

"I'm sorry, I don't understand."

"Said, were'dye ca'fra, hey?" The woman spoke even more loudly and slowly.

Cordelia couldn't bear to ask the woman to repeat herself, so she simply nodded and smiled.

The woman looked at her for a moment, then shrugged, "I s'pose you're not right in ta head." She tapped her head with a finger, "not right, hey?"

This Cordelia understood perfectly. She nodded and wished she were elsewhere.

The woman set tea in front of Cordelia and continued standing and staring for a minute, but after a while the activity obviously paled, and she sat down in the place where she had been when they came in, and turned on a radio. It was the Radio Maria station for ultra-Catholicism and right-wing propaganda. A nun with a crabbed, monotonous voice was giving a caller a recipe for pickled herring salad. Pine bark sounded more appetizing, thought Cordelia with a sigh, warming her hands on the glass of tea. The nun was succeeded by a series of righteous or angry voices. The woman in the corner listened, gave Cordelia occasional glances, sighed sometimes, and was still. Cordelia was aware that the woman wanted her gone. The minutes, as shown on a small plastic clock, ticked by at an agonizingly slow pace. They couldn't stay here forever, and there seemed to be no way of leaving.

Well, she could retreat, always, into her own thoughts. She had now two months of memories, the two months since she had met Darek, to be carded over. There had hardly been time for reflection in that space.

Most recent were those from her honeymoon. She glanced at the woman in the corner, mouthing a prayer in response to a cue from an unctuous voice on the radio. No, she couldn't think about the events of her honeymoon, couldn't bear to have this woman's presence, heavy and crude, intruding itself into images of entwined limbs and shared intimacy. She put a hand up and began to twist a strand of hair to keep certain thoughts at bay. Some memories were so private they could only be fully savored when one was alone; and yet, she remembered every moment, from the time she met Darek; every moment, and how he looked and what he said, and what she said, and everything else, from the moment they had come to an understanding that evening, after the events in the town hall.

15

"I'll call you tomorrow," he had said, when the taxi had deposited them before the villa far into the evening of that day six weeks ago after their civil marriage and the shooting in the town hall. "I don't know when. It might be rather late in the day. Is that okay?"

Of course she had agreed it was okay, everything was okay, everything was wonderful – she was going to marry him, he had asked her to marry him for real. She was delirious with happiness and dropping with exhaustion. She was barely able to ask a question about the security car drawn up in front of the house.

"Just for a while, just to be on the safe side," he answered. "I don't want you to be harassed by reporters or anybody else. Don't worry about it."

It was true; she had just been given, very publicly, 20 million euros worth of assets. She supposed it did make her somewhat of a target. But she had no energy to spare for the worry. She was subject to fatigue and she had spent a day that would have tried the nerves of the most robust. But there was her mother. If her mother was still up she would have to take care of her, she couldn't leave it to her brother; he'd been with her all day. And yet, she so much wanted to lie down and sleep.

But she found that Darek had solved this problem for her as well. Sometime in the course of the evening he had arranged for a woman to come and spend the night looking after her mother. Later she had been amazed at his foresight. At the time she hardly noticed. There was nothing for her to do but assure her father and brother – who actually hastened to meet her, met her in the stairwell as she came in the door, an extraordinary occurrence – that yes, in spite of what they'd seen on the television, she was all right, quite all right, splendidly all right, absolutely and positively overflowing with all-rightness and to leave them gaping, and climb the stairs slowly and drop wearily and exultantly into bed.

And the next day she waited for him to call, waited all day in nervous expectation, wondering if she had imagined it all, if perhaps he might have changed his mind overnight, thought better of it, if perhaps he had only been carried away by the events of the day, told her she was the one he wanted to spend his life with only in a sort of reaction to the relief of no longer being pursued by the law.

She didn't say anything to her father or brother about what had happened between herself and Darek. Of course, they had seen the news the evening before, so they knew the public part of it quite well, but she didn't tell them about anything that had happened afterwards, about Darek's declaration to her. She wanted to see him again to make sure he hadn't changed his mind.

And there was the news, of course. The events of the preceding day were endlessly recounted and commented upon. She saw that Darek had been interviewed again, as well as various government spokespersons, but there was nothing really to add to all that had been said before. It had been a fiasco for the party in power, their popularity in the polls had taken a dive, and they were trying to smooth things over as well as they could. Cordelia knew she should feel triumphant; knew she should be pleased that the ruling party's success in the coming elections seemed a little less secure, but all she could think about was her quasi-husband.

She stationed herself beside the telephone, afraid when any necessity called her into another room that she might miss a call. When the telephone rang, she jumped for it. She jumped for it three times, in fact, with pounding heart, only to be disappointed by the voice of one or another of her father's colleagues – who were doubtless surprised by the vibrant eagerness of her greeting and the quickly succeeding change of register – before she heard Darek's voice on the other end of the line. She had wondered if she would recognize it, since he had never called her before. But she found that she knew at once who it was, and not only because he spoke in English – there was that undercurrent of amusement which only rarely and very temporarily deserted him. She knew him even though he only said 'hello, Cordelia?'

"Yes," she said, not knowing how to go on, really. Yes, Darek? Yes, *Pan* Zaremba? She had only spoken formally to him in the past, but now everything was different – if it was. She twisted the telephone cord.

"I'll still be busy here at the office for another hour, but I'm sending Mariusz for you in the car and by the time you get here, I should be done, we can have dinner together, okay?"

It wasn't a lover-like speech, but it would certainly do, Cordelia wasn't picky. "Okay," she answered breathlessly.

"Good," he said, and the phone went dead.

She remembered the office building, when they arrived before it – she and Mariusz – after a rather awkward ride, in which he had made one or two comments about the events of the previous day, and she had replied stiffly and then neither had known what to say. She knew he found her odd but was polite to her because of Zaremba. He drove around to the back when they arrived at the building, stopped the car beside a loading ramp, and unlocked a service door for her. "*Pan* Darek said to come in this way; there are some reporters out front." She remembered the building's glass doors and the security guard and the elevator, as she stepped into it. She remembered, but only in a fleeting moment, as it crossed her mind, riding up in this elevator when she had come for the job interview a year and a half ago. On that day she had been nervous in an ordinary way, flustered and embarrassed by what were for her unusual circumstances, but knowing after all that the outcome of the interview wouldn't really matter, that life would continue pretty much as before, whatever happened to her in the next half hour. Now everything was different, and vitally important, and she was as taut as a stretched wire.

The main thing was whether he still felt as he had felt last night. It seemed incredible that he could care for her, but still, she thought his asking her to meet for dinner sounded encouragingly solid. Surely, if he had wanted to tell her it was all a mistake, he would have suggested a quick drink in a bar or something from a takeout booth, to be eaten on a street corner, where he would leave her standing, with a forgotten french fry clutched in one hand, as he walked away.

She would probably know by the way he looked when he saw her – would he appear uneasy, as if he wished he could get out of it? – or would he smile at her? She took a deep breath as the elevator stopped, and stepped out, putting her crutch down carefully so as not to make any noise. There was the sign on the door that had given her pause that time before: 'Z. Devel.' Zaremba Development. She wasn't quite sure yet whether the abbreviation was accurate or not. She shifted her crutch into her withered arm and opened the door, stepped through. There was the same cool secretary; she had a different hair color, but Cordelia remembered her anyway.

"*Dzien dobry, pani*," Cordelia said and then hesitated; how did she introduce herself? Cordelia Fogg? Cordelia Zaremba? "Um..." But her explanation was unnecessary.

"*Pan* Zaremba is expecting *pani*," said the secretary, rising with a marked increase in respectfulness over the year previous. "But he's in a meeting; he'll be just a moment. Can I bring you tea or coffee?"

"No, no, thank you, I'll just wait," Her heart fluttering, Cordelia crossed to the line of chairs where she had waited before. In a moment, perhaps, he would come through that door.

She twisted the handle of her crutch, tried to be calm, saw the door to his office beginning to open, heard voices. She rose and stood waiting, looking at the ground. She was aware that he was emerging with two other men, was coming towards her. She was looking down; she had missed, she realized, the moment when he first saw her, and now she would never know if he had looked pleased or not. Her eyes hardly got as far as his face, she was only aware of his presence. He was introducing her to two foreign men – 'my wife' – even in her preoccupation with the introduction, the awkwardness of having to shake hands left-handed, the necessity of stammering something polite, she was aware of the words, and then he was seeing the men to the door, they were gone, he was saying to his secretary that she could leave, that he would lock up, the secretary was gathering her things, saying goodbye and leaving, and all this time, Cordelia stood and waited, looking at the ground.

The door closed on the secretary. Cordelia heard it click shut. They were alone. There was silence. She felt more than saw that Darek was seating himself on the secretary's desk, that he was regarding her steadily.

"You know," he said slowly, "what kind of wife are you going to be?"

She began to tremble.

"Someday I'm going to get up in the morning and leave home with shaving cream on half my face and my shirt on backwards and you won't have set me straight because you won't even have looked at me."

She raised her eyes then and saw that he was laughing at her, and she smiled back rather tremulously.

"Come here," he said, and held out his arms. And she went towards him, but dropped her eyes again, when she reached him, before the depth of his gaze and something that loomed towards her, cut off her breath.

And yet she found that she could breathe, just.

"You must have been very busy today," she said, after a time, into the shoulder of his shirt. "Is it going okay?" She meant the business, the interviews.

"Hm. Very wifely," he said appreciatively, into her hair. "I've been working to repair damage all day. Some things are probably irreparable. But one or two good things are in the offing anyway. Those two fellows – " he broke off suddenly, "but I don't want to talk about business now, we've got more important things to talk about...I dreamt about you last night."

"You did?" Cordelia hesitated, "um…a good dream I hope?"

"Very satisfactory, thank you."

Cordelia was glad she didn't have to meet his eye. She made a slight move to withdraw from the circle of his arms but finding them unyielding, subsided. Now seemed the time to get matters clear.

"I wasn't sure," she said tentatively, "whether you'd still feel the same today. I mean, I wasn't sure I hadn't just dreamt it all myself.'

He didn't speak at once but let her go and took her hand, turning it over to examine the device of string running from her finger to her wrist by which she had secured her too-large wedding ring. "I suppose the first thing I'll have to tell you every day for the next ten years is 'I still feel the same'…But I see you had faith enough in me to hang on to the ring this time. We have to get this repaired. Come along."

He stood from the desk, suddenly large beside her, and ushered her towards the door.

"There's a jeweler," he said, as they got into the lift, "who's agreed to wait after hours."

"Oh," she said, a little surprised and not knowing what else to say; it was probably another one of his friends, he seemed to have a great many acquaintances, and she had to remember that he was rich enough not to have to think much about an expense like having a ring reduced to size. It had fallen off once last night.

They got in the car, the same company car that Mariusz had been driving, still parked close to the back entrance, and as she sat beside him and they drove toward the center of Warsaw, she thought that all her brief acquaintance with him had been punctuated by drives in the car. She liked these rides; and today it was easier to talk to him when his attention was necessarily directed away from her in part at least, and soon she found herself chatting gaily with him about their shared adventure of the day before, and then more seriously about politics, power struggles, and the use of adversity and the media. Their personal situation retreated for the time being before the importance of the outer world, until they reached the heart of the city and Darek was stopping the car.

They parked on a busy street where the shops had closed up and the working day was over, but there were still many people about, couples strolling in the evening to a restaurant, groups of young people in search of a café, apartment dwellers walking their dogs. Darek came around and opened the door. There was a jeweler's shop in front of them, with a light showing inside, although the grill was down over the window.

"I've never been in a jewelry shop before," said Cordelia as they crossed to the door.

"Never? You don't like jewelry?"

"I don't know. I never thought about it. I never had any."

Darek stopped before the door of the shop, "But didn't anyone ever give you any? Your father, your brother at least? For Christmas or your birthday?"

"No. Antek hides at Christmas and never remembers my birthday. My father gives me books – usually something elliptical and New Yorkerish. He likes that kind."

Darek gave her a look.

"I like books," she added loyally.

"But you don't object to jewelry? It's not against your principles or anything?"

She shrugged, "No, why?"

298

He knocked and put his hand on the shop door. "Because I'd like to buy you an engagement ring. We sort of skipped that part in the rush."

"Oh," she said, taken aback, "No, thank you, you don't need to, really."

"But I'd like to," he said, and the door opened and so she did not reply and soon she found herself seated on a red velvet chair, while a man took her wedding ring into an inner workroom to reduce it and a woman brought a tray of rings. Darek hovered, keeping one eye on Cordelia, while picking up various items from the counter and examining them, or shifting from foot to foot; immobility was not natural for him. His broad and muscular form, with the athleticism that comes from hard and early physical labor, was out of place in the surroundings but he seemed serenely unaware of the fact.

"Which do you like?" said the woman, advancing a number of different shapes of what Cordelia assumed at first were diamonds, and then decided that after all, they must be that other thing, what was it? Zircons probably, otherwise how could they be so large and brilliant? She had never seen anyone wearing anything like that. She picked up one that was not so large but had an intricately worked setting. It was really very pretty. By far the prettiest. She turned it over in her fingers, saw it catch the light and sparkle, admired it as an object, almost wanted it, had a very faint desire to possess it. But after all, she didn't need a diamond ring, however much it might be a zircon.

"Which do you like best?" asked the clerk again, "that one?"

"Yes, I like this one," said Cordelia, "but..."

"See if it fits."

Cordelia blushed, the clerk didn't realize that she couldn't easily put it on by herself, one-handed – there were always these embarrassing moments when she went out in public, it was one of the reasons she stayed home and avoided people – but Darek stepped forward and helped her. It fit. She admired it for a moment, to be polite; in just a second she would hand it back and shake her head. The man was emerging from the workroom with her wedding ring. She had both rings on and Darek was handing over a bank card, was saying they'd take it.

No, thought Cordelia, please don't, and opened her mouth to speak, and then stopped; she didn't want to embarrass him by quarrelling about it in front of the shop people and presumably it wasn't that expensive. Nothing he had ever said or done had given her the impression that he was a man of extravagant habits, quite the contrary. She waited with bent head, feeling half pleased and half guilty, while the jeweler got out the card machine. Her eyes fell on the tray of rings. One of the price tags caught her eye. She gasped, felt faint for a moment. That couldn't be right. The other tags were turned over; she raised a shaking finger and flipped one so that she could see it. As much as she made as a translator in two years. The enormity of it held her speechless for a moment. Then:

"No!" she exclaimed, rising. Darek and the man and woman turned to look at her. "No," she said to Darek, "thank you anyway." And to the shop people, "I'm very sorry, I didn't realize what it cost, I don't want it, thank you anyway." She grasped the ring in her injured hand and managed to tug it off on to the counter. "Here. Thank you anyway." She turned and left the shop.

Outside the night air of autumn was cold on her hot cheeks. She stood alone and lost for a moment, thinking of nothing but the look Darek had given her as she left. She glanced back uncertainly toward the shop, but she saw only the back of his head and shoulders, dimly, through the glass. He had looked angry. She stood for a moment more, uncertainly, as the evening walkers passed her on either side unnoticed. Of course he had been angry, she had created a scene and embarrassed him. But what else could she have done? It was crazy to spend that kind of money on a ring. But perhaps she should have done it differently, she thought miserably, done it in a more polished manner?

She looked back at the shop again. He was talking to the jeweler. He was probably avoiding having to come and meet her. She might as well go home. There was a kiosk nearby, it appeared to be open. She hobbled over to it, thinking, by the time she reached it, that after all, she was wrong, that the money was his, and she had no business telling him what to do with it. He was the one who had made himself into a multi-millionaire, not she, and in any case, if he wanted to throw his money into the Vistula, bill by bill, that was his affair. The idea that she was in the wrong was unusual and not comforting. She bought a ticket, and when she looked up, he was there, waiting for her on the sidewalk in front of the shop.

She walked slowly towards him, came to a stop some feet away.

"You're going to take the bus home?"

She hadn't intended to, really, the ticket was only a sort of insurance. But since he asked, maybe he was hoping. She raised her chin (only it was quivering) "yes."

And since he didn't say anything, she stammered, "I mean, maybe you'd prefer it, maybe if you're upset, maybe it would better..."

"And maybe you should stop talking nonsense and get in the car?" Since his tone wasn't angry, his bluntness was reassuring.

She got in. He got in too, rolled down the window, took out a cigarette and began to smoke it.

"I suppose," he said thoughtfully after a moment, rubbing his temple with the thumb of his left hand, "that after a time you're going to make me give up smoking."

Cordelia's acquaintance with him was brief, but it was long enough so that she recognized this as the opening gambit in a conversational chess game that would actually have nothing to do with smoking, everything to do with the ring, and would lead in short order, whatever answer she made, to her checkmate. But, she thought, there was no need for his maneuvers this time; she owed him an apology.

"No, I don't think I have a right to tell you what to do. Not about smoking, or anything else. I was wrong – in there." She jerked her head towards the shop, played nervously with the handle of her crutch. "I'm sorry."

And then, since he didn't answer at once, but was regarding her with a look of what might be perplexity or even, oddly, anxiety, she added in explanation, "It was just such a huge amount of money. It didn't seem proper."

"It's not a lot of money to me. Perhaps I should just have bought it and given it to you, only I wanted you to choose what you liked."

This was awful. "It was very kind of you – "

He stubbed out the cigarette. "Well, yes, but that's not the whole point."

She looked a timid question at him.

"When you told the reporter yesterday that ours was an 'abuse of power' story not a 'love story,' that was a

302

brilliant answer in the situation, but it does rather leave us – publicly, I mean – in an odd position."

"It seems to me," said Cordelia, considering, "that our feelings or – intentions – are our private affair, anyway."

"Yes, but marriage is a public institution. We live amongst other people and for the ease of social intercourse our relationship needs to be clear. I think a civil ceremony after ten days acquaintance followed by a declaration that our marriage was for reasons of political resistance manages to muddy the waters considerably. That's why I think – if you don't mind – that a church wedding as well would be good, and that some public proofs of my affection are in order. That's why I wanted a ring that would make a statement."

"Oh," said Cordelia, marveling once again that he could express himself, frequently, in the earthiest of terms and then again that he could formulate thoughts at this level. She didn't suppose he believed a bit of it. "But surely there are other – maybe cheaper – ways of proving one's affection to the world? If it really needs proving?"

"No doubt. What would you have me do? Come, a public demonstration – speak and I obey." She could see the corners of his mouth beginning to curl, the laugh lines around his eyes.

"No, there's nothing, I – "

"No? So we'll think of something else later. In the meantime, are we agreed? There's no reason not to start with a ring?"

"Um – ," said Cordelia.

"Excellent," said Darek, taking the ring out of his pocket and putting it on her finger before she could do more than take a breath of surprise and objection.

Cordelia looked at the ring on her finger. It was a beautiful ring. He was waiting rather apprehensively. She smiled at him. "Um, thank you."

He gave her one of his quick grins. "I'm glad we're learning to compromise so early on."

"Do you mind where we go to eat?" he asked a while later, as the car took to the traffic again, "I'd like to catch the news, see what they have to say about us today – although I've been keeping tabs and there doesn't seem to be anything new. There's a sort of pub with a TV screen not too far from here. The food's not too bad either. But I don't know – maybe you want something more…with candles and that sort of thing?"

Cordelia assured him she didn't need candles and didn't mind the 'sort of pub.' She glanced at the unaccustomed ring on her finger, sparkling in the light of a street lamp as she raised her hand to her hair, and thought she didn't mind anything, could not have cared less where they ate, so long as she was with him and he was satisfied.

And later, after a meal she didn't notice:

"Will you come up to my apartment?" he said, pulling the car up alongside a parking place. "It's here."

She gave him a startled glance.

"Don't look at me like that, I'm not suggesting – anything except coffee. I want to talk to you about money, and I don't want to do it in a public place."

"Aren't you afraid your apartment might be, er, bugged?" His apartment, she knew, had been searched.

"No, I had it checked by two different outfits this morning. It should be all right. There was a considerable mess last night though. My belongings thrown all over, things pulled out of drawers – it would have been worse

304

if the neighbors hadn't interfered. It took a couple of hours to clean it up."

She walked with him into the building, stood staring at the floor as the elevator went up, stood beside him as he put the key in the lock and pushed open the door for her. His apartment. She had tried to imagine how it would be – and it wasn't far different. It wasn't exactly a minimalist interior, but very orderly and lacking in clutter of any type. It was spacious for a Warsaw apartment, the furniture new but good, and there was a view of the Palace of Culture. It was very different from the old and worn and book-strewn, paper-piled interior of her family's villa. He had told her he hardly spent any time in his apartment and it showed. She wondered suddenly if, in spite of the thickness of his psychological armor, he ever found the place lonely. Even though they had talked to each other a great deal about themselves in the past days, it wasn't a question she felt she could ask him now; she felt her shyness growing again by leaps and bounds.

"So," he said, "let me show you around – you can decide later if you want to live here or if we should look for something else. This, obviously, is the living room, this way…"

She followed slowly after him, not daring much to look around. This was where she would be coming to live. With him. He had said it so casually, so matter-of-factly. It seemed an incredible thought. She was conscious of his every movement, the texture of his clothing, the rise of muscle as he waved an arm.

"The bedroom – again, obviously."

She took a quick glance, a quarter of a glance, and stepped back, made as if to move on.

"How did you get to be so prudish?" he asked, laughing at her as she took a hurried step away.

"I'm not."

"Shall I prove it to you?"

"No!" she looked at him in alarm, but saw that he was joking.

"Bathroom." He waved towards a door, showed her another room or two which she hardly took in, then steered her back towards the living room, and seated her in a leather-upholstered chair at a heavy round wooden table. He went to make coffee, and she sat feeling out of place and wishing she could leave. She was like her brother Antek, she realized suddenly, almost as eccentric and socially inept, and her first reaction to any stress was a desire to run and hide. She was being given a chance for normality – and she would certainly do something to wreck it, she thought with the beginnings of panic.

He reappeared. "Sorry, I'm a bit out of supplies – thanks to your keeping me for the last while. There's nothing for dessert but these biscuits. I think they're all right." He looked at them dubiously as he set them down. "I've got some yellow cake – you know, one of those kind in a foil tray – left from two weeks ago, but it's growing a bit of green mould, so I won't offer it to you – even if it would meet your ideas of thrift."

He looked at her, but she didn't rise to the bait, didn't appear even to hear him but sat staring at the table top. He set the coffee down in front of her. Then she reached for it clumsily and her shaking hand spilled it, so that the cup clattered on the saucer and the coffee splashed onto the table.

"Oh," she exclaimed, distressed, "I'm sorry, how stupid of me."

He stopped smiling, picked up the saucer and retreated with it wordlessly, returned and mopped up the table, left and returned with a fresh coffee. He set it down again and stood beside her.

She didn't know what he was thinking or why he was looking at her like that. She gave him a frightened glance and apologized again.

He pulled the chair beside her away from the table, dropped into it and pulled her own chair around to face him.

"Tell me, Cordelia," he said rather sternly, "why have you started looking at me like that? All last week you never looked at me like that or spoke like that. You gave me angry looks, and compassionate looks, and distrusting looks, but I never saw that you were afraid. Yesterday you were so brave – you stood your ground like a hero. I asked you to do the most outlandish thing and you never gave me one look as full of fear as you've been giving me repeatedly this evening. Why? What have I done? Because of the ring? Was I overbearing?"

"No," she said, embarrassed and not wanting to look at him. "No, it's none of that. Nothing you've done."

"So what's changed?"

She hesitated but he was waiting for an answer. She answered him honestly because she couldn't imagine doing anything else. "Last week," she said finally, in a constricted voice, "I had nothing to lose. Even after I…after I, um," – 'fell madly in love with you,' she thought but didn't say – "started having, um" – she paused to select safer words – "feelings for you, I never truly expected that you might wish to have anything much to do with me after your, um…problem was solved."

She glanced at him, but he was listening with bowed head. "And now," she went on, somewhat emboldened by not having to meet his eye, "I'm every moment afraid that I might do or say something and you will look at me and suddenly see me as I really am…and then it will be all up with me…and…" she trailed off.

He didn't raise his head but grasped her knees between his hands, his fingers along her thighs. She flinched and tried with her good hand to pry his fingers away, but they wouldn't budge, and she gave up.

"How are you really?" he said, and she could hear the slight amusement in his voice, and something also that might have been pity.

"I don't know. I can't judge myself. Presumably repulsive."

He raised his eyebrows. "Why do you say so?"

"My arm, my leg. People are repulsed, I know they are." There had been that man who had said so, just last night – one of his friends whom she had overheard, but she wouldn't tell him that, only the memory stabbed, painfully.

"Tsk, Cordelia, such minor details…And you must have had boyfriends before – they must have told you how beautiful you are?"

"No. I never had a boyfriend before."

He looked up at her then, startled. "What, never?"

She began to tremble, shook her head. "No."

And then when he didn't speak at once, but only stared at her, so that she could feel herself growing red under her gaze, she whispered, looking down at his hands along her legs, "Does it matter?"

"Uh…" he said, and she knew from his being at a loss for words – he who was almost never at a loss – how deeply he was taken aback. But he hadn't removed his hands from her knees, and she was oddly comforted by the fact, even as her eyes sought for her crutch so that she could leave, run away.

But he could read her mind. He straightened, reached for her crutch and placed it along the wall, out of her reach.

He turned back to her, answered her. "I know you've led a very secluded life in the last years, so if you'd told me you'd had a dozen boyfriends, I would have been surprised, but I would have thought it normal. It wouldn't have mattered to me. I assumed that there had been one or two at least, at some time. But now you say there was no one...And I thought I'd already had every bad thought it was possible to have about my compatriots..." He paused. "You've never slept with anyone?"

She shook her head.

"I wouldn't have, anyway," she murmured, "not out of marriage. I don't like the idea." She said so, and it was true, but at the moment she wished, oh, that she'd had lovers by the hundred, if it would have raised her in his view.

"You don't like the idea?" He repeated in a voice in which dismay struggled with amusement.

"No. Not out of marriage."

"*Kurcze*...And within marriage?"

"I – I wouldn't know, would I?

"*Kurcze blade*...No, I guess you wouldn't....So when I kissed you last night – that was a first kiss?"

She nodded, not meeting his eye, her heart pounding.

"I'm sorry if you dislike it," she whispered.

He took a deep breath, pulled her chair sideways and closer, pulled her into his arms, and as her heart beat even faster, said over her head, "I don't dislike it, I'm rather chuffed. But God, Cordelia, you've got a lot of wasted time to make up for." And began to kiss her.

And then, after a time, he had let her go, and had brought paper and a pencil, and had talked to her in a very business-like manner about finance and their future.

Then later still, when her head swam with figures and the effort to remember everything he was saying, he had paused in his explanations.

"It's late," she ventured. She wanted to go home and she thought he might drive her there, but, as she didn't know really, what to expect of him, she didn't like to assume it. "Do you know where I can get a bus from here… or do I need to take a taxi to get home?"

"Don't be silly, I'll take you, of course." He pushed back his chair. "Here, stop struggling with all this," he reached for a paper and put it aside. "I wouldn't have bothered you with it tonight, only – like I said – we can't leave the money sitting there."

"I'm sorry to be so stupid about it all."

"Cordelia, you have no idea. No idea at all."

16

Cordelia looked up from her memories to find herself still in the unknown kitchen. The radio was still droning; the woman appeared to be dozing. A log crackled in the stove. There was frost still clinging to the outside of the window, making lacy patterns in the corners of the lower panes. Through the murky glass, she could see, occasionally, her husband or the homeowner passing in the yard. They seemed to be conferring over various bits of machinery, to be picking things up and putting them down and carting objects back and forth. Perhaps, thought Cordelia a little wildly, they were trying to build a car from scratch.

She wasn't far wrong. After what seemed like a very long interlude, her husband and the man reappeared, bursting into the kitchen in a stream of cold air and misty dampness, slapping their hands together for warmth, exclaiming jovially, and obviously now the best of friends.

Darek turned down the man's offers of a little drink – or two, or three – before they went, and grinned at Cordelia. "You're going to like the vehicle," he said.

"Is there a car?" Cordelia asked, rising with sudden hope.

"Well, let's call it that, for lack of a better word."

Cordelia thanked the woman for her hospitality, received a sleepy nod in reply, and followed her husband out into the cold yard with its manure heap and wind and debris. A *mały* Fiat stood in the lane. It was a tiny car, a car for dwarfs, rusted and crooked and looking as if it had stood for many years in a field. There seemed to be some hay or straw still sticking to the bumper.

"Does it run?" said Cordelia, eyeing it with distrust.

"Well, not yet, but we hope it will. We're going to try to jump start it by pushing, and if it catches I don't want to stop, so you'll have to be inside." He opened the door for her.

There were no seats, but either her husband or the other man had provided two upturned plastic buckets for seating. The floor looked as if it were crumbling in a place or two. Still, she had thought the Jaguar the height of modern luxury and look where it had landed them. She wedged herself into the car's tiny interior and seated herself precariously on a bucket.

And then she was being pushed; the car was hurtling down the track, the man pushing behind and Darek pushing in the open door, the dogs pursuing, still barking, and it was picking up speed, he was jumping in, banging his head, swearing, the car was starting, rumbling and sputtering like a bad-tempered lawnmower with the hiccups. They were off. Darek put his head out the door and yelled his thanks back to the man, then swung the door shut, only it wouldn't quite latch, but rattled there; the entire car rattled, and the buckets beneath them rattled on the floor, and the windows rattled in their frames, but they were moving, ripping down the dirt road at fifteen, twenty miles per hour, on and on past fields and woods.

A van was approaching them from a distance, coming at a dangerously fast clip along the lane.

"Cordelia," said Darek, shouting a little over the engine and the clanking, "duck down and stay down."

Cordelia ducked as well as she was able.

"Stay there," he said, so she stayed.

The van passed by. "Okay, you can come up now."

"What was it?" she shouted back, rising up. "Why did you tell me to do that?"

"I don't know. Just a hunch that van might contain my Jaguar. Maybe not. Probably not. But I'd rather not take chances. Me, I look like any other Pole, no one would recognize me. You're very distinctive, however."

Cordelia looked over her shoulder. "They're gone anyway."

"Yes, don't worry about them. It was probably just a van."

"Going to the farmer where we were?"

"Why not?"

She shrugged. He knew as well as she that the farm had been at the end of the lane and there was no obvious reason why a large delivery-type van would be heading there.

"Did you get the license number?"

"Yes, but it won't do any good. Forget about it, Cordelia."

The small engine kept churning; the lane reached the highway and they swept past a stop sign and onto the pavement without a check and ran on, hugging the shoulder, at perhaps thirty miles an hour.

"We won't make it all the way to Warsaw in this," said Darek after a time, in which they had been passed, very fast, by a number of other cars.

"Good!"

"Hey, I paid 200 zlotys for it – it's a great car!"

"You're the expert," she shouted back.

"Well, it won't make it to Warsaw. I'm really hoping it'll make the nearest gas station."

"What do we do there?"

"I'll try to find someone to see what's with the Jaguar; I'll also try to get a hold of the police. Then, I suggest we abandon this – lovely – machine and try to persuade a truck driver to give us a lift home. What do you think?"

"Fine. Where *is* the nearest gas station?"

"Aren't you enjoying the ride?"

"Enormously, but I have doubts about the safety of this thing."

"Well, it doesn't have lights, so we'd better arrive before dark, other than that – our recent experience notwithstanding, it's the things people do at the wheel that cause accidents."

"Well, it's true, I don't think we're going to be speeding in this."

"No. Although there are other things we could do, if we wanted to, er, enliven our trip. For instance, I was reading recently in a car magazine that traffic patrolmen are reporting an increasing incidence of accidents due to persons attempting to have sex while driving. Seems to be a fad."

Cordelia considered this statement in silence, trying to imagine, from her limited experience, the gymnastics that would be involved.

Darek gave her a provocative glance, "I, however, am a competent multi-tasker. I would not have an accident."

Cordelia considered the dimensions of the car. She knew she was perfectly safe. "Yes, let's," she answered wickedly.

The car wobbled on the road in response to Darek's surprise. Cordelia started to giggle and Darek joined in her laughter, shaking the car so that pretty soon Cordelia cried out, "Stop! Stop laughing, the windows are going to fall out – and this door's coming loose."

And suddenly, Darek wasn't laughing. He had straightened and was looking grimly and silently in the rearview mirror. With a whine and a roar, the car accelerated to twice its speed, a crazy speed that would surely and shortly cause its total disintegration. Cordelia looked at him for a moment in surprise and then glanced behind. She almost screamed. The grill of a large vehicle, a delivery van, appeared to be hovering over their small car, roaring down upon it, wheels and bumper almost touching.

"Wha – ?" started Cordelia, and then bit off the words. It wouldn't help to distract Darek.

She looked back again. Did the driver want to run them off the road? Was it a bad joke? Or road rage? Or did someone want to kill them? Fear and adrenalin coursed through her veins but there was nowhere to run.

The driver of the vehicle blew a long blast on his horn. Cordelia looked back. The driver, a faceless dark form behind the windscreen, was signaling for them to pull over. His bumper was inches from theirs.

"He wants you to pull over," Cordelia shouted.

"*Kurwa mać!*"

The jolt as the van bumper struck the back of the Fiat sent Cordelia flying forward; she cracked her forehead against the windscreen, as Darek fought to keep control of the small vehicle.

The van had backed off but was coming again. Darek hastily signaled that they were pulling over. They were slowing, slowing, with the van behind them. Cordelia sat crumpled against the door and her heart pounded in her chest.

They were coming to a stop along the edge of a frozen lake and marsh, on the gravel edge of an embankment; Cordelia saw nothing beyond; her whole concentration was on the vehicle behind them. Who was it and what would they do? She didn't need any explanation to know that they were in danger; that someone, for some reason, wished to harm them. And there was no place to hide, no escape.

They were almost stopped, the van behind them, they were barely inching forward. "Hang on, Cordelia," said Darek quietly. She caught her breath, sought for a handhold on the dashboard. Behind them the van had stopped, its doors on both sides opened and slammed shut again. Men were approaching. Cordelia couldn't see their faces, they were hidden by the angle of the back windscreen; she had an impression of bodies, coming at a near run from both sides.

And suddenly the Fiat shrieked into motion again; it jerked forward, then turned and plunged down the embankment. Cordelia's stomach dropped as the car dropped, jolting over the gravel; the car tilted and Cordelia's hand was torn from the dashboard as she fell off her bucket in a heap. Something that might have been the report of a gun exploded behind them, once, twice. They were whipping through marsh grass, sliding on ice; canes or willows were slashing at the car windows, at the doors; the car was fighting its way up a frozen bank across a meadow of hummocky grass, dropping down again to career across another expanse of ice and into the tall reeds. And then they were slowing but continuing onwards, slowly, slowly, seeking for a way forward, every rough patch of ground spelling the possible end. Cordelia crouched on the floor and held her breath. The van could not follow, but if the Fiat stalled the men would easily catch up to them on foot, or the car might simply drop through the ice into the water and they would surely be trapped in it and go down too.

How far had they come from the road? She didn't know, she didn't know how long they continued onwards through the swamp, emerging sometimes onto higher ground, and then, blocked by the undergrowth or open water, forced to turn and seek another route, wondering, all the time, whether the ice beneath them would hold. And yet, luck was with them. Had they been moving this way for a quarter-of-an-hour, a half-hour? She didn't know.

The sun, the pale and tired sun of late autumn, was already sinking to its knees as they emerged onto a meadow and bumped in the gathering dusk over the short frosted grass, obviously much cropped by cows at a recent date. On crossing the meadow they found a lane, and in jolting through the smallest of ditches to the lane, the Fiat gave a last cough, and a hiccup, and died.

Darek sat in the car, in the silence, very still. Cordelia made an effort to rise from the floor, to regain the dignity of her bucket seat.

Darek looked at her then as he reached to help her, and swore, swore in a way that she had never heard from him before, so that she realized he was furiously angry, more angry than she had ever seen him even in the days when he was having troubles with the Anti-Corruption Bureau. The fact was unnerving. She looked at him with a sort of dread but all he said was, "You're bleeding."

Cordelia put a hand up to her head. She'd forgotten about the crack on the dashboard. She could feel a lump growing, and a slither of something wet, that showed itself to be blood when she pulled her hand away. She felt very ill, but more, she thought, from fear than from her injury.

"It's all right."

Darek swore again as he put his hand under her chin to turn her head towards him.

"Who are they?" she asked in a shaking voice as he examined her injury.

But a car was coming. Darek let her go, was jumping from the Fiat, stepping into the lane to flag down the vehicle.

The car contained a pleasant young couple. An accident? And *pan*'s wife was injured? Certainly they would give them a lift, no problem at all. To the nearest gas station? Yes, certainly, they were going that way, no, no, not the least of an inconvenience. But it was a ways — 40 kilometers or so.

Cordelia sat beside Darek in the back seat of the car, in the warmth, with his arm around her and a handkerchief pressed to her forehead, and thought that what she really wanted to do was close her eyes and pretend that none of it had happened. Here, in this car, with these nice, normal people, it seemed unreal. But it had happened.

17

Still, as the minutes passed, and nothing untoward occurred, they only drove onwards and Darek chatted with seeming calmness to the couple, putting the accident down to his own inattention at the wheel, making light of it, she began to relax. They would be home in Warsaw tonight. They had had a horrible adventure but it was over. The criminal element that had set upon them had been eluded and would presumably be seen no more. She took a deep breath. Her forehead had stopped bleeding. She crumpled the handkerchief in her hand, hoped that none of the blood had dripped on her new coat, and began to feel more herself.

She began to wonder if they would go first to her family's villa or to Darek's apartment when they reached Warsaw. She had been living so entirely in the present, in the delight of the passing moment during the past weeks that she hadn't thought of it before. Now she had a sudden intense longing to see her father and mother and brother again. She would have to get a grip on herself before they got home. Antek had been pleased for her. She had wanted to show him how happy she was – that it was possible to be happy in this world. It wouldn't do to turn up from her honeymoon with a grim and battered face. Her father hadn't really had time to grow reconciled to her marriage. She remembered how they had told him, that second day of her engagement, well, of their marriage really, the period between the civil ceremony and their church wedding.

That day she had risen late and, feeling refreshed, made her way downstairs, stopping in the salon to speak to her mother, who was there with one of the two women whom Darek had miraculously summoned to act as caretakers. Cordelia didn't know how it had been done; she supposed through his many contacts.

The caretaker was a pleasant middle-aged woman; she looked up as Cordelia came into the room and greeted her mother.

"*Pan* Zaremba is here, *proszę pani.*"

"Here?"

"He's boiling the dog," said Cordelia's mother with a vague smile. She turned to the caretaker, "We had some this morning."

"He's in the kitchen then?"

"Yes, *proszę pani*, he's been waiting for an hour, but he said not to wake you."

An hour! Cordelia gasped and hurried to the kitchen, drawing up short in the doorway. Darek was sitting at the table with a glass of tea, as if he'd always lived there, instead of only for ten days, and Hempseed, somewhat too large to be a lapdog, was perched precariously on his lap, and he was feeding him bread and butter.

"Hi."

She caught her breath as he looked up and smiled at her. Forty-eight hours ago he had still been, essentially, a stranger; she had known his views on many subjects but not what he thought of her. Now she was assured of his interest, knew the feel of his arms around her, his lips on hers. He was familiar and yet – not.

He tossed the last bite onto the floor, where the dog followed it in a flurry of fur and toenails, and rose to greet her.

"Cordelia, I still feel the same."

"What are you…I thought you'd be at your office today?" she asked.

"Mm, I'm going. But you seemed hesitant about telling your father our plans, so I came along to help."

"Ah," she said, pleased, and yet wondering if that were really a good idea. Her father and Darek had never got off on quite the right foot, somehow. The fact that her father owed Darek his life constrained him to politeness but was an additional irritant.

"Help what?" said Cordelia's father, coming into the kitchen at that moment and seating himself at the table. "Good day, Mr. Zaremba. We meet again. I haven't had the opportunity to congratulate you on the, er, fortunate outcome of your tribulations, but all's well that ends well. Cordelia – the intruding female is still in command of my salon. Is this a situation that is likely to prolong itself? She was there yesterday, too."

"Shh. She'll hear you. No, that was the other one. A different woman," said Cordelia, "They both seem very nice though," she added positively, and with a sinking feeling, "Mom likes them, I think."

"They are indistinguishable. Your mother can not distinguish them, I'm sure."

"She can't distinguish me, either, Tato." Cordelia felt that this was not going to go well. Her father obviously in an unusually testy and combative mood.

"We are not talking of you. We are talking of the invasion of my house. When will it return to normal, I ask you?" And then, changing tack abruptly, and swinging round on Zaremba, "Help what?"

Instead of answering, Cordelia and Darek silently pulled out chairs and sat down at the table beside him, while he eyed them with growing distrust and disapproval.

"I'm not going to like this, am I?" he said finally.

Darek said, "The subject is this: You've had Cordelia at your beck and call for a long time now, haven't you?"

This was unanswerable. Cordelia's father opened his mouth and shut it again.

"So it's my turn now," Darek continued, "I want her at mine."

Cordelia glanced at Darek and he gave her half a wink and continued to her father, "But as to helping, as your son-in-law, I naturally desire to make everything as smooth and easy and bob's-your-uncle as possible – "

"'Bob's-your-uncle' – where do you get such words?" Cordelia's father stared at Darek through his glasses and began in a tone that made clear he thought he was fighting a rear-guard action. "And speaking of words, I thought it was clear that you were a son-in-law in name only, a temporary son-in-law – let's not have any talk of son-in-laws."

"No, I intend to marry your daughter again."

"I knew it! A repeat offender!"

"I'm sorry if it offends you, sir, but your daughter seems pleased enough with the idea," said Darek calmly. "We thought a church wedding, about as soon as it can be arranged, maybe in three or four weeks."

Cordelia's father looked at Cordelia.

Cordelia nodded her head vigorously.

"You want to marry him? For real?" he asked her in genuine puzzlement.

Cordelia glanced uncertainly at Darek, embarrassed for his sake, but he seemed unfazed. "Yes."

"But why?" Cordelia's father was not known for tact at the best of times, and now he was too upset to care.

Why? thought Cordelia. Why? Because Darek had all the force and vigor she lacked; because he could walk circles around her mentally and physically; because he filled her with a sense of her own inferiority and exalted her with the feeling that he admired her; because he was responsive and kind and exciting; because instinct told her that if she asked him to do something or told him she wanted something he would leap to satisfy her desires; because she only desired his company and his company left her shaken and thrilled; because she never felt she was living before he came along.

"For his money," she said.

Darek smiled.

Cordelia's father stared at her. "'It's a wise father knows his own child,'" he muttered at last, and Cordelia knew he wasn't referring to her answer at all.

"I think once you get used to the idea you'll see it's a good thing," she added gently, glancing uncertainly again at her husband-to-be. Hopefully she would be able to make him happy.

"We are told," said her father in an indignant mutter, "that marriage is a desperate thing, an evil, a noose – and you go to it like there's no tomorrow. You aren't even going to take the leisure to repent a little first before you hop to it again? Cordelia, think what you're about!"

"I have thought," she said. She had thought of nothing else, every waking minute, and often most of the night, when she should have been asleep, for the past twelve days. She knew there was nothing else as important to her. But her family was important too – Her father was looking old and unwell; it hurt her. She opened her mouth to reassure her father, but he starting speaking first.

"So the intruders will be a permanent feature then?" asked her father. "These 'fat, white women whom nobody loves'?"

"They aren't fat – " retorted Cordelia indignantly.

But Darek interrupted her suavely, submissively, "Would you like me to procure you thinner ones, sir?"

In the stunned silence that followed, while Cordelia's father was still recovering, and Cordelia was wondering frantically how to smooth this over, Darek was able to add, "But I don't mean to take your daughter away from you entirely, you know." He continued: "I'm aware that she'll want to spend a lot of her time here with you and I'll make sure that it's possible." He went on to talk of ways and means and Cordelia listened in surprise and gratitude and the hope that her father would eventually come round.

Antek's greeting of the news, when she told him later that day, had been more positive. He had been pleased for her, perhaps even very pleased. "It might work," he said, "His style will be somewhat cramped, and you'll have to close your eyes at times, but I think you have as much chance of making a go of it as anybody…"

"That's not very encouraging, Antek," she had said, although this was possibly high praise coming from him.

"Why? All I mean is that I suppose he'll push too hard at times and you'll explode, and then he'll have to work you back into a good mood. He's adroit. He'll do it."

This image of her future relations with Darek had seemed too ridiculous even to warrant protest.

Her father had given her away in church, had wished her happiness afterwards with a touching attempt to appear pleased for her. But she had not seen any of her family for two weeks; it would be good to see them again.

And now here they were, pulling up to the gas station. Home was getting closer; they would find a truck driver and beg or buy a ride to Warsaw. They shouldn't have to wait long. The parking lot, dimly lit, was full of large vehicles of a type that usually looked rather hulking and sinister to Cordelia, but today only looked like possible means to their journey's end.

The station was small. The couple dropped them under the canopy covering the gas pumps and departed. Cordelia stood beside Darek on the sidewalk and breathed in diesel fumes and cold air. Now she could ask the questions she had stifled in the car, in the presence of the unknown couple.

"Who do you think they were? Those people in the van," she asked, trying not to let her voice shake at the memory. "And why did they do that? It wasn't about the Jaguar, was it?"

He answered shortly. "No, it wasn't about the Jaguar. I don't know who they were. I don't know any more than you do. But Cordelia – did you hear, when we stopped and then I drove down the embankment – just before they shot at us – that someone shouted in English?"

"No. Did they shoot at us? I wasn't sure. I thought it was maybe just my imagination."

"Yes. There were definitely two shots. Warning shots, I presume, or someone was a really bad marksman. They could hardly have missed the car; they had several seconds I suppose to take aim before we were out of sight. I don't know why they quit – maybe another car came along and they had to stop because of the witnesses...So you didn't hear anyone shouting in English?"

Cordelia shook her head. "Maybe they were just swearing in English. Lots of Poles think it's cool to do that."

"Maybe. I thought I heard someone shout 'stop you...' but, well, never mind, it was probably just some trick of the wind or, as you put it, imagination. Let's go inside. I'm going to call the police. It won't do any good in terms of finding out who or why, but I want these events to go on record."

Cordelia nodded, all the fears that had begun to be lulled springing up again and catching at her throat. She didn't want Darek to think she was hysterical though, so she put her chin up and preceded him with a semblance of calm into the station.

It was one room filled with shelves holding car oil and candy bars and magazines of the kind men read. A couple of drivers were purchasing items at the counter, and two weedy young men minding the cash register looked up in curiosity as Cordelia and Darek entered. Cordelia asked for the restroom. "It's outside, around the back," said the man, staring at the bruise on her forehead.

"He thinks I beat you," Darek whispered to her, his anger softening for a second of amusement.

Cordelia gave him the ghost of a smile, hastily shifted her crutch to take the key the man was holding out to her, and turned away again, catching her crutch awkwardly in the door as she slid through and hurried away. Behind her she could hear Darek asking for the number of the nearest police station.

It was eerie around the back of the station, quite dark, with a number of vans parked along the curb to one side. Any one of them could have been the van that attacked them, thought Cordelia. And then she thought that that was ridiculous: they couldn't all be suspect. But she was very alone here. Anything could happen to her and no one around front would ever know about it. She found the door to the restroom, fitted the key in a greasy lock, and pushed open the door, glad when she found the light and was able to push the door shut again and lock it.

At least it was tolerably clean. There was a good-sized mirror over the wash basin; her reflected image rather startled her. It wasn't the bruise on her forehead that was unfamiliar so much as her clothing. Her new winter coat had been made by a Russian designer with a flair for the romantic; it was made of plush and down and was long and light and draped like an ermine cloak. It had been a present from Darek just before their wedding. Her face, rising out of the broad collar, looked pale and injured but still, somehow, cosseted. She ran water onto a paper towel and sponged the dried blood off her forehead. She'd left her hat in the Fiat, she realized; and all their luggage had stayed behind in the Jaguar. It didn't matter. They were safe.

She brushed out her hair, decided with another glance in the mirror that she'd do, and, with some reluctance, opened the door and stepped out again into the darkness. She didn't like turning her back to lock the door again, but she did it, and then she was hurrying to get around the building. A large semi truck rolled past, loud in the silence, and an unsavory-looking person, with a paunchy stomach and a shaven head came round the corner of the building, but she had reached the light again, was around the front of the station, reaching for the door and once again inside the station, in its warmth and light and enveloping scent of automotive rubber.

Darek wasn't there though. She supposed, without apprehension, that he'd gone to the restroom as well and she hopped to one side of the station to wait, out of the way. When he didn't reappear at once, she looked about and found that there was a low window sill where she could perch. She hoped the attendants wouldn't mind – it was difficult for her to stand for long periods.

She didn't know how long she waited. Beyond the station windows, the cars and trucks came and went, pulling up to the pumps with a flash of headlights, pulling away again, their taillights glowing till they reached the highway and disappeared. Drivers came and went in the station, fat men and thin men, tall and short; rarely women. Cordelia watched them with a sort of apathy, waiting only for Darek.

Her mind was mostly occupied with their present circumstances, and yet it wandered back too. She had waited for Darek before. There had been a day, maybe a week before their marriage, when she had waited for him in a café, waited and waited, for one hour and then two, and he had never shown up. She had become convinced that something terrible must have happened to him. Before she finally left the café she had had time to imagine all the details of his death in a dozen different circumstances. She had been walking blindly along the sidewalk, when Mariusz pulled up in the company car.

"*Pan* Darek asked me to pick you up. He had some important business underway."

So he was all right then. She said a little internal prayer of relief, got in the car and asked to be taken home.

"Well," Mariusz said, embarrassed, "he asked me to bring you to the office. So…"

"That's okay," said Cordelia, although she was fatigued by now and would rather have gone home.

When they reached the office, Mariusz called Darek on his cell phone. "We're here…Yes, she's all right." He glanced uncertainly at her, "she looks pretty upset though."

Cordelia gasped and shook her head at him – he shouldn't have said that – but he was already getting out of the car; Darek was trotting out of the building, sliding into the driver's seat. He didn't speak to her, not even a 'sorry,' but simply jerked down the gear stick and drove the car through the parking lot and pulled it up brusquely on the far side, behind a utility shed, away from other people. Cordelia stared at him.

"So," he said, turning to her, as he switched off the ignition. "Let's have it."

"Have what?" said Cordelia, continuing to stare. "What's wrong?"

"The recriminations," he said rather defensively, "The what-a-no-good-etcetera I am to have left you there. All that. Mariusz said you were angry – so say what you want to say and let's get it over with."

"He didn't say I was angry," said Cordelia, bewildered, "he said I was upset. I was – I thought something had happened to you."

"Happened to me? What could happen to me?"

She explained patiently: "You could get run over crossing the street, or a crane could collapse on you at a building site, or you could fall down a stairway and break your neck, or a cable could break in an elevator shaft or – lots of things."

"*Kurcze*," he said, with mock gravity, "I never realized."

"And I'm so glad you're all right."

He had made a slight move towards her then, shaking his head and half smiling, and she had thrown herself on his neck, her first spontaneous gesture of affection towards him. He was all right.

He had been surprised and pleased but after a moment he had held her away from him and looked at her in puzzlement.

"I should stand you up more often. You really aren't angry?"

She shook her head.

"I had a girlfriend once," he confided, "who used to go ballistic when I wasn't on time. Once in a restaurant – this was the last time – she threw a plate at me when I showed up late for dinner."

"Goodness."

"So – well, I didn't think you'd throw things, but I was expecting a bad time from you too."

"No, I thought something had happened to you. I'm so glad you just forgot me."

"Yes, I admit – I did. But I was busy selling a piece of land I expected to have difficulties with to a couple of Syrian businessmen – those fellows who came to my office a couple of weeks ago – I introduced you to them, I don't know if you remember." He released the emergency clutch. "Come on, let's go get something to eat, and I'll tell you all about it. You'll forgive me when I tell you about the deal I made."

"I'd forgive you anyway."

He put the car in motion. "You're not going to make me grovel?"

"I don't believe you ever grovel."

"No, I never have – but I sense you might be able to make me."

"No!...But I suppose I can deduce from your girlfriend that it might happen often – that you might keep me waiting?"

He tilted his head to the side in a noncommittal manner. "It could happen sometimes."

"Then I guess I'd better always bring a book with me," she said humbly.

"God, Cordelia!" he laughed, "You've actually made me feel guilty."

And yet, surely it had been a long time, she thought, after a while. She didn't have a watch. No doubt it was nothing like so long as it seemed. She counted another ten cars come and go, and still Darek hadn't reappeared.

From her purse she extracted the small cell phone that he had given her, after that day when he'd forgotten her, and put it down beside her on the sill, pressed in his number, then quickly raised it to her ear again. A woman's voice answered, a recorded voice, telling her that 'the subscriber was temporarily out of reach.' She dropped the phone back in her purse. Quite a period of time had passed, she was sure.

She began to grow uneasy. She became aware, too, that the two young men at the counter were giving her odd glances. She hobbled over to them.

"Excuse me, did my husband ask for the key to the restroom?"

The two stared, glanced at one another, shrugged, shook their heads.

"You're sure?" she tried to keep the anxiety out of her voice.

"Sure," said one, "it's right here, see?" He held up a key.

"All right. Thank you." She turned away. Perhaps he was outside, talking on his phone. That must be it. He was probably just around back, or to the side, where she couldn't see him. She struggled with the door and stepped outside. He wasn't anywhere near the front of the station. Here there was only wind and the greenish lights over the pumps and the two parking lots to either side, empty now. She went on around to the back of the building. One man was getting into a passenger car, buckling his seat belt; another was standing smoking beside a truck. There was no sign of Darek. Stifling her rising panic, she circled the station and went back inside.

"Please," she said to the attendants, "do you know if my husband called the police? I heard him asking you for the number."

"Yes, he asked us for the number and we gave it to him. But we told him the police wouldn't come out here – not unless it was an emergency – and maybe not even then. They have to come all the way from town, it's half an hour and they have limited gas allowances, you know. We told him it wouldn't do any good. If you have something to tell the police you have to go to the station."

"But do you know if he called?" Cordelia asked anxiously.

The two shook their heads, shrugged. "He went outside. We don't know if he called."

"He's not there," she said, her voice beginning to shake. "Please – when did you last see him?"

But they shook their heads again, spread their hands, they hadn't been paying attention.

She went out of the station, around to the back, swinging briskly on her crutch. The man was still smoking beside the truck, but only just. He dropped the butt on the pavement and ground it out with his heel, turned towards his truck. She hailed him.

"*Proszę pana!*"

He turned.

"Please, did you see – did you by any chance see a man, my husband, he was wearing a tan coat…"

The truck driver nodded. "A strongly-built man?" He gestured to show a breadth of shoulders. "About your age – or maybe a little older" he added with belated tactfulness, "and not from around here. He was with some other men."

"A man, yes, in a tan coat. I don't know about the other men. Maybe he was talking to someone."

"Yes. There was such a man. He was with some other men. Three or four of them. They were showing him something, it looked like. I don't know where they went though. I got into the cab to look for my cigarettes, and when I got out again they were all gone. What, has your husband disappeared?" He laughed a little, as if making an absurd suggestion.

She nodded, willing down the panic.

"Where's your car?" he asked.

"We didn't come in one, we got a ride here."

The man looked at her in sudden sympathy, but no particular concern. Cordelia saw his eyes rest on her forehead, slide downwards. A quarrel, she could see him thinking: first the man batters his wife then he walks out on her. "Was he drinking? Maybe he's laid himself down in the grass somewhere."

"He wasn't drinking," she whispered. "I'm afraid he's been kidnapped."

"Kidnapped! *Proszę pani*, what an idea! I was right here!" He shook his head emphatically, "If anything like that had happened, I would have noticed. Being on the road, you know, you have to be aware of what's going on around. Anything odd and I would have sensed it. Like I noticed there was something strange about your husband – not a man from these parts – that was obvious at once – and the other men weren't either. But there wasn't any foul play, that's certain. There would have been sounds, you know – of a scuffle, of, of, well, you know, sounds…He wasn't kidnapped, *prosze pani.*"

"Then where could he have gone?" she spoke more to herself than to the truck-driver, but he answered her with a shrug and a half-laugh and a shake of the head.

"*Prosze pani,* it looks like he's left you here. Not nice of him, I must say. I wouldn't treat a lady like that – even if she was my wife."

Inside her purse, her cell phone was ringing.

"There," said the man, looking relieved for her, "that'll be your husband. Didn't I tell you?" He turned away and walked towards the station.

Cordelia dropped her crutch, hastily pulled out the phone, held it up to her ear, but no one was there. A text message from Darek. Her eyes were blurred by the wind; it took a second of concentrating before she could make out the letters. She read:

"*I can't take it anymore. It's been lousy and you know it was never meant to last. I would have chosen some other moment, but that's how things worked out. Don't wait for me and don't look for me because you won't find me. Don't go to the cops or anyone else. I repeat, don't go to the cops. It'll just make matters worse for us both. I'm outta here.*"

She stared at the words. However long she stared they said the same thing. She lifted her eyes, looked back. The message was still there. She held it in her hand and it stayed there. She felt nothing, not anything, not belief, or disbelief, or anger, or fear, or loss. She was like a person who has sustained a terrible injury and for some moments fails to feel the pain. She stood as if paralyzed, while her limbs slowly turned to ice, and the cold began to seep upwards and inwards, into the pit of her stomach.

18

Last night at the hotel, she thought, memories swirling haphazardly through her mind, and this morning too, and now this? It couldn't be true. She looked around as if Darek would surely appear from behind the corner of the building, would walk toward her. But he didn't come, he wasn't there. She had been abandoned.

A large vehicle swung in a turn that narrowly missed the sidewalk where she was standing, lifting her hair with its passing and buffeting her with cold. She didn't notice.

Finally she became aware that someone was speaking to her. It was the truck-driver.

"Lady? Do you want a lift somewhere? They're about to close the station."

And when she didn't answer, but just stared blankly at him. "Come on, I'll give you a lift. You can't stay here – they're going to close the station," he repeated with kindness, "you'll freeze to death here."

"My husband…"

"He's not here. You better come with me."

Cordelia nodded at him numbly. No, there was no point in staying. She followed the truck driver to his truck.

The cab was very high. She couldn't possibly climb up there alone. Darek would have simply lifted her up. Darek was gone.

"I can't climb up there," she said flatly to the truck driver. "I'll stay here." She half turned away on her crutch. All she wanted was to find someplace to lie down and die.

"Lady, you can't stay here," he answered patiently still, but with the beginning of exasperation, "look. The parking lot's empty. There's no one around. Come on, I want to get going. Your husband isn't here – he's left and gone off someplace."

No, thought Cordelia, he wouldn't have left me here, I don't believe it. And then, the half-conscious thought came that if she lay down and died, she would never know the truth. She turned to the step of the cab, handed her crutch to the truck driver, and with a superhuman effort, a great deal of bruising flailing, and an ignominious boost from her helper, managed to scale the height.

The truck pulled out of the station and onto the highway. "Where are you going?" asked the driver, guessing the next large town along the way.

"Warsaw," said Cordelia.

"Warsaw!" he answered, "that's a ways a way. Well, we've got a night of it ahead then – I'm going to Warsaw myself. Delivering washing machines – from the Czech Republic."

Cordelia leaned her head against the glass of the window. She had scraped her arm badly in making the climb and wrenched her leg as well. She didn't notice the pain; she didn't feel anything really, except a vast emptiness, an emptiness so large it was crushing her and soon there would be nothing left.

The truck driver was making small talk but she wasn't listening. He gave up on her and took out a cigarette and began to smoke.

The kilometers passed one after another, dark fields and woods falling away beyond the window, and Cordelia didn't move. It wasn't until the truck braked sharply to avoid hitting a passing car that cut too briskly in front of it that Cordelia roused herself. She pulled her cell phone out of her purse and looked at it again.

Darek couldn't have written that. Maybe he had been kidnapped and the kidnappers had written it on his cell phone. She was grasping at straws. But kidnappers wouldn't have written in English. Although Darek had said – he'd said he thought he heard the men from the van swearing in English. She closed her eyes and leaned her head against the window again. And she'd said that lots of Poles swore in English, and he'd agreed that that was true. And they wouldn't write idiomatic English like this, even if they knew some words or could speak the language fairly well. There wasn't a grammatical error in it, however improper the style for the moment. 'I'm outta here' – any Pole might come across that on television or the internet, but none of the criminal class was likely to come up with 'would not have chosen.' She stared at the words. 'I'm outta here.'

She had never heard Darek use that expression. It didn't sound like him. Neither did 'cops.' He said 'police.' Or did he? But after all, how well did she know him? She had known him two months. And yet, his manner of speaking was one of the things she enjoyed about him. His speech patterns were a mixture of the lapidary quality of the Polish street and a vocabulary garnered from extensive reading on a range of serious subjects. He was a very clever man and he expressed himself with great

338

clarity at all times. This message sounded like...like what? Not like him somehow. And yet he must have sent it....'Lousy' – Darek said 'lousy': he had said her father was a lousy driver and she was a lousy liar, and that many other things were lousy. But he wouldn't have said it of his time with her, even if he had thought it. He wasn't that cruel. He wasn't cruel at all. He could only have said it because he wanted her to be convinced. But why? Why?

Because he really wanted to be free of her. She caught her breath. Was it possible? After all his kindness, gentleness, his show of infinite tenderness? Impossible.

And yet he was gone. And the message was here. So none of it had been real? Had been only for some purpose of his own? Could he have faked it all? No. She thought of this moment and that moment – he had been sincere, she hadn't doubted him, he had meant it. Hadn't he? He loved her. Didn't he? But he had left her – like this. Pain washed over her in a wave.

Unless he had been kidnapped and the kidnappers made him write that message. But why would they do that? Wouldn't they write, if they were kidnapping him for money, 'bring the ransom money to such a place?' and if they were kidnapping him to kill him – her throat constricted even further at the thought – then surely they would just have him write, if they let him write anything at all, 'don't go to the police or my life will be in danger...' and not something about leaving her? It didn't make sense.

She turned to the truck driver. "*Proszę pana*, could you tell me, please, about the men you saw my husband with? What did they look like?"

The truck driver thought a moment, hesitated, shook his head. "It was the fellow in the tan coat – your husband – I noticed, not the others particularly."

339

Yes, thought Cordelia, Darek always thought he looked like everyone else, but he stood out, people noticed him without knowing why, there was a sort of magnetism about him.

The truck driver was continuing "They were all about the same age, I guess, thirties, probably. If they had been in uniforms I might have thought they were police, I don't know why, just an impression – maybe they weren't Poles, maybe Germans, maybe that's why. I think they were wearing dark coats, nothing special." He shrugged. "Why?"

"You're sure you don't remember where they went? What sort of a car they got into?"

"No, like I said, I didn't see."

"And you're sure he was walking with them?"

"Yes, I saw them walking together across the parking lot, like I said. They were talking. Then I went for the cigarettes, and when I got out of the cab again and looked around, they were all gone. He probably hitched a ride somewhere, like you're doing." He continued, trying to cheer her, "You'll find when you get home that he's there waiting. He'll have cooled off and he'll be very sorry and you can give him the cold shoulder for a while – make him suffer a bit, the bastard – begging your pardon, ma'am – and then in a few days you can make up and everything will be lovey-dovey again, you'll see. I know how it is in marriage. I was married twenty-five years. My wife's dead now, been dead five years, but when I get to heaven she'll be there waiting, I know."

He stubbed out his cigarette suddenly. "Better take care of myself," he muttered musingly.

Cordelia didn't respond. He tried again.

"You've been married long?"

"Two weeks."

The truck driver jerked his head around to look at her then shook his head. "*Kurcze*, some honeymoon."

It had been the perfect honeymoon – she wouldn't have changed any part of it. She had been blissfully happy. And it had all been unreal? Something inside of herself, something of utmost importance, began to writhe and shrivel.

The dark miles followed each other, the headlights on the road, the crosses marking road accidents, caught by the headlights between the trees and then slipping past, until eventually they were approaching Warsaw, there were more lights, more houses, endless fences, endless suburban houses, city streets. Soon she would have to face her family.

"Where shall I put you down?" asked the truck driver.

Cordelia came to, looked about. "Where is this?" She didn't know where they were in Warsaw, didn't recognize anything, wasn't fit to recognize anything. "It doesn't matter," she said. "Here is fine. You can let me out here." She struggled to say something appropriate. "You've been more than kind," she added.

The truck driver regarded her with patient irritation, shook his head. "Where do you live, lady?"

She thought and eventually remembered her home address.

The truck continued on through the city, to the outskirts, turned down a tree-lined street, and pulled up before her family's dilapidated white villa.

"This it?" The truck driver craned his neck.

This was it. Now it was really time to make an effort and thank him properly. Cordelia made an effort. There was only, now, the problem of getting down from the cab. The truck driver climbed up and opened the door for her. She had to make it down the ladder. She looked down at the ground. She supposed she'd fall all the way and she didn't care. She hoped she'd be knocked unconscious and swung herself out of the cab. The truck driver caught her with a curse at the bottom and deposited her on the sidewalk. He had really behaved beyond the call of duty. Cordelia thanked him again, standing on the sidewalk, and with relief, he got in his truck and roared away.

Behind her the house was dark. It must be the middle of the night and they would all be asleep. Suddenly she wished she'd gone to Darek's apartment. Anything rather than to have to meet her family, have to tell them. Perhaps she could get a taxi and go there now. And then she remembered – she had no right, no claims to that apartment anymore, she didn't belong there, Darek had left her.

She put her hand on the gate handle. Darek had left her. She leaned her head against the gate's iron bars. He couldn't have. He had. She began to sob, painfully, so that her whole body was wracked.

Inside the house, Hempseed began to bark. A light sprang on. Someone was looking out a window, but she didn't notice. She couldn't go in, couldn't move.

It was Antek who came out of the house and along the path in his shabby dressing gown and bare feet on the ice. He peered towards her. "Cordelia?" his voice was full of amazement.

He opened the gate. She didn't move, but made an effort to stop sobbing, to catch her breath. He was staring at her. His deep and silent concern and his inability to respond were almost more than she could bear, she began to cry again.

"You'd better come in," he said at last. And then, as if he didn't want to know, but had to, "was there an accident?"

She shook her head and then nodded, and he forbore to ask more questions, but only tugged her towards the house.

He opened the door, pulled her by the sleeve inside, and she was greeted with wild effusion by Hempseed, who leapt about, clawing at her and wagging his tail madly. She paid no attention, and he shortly subsided, ears cocked and a puzzled expression on his face.

Cordelia's father appeared, coming heavily down the stairs in a dressing gown as well. "I thought I heard someone..." he began to Antek. Then he caught sight of Cordelia and stopped. He took in her battered appearance, her stained and tearful face, in amazement and utter silence.

Cordelia made an effort to pull herself together.

"I've come home," she said unnecessarily.

Cordelia's father had regained his breath, and he began on a rapidly rising tide of anger: "I knew it! *Boże kochany!* He hit you? *Boże, Boże!* He couldn't even wait for the honeymoon to be over! May he be damned from here to Eternity, damned like an ill-roasted egg, damned in boiling oil, damned..."

"Yes. Stop," said Cordelia, gulping. "I get the picture."

"May he rot in hell, may he rot from hour to hour! may he..."

"But I don't want him to rot!" Cordelia quavered.

"Well, where is the damned rotter anyway?"

"I don't know," she answered, and then, as she gave way to tears again, he became helpless and agitated: "Well, well! – Antek, do something for your sister! Warm

343

milk or hot water or something! What happened? *Boże kochany!* Why doesn't anyone tell me anything? I knew it! I knew how it would be!..."

"No, please," Cordelia broke away from them. "I just want to go to bed, please. I'll tell you about it in the morning. I can't talk now." Followed by a torrent of words denouncing Darek, she heaved her way up the stairs to the first floor and into her bedroom.

She closed the door and carefully hung up her coat. The coat from Darek. She hung it in the closet beside her long white wedding dress. She sat down on the bed and took out the cell phone again. The cell phone from Darek.

"I can't go on with this," the screen still said. Darek, of all the people she had ever met, had extremely clear ideas about what he wanted in life and how to get it. He wouldn't get involved in a situation, and then decide, suddenly, that it wasn't for him. He hadn't been struck by a sudden indecisiveness about the future on the road home and skipped out on an impulse. That was completely unlike him. He must have planned to leave her from the beginning.

And the ring? She felt it on her finger. He must have had his reasons for making their marriage appear real. Who knew what they were? He didn't tell her everything. He never had. And yet they had talked so much.

She rolled over on the bed, her hand twisting in her hair. The memories wouldn't go away. There had been that time, a week or so before their church wedding. She remembered it as if it were yesterday, a sweet memory and now...

He had been driving her home, after an evening in which they had talked and talked, and in the car they were still talking. Until at last there was a pause and she leaned back against her seat, as the car bore her smoothly through Warsaw, and said idly and dreamily, "We talk so much that by the time we're married there won't be any topics left. I wonder what we'll do?"

"We'll make love," Darek answered.

There had been a slight pause, then, "okay," she had said, with a pretense of calm and a slight smile, looking out over the dashboard.

Darek had pulled the car over to the curb abruptly and leaned against the steering wheel. "Look at me, Cordelia."

With a tremendous effort, she had raised her eyes to his and kept them there, in spite of the extreme tendency of the lids to sink and protect her from his gaze. She had smiled and looked into his eyes for almost five seconds. Then she had looked down and caught her breath.

"Oh, bravely done," he had whispered.

She didn't answer.

He had reached out for a strand of her hair, played with it gently. "It will be all right, Cordelia."

"Okay."

He had leaned closer, said softly, reassuringly, "Cordelia, we won't – run out of conversation."

She had laughed – he had meant her to laugh.

Only it had been no more than skin-deep, all that kindness? And yet she had always felt it was too good to be true. Darek had thought she didn't trust him – she hadn't trusted herself. She hadn't believed she had any quality that could interest him, couldn't ever quite believe that he could love her. Men of his sort, she thought, married achievers like themselves or trophy wives. She wasn't either. She hadn't scaled the lowest rungs on any ladder of achievement: she hadn't been made a partner in anyone's law firm, or even an employee, hadn't won a Pulitzer prize, or any prize, hadn't organized a relief effort, or even the household very well, had no social graces, no career, no income of note. She had a twisted arm and a twisted leg and needed to rest all the time. He had said he loved her.

She began to cry again, she couldn't seem to stop. Hempseed jumped onto the bed beside her and lay still, his muzzle drooping on his paws. The door opened and her mother came in, looking as disoriented as usual but as if she realized something was needed.

She sat down on the edge of the bed.

"Mom," said Cordelia, lifting herself up, trying to control herself, to speak normally.

"Maria?" said her mother.

Cordelia went back to crying. Her mother began to look alarmed, and then frightened. She began to sniff and soon she was crying too, loudly. Hempseed began to howl. After a time Cordelia's mother stopped crying and began to sing, something that might once have been operatic and funereal but now was merely wailing.

Cordelia clasped her hand over ear. She had returned to the madhouse. She had almost escaped and now she was back. She stifled a desire to shriek.

She woke in the early morning, in the wintry dark, and felt first the icy coldness of the room biting at her from beyond the covers and then the icy coldness of her heart. She reached out her hand for the cell phone, turned it on. There were no new messages. Only the old one. She lay still; there was no point in getting up, no point in living. And yet, as the darkness turned to a watery grey light on the bare branches beyond her window, she realized that she was not going to die, and that she would have to carry on. She could hear her mother moving about. Someone should attend her. She wondered what had happened to the caretaker, the woman hadn't been in evidence during the night.

And some time later, in the salon that had become much more cluttered in her absence, she explained her circumstances to her father and her brother.

"So let me get this straight," said her father, "You were chased and struck by a large van and then Darek left you. What do you call that!?"

"I'm truck-struck and he's a weasel," she said, with a sound between a giggle and a sob, as she stared out the window.

"Yes," said Antek impatiently, "if it's as it seems, but —"

"You're making jokes?" cried her father indignantly.

Cordelia shrugged.

Antek opened his mouth to speak, obviously thought better of it, and retreated on faint footsteps toward his room, and her father asked her if Darek had also received a blow to the head?

"No."

"He just went bonkers on his own?"

She shrugged again. "Maybe he was bonkers before, when he asked me to marry him. Maybe he just returned to his senses. I don't know what to think." She hoped vaguely that he would contradict her.

"*I* know *exactly* what to think," her father muttered angrily, polishing and polishing his glasses. "And I knew what to think then — I thought you were both touched in the upper story, and I told you so at the time. You're totally different sorts."

"I guess so," said Cordelia.

"You were besotted. I never saw anyone so besotted," said her comforter.

"Yes, that's the word, I suppose,'" she agreed in a monotone.

"What? You agree with me? Don't start agreeing with me, Cordelia, it's completely unnatural in a daughter."

"Anyway," said Cordelia wearily, "you said marriage was a noose – I guess I've escaped."

"Yes," said her father, changing position, "but when you were so clearly meant for the gallows, I don't like to see you turned away."

She raised her hands in a gesture of helplessness.

Boże, boże, he muttered, shaking his head. Then he shrugged hopelessly at the inexplicability of the world; all this was beyond his comprehension and better just to ignore. He sighed heavily several times and said – since it appeared she was home to stay – that perhaps she could locate his notes on Kamińska – they were somewhere about.

She rose mechanically to do his bidding. "Why is it so cold in here?" she asked, shifting a pile of papers. "Mom will be cold."

"It's called winter, Cordelia. You've been away too long, you've grown soft."

She began to sort the papers. Had she really forgotten, in just two weeks, what it was like in that drafty villa? Darek had admired the house but none of what he'd said about its condition had been complimentary. He had said they would renovate in the spring. Why, if he'd been intending to leave? She didn't care now, if she froze to death. But she had responsibilities; her mother was shivering in spite of the blanket around her shoulders.

She rose and went to the fireplace, began to stack kindling carefully, with fingers that trembled with cold or nerves. Her father came to help her and began to toss in wood and papers at random.

Cordelia knelt on the ground and watched his ineffectual fire-making efforts without a word. Her head ached, but she didn't know if it was from crying all night or from the bump in the car. She roused herself.

"Tato – isn't that your paper?"

"What?"

"That paper you just threw in – aren't those…" She reached and snatched out a paper just before the flames took it. She handed it to her father. "Your notes on Kamińska."

He took the paper, put on his glasses to read it – "ah, ah, yes, thank you." His usual cheerfulness began to return. "You know – it's good to have you back, Cordelia."

Cordelia didn't hear him. She stared into the dwindling fire, not caring if it went out or not. She wanted to go off someplace and be quite alone. But she couldn't, she remembered, because of her mother. "And the women who were looking after Mom? What's become of them?"

Maybe they wouldn't come when it was so cold in the house.

Her father looked up from his reading, "The one who's supposed to come today called and said that neither she nor the other woman had been paid. Don't look at me! That wasn't my affair. They were supposed to get paid yesterday and it didn't turn up in their accounts – they wanted me to straighten it out, but how could I? I said to wait until you got back."

But that was bad – if they hadn't been paid she would have to go to the bank and set that right. Probably some employee had made a mistake. Of course though, she would have to tell the women that she couldn't afford to continue their employment. She would also have to get in touch with the translation agencies she had worked for before and tell them that she was available again. She made an effort to hitch her mind back onto the routine of her former life. She couldn't do it.

Darek had asked, that time she had gone to his apartment and they had talked about money, if she wanted to continue working. And she had said that she had to work – she had to contribute to the family's support.

"Yes," he had said, "but do you like to work? Does it give you pleasure?"

"No," she had said frankly, "I hate it."

"You hate it? You feel that badly about translating? Then why do you do it?"

She had shrugged, "It's the only thing I know how to do. One has to work."

"You don't. Let me take care of the bills. We can find more interesting things for you to do."

She hadn't thought anything was more interesting than Darek.

Now she should be glad she had an occupation she could return to. She didn't feel in the least bit glad though, only unutterably empty.

Her father was leaving the room; he looked at her and shook his head. "'Wise women/Have erred and by men been deceived' – Milton, slightly rephrased," he murmured for her benefit. "Yours isn't an unusual case."

But she wasn't listening. Amongst the papers her father had been about to throw on the fire was a stack of letters; most were opened, but one, still sealed, caught her eye as it lay on the carpet. It had her name on it and an Australian postmark. She picked it up. From Darek's mother. Darek's mother hadn't come to the wedding; only her family and a few other people had been there, the ceremony had been very private. She had wanted it that way – Darek had proposed a large wedding but had submitted with good grace to her suggestion that she'd had all the publicity she wanted at the town hall. Why had he wanted a large wedding if he'd intended to leave her? Why had they made those plans about going to visit his mother in the spring? And all those other plans? Because talking was easy for him, she supposed.

She opened the letter and read. It was the letter of an uneducated woman, a woman struggling with writing, but a warm letter, a welcoming letter, in which she read, with slight wonderment, overtones of Darek's own turns of phrase. Darek, said his mother, had spoken so highly of her and was clearly so much in love with her that she had no fears for his future happiness. She was eager to meet her new daughter-in-law and looking forward to their visit in March. Cordelia folded up the letter again. It seemed cruelly inappropriate to the day. But from everything Darek had ever said, she believed he was very attached to his mother. Surely he wouldn't have told *her* these things unless he meant them? Where would be the point? But maybe she, Cordelia, didn't know or understand anything about him?

Or what had happened?

She looked at the cell phone that she was carrying about with her, but nothing had changed. She read the message again, and then stared unseeing at the frosted panes of the windows. Time passed, and she didn't know how much later it was that she became aware that Antek was standing beside her.

"He wouldn't have left you," Antek said hesitantly but with conviction. "Something happened to him. He loved you, Cordelia."

Cordelia swallowed the lump in her throat, blindly handed him the cell phone so that he could read the message.

"It's in English, Antek. He must have written it. Who else would write it and why?"

Antek took the phone and read. Silently he handed the phone back. Silently he turned away and sat down in a chair. He had a camera in his hands and he began to click the shutter, loading and releasing it, loading and releasing.

The noise jangled her nerves; she wanted to scream at him to stop.

She looked at him, and he looked back. "I still don't believe it," he said, and went on clicking the camera.

Somehow the day passed. Cordelia clutched her cell phone in her hand, but it never rang. Darek's number was always blocked.

She would grow old in that house, she supposed; every day would pass like the one before it; as it had for ten years. And in her old age? She used to worry about growing older, she had particular reasons for it.

She had told Darek so, on the first day of their engagement, in the pub before they ate dinner.

She had waited only for the waitress to depart after handing them the menus. She had taken a deep breath. "There's something I think you should know," she said, "I should have told you before you bought the ring."

He looked up from the menu, with eyebrows raised.

"It's about my disability," she began and stopped.

"Go on."

"It may come back – the polio, I mean – when I'm older – in my fifties, maybe, or later. I may become even more crippled than I am. I may become a total invalid." She gazed across the room, not wanting to see his expression.

"Yes, I know." He returned to his menu.

She looked at him sharply. "You know? How do you know?"

"I checked it out, of course. Days ago." He made a wry face, "I always investigate my acquisitions thoroughly. What do you want to eat?"

She didn't reply but watched him while he read the menu calmly. "Doesn't it bother you?" she asked finally.

"Of course it bothers me. I hate to think you may have that ahead of you."

"I could be a terrible burden to you."

"Yes. Or a number of other things could happen," he said with a smile, "*I* could become a terrible burden to *you*."

"No!"

"Thank you – you're sweet, Cordelia. But listen: it may not happen, or there may be treatments by then, or, if it does happen, than you'll be better off with money to make life easier. Don't worry so much."

He had promised to take care of her all her life and he had left her by the side of the road after two weeks.

I am free, thought Cordelia suddenly. I have no more fears for the future. I have no more hopes. I do not care what happens to me when I am old; I do not care if I live or die. I am free because nothing can touch me any more. The thought should have brought comfort, but did not.

The telephone rang. The stationary telephone. Cordelia leapt for it, heart pounding. It was a woman's voice, and it took Cordelia a moment to make sense of the words. It was one of the caretakers, explaining about the bank, and her father, and not coming. Wearily, Cordelia found herself promising to go to the bank and straighten the matter out. Yes, she would do it that day, she assured the woman. She would leave soon, she was leaving now. She hung up the phone. How odd that life went on.

There were few people about in the bank. Two or three other customers were standing in line for the counter when she entered. She crossed the marble foyer to a desk, asked to speak to someone about the account, and soon found that the manager had appeared and she was being ushered into a small office.

There had been an error, said the manager, in some confusion. Someone – not himself, certainly – had thought that the funds might be frozen.

"Why would they be frozen?" asked Cordelia in surprise.

The manager shuffled papers on his desk. It had been an error, he said, they were very sorry to have caused any inconvenience. *Pan* Zaremba had been banking with them for a long time and they were very pleased to have his custom.

Yes, thought Cordelia, the man had been all affability and helpfulness when she had come here before with Darek.

"But I don't understand. Please explain this to me. Why would our account be frozen?"

"I'm sorry. It was someone – I don't want to say who, one of our employees – who made assumptions, overstepped her duties. It would appear that there were journalists here, asking questions yesterday. About that very large sum that came to your husband, two weeks ago – from some foreigners, right? You know about that?" He suddenly looked uncertain whether he should be discussing it with her. "It was really improper and we apologize; the transfers will be made."

"What questions were they asking?"

The manager didn't answer, pretended not to hear. "And how is your husband? Well, I hope? Good, good." He was standing up. She was expected to leave. She stood, but tried again.

"What were the journalists asking about?"

"I'm sorry. I really couldn't say. I wasn't here then, anyway. It was my lunch break," He confided this last with relief, so that she supposed it was true.

"But you heard your employees talking?" she prompted.

"I'm sorry, *pani*, I really can't talk about it."

Darek, she knew, would have persevered and would have winkled out what he wanted to know. She had no such abilities or habits; she gave the man a dubious glance and allowed herself to be shepherded to the door.

And soon again she was standing, in a confused reverie, outside the bank. What could he have meant? She had to get home and search the news. Her head hurt more than ever.

She sat at the bus stop. The wind bit at her and the other passengers gave her repeated glances – her coat, her crutch, her bruise, her beauty. She noticed none of it. Could it be that the government was pursuing Darek after all? When they had thought that everything was going to be all right? Had he known and decided to run, to escape abroad? But that was so unlike him – he hadn't run two months before. The truck driver had said – she remembered his words now – that the men Darek had been talking to had looked like policemen, had given him that impression anyway. She hadn't paid attention. Maybe they were policemen. But no, that didn't make sense either. If they were from the police, and Darek had been arrested, he wouldn't have written those words. He would have sent a message saying 'contact lawyers.'

She had paid the caretakers out of her own savings, in the end. She didn't want to touch his money. But she had never had a great amount. If he needed a lawyer how would she pay for it? Well, for that, of course, she could use his money. But no, again, she was grasping at straws, she was forgetting. He couldn't have been arrested.

She got on the bus and rode through town and got off again, hardly noticing her surroundings. She limped along the street to her house, head down, looking at the pavement and leaning heavily on her crutch.

They were upon her, like hounds on a rabbit, before she realized they were there. Cameras flashed right and left and she jerked her head up. She was surrounded. More cameras flashed. Someone was filming she saw. There was a film van, like the one that had come to the town hall that day. A journalist was holding a microphone out; she was surrounded by journalists. The gate to the house was still a hundred feet away.

"*Proszę pani*, welcome back from your honeymoon."

"Er, thank you," she began to say, but was cut off.

"Do you have any comment to make about the recording?"

What recording? thought Cordelia, what are they talking about? She didn't answer.

"*Proszę pani*, could you tell us where your husband is?"

"There are rumors that your husband has left the country, is this true?"

She tried to walk on but they were blocking the sidewalk. They were all talking at once; she couldn't have answered them if she'd wanted to. They came to the same realization: "In turn, then," said one of the journalists to his colleagues.

"Now then, could you tell us where your husband is?"

"No."

"No, you can't tell us or no, you won't tell us?"

"If you have questions for my husband you must speak to him directly." She spoke politely but firmly.

"Where is your husband?"

They were crowding her.

"I'm sorry. I am not a public information booth." She didn't know where the crisp words came from. The journalists backed off a little. "Please stop harassing me."

"I see you've been injured – how did that happen?" someone was persisting.

"An accident. I am liable to accidents. Perhaps you would allow me to proceed, before another happens."

At that they cleared the path for her and she hobbled on, as fast as she could, to the gate, pursued by cameras, and made it through the gate and almost slammed it on one pursuer as he tried to slip through with her, and turned to run towards the house.

Someone called after her, "*Proszę pani*, have you seen the recording on YouTube?"

She stopped, turned around. In spite of herself, she couldn't help asking: "What recording?"

"The one that was placed on the internet three days ago. We were informed of it this morning. A recording of your husband discussing the sale of yellow cake."

"My husband sells land not cakes," she answered slowly, staring, and realizing, even as she spoke, even as she saw the reaction in the faces of the journalists, that there was something here she didn't understand and something too, that rang a faint chord of memory.

"Your husband..." someone began.

"You've met the Muslims involved, I believe," said another. "The secretary at the Zaremba Development office said..."

"If you have any questions, you must ask my husband," she said firmly and turned away.

"Yes, but where is your husband?" someone called after her, but she did not turn again.

She closed the door to the house and leaned against it.

"Darek!" she wanted to cry, Darek, what is it all about?

19

The first thing to do was to search for a recording on YouTube. She stumbled up the stairs into her bedroom and sat down at her desk without even taking off her coat. The laptop had a fine layer of dust on it and took a long time to boot up; she waited impatiently: YouTube, Dariusz Zaremba. And there it was. '*Filmiki* - Dariusz Zaremba talks business with terrorists.' Darek talking with terrorists! Impossible. The fine hairs rose on the back of her neck. She clicked on the title; a picture appeared on the screen – Darek, a video taken from a distance, probably in front of the building where he had his office, in the company of two rather dark-skinned men. They were walking, stopping for a moment to confer, and there was his voice, unmistakably his voice, in an incomplete and one-sided conversation as if he were talking to someone and only his words had been recorded, with pauses while his interlocutor spoke. From the fact that he was speaking English it could be inferred that he was speaking to the foreigners in the video.

"*Let me show you...I don't have anything else, I'm afraid...I've got some yellow cake...I would offer it to you.*" A long pause, and then: "*Such minor details*" – the voice was dismissive, almost irritated –"*It would meet your ideas...You can decide later if we should look for something else...If you want to prove it like a hero...To the ground...If you want them...full of fear...*" – this was said with particular emphasis – "*You hate it...I'd already had every bad thought it was possible to have about my compatriots...Yes...overbearing...Yes...because of the ring*" – a slight questioning here, and then decisively – "*Come, I wanted to talk to you about money.*" And then, a number of large figures and the names of banks, given after pauses.

Cordelia leaned back in her chair. If she had felt cold before it was nothing compared to the chills that now ran down her spine. Not that she believed it. She didn't believe it for a moment. She might have doubted Darek's love – that had to do with her estimation of her proper worth – but she had an absolute conviction that, however he might sometimes lack patience with fools, he was compassionate and concerned about other people, and he would never compound with terrorists or criminals of any sort. It went against everything she knew about him. It was impossible.

And besides, she knew, all of a sudden, with a wave of humiliation, as she turned over one word and another – 'compatriots,' 'full of fear,' 'hero' – he had said that she had 'stood her ground like a hero' – where the conversation came from.

But if someone were making this kind of falsification about Darek than he was in trouble – that was what had set her heart racing and caught her breath in her throat. She stood abruptly and went to the door. "Antek?" she called hoarsely, "Antek?"

Her brother did not answer.

She stumbled down the stairs and into the salon. Her parents were there. Her mother was holding a book and pretending to read, and her father was standing at the window with a glass of tea in one hand and a journal in the other, looking out towards the fence with more than an appearance of enjoyment.

"Tato? Where is Antek?"

Her father waved a hand towards the window, chuckling. "Dealing with the paparazzi. They're getting what they deserve, hmm."

Cordelia crossed to the window hurriedly, looked out.

Her father was continuing, "The fact that your brother looks like a male model in an Italian advertisement is delightfully suggestive. The tableau is full of semiotic ambiguities – one is reminded also of the work of various Latin American writers – . "

The fence was lined with journalists, still holding cameras, apparently waiting for someone to emerge. Antek had approached the fence and pulled out his own camera. Now he was angling it close towards the nearest journalist, tilting it for the best shot. Click, click. It was a manual camera, it made a lot of noise.

Cordelia couldn't hear it from inside the house, but she could imagine it. "Reflections of reflections," said Cordelia's father appreciatively.

The journalist looked vaguely irritated, while his colleagues looked rather amused, but as Antek moved on to the others, photographing them as if they were the insects that were his usual photographic prey, they became more and more uneasy, and while some were obviously objecting verbally, most decided to seek the security of their cars. Antek's lens pursued them. Quickly they began to leave.

"No!" said Cordelia to her father, "He shouldn't do that – we can't make them angry – who knows what they'll do!" And in spite of the fact that she had been quite brisk with the journalists herself, just moments before, she hurried away to stop Antek, not heeding her father's cries to let him be, let the fun go on.

She had to talk to them, tell them it was false – that she knew what that conversation was about, that it hadn't gone like that at all. She had to tell them, and yet, on the very thought, she was suffused with mortification. How could she tell them? And still she was hobbling for the door as fast as she could.

By the time she had reached it and stepped out in the garden, the last holdouts had given up and retreated to their vehicles. The fence was cleared. Antek flourished the camera and returned with his slow and lanky step to the house.

"Wait!" cried Cordelia to the departing journalists. "Wait!"

The wind carried her thin voice away. By the time she made it to the gate, the last ones were driving away.

There was nothing to do, now, but search the computer for information. First of all the news – but there was nothing – and then 'yellow cake.' Google provided the information that it was an ingredient used for nuclear reactors and also for nuclear weapons. Yes, now she remembered, that's what it had been falsely claimed the Iraqis were procuring from Niger. And on the Google page, below the entries for uranium extract, there were listings for cake recipes. He had spoken to her of yellow cake for dessert, that evening she had gone to his apartment, and someone had been recording their conversation. Someone had recorded the whole of their very private, very intimate conversation. She felt her face burning with shame and anger and a sense of outraged privacy and dignity. To think that anyone had been listening to that! Listening and no doubt snickering – she gasped.

Antek appeared in the doorway, hovering uncertainly, still clicking some lever on the camera nervously. She gestured to the screen and clicked on the YouTube recording. He came and stood behind her, listened with bowed head. He had become so much more definite and assertive again lately – Darek had done that, Darek had changed him too. But Antek said nothing when the recording finished, just turned to move away, with a hopeless shrug. "So maybe I was wrong about him," he said very quietly. "My mistake."

"No!" Cordelia cried, "Antek, no! It's not real. It's a chopped-up version of another conversation – a conversation…" She panted twice, "a very private conversation we had. And they must have been taping it – and then they took some of the words and stuck them together differently and put it with the video – and they made it into this."

"Oh," he said, looking encouraged. "Oh, well, that's good, isn't it?"

Cordelia didn't think it was good. And she was afraid.

"Is there anything else?" Antek asked, "in the news?"

She shook her head, she hadn't found anything.

"And these two that we're supposed to think are terrorists in the video – do you know them?"

"They're Syrians. They bought some land from Darek a week or two before our wedding. He told me about it. They want it for a pharmaceuticals factory. It's all quite legitimate – they have a permit from the government."

"So where is Darek?"

"Oh, Antek, I don't know. What do you think I should do?"

But Antek had used up his store of determination and energy for the day. The quixotic humor that sometimes gleamed from him and that had sent him to vanquish the journalists had evaporated. He was shaking his head and already retreating. Cordelia knew he was going to make a run for his room in the attic – that he would pull out an old camera, take it to pieces, and immerse himself in the minutiae of its springs.

"Nothing you can do," he said quietly as he went out. "'Their strength is to sit still' – I read that somewhere."

Sit still, thought Cordelia, all my life I've been sitting still, until I met Darek. But Darek had left her. Maybe he *had* run away, after all? Perhaps he was just in hiding for a time and would return, when he had plan of action? But then why the message? Why had he left her at the station?

Sliding between the sheets of her bed was like going to sleep in a snow bank. Cordelia curled in a small ball, trying to marshal the utmost warmth; to stretch a leg down to the lower regions of the bed was afflictive. She lay still in the dark, listening to her own heart beat and watching the vaguely silhouetted branches outside her window claw slowly at the night air. She was exhausted and she didn't suppose she'd ever sleep. Two nights ago – only two nights! – she had been with Darek in the hotel. He had told her, as she lay in his arms, a great many lovely things – all lies, she supposed now. And it didn't change anything, she realized – if he would only return, she would forgive him all of it.

She rose in the morning with a sense of determination edging out a little of the emptiness. She huddled on her Russian coat over her nightgown and, not noticing the darkness beyond the frosted panes, the faint streak of bronze-gold in the eastern sky, sat down in the chair at her desk with her bare feet on the frigid floorboards. The first thing to do was to check the newspapers on the internet. There was more information today. It was a small item on some sites, larger on others. She caught her breath at the headlines. '*Zaremba Involved with Terrorists?*' said the most respectable, and continued in a rather cautious vein.

'*Although the police and prosecutor's office deny all knowledge of the matter, journalists at this paper were tipped off yesterday to the appearance on YouTube of a recording purportedly of the voice of Dariusz Zaremba, the millionaire real estate developer involved in September in a controversy with the Anti-Corruption Bureau. The recording appears to be a conversation between Zaremba and two foreigners in which the sale of yellow cake – an ingredient in nuclear weaponry – is discussed. The conversation would seem to be referring to the desire of the speakers to cause harm and fear. It is not known who placed the film on the internet or for what purpose. What would seem to lead verisimilitude to the conversation is the fact that it is known that Zaremba recently received a large sum of money from certain Arab businessmen (visible in the YouTube clip), who are purportedly in Poland to consider investments in real estate. Although Pan Zaremba's newly-wedded wife has returned to her family home, Pan Zaremba himself was unavailable for comment, and sources have indicated that he may have left the country.*'

The less respectable papers were not so cautious. '*Zaremba in League with Terrorists!*' shrieked *Śmiećpospolity*.

'*Dariusz Zaremba, multi-millionaire real estate developer who was last seen evading the grasp of the Anti-Corruption Bureau, has been caught colluding with Muslim terrorists in Poland. Although the police are failing to pursue the matter, a recording clearly catches Zaremba making a deal for the sale of nuclear raw materials for the use of nuclear bombs. 'If you want it [razed] to the ground' he says, he has the stuff. If they want to spread 'fear' and 'harm' he's willing to talk business, he says. It would seem they were willing. A very large sum of money has recently been transferred to one of Zaremba's many bank accounts. The only question is why the police aren't acting and why Zaremba is still at large. One answer to this last may be that he has fled the country. Are any of us safe? The Ministry of the Interior is declining to comment.'*

The articles in the other news sources were in either of these same veins.

So she had two possibilities, she thought, hugging her coat about her. She could sit still and wait for events to unfold – and perhaps they never would, perhaps she would sit waiting for the rest of her life, and never know anything: that was the galvanizing probability. Or she could decide not to acquiesce, not to wait, not to be passive. And in that case, what should she do? Carefully, trying to foresee the consequences, she spent an hour thinking through the possibilities. Then she rose and began to dress hastily. If she thought any more about the chances of making a dreadful mistake she wouldn't be able to proceed at all.

She would refute the stories. She didn't have a printer, so she would have to write it out by hand. She would make several copies, and by then hopefully the bank would be open. She was going to need money for what she intended to do. First she made a number of phone calls, and then, filled with a sense of urgency, she began to search for paper.

"I would like," she said to the bank teller, "to withdraw all the money in my account. In cash, please."

The teller gave her a look and asked for her account number. Cordelia gave it to her and waited while she typed it in a computer.

"You want to withdraw all of it?" the teller looked up at her.

"Yes."

The teller asked her to wait a moment and faded away towards the interior of the bank. In half a minute the manager had appeared, was once again ushering her into his small office.

"I am told," he said, "that you wish to withdraw all the money in your account."

"That's right."

"In cash?"

"Yes."

"Uh – er," he stammered, his curiosity obviously very piqued; Cordelia could see that he wanted to ask her for what purpose, but didn't quite dare. He squirmed. "It's awkward. Bank regulations, you know, only allow you to take a certain sum in cash on any one day." He spread his hands, "Unless you inform the bank ahead of time."

"But it's my money. Surely I can take it when I so desire." She was only asking for her own savings, not Darek's.

"Well, yes, but the problem is, we don't keep large amounts of cash in the bank. For security purposes, you know. This is only a local branch."

She stared at him impassively and he squirmed some more, and argued some more, and eventually went to check on something, and when he came back he said, "I could let you have half that, as a special favor, since you're such a valued customer."

"So I'll take that, then. And tomorrow I'd like the rest."

The bank manager nodded. "All right." He began to fill out papers for her.

She watched him for a moment, and then added, "and there's one other thing, please."

She had asked Antek for one of his small bags, one that strapped around the waist and had a zipped compartment. She had put the money in there; it was too heavy to carry in her purse, she carried almost nothing there, and she didn't want to risk having it stolen. Her sweater covered the bag nicely, so she had no fears in that direction. She left the bank and hesitated for a moment on the pavement. She could take a taxi, but that would mean dealing with the taxi driver, and she hated talking to strangers – she would have enough of that today anyway. The tram line was just here, it would take her straight to her destination. She decided for the tram.

There was one pulling up, it was the right one. She hurried along the platform and got in, in the last car as she was slow and couldn't make it to the others in time. She was the last passenger to board, and the car was empty except for an older woman with a pull cart, sitting well towards the front. She was dropping into a seat and the doors were closing, when they were burst open again by a party of young men. There were five of them in their late teens or early twenties, burly fellows with very short-cut hair and baggy pants, typical young men. And ordinarily, such a group of young persons would not in any way have attracted her attention or her anxiety. This time she glanced up at the young men and somewhere in her mind a series of warning bells began to ring, at first gently and then more and more clamorously. Was it a sense of smell, a subconscious notation of gesture, or simply sharpened perception? One thug – she knew they were thugs – sat down behind her, and one in front. The other three remained standing, holding onto the ceiling straps, so that she was surrounded. Her heart rate accelerated to an adrenalin-filled pump. She was their prey, she knew. If they got her money, her plans would be spoiled, and she didn't know – time might be important. Time was passing. The tram lurched on its railings and the men didn't move. The money was safely out of sight, she hoped, and looked around the tram. There was only the older woman. She sought the corners of the tram – no cameras. They were coming to a stop, were stopping. The woman was getting off, there in the front. Cordelia rose too. This wasn't her stop, far from it, but she would get off, if they would let her.

"Excuse me," she said to the young men, who were blocking her way. They didn't move.

"I'm getting off, please," she said. But they didn't move or answer, forming a wall between her and the exit. Now her heart was really pounding. The tram doors slid shut and the tram left the stop, was picking up speed.

She couldn't keep her balance while the tram was moving. She sat down again, half falling back in her seat. One of the young men was reaching for her purse, but the strapped crossed over her shoulder.

"Give it," he said, leaning close. She could sense the animal excitement on him. She nodded, fumbling to pull the strap over her head. He jerked it away, ripped open the zipper and began to go through the contents. There wasn't much. She couldn't carry much. There was a comb, some papers, her ID, and the cell phone. That was all.

The young man swore angrily, "There's nothing here!"

"How nothing?" another asked, snatching the bag away and looking. "She came out of the bank."

More swearing. "Take the cell phone," someone said, reaching for it.

They would take the phone, and then – what if Darek called?

"It has a tracking device on it," she lied hastily – was one allowed to lie to thieves? – and not knowing if she was talking nonsense or not. She had no idea if it had a tracking device.

Obviously the young men didn't know either. More swearing. "Throw it away," someone said. The young men, thwarted of their reward now, angrily pulled open the door by force.

"No!" shouted Cordelia.

Someone hurled the phone through the opening and it flew out, far behind the tram, struck a landscaping bush, bounced, slithered across the street, narrowly missed a passing car, and came to a stop amongst the traffic.

Cordelia had risen and was clinging to one of the young men.

"Let go, *kurwa*!" he jerked away from her, sending her stumbling into another. And instantly, the little bit of violence changed everything.

"Throw the *kurwa* from the tram too, *kurwa*!" said someone, pushing her back, and instantly she was being grabbed, being shoved towards the entrance. The door was being held open and she could see the ground whizzing past beyond – gray pavement and iron bars and gravel. She had a moment of disbelief – they wouldn't really throw her out, would they?

"No!" her cry was panicked, pitiful, as she wriggled in their grasp. She clamped her teeth shut. This couldn't be happening.

"Go on, go on, throw her out!"

They were pushing her towards the entrance, she was out the door, almost out, she was dangling in their hands over space and rocks.

She opened her mouth to scream, and shut it again, twisted so that she caught hold of someone's sleeve in her good hand.

"Stop!" cried someone. "*Kurwa, stop!*"

"Let go!" shouted the person she was clinging too, on a note of rising fear, "let go, *kurwa!*"

The mass of limbs swayed towards the opening. They were going to lose their balance and they would all fall out. They were all shouting. The tram was pulling up, it was slowing, it was stopped. Cordelia landed hard on the platform, and the young men jumped around her, they were running – only one turned and threw her purse to her.

"It was a joke," he said, and ran.

People were surging out of the other cars, everyone was looking to see what the shouting was about. The young men ran the length of the platform pushing other passengers aside, vaulted over the railings, and disappeared across the street.

Someone was helping Cordelia up. Someone was handing her her crutch. Several people were suggesting that she should call the police immediately.

"You shouldn't ride in a car by yourself. It's asking for trouble," someone was informing her helpfully.

Cordelia straightened herself, shook off her helpers, thanked them, and headed down the platform as fast as she could. The thug had thrown the cell phone into the street half a block down. Please don't let it have been run over, she thought, please.

She arrived panting. It was there. It was lying in the street, a little off the centerline. It hadn't been run over yet. The traffic was heavy here; how could she reach it? She waited impatiently for a break in the cars. She was two lanes from it. It was sixteen feet away and she couldn't reach it. Every car that passed she marked the space between the wheels and the phone. One foot, six inches, three. 'The toad beneath the harrow knows/where every separate tooth point goes.' The cars were coming too fast. If she stepped out they wouldn't stop in time. And now the phone was ringing – ringing as it lay in the street. It must be Darek. Only Darek called her. There was a slight opening between the cars. She leapt off the sidewalk, and swung towards the centerline. The phone was there, she was dropping her crutch, reaching for it, holding it up to her ear as the cars went by on either side, horns shrieking. She couldn't hear. A text message. She stared at the screen: 'this is ERA with a promotional offer for your cell phone account...' It was an advertisement. She had risked her life for an advertisement. The cars were stopping, honking. She returned to the sidewalk amidst a storm of angry gestures and unheard shouted words. Once safety was regained, she took a deep breath. She put the cell phone in her purse, and set out once again. She had things to do – nothing was going to deter her.

20

Bzikowski's offices were on the tenth floor, but she was stopped in the lobby by a security guard in black combat gear.

"Where are you going?" he barked.

"To *Pan* Bzikowski, on the tenth floor," she answered, looking in some surprise at the man.

"Do you have an appointment?"

"No."

"So what's your business?"

"My own, I believe," she responded with some asperity.

"Wait a moment," he ordered and made a call on a cell phone. She heard him saying that there was a lady wanting to see Bzikowski. A lady without an appointment. What kind of lady? He looked her over, running his eyes up and down her, while she raised her chin. A lady with a bruise, but respectable-looking, he admitted, grudgingly. With a crutch.

"Okay," he said, putting away his phone as if he'd done her a favor, "you can go up."

She got in the elevator. At any time in the past ten years, she would have been dissuaded from any plan by a fraction of the discouragement she had just received on her way to the private investigator. Now she was determined on her path. In the privacy of the elevator, she took the money from her waist pouch and placed it in her purse. Hopefully it would be enough and hopefully she – or it – would persuade him to help.

There were more of the security guards standing outside the door to Bzikowski's offices. They were mountainous men, broad as well as tall, with no necks, who also appeared to be armed. They blocked her way.

"I've come to see *Pan* Bzikowski," she repeated, her eyes seemingly on a level with their stomachs.

"Wait here."

Again the cell phones came out, again the eyes looked her up and down. Then they nodded and moved infinitesimally to the side, letting her pass and letting her struggle with the door herself. What, she thought, had she expected? She had known that she was entering the sleaziest of worlds. She felt a strong revulsion, which was not in any way allayed by the outer office, where there were more men about, and a lot of electronic equipment and pizza boxes in an atmosphere of squalor and jack-boots. The walls were hung with a great many photos of a man in action poses. She was shown into another office.

"*Pan* Bzikowski?" she said, to a heavy-set middle-aged man behind a desk, the man of the photos.

"The same," the man answered, leaning back in his chair and looking her over as his minions had done. "*Pani* Zaremba, I presume? This is a surprise."

"Yes. How did you know my name?"

"Saw you in all the news a while back," he drawled, "Some show you made with your husband – a regular *bigos*. And now you're in again – I saw it in this morning's paper. Regular wheeler-dealer, your husband, isn't he?"

She didn't answer. She instinctively found the man loathsome and felt her distaste increasing with his every word.

"What can I do for you, *Pani* Zaremba? What brings you here? Oh – sit down."

She perched on the edge of a chair. He picked up an object from his desk and began to play with it. She realized with a shock that it was a gun. She shuddered and he pointed the gun into the far corner of the room, as if he were pretending to shoot at something – or someone?

Maybe she should leave, she thought; she wished she could leave. But everyone said this was the best private investigator in Poland. She had called Darek's friend Zbyś – he had said to go to Bzikowski – Bzikowski had contacts everywhere; in the police, in the government, in the underworld. If Darek's disappearance had to do with any of those milieus, he might know people who would know, and for sufficient money he wasn't likely, in Zbyś's opinion, to have scruples about the information. The man was probably unbalanced, but what did it matter what kind of man he was, if he could help her find Darek? But would he be able to do anything? Or was she wasting her time and money?

"Well?"

"I'd like you to help find my husband," she said as steadily as she could, "He disappeared the day before yesterday, in the evening, from the fuel station on the highway between Ostranica and Kiczera Dolna."

"Why don't you ask his Arab friends where he is?" The man put down the gun; he was half-chuckling and half-sneering.

"He doesn't have any Arab friends – I mean, he may have many…" What did she know, after all? "I don't know where he is," she repeated in a small voice, "and I'm afraid something may have happened to him."

"Sounds like he left the country."

"That's what the newspapers say, but I'd like to know for sure that he left the country and that he's all right. That nothing happened to him."

"What do you think happened to him?"

"I don't know."

The man picked up the gun again, began to twirl it on his finger thoughtfully. "It'll cost you a lot."

"How much?"

"A lot. But your husband's a rich guy, he can afford it."

"Yes, but my husband is gone. I am not rich. I brought 30,000 zloty. Tomorrow I can bring you the same. It's all I've got. Please – I hope you can help me." Please let it be enough, she thought, hating herself for begging, hating the man for his uncouth manners.

"Let's see."

She opened her purse and pulled out the money, but some instinct prevented her from handing it over at once.

"And you think you could find out something?"

The man gave her a disapproving look, "Of course I can find out something," he said, reaching across the desk for her stack of bills, taking them from her hand. He counted them briskly.

"It's not enough," he said, finally.

"If you can bring me some information by tomorrow, I will bring you more."

He gave her a sharp look and she looked back at him, her heart thudding.

"That's not much time."

She didn't answer.

He appeared to consider. "Okay," he said finally, snapping the gun down on the desk so that she jumped, "you bring me another 30,000 tomorrow and I'll see what I can do."

When she came out of the building, it was beginning to snow, hard pelting flakes blown by the wind and striking briskly on the pavement and on car windows. The sky was lowering itself down over the city like a lid on a pot. She ran for the shelter of a porte-cochère and stood there for a moment, steadying herself, taking in her surroundings. The meeting with Bzikowski had been so stressful she hardly knew where she was. Bzikowski had been almost worse than the thoughtless young thugs on the tram. But yes, she could calm herself; she recognized the street – on one side there were nineteenth-century buildings with ornate window frames and balconies, on the other a row of modern glass constructions stared back at their forebears. She had planned her day around the location of the private investigator's office. The café where she had asked the journalists to meet her was at the end of the street and across the corner. She had asked them to come at noon and she had five minutes. She put down her head and dashed out into the snowflakes.

She had thought, as she was writing that morning, that she was beyond feeling; that she could not feel any more mortification or embarrassment; that it would be all right, that she would keep her mind on her goal. She was wrong. They were waiting when she arrived. She would have recognized them as journalists, even had they not all turned and looked expectantly at her. She approached their table and someone pulled out a chair for her, helped her out of her coat. They were people of her age, three men and two women – interesting people perhaps, with rich and varied experiences and education, kindly people perhaps, people she might have liked had she met them elsewhere. Somehow that made her task seem much worse. A little revulsion, as in the case of Bzikowski, would have hardened her resolve. Now she quailed, and felt her cheeks grow hot and red as they waited for her explanations.

"I asked you to come here," she said, "because I wanted to set the record straight about the conversation on YouTube with my husband. That is, the one where he's supposed to be talking with a terrorist."

The journalists looked at her with interest.

"I," she said, "was that terrorist."

"You, *prosze pani?*" someone asked with a slight laugh.

"Yes," she said as she pulled out of her purse a number of papers. "I wrote down the conversation as it really happened. And I underlined the parts that were used to make the recording. You can see for yourselves." She handed out the copies and then sat looking very hard at a crack in the marble table while the journalists read her handwriting. To think that they were reading that – .

"When did you have this conversation?" asked one, looking up.

"It was the evening after – after the events in the town hall." The journalists all nodded, they knew all about it. "It was in – in my husband's apartment. It had been searched and bugged," – the journalists were still nodding, they knew that the apartment had been searched, it had been on the news – "and my husband had had the place checked by two outfits, to remove the bugs or whatever it is that is used for surveillance, but, I guess they weren't competent…"

"No," agreed a journalist, "you should have gone to three outfits. In Poland, it always takes three workers to do one job."

"Oh come on," retorted another, "that's as bad as the light-bulb joke."

The journalist shrugged, "still true."

"It isn't true," said another, "think about all those plumbers who go to France. The French love them. Poland produces some very good workers."

"I don't agree," said another.

Cordelia leaned back in her chair, forgotten. Some things in Poland never changed, no matter what the circumstances. Five Poles would always have ten opinions, and one could always be certain in recounting a problem that one would be told either that it was one's own fault for not being sufficiently careful, or foresighted, or cunning, or that one was actually quite lucky because it could have been much, much worse.

"Well," said a woman journalist, "you were lucky anyway to get out of it all as easily as you did. If it hadn't been for the elections, the CBA wouldn't have given up so quickly. I don't mean to imply that your husband was guilty – just that he was very fortunate everything ended the way it did."

Cordelia didn't answer. Darek had been right that he would never be entirely free of the damage to his reputation done by the machinations of those politicians, by the media. It was mortifying to think that people could doubt one's honesty – she was as much involved by now as Darek. And what was her embarrassment over a private conversation in comparison to that? She was ridiculous anyway to have thought it was of any interest to anyone. And yet it would always hurt that the journalists had read it and it would always be a memory of shame, and right now, as they dropped their argument and all bent over her words, it was hideous, hideous, horrible. She watched the strangers reading, heard in her mind Darek saying '*let me show you around – you can decide later if you want to live here or we should look for something else...*' '*...And I thought I'd already had every bad thought it was possible to have about my compatriots...You hate it? You hate translating that much?*' And so on: she had made what omissions she could; she had put down only as much of it as had been necessary to carry conviction about the true context – but still.

The three men finished reading and looked vaguely embarrassed themselves. The two women glanced at one another and Cordelia saw one pointing to a line and raising her eyebrow at the other. They didn't believe her, she knew, or they thought her behavior or her ideas too ridiculous, or felt resentful towards her because her morals were different than theirs. "Because she's like she is," the other mouthed back, as if Cordelia had problems hearing as well.

"Well," said one of the men to Cordelia, "you say all this – and I agree it looks convincing – I, at least," he glanced at his colleagues, "am convinced, but we have only your assertion – do you have any proof?"

"Yes," she said, trying to speak calmly, "those sums, at the end of the conversation. It was – my husband was telling me what he wanted to do with various accounts, and with various pieces of property. If anyone wants to see – I have here, from the bank, a statement of the transfers in our finances – you can see that that's what we were discussing – that those weren't sums to be paid by other parties." The journalists looked and appeared to believe her.

"But if it's all a falsification, you must know then who placed the recording on the internet?" someone asked. "Or at least have suspicions?"

"No," she said, "I have no idea at all. I was hoping *you* would be able to find out."

The journalists looked at one another, some as if seeking information and others rather jealously, and made noncommittal replies.

"Have you filed a complaint with the prosecutor's office? It's a crime, you know," said one.

"Yes, I know it's a crime – at least, I should hope it is. And no, I haven't reported it. I thought maybe it would be easier for you to make your enquiries, to find out – whatever there is to find – if I hadn't done so." She added: "So I'm counting on you."

The journalists looked at her assessingly and perhaps with the beginnings of respect.

It was dark by the time she made it home, limping up to the gate with groceries dangling in a plastic sack, as she had done for years. She had been away two weeks, and she hardly remembered how to cook. Not that she had been cooking in the weeks previous either, she had gone out almost always with Darek and the caretakers had gotten meals for her family at home. She had arranged with the women that they would return tomorrow and would stay for one more month, or until they found other jobs – it had seemed only fair to them, although it was an expense she could ill afford now. In the meantime, she must carry on.

She found her family gathered around the fire in the salon. Her father looked up from a book and asked her where she'd been all day.

"I...held a press conference." The slightly pompous words made it seem a little less real. She moved to the fire to warm herself. Her father stared as if dumbfounded,

"Marriage is complicated," said her mother, nodding and almost on target. And then brightly, as if remembering: "Zembara." And then, more hesitatingly, "Zerbemba?"

"Yes, Mom," said Cordelia, pleased at this show of near comprehension. "That's it."

She went to the television. It was an aged model; Darek had said it belonged in the Palace of Culture's dinosaur display. The remote wasn't in evidence, so she switched the knob to turn it on. But nothing happened.

"It's broken," said Antek, raising his head from a magazine.

"Broken?" she repeated in dismay, feeling as if this might be the last little straw that broke her spirit.

"It gave out last week. We thought about having it repaired but we didn't get to it," said her father

"It's just laisser-aller, laisser-aller all the time," grumbled her mother quietly and perfectly on target.

"I suppose you think you want to hear about yourself," Antek murmured sympathetically, "but do you really? It probably won't be pleasant. Better not to know anything, I'd say. You know the quote: 'there is not a more mean, stupid, dastardly, pitiful, selfish, spiteful animal than the Public'...I think I skipped some adjectives...."

"Envious and ungrateful," supplied Cordelia's father.

"So my point is," continued Antek, "you don't want to be captive to anyone's opinion."

But I am captive, Cordelia thought.

"It's definitely a case of what you don't know won't hurt you."

Maybe, thought Cordelia, but it could hurt Darek. But she didn't say anything; she just left her family to their reading and went to put the groceries away. She had to wait until mid-evening to get the news off the internet. She skidded past reports of snowstorms and closed airports in the Bieszczady region to find the name 'Zaremba.'

Three of the journalists with whom she had talked had persuaded their publications to print cautious explanations: '*it would seem that the recording placed on the internet, purportedly of Dariusz Zaremba discussing the sale of yellow cake, was a hoax, and was no more than a rehashed recording of Dariusz Zaremba discussing dessert with his wife. Cordelia Zaremba was able to give a full reconstruction of an innocent conversation between herself and her husband...etc.*' The perpetrator of the hoax was unknown, they said, as were the reasons why anyone would want to further – 'further,' noted Cordelia – damage Zaremba's reputation. There was no word about the foreign businessmen who were also affected by the recording, but Cordelia noticed that point with only a small fraction of her mind. She felt a sense of accomplishment – she had had a plan of action and carried it through successfully. She clicked on the fourth site.

'*Cordelia Zaremba, disabled wife of mega-rich real estate developer, Dariusz Zaremba...*' – Well, not *mega* rich, thought Cordelia with distaste, before she was aware that that was the least of it. As she read on she realized that the journalist from *Śmiećpospolity* had somehow, somewhere, heard the real recording or had access to the whole conversation and had rearranged it, removing the false criminal element of the YouTube recording but chopping their words to loathsome effect. Cordelia read the column with shock and a sort of nausea.

'Cordelia Zaremba, disabled wife of mega-rich real estate developer, Dariusz Zaremba, claims the recent recording on YouTube under the heading 'Dariusz Zaremba talks business with Terrorists' was all a hoax. She admits the voice and words are those of her husband – currently out of the country and unavailable for comment – but claims that the conversation, far from being a deal for nuclear material between Zaremba and an unknown caller, was a love quarrel between herself and her husband after their wedding ceremony in the town hall on Turawska Street in late September. (Our readers will remember that Pan Zaremba had been pursued, under suspicion of fixing a tender and corrupting a public official, to the Town Hall by the Anti-Corruption Bureau, and that Pani Zaremba's interference caused a shooting accident that could have cost many lives). Our journalist was able to trace the recording to an anonymous source. As Pani Zaremba herself described the conversation to us in detail, we have decided to set the record straight by providing the transcript here, in translation, with certain necessary omissions for the sake of public morality:

DZ: "Sorry, I'm a bit out of …keeping …" [omission]

DZ: "I've got some yellow cake – you know, one of those kind in a foil tray – left from two weeks ago, but it's growing a bit of green mould, so I won't offer it to you… [omission]…even if it would meet your ideas.

CD: "Oh… how stupid [omission]"

DZ: "why have you… started looking at me like that? All last week [omission] you gave me angry looks [omission] but you stood your ground like a hero. I asked you to do the most outlandish thing and you never gave me one look as full of fear as you've been giving me repeatedly this evening. Why?[omission]because of the ring? Was I overbearing?"

CZ: "No it's [omission] repulsive."

DZ: "Tsk, Cordelia, such minor details [omission] And you [omission] have had boyfriends before[omission]… I thought I'd *already had every bad thought it was possible to have [omission] You've [omission] slept with anyone...*

CZ: "[omission]I don't like the idea."

DZ: "So when I kissed you last night [omission]"

CZ: "I'm sorry if you dislike it."

DZ: "Don't be silly, I'll take you, of course...Don't struggle [omission]"'

Oh, thought Cordelia, oh *God*. Taken out of context, these bits of speech made her into a loose woman grown reluctant over something kinky and Darek into a brute. And there was no way the record could ever be set straight. She had thought she had handled the matter and she had only messed everything up and made it much, much worse.

But there was more. *"Perhaps"* the writer had concluded righteously and hypocritically, *"someone should inform Pani Zaremba that there are organizations for abused wives (see photo of Pani Zaremba) and perhaps someone should inform Pan Zaremba that there are laws protecting women from the necessity of engaging in unwanted sexual activities."*

Cordelia sat as if paralyzed. It was humiliating beyond anything she could have imagined. And Darek would be furious with her if he knew. She bowed her head until it came to rest against the table. It was horrible.

It was many long minutes before she could bear to check the last site. There, however, a respectably written article stated that a reporter had traced the recording through anonymous sources in the telephone company to a computer in a government office. It was believed, said the writer, that the recording had been falsified, but it was not known why it had been placed on the internet, nor precisely by whom, nor whether *Pan* Zaremba intended to press charges.

Why, she wondered, had the makers of the original recording given it to the journalist? Perhaps because she had persuaded the other journalists to call it a hoax – this way, the makers could produce still a little more damage.

After a time Cordelia became aware that the evening was passing, that it was well past time to be making dinner. She hated the idea that she would have to meet her family, that they might have read this too – and yet, there was nothing for it but to rise and go to the kitchen and pick up pots and pans and wield them – however thoughtlessly – on and off the fire.

No one mentioned the subject until half-way through the meal. Cordelia picked at her food without eating, not looking at anyone.

"Well," said Antek resignedly, "life's just one damn thing after another."

"So you saw that article, then?" Cordelia asked him sharply.

"No, no, I was only speaking of this chop," he temporized, attacking a burned portion with renewed vigor.

"Antek!"

"Yes, yes – but it doesn't matter," he muttered in embarrassment.

"It wasn't like that! They twisted it! It – the conversation – it wasn't anything like that at all. Not the way they make it sound."

"I didn't think so."

"What? What are we talking about?" said Cordelia's father.

Cordelia and Antek became very busy sawing at their food.

Cordelia's father began to quote, in his rich tones:
O earth, so fully of dreary noises!

O men, with wailing in your voices!
O strife, O curse, that o'er it fall!
God strikes a silence through you all.

'Through you all,' he repeated questioningly, looking at Cordelia and Antek, who remained perfectly quiet. "Cordelia, you don't seem happy," he remarked as if just noticing.

"No," she said, "I'm so full of dreary noises, I can't hear myself think." They all went back to eating then, a sympathetic sort of chewing of an inedible meal, and Cordelia, if she might wish that her father could summon a better response to a crisis than another quotation, or that her mother weren't mentally absent, or that Antek were sturdier, yet took some minute comfort in the presence of her family about her.

21

The next morning she visited the bank again, and then another tram ride set her down, without misadventure, in the heart of town, where she threaded her way through a confusing rush of passengers moving in all directions and into a quieter street with high iron fences and greenery and an arcaded church. She had a ways to walk. If Darek had been with her he would have talked to her about the architecture, and architecture would have taken him to history, and from history it was only a hop to politics and current events. He had said he wanted to enter politics. They had talked about it that last morning in the hotel. Why, if he had intended to leave? He would have made a good politician, she thought; he wouldn't have had connections in that vague milieu where the underworld met with authority. He wouldn't know someone like Bzikowski. Or would he? A sudden awareness of the totality of her ignorance on all but the most cultivated and useless of subjects rushed towards her like an enveloping storm cloud and almost swept her from the sidewalk. She faltered and then walked on, until she found herself in front of the building. She took a deep breath and went in.

The bodyguards allowed her to pass, without ado this time, into the office. Again Bzikowski did not rise but sat leaning back in his swivel chair, rocking it a little from side to side. He looked pleased with himself.

"Sit down," he waved her to a chair.

She sat, grasping her crutch firmly and waiting with bated breath. He didn't speak at once, obviously enjoying the sensation of keeping her waiting. She out-waited him.

"Read all about you in the papers," he said with a little laugh.

"Not really." She spoke calmly, willed herself not to blush.

"No? Sounded pretty good to me," he chuckled.

She did not respond, which obviously irritated him.

"So – you want this information or not?"

"Did you manage to find out something?" she couldn't keep the surprise and eagerness out of her voice.

"Of course I found out something. You know, you're rather insulting. That's going to cost you another, let's say, 1000 zloty."

How much, Cordelia wondered, with an inward surge of fury, would it cost me to be really insulting? If I had the money – but she was here for Darek – the anger passed in a second.

"Please tell me what you know," she forced a note of supplication into her voice. "Or – I don't know the etiquette – do you give it to me in writing?"

"No, lady, this is strictly off the record. And first the money, like we agreed."

She handed over nearly the remainder of her life savings, and he counted it, dropped it in a drawer.

"So – " he stopped tilting the chair, leaned forward onto the desk. "Your husband made somebody angry, right? When he set all that up with the media at the town hall. You probably thought you were very clever, but people in positions of power, see, they don't forget things like that. So someone wants a little revenge…" he paused.

"Who?" said Cordelia.

"No, I'm going to tell you what happened, not who did it. That's confidential, see? I have my own interests, my own lines of information, to protect."

Cordelia waited and after keeping her in suspense a little longer, he continued.

"Someone wants revenge, someone in a government position whose nose got put out of joint. So he and his friends make that recording, right? And it was supposed to end there, with the unpleasant publicity and the suspicions – but this someone, see, having made the – shall we say – 'terrorist recording,' suddenly comes into contact, more or less by accident, I think, with a certain CIA operative who is here doing – whatever it is that they're doing here – nobody knows, you know? And he passes on this information – wouldn't you in his place? It's so easy now. The war on terror has made it so easy."

Cordelia didn't respond, but sat staring.

Bzikowski continued, "So there you are. The CIA guy believes it. Why wouldn't he? A government official, very creditworthy. The government official knows about your husband's deal with certain Arabs. That makes it look even more believable. Big amounts of money changing hands, right? Talk of a ring. So they tell the CIA guys that Zaremba's an Arab too – no, excuse me, they said he was Iranian. A fellow of Iranian descent." Bzikowski laughed.

"No one would believe that!"

"Darioosh Zaremba – sounds Iranian to me." He continued to chuckle, a wheezing sound.

"They couldn't be that stupid!" Cordelia exclaimed, and then she thought, yes, they could, from everything she'd ever read, they could. She could hardly breathe.

"Are you all right, lady? *Cholera*!" he sat up straight in his chair, "you're not going to faint are you?"

She shook her head.

"You want me to go on?" Bzikowski asked.

She nodded dumbly.

"So the CIA guys think they're really onto something – they don't have much time, but they find out where he is and decide to grab him while the grabbing's good." He leaned back in his chair, picked up the gun that had been lying on his desk, stroked it thoughtfully. "He'll end up in a jail in Egypt, I suppose, or maybe Morocco. They must want to question him, otherwise….either way, I wouldn't like to be in his skin."

Cordelia stared at him, her lungs constricted.

"But you won't see him again, so the sooner you get used to widowhood the better. Hey – you'll be rich, you can enjoy yourself."

"You mean," she repeated slowly, "that it was CIA agents who were pursuing us on the highway? That my husband was abducted by CIA agents? Because they think he's a terrorist? I don't believe it!"

"Okay, don't believe it." Bzikowski shrugged, swiveled his chair back and forth.

"How can that be? How can that happen?"

"*Pani*, don't you read the news? It happens all the time. The US and other countries – Israel, for example. All over the world. True, not so much in the last year in Europe, the American rendition program was supposed to be closing down here – but before that, those aren't small numbers, they were snatching people up right and left, you can see the routes for disguised flights on the

391

internet: a regular migration flow of abductees. And I suppose someone like your husband – yellowcake, you know – that's heavy stuff – he was too good to pass up."

"But it's totally untrue! He's not a terrorist!"

"I don't think that's ever stopped them."

"What can I do?"

"Nothing you can do." He shrugged, "Okay, you can try talking to various people in the government. But right now, you know, with the new government, you'll have a hard time. The old crowd certainly isn't going to want to help – and the new ones – those are unknown quantities. The new Minister of the Interior – you could try him, or the new Minister of Foreign Affairs – but he's unlikely to help – he was part of the government that refused to cooperate when the delegation from the European Parliament came asking questions about CIA renditions from Szymany; also he has very close ties with America, he was associated with the American Enterprise Institute for years – those are the freedom by force guys, the freedom-over-your-dead-body guys," he chuckled again. "I'm a fan myself. They've got the firepower, you know, they're just lacking the brains." He tapped his own head. His tone held both admiration of a superior power and the vanity of his own superior abilities.

Cordelia had difficulty following him. "You're telling me there's no one I can turn to? Not the police, not anyone?"

"The police?" he snorted, "What can they do? He's beyond their reach." He considered a moment: "Maybe the Australian ambassador? I can't see what he'd do though. Lodge an official complaint that no one will ever notice. Your husband'll be long out of the country by then."

"Do you think he's still here, in Poland?"

"No, not likely. It's been what – how many days?"

"65 hours."

Bzikowski shrugged, shook his head.

"But if he were – where would he be?"

"How should I know? The intelligence training center at Stare Kiejkuty is one of the places where the CIA is supposed to have held prisoners before transporting them from the airfield in Szymany. That airfield is closed now though, so it wouldn't be there. There are other fields – Bieszczady-Bladowo, for instance, is the most likely in this case – if you want my humble opinion. It's not too far from where your husband disappeared. And it would be easy to arrange. A little money spent in the right place – or maybe it's not even a matter of money – maybe it's a matter of loyalty – helping out the Americans – or ideology – helping out in the war on terror. Someone very high up makes a phone call, says 'a plane is going to land and take off, no one's to go near it,' and that's all that's necessary, a prisoner is loaded onto an airplane, the airplane takes off and no one at the airfield knows anything."

"If they haven't left Poland yet, he'd be there, or near there?"

"Yes, maybe, but you'll never find him, lady. Never."

She left Bzikowski's office blindly, stumbling down the corridor into the elevator and out of the building. All those articles about persons on whom suspicion had fallen for some reason, persons snatched up, innocent or guilty, without trial, and whisked away to torture and jail and no recourse and often no return – those articles she had merely glanced at, had thought 'how shameful' and turned the page. They had been small news items, usually, not front page news, few people in Europe or America had cared very much that people had been, were being, taken from various countries and disappearing. Darek had cared. He had said – she remembered the flash of anger that injustice always seemed to evoke in him – that those responsible, at the highest levels, should be tried for crimes against humanity. She hadn't disagreed certainly – it just hadn't seemed very pressing or essential in comparison with their own recent difficulties with the Anti-Corruption Bureau and the looming exigencies of their personal plans. And the subject had only come up once, as an offshoot of a conversation about something else entirely. Neither of them had had the slightest idea, the remotest, minutest conception that he might himself be a victim. A victim – she stopped dead as all the associations of the word flocked through her mind. She thought of him being locked for years in a cage, with no contact with the outside world, no help, no hope. An image arose before her mind of a captive in a black hood; nameless, faceless – it could be anyone. It could be Darek? Beaten and waterboarded? Darek?

Someone was speaking to her. "*Pani? Proszę pani?* Are you all right? Do you need help?"

A man and woman were standing beside her, speaking loudly to her. She managed to focus on them, shook her head, wondered vaguely why they didn't move on.

"Because," the woman said, "*proszę pani*, you're standing in the middle of the street and the light has changed. You're going to get run over."

"Come, come out of the roadway," said the man.

She allowed herself to be led to the sidewalk.

Once set in motion, she continued, her crutch seeming to carry her forward of its own accord, one step after another. Was it true? Could it be true? But why would Bzikowski have invented something like that? If he had wanted merely to take her money there were many more plausible stories he might have invented. And then she remembered the words of the truck driver, describing Darek walking across the parking lot in the company of a number of other men: "I noticed there was something strange about your husband – not a man from these parts – that was obvious at once – and the other men weren't either," and later, when she'd questioned him in the truck: "If they had been in uniforms I might have thought they were police, I don't know why, just an impression – maybe they weren't Poles, maybe Germans, maybe that's why."

Maybe they were Americans – and if they were Americans that would explain the shouts in English Darek thought he heard when the Fiat went down the embankment. Had the men in the van been CIA agents? Had they approached him at the fuel station and told him to come quietly, and he had done so? But then why would he have sent her that message? Why not send a message saying 'get help'? Unless he hadn't written it at all? Her heart leaped at this thought, but only for a second. The matter was too serious to care, right now, about her own feelings. But why would the CIA men have bothered to write anything to her, good or bad? Or maybe Darek had written it because he didn't want her to do anything? Maybe he thought if she did something it would make matters worse? She stopped for a moment in a state of horrible indecision then continued blindly on her way.

"*Matko Boska!*" someone was exclaiming loudly, grabbing her arm, pulling her roughly to a stop. "She's not safe to be let out alone."

It was the same good Samaritans who had helped her out of the street. "*Pani*," said the man, letting go of her arm "you almost walked into that scaffolding."

Cordelia looked; there was indeed, right in front of her face, a large iron structure, covered in warning tape.

"Maybe she's not all here," said the woman in a whisper to the man, "what do we do? Call the authorities to take care of her, or what?"

Cordelia pulled herself together and assured the two that she was quite all right now, that she had only been momentarily distracted, thank you very much, and hurried away, leaving them shaking their heads behind her. She had things to do; she had no time to waste.

Every action seemed to take place in the slow motion of a very bad dream, but actually within an hour, she had caught a taxi, made phone calls, been to one of Darek's banks – where she had had a set-to with the manager and prevailed – had summoned another taxi, and been stuck in traffic, and jerked out some of her hair, and now was being set down in front of the central train station. She thrust a large bill at the driver, a much too large bill, and left him without a backward glance as he stared after her.

She rushed into the building, scanning the departures board for possible trains. Behind her the large open space of the hall echoed with noise and bustle, but she noticed none of it. An express was leaving in fifteen minutes. It would take her most of the way – if she didn't make that one she would have to make a series of changes on slow local trains; it would be tomorrow before she arrived. Tomorrow might be too late. Even now they might be loading Darek on a plane – in which case it was already too late. No! she wanted to shriek. She had to reach him first; she had to catch that train. Fifteen minutes, only fifteen minutes! She tried to calm herself: fifteen minutes – it would be enough to buy a ticket. But there was a line in front of the wicket. Cordelia rushed towards it, but before she reached it, just as she was coming up to it, a party of young people, with large backpacks, sauntered slowly over, and without a glance at her, joined its tail ahead of her. Her waiting period had just grown longer by five persons. She bit her lip. The line moved forward six inches. She shuffled forward too. Four minutes passed. Then two more. She was still six persons from the wicket. Hurry, she thought, hurry, please. But the ticket seller was in no hurry: she slowly counted out money, talked to her colleagues who were sipping tea, slowly answered questions about reservations and connections. The travelers, once arrived at the front of the line, seemed to be in no hurry either. Cordelia's stomach twisted. Three minutes left. She would ask the people to let her through, she couldn't bear it; she couldn't miss the train. There were only the young people ahead of her.

"Please," she said, to one. "Would you let me through ahead of you? It's terribly important."

Half the party moved instantly aside, with polite murmurs and gestures that she was to go ahead, certainly, no problem. One young woman, however, decided to stand on her rights, "Why? Why should we move aside for you? It's important to us too that we not miss our train."

"But Ania, we have half an hour," said someone.

"But it's the principle of thing," she insisted, "if it's so important, why didn't she come earlier? Why does she have to take our place? It's conscienceless."

"Yes," said Cordelia, "I agree with you. You're entirely right. I'm so sorry, so extremely sorry. I can't tell you how sorry and how deeply conscious I am of the impropriety of my conduct. I assure you I will make every attempt to improve in the future. I am most humbly grateful to you."

The young people gaped.

She was at the counter, she was handing over her money and getting a ticket, wheeling about and scurrying for the stairs to the underground platforms. The stairs were long and she went down too fast; if she slipped, if she made one misstep, she knew, she would be badly hurt – she had no way to reach for the handrail, with the crutch in her good hand. She couldn't even slow down, once she was started, it was sort of like a headlong fall – and yet here she was at the bottom, panting, and the train was there at the platform, everyone was already on. She had only to make it across the gap between the platform and the train step, and not think about falling onto the rails, and she was on. She leaned back against the compartment wall as the doors shut and took a deep breath. The train wasn't pulling out. She had had a good two minutes to spare. Darek would have kept his cool. She unbuttoned her coat and fanned herself with her ticket.

The train gave a tiny jerk. It was going to move. Through the door she saw two men come running along the platform. They looked like foreigners, somehow, Americans she guessed, their disproportion of lower face to forehead accentuated by rather military haircuts. They were wearing dark overcoats like businessmen, and yet they didn't look like businessmen. There was something rather odd about them, but she couldn't have said what. They leapt onto the car adjoining hers and disappeared. They had barely made it to the lower levels of her consciousness.

The train began to move, sliding faster past the platform. She needed to find her seat before the swaying of the train made it hard for her to keep her balance. She looked at her ticket, and then at the doors of the compartments. Ahead of her, at the other end of the car, a group of men was standing, looking out a window. Those closest were doubtless Poles, those behind might be foreigners. She hardly gave them a glance, and yet when she found her compartment, it was empty. Normally she would have rejoiced, normally she would have much preferred to have a compartment to herself, but since her meeting with the thugs yesterday she was cautious. She moved on and found the next compartment was occupied by an elderly couple and a single man; she summed them up at a glance: retired teachers and a computer technician. "Is anyone sitting here?" she asked, gesturing to an empty seat, and the older man replied politely that no one had claimed it yet and that as far as he was concerned she was welcome to it. She sank down gratefully in the corner.

Outside her window the city was passing; she watched it with unseeing eyes. Embankments with tired grass, the backs of tall buildings, streets, bridges, a church; then the backs of small brick apartment buildings showing dilapidations, trees, bare and dark-branched mostly, but here and there one with a brown or gold leaf still clinging; little hideouts amongst the bushes where drunkards had come and left a litter of bottles and maybe a shoe or sodden jacket. The names of suburban stations slid past in a blur, the train did not stop. Soon there would be open country; field and farm and country road. She could not have turned back if she had wanted to.

It did not at first occur to her that she might want to turn back. She only thought, as the train beat out its rhythm with increasing speed, that she wished she were there already, prayed that she was not too late, and did not think at all about what might happen to her. She was going to rescue Darek – how, she didn't know. But she had to get there before he was taken from Poland. She was going, she knew, on a forlorn hope, on the off chance that she would find him, that she would be able to persuade his persecutors to let him go. No one, Bzikowski had said, had ever managed to do so. For an hour, she had been filled with determination. She was going to try.

And yet, after a time, as her world was reduced from the rush and impetus of departure from the city to immobility in the compartment, the motion of the train, and the swift-passing countryside, she began to doubt, more and more strongly. Suppose she was going to the wrong place? Bzikowski had said Bieszczady-Bladowo was the most likely, but what if he had been misleading her, or were simply mistaken? The agents could easily have chosen some other spot; Poland was filled with unused or partially used former military air bases, and many were in remote locations and many would be suitable for such an operation.

She wavered, turning over the possibilities. Yes, she began to think, she had made a mistake. She should have gone instead to the Australian embassy, to government officials, to the media. She had indeed called one of the journalists, the most sympathetic-seeming one, and she had told him what Bzikowski had told her and what she hoped to do – but she didn't know what use he might make of it; she had only had a vague feeling that the more people who knew, the better. Now she should have stayed to mobilize what help she could find. She had made a terrible mistake. She had been mad to come; she would never find Darek. Indecision tore at her.

She dug in her purse. Just as she was leaving, Bzikowski had tossed her a slim stack of papers – "here, I like my customers to be satisfied. I had the boys make you up a report on renditions." She hadn't had time to read it before, now she ran her eyes down the pages:

"*They picked up the wrong people, who had no information. In many, many cases there was only some vague association* [with terrorism]'" – CIA officer quoted by Dana Priest, *Washington Post*

'*To carry out its mission, the CTC relies on its Rendition Group...Their job is to figure out how to snatch someone off a city street, or a remote hillside, or a secluded corner of an airport where local authorities wait...Their destinations: either a detention facility operated by cooperative countries in the Middle East and Central Asia, including Afghanistan, or one of the CIA's own covert prisons*' – Dana Priest, *Washington Post*

'*...the two countries did host secret detention centres under a special CIA programme established by the American administration in the aftermath of 11 September 2001 to "kill, capture and detain" terrorist suspects deemed to be of "high value". Our findings are further corroborated by flight data of which Poland, in particular, claims to be unaware...*' – Dick Marty, rapporteur for the Council of Europe

"*D was like our default option: Detain. Like if we pick up some guy in a raid where we also got one of the HVTs* [High Value Detainees]*... and maybe we've got nothing on this guy, but obviously we're still gonna hold him.*'" – source quoted by Dick Marty, rapporteur for the Council of Europe

"'Poland was picked...Polish intelligence officials were eager to cooperate. "Poland is the 51st state," one former C.I.A. official recalls James L. Pavitt, then director of the agency's clandestine service, declaring...'" – Scott Shane, *The New York Times*

'*... the idea was to act on tips and leads with dramatic speed.*' – Dana Priest, *The Washington Post*

She was unaware that the younger of the two men in the compartment was giving her repeated glances, and was startled when he spoke to her.

"Excuse me, *pani*, but aren't you that *pani* who was on television a while back? In the news? The one who was given..." he hesitated, obviously feeling it might not be good taste to mention money, "...who was married on television – when there was the accidental shooting in the town hall?"

"Yes," Cordelia answered grimly. She would rather not have been identified, but it never occurred to her to deny the fact.

"What a horror!" said the elderly woman sympathetically.

"Let the *pani* be!" said her husband, "You can see she doesn't want to talk about it."

"It's all right," said Cordelia politely, but she rose, in spite of the swaying of the train, with the intention of standing in the corridor for a moment, as if to look out the window.

She steadied herself against the wall in the corridor. The young Poles who had filled one end of the car before had disappeared; there was only one of the businessmen-not-businessmen foreigners she had seen running for the train. He was standing watching the landscape pass, but he turned and looked at her. She avoided his gaze, as she always did with strangers, and turned to stare out the window at the landscape, as he had done. The ride to Przestrzyna was supposed to take four hours; there she would have to find another train or a bus to take her the rest of the way – if she went the rest of the way. Perhaps she should turn around and go back. And yet somehow she knew she was going to carry on to her goal and also, with certainty, that she would find nothing. Darek would be gone – but she couldn't think about that, she mustn't.

It was hard to stand up when one was just an empty shell. She turned to go back to the compartment, and was surprised to see the same foreigner at the other end of the corridor. She hadn't noticed him passing her in the narrow corridor and surely she would have done so? She turned her head in the other direction. No, there were two of them. One at each end of the car. The one to her right started towards her.

Without knowing why, Cordelia hurried into the compartment, and found her heart pounding. She sat down in her corner and closed her eyes to prevent more inquiries from the other passengers, but not before she saw one of the foreigners pass beyond the door. He paused there for a fraction of a second and looked in at her, with an expressionless face, then went on. Why, she wondered, behind closed eyes, did she feel, in the Polish phrase, as if someone had walked on her grave? She was imagining things, surely. She resolutely did not open her eyes and concentrated on being calm.

Darek was always telling her that she worried too much. Every worry of the past seemed microscopic in comparison with her current preoccupation. If he were restored not to her love – she had never ceased to love him – but to her good opinion, then his fate was so much more unbearable. She shook her head to get rid of these thoughts; they would only hamper her at the moment.

Someone was pushing open the door. Cordelia's eyes snapped open. It was a man in uniform – selling sandwiches, coffee, and cookies. Cordelia breathed a sigh of relief. She had no appetite, none at all, but she realized she would need her strength in the hours ahead. She bought a cup of coffee and a packet of gingerbread, and forced herself to swallow one slow bite after another, ignoring the glances of her fellow passengers, who, as they consumed their own snacks, were obviously consumed with curiosity.

Finally, as she was finishing her last piece, washing it with the hot coffee past the lump in her throat, the older man spoke again: "Are those your bodyguards? They can come in and sit down if they want, it won't disturb us." His wife and the other man nodded.

Cordelia's head snapped around to the door again, the two foreigners were standing just outside the door, staring in. They were wearing dark glasses now.

"I don't know them," she said, with a prickling of fear, "I don't have bodyguards."

At this moment the door opened and the two men came into the compartment. They sat down facing Cordelia. She had the uncomfortable feeling that they were staring at her from behind their glasses. Were they agents, or was she just morbidly, wildly imaginative? Were they after her, or were they ordinary people traveling somewhere on their own business, no harm to anyone? Surely, surely, it was only because she'd been reading that report that she had such ideas.

And yet, as one of them shifted in his seat, she noticed that there was a bulge under his coat, a hint of a gun holster. She had seen such a holster recently, openly, on Bzikowski, or she would not have recognized it for what it was. So that settled it. She looked around the compartment, but there seemed no way of escaping them. She couldn't run even if there had been anywhere to run to. She felt her blood beating in her eyes, in her ears. Would they take her, at least, to Darek? Or would she never see him; would he end up in a jail in Afghanistan and she in Morocco?

One of the agents suddenly turned his head toward the other passengers: "Does anyone here speak English?" he asked.

The three shook their heads. The man turned to Cordelia. "Do you?"

She nodded, realizing too late that this was a mistake.

"So where is this train going?"

She had a wild urge to burst into laughter. But how absurd – they had got on the train after her and had no idea where it was going. How Darek would be amused, if only she could tell him. But maybe she would never see him again. And the man was waiting for an answer. The thought of Darek was steadying: she would need her wits about her; she found that she could answer calmly enough.

"*Na południowy-wschód*" – to the southeast. They didn't need to know more than that.

"Nap – *what?*" repeated the man, in irritation.

"*Na południowy-wschód.*"

The man stared, obviously not knowing what to do with the information, and the younger Polish passenger seized the opportunity to jump into the conversation. He addressed himself to Cordelia politely:

"I'm sorry if I disturb you by mentioning it, but I want to tell you that you have my sympathy for everything that happened to you and your husband. I've been following the recent events too – the recording and all that. I'm interested in such things, you see – in how the internet can be used to destroy people's reputations. Anybody can be accused of being a terrorist – "

The agents' heads whipped round at the word '*terrorysta*,' and Cordelia could see them wondering if this word meant what it sounded like.

" – or a child molester, or any other disgraceful thing, and without recourse. I'm glad you managed to get it set straight in some of the papers. I hope you intend to find who did it and press charges. This sort of thing is occurring at an alarming rate – it shouldn't be allowed."

The elderly woman interposed, saying she didn't know what the man was talking about and asking, eagerly, to be filled in. The man obliged and she was then voluble in her disapproval of the internet in general, of persons who made recordings, of the government, and of 'them' in general, whoever 'they' might be who made life miserable for ordinary people. There were even people who committed suicide because of some slander about them on the internet…

"Wait," said Cordelia, to her well-wishers, "I must translate for these foreigners, if you allow me." They nodded and waited with eager curiosity for the expressions of the foreigners.

With an upsurge of courage, Cordelia turned to the two agents: "You might be interested in what your fellow passengers are saying," she said politely, "and I wouldn't want you to feel left out – so I will translate for you what they have said." Their expressions were not encouraging, quite the contrary, but she talked on boldly anyway.

When she was done, and when she had additionally told the agents everything she knew about the recording and who had placed it and why and the private investigator's conclusions and the corrections in the newspapers – which they could find themselves if they were interested – the agents continued to stare at her, or so she thought, because she couldn't see their eyes, and their faces remained impassive. They certainly didn't respond. She had been naïve, she realized, with a mental cringe of mortification, to think they would listen to her.

In fact, the agents' non-response was so palpable, so positively rude and threatening seeming, that after a long silent pause, that drew itself out and filled the train compartment with its echoes, the elder man suddenly said to his wife in a whisper – "come," and pulling their bags down briskly from the overhead rack, he shepherded his wife from the compartment. The younger man watched them go with unease; he looked at Cordelia, sitting frozen, her eyes on the floor; he shifted in his seat, with increasing nervousness. The agents turned their heads and stared in his direction. Cordelia read his thoughts: it would have taken more experience and resolution than he possessed to know what to do in such a situation. And part of the problem was the uncertainty of whether there really was a situation; it was perhaps better not to find out. He rose.

No, thought Cordelia, don't go, don't leave me here alone with these men. She should ask him for assistance, ask him not to leave; but it was too unfamiliar to ask for help – maybe she was imagining it all? – her inhibitions rose, she hesitated; she was opening her mouth to speak, but he was already sidling apologetically out of the compartment. Too late, she rose to follow him; the door snapped shut on his departing back. She wouldn't stay here, she was standing unsteadily and reaching for the door, when one of the agents rose too, and she was jerked roughly back onto the seat.

"Don't scream or you're dead," the man said.

She believed him. She pulled her arm away and sat still, while he remained menacingly beside her. So that settled it. She hadn't imagined it. She was a prisoner of the CIA. Outside, the other passengers had disappeared. None had noticed what had happened behind their backs. The corridor was empty. Outside, the fields still fell away, one after the other. Her heartbeat was outracing the rhythm of the train.

She was alone with the two agents.

"So where are we going?" said one of the agents.

"*Na południowy-wschód.*"

"I know you can speak English – you just did," he responded sharply. "So, for the third time – where are we going?"

"I cannot comprehend how I should be apprised of the travel plans of unknown gentlemen," Cordelia murmured.

"What?"

"How should I know where you're going? I never met you before in my life," Cordelia simplified.

The response was not polite.

"I don't think you should swear at me," said Cordelia softly, "I don't think that's in the manual of proper agent behavior."

They were quite silent.

"Go find out where we're going," said one to the other after a time. "The first stop. Get somebody to write it down." The second man, the man Cordelia thought of as Military Cut, stepped out of the compartment. That left Blandface. He was the more terrifying character, Cordelia thought, and also, apparently the leader.

"So where's your husband?" he asked.

408

It took a moment for the import of the words to register then Cordelia felt a wild surge of joy. "Ah," she cried, "he's escaped! I'm so happy." Tears began to roll down her face. "So happy." She sought in her purse for a kleenex.

The man looked decidedly irritated. "I didn't say he'd escaped."

"But I can deduce it. I'm crippled you know, not stupid." Her relief was making the words tumble out, she realized, but she couldn't seem to stop. "And you should be glad too, because he's completely innocent and I'm sure you wouldn't want to be responsible for abducting an innocent person." Never mind, she thought, that he shouldn't be abducting anyone, innocent or guilty – in her relief she could be politic.

"Your husband's about as innocent as a rattlesnake. Your husband's a bastard. But I didn't say anything about abducting anyone."

"Not to mention," she continued, the combination of surging contempt and joy making her suddenly reckless, "that your behavior has been illegal and immoral and *scandalous*."

"Shut up."

She gave the man a level look and a smile. "I hope you reform."

"*Shut up, I said!*"

This was said with enough vehemence that Cordelia took warning, in spite of her effervescent relief – Darek was free. But of course he would get free – what could be more like him? She hadn't considered the possibility, but certainly if anyone could get away it would be he. From dozens of war-time escape stories, every Pole knew that the thing to do was to seize the right moment and *run*. Is that what he had done?

And then other considerations began to crowd into her mind. He was free, but would they catch him again? And what did they intend to do with her?

Military Cut returned to the compartment and handed Blandface a piece of paper. The two puzzled over it. "Every name here is just a bunch of 'z's," Blandface grumbled in disgust. "But it starts with a 'P'. That's good. If it's the town I'm thinking of it's suspiciously close." He appeared to consider. "Hell, could be the total opposite direction though."

The two men looked at her.

'Przestrzyna,' Cordelia knew it said. The train stopped first in the town of Przestrzyna. She had never been there before. She had no idea whether the station was in the middle of town or far removed, in the wilderness. What would they do when they got there? Would they make her get off with them? And then what?

"Where's your husband?" Blandface began again.

"I don't know."

"Is he there in Pereze – " he waved the paper at her, "this place?"

"I don't know."

"You really should tell us – it'll be better for you."

"Why, what could happen?" She didn't want to know, but silence would seem like fear.

"Things you won't like."

Boże kochany. Cordelia quailed inwardly. "But it's hard," she suggested tentatively, "to understand how…whatever you might do to me…will make me know something I don't know. I don't know where my husband is. So I can't tell you, even if I wanted to – which I don't."

The two men were silent, an unpleasant silence. She was very afraid and her fear built slowly on itself. If Darek were free then if she could get free, then – she began to make hasty calculations, the stakes for the future suddenly growing very much larger. If she waited until someone passed in the corridor, and then she screamed – screamed at the top of her lungs – would they really kill her? Yes, she decided, they probably would. The man had mimed a short chop to the neck. A blow like that – she remembered reading in some spy novel – could easily go unnoticed in a crowd. The victim just dropped to the ground and rose no more.

She couldn't escape. It was useless to think so. What was it one was supposed to do in such situations? However unsavory they were and however humiliating it was, she had to talk to them; she had to put it to them again that her husband was not what they thought he was. Maybe they weren't listening but maybe some little wedge of information could be pounded into their minds. "Look," she said to her captors, carefully, patiently, trying to speak simply because they seemed to her limited, like automatons that had been set in motion and were carrying out a task, self-set or appointed: "my husband is not a terrorist. He is not involved in selling yellowcake; I don't suppose he knows any more about the stuff than you do or I do, or all those people at the CIA do. The recording you heard was a hoax. It was in all the papers, yesterday and this morning, that it was a hoax. Did you read them? Surely, if you people are in Poland, someone in your organization can read the language here?"

Blandface made no response. Military Cut suggested she watch the scenery.

Cordelia took a deep breath and went on: "You were fed misinformation by someone who wanted revenge against my husband. It was nothing more than that. My husband is involved in selling a piece of land to some men from an Arab country. That's not a crime. It is

411

perfectly legal. My husband is a legitimate real estate dealer and developer, nothing else. He's not a criminal; he's not involved with criminals. Don't you think that if there were any proof against him that the Polish authorities would have acted themselves?"

She paused to draw breath, all her wits concentrated on her argument, waiting for them to suggest that a lack of proof didn't necessarily mean that someone is innocent, because she had an answer to that – 'yes, but it's necessary for the rule of law to proceed on that assumption'…But no one answered her at all. She was about to continue, "He doesn't wish or intend harm to anyone…"

She was interrupted. "You're just like your husband, aren't you?" observed Military Cut glumly. "He wouldn't shut up either. He kept talking and talking. All day and all night. Drove me crazy. Ma'am, we had to…"

"Never mind that," snapped Blandface.

Cordelia stared angrily at them; she hadn't made the least impression on them. They hadn't even been listening. "You, on the other hand," she continued, "do wish people harm. I wonder why? Did you have very unhappy childhoods?"

"Ma'am," said Military Cut, "we're just doing our job. Trying to make the world a little safer."

"Curiously, I don't feel very safe."

"Shut up," said Blandface.

Cordelia was silent. Obviously she didn't have what it took to talk to – well, to anyone really, except Darek. But she didn't want them to think she was afraid of them. She had an instinctive feeling that they were the sort of men who would be excited by their victim's fear. The thugs on the train had been better – they had had limits; these didn't, she suspected.

"If I'm your captive, where are we going?"

"Never mind," said Blandface.

"I think I have a right to know."

"No, ma'am, you don't have any rights," said Military Cut.

"Because you're criminals?"

"You know, you better watch your tongue. You're starting to irritate me," said Blandface.

She was silent for a minute but after a bit she couldn't help asking: "Do you know Tennyson's poem about the light brigade? No? It has this great line: *'someone had blundered.'* I don't know why, but I can't seem to get it out of my mind."

"Shut *up!*"

Cordelia bit back further comment. She was like her father, she realized with a jolt; here was a crisis and all she could do was summon up someone else's words. What was the point of baiting and angering these men, even if they were persecuting her? It was the wrong tack entirely. She'd just failed her crash course in how to deal with the media and now she was failing her crash course in abduction. *Darek*, she thought, *help me.*

And then it occurred to her: If Darek were free, surely he would have called her? But she hadn't heard her telephone ring. Maybe it had rung while she was running for the train, or while she was in the midst of traffic, in the taxi, and she hadn't heard it? She had to check it. She rose.

"Where are you going? I told you to sit here."

"No, I don't remember that you did. You jerked my arm and made me sit. I don't remember anything about a request. I need to go to the toilet – the restroom," she corrected, remembering the American term. There she could look at her phone in privacy.

413

"You can't."

"But I do." She swallowed her distaste, and added "Please." She stared at the floor; this was humiliating.

"No."

She waited three minutes and then began again.

"I have to go to the restroom, please."

"No."

She repeated the request every three minutes for half an hour and eventually Military Cut swore, and Blandface said grudgingly 'all right,' and they all three rose and left the compartment.

The toilet was at the end of the car. One stepped beyond the door to the corridor, and there was the toilet on one side and the door to the outside on the other. They came through the corridor, and she was on the far side of the agents, closest to the opening; she looked at it and instinctively shuddered and shied away. Her experience on the tram had given her a horror of doors and rails and rushing ground and she was unsteady on her crutch in the moving train. And yet, it was a dreadful mistake to have flinched; her horror was communicated; she saw it in a flash. The idea leapt from her mind into the minds of her captors. She saw it even as she tried to retreat, dropped her crutch and reached hurriedly for something, anything to hang onto. Too late – Blandface was already grabbing her, crowding her; she opened her mouth to scream and his hand closed over it. He was twisting her good arm behind her back, shoving her towards the opening. It was happening too fast, she had no time to think anything except – No. But without her arm she was helpless, her other hand wouldn't grip; she was pushed ineluctably towards the entrance. She jerked her head to try to free it from his grasp, to scream, but he pulled her neck back. He would break it before he pushed her from the train. The ground was passing too quickly to see. She would never survive.

"Where's your husband?"

She was being held over the edge of the car, she felt her feet losing touch with the floor.

She didn't answer. She couldn't. He didn't seem to realize that she couldn't. He was still speaking in her ear. They were half out of the train and the sound was born away by the wind. No, she thought, no. Images rushed through her head: her mother, Antek, Darek. He'd think she'd killed herself. She writhed in her captor's grasp but there was nothing beyond or below her but space.

And then her telephone rang.

She was jerked back from the void; Military Cut was fumbling in her purse, trying to find the cell phone. Blandface still had his hand over her mouth. If it was Darek, she couldn't let them talk to him. She writhed in the grasp of her captors, and Military Cut dropped the phone. It fell onto the last step, beyond the open door.

For a split second they all watched as it rang again and the motion of the train edged it toward the abyss. Then Military Cut lunged and grabbed it.

Military Cut was staring at the phone. A text message and he couldn't read the Polish text. He held it out to her. "Scream, ma'am, and you go out the door. What does it say?"

Blandface took his hand off her mouth. "This is a promotional offer from ERA," the phone said. She tried hastily to think, and all that passed through her mind was that she wasn't dead. But they were waiting; she had to think, think fast: it should say something to put them off. She read aloud, in a shaking voice: "All requisite authorities are coming to your assistance and the agents will be apprehended."

The agents put their heads together over the small screen. Blandface said "ERA – that's the cell phone company."

Military Cut turned to Cordelia, with seeming disappointment: "Ma'am, you just lied to us."

"And you just tried to kill me!" she snapped back. She made an effort to regain her crutch and added resentfully, "I suppose you're going to tell me this was a joke?"

Blandface looked blank; Military Cut was of a literal turn of mind and answered her seriously: "No ma'am, it wasn't a joke."

"In fact," said Blandface, his hand closing over her mouth again, and swinging her towards the door. But the ringing of the telephone interrupted him again.

"Hello?" said Military Cut, and his voice suddenly became charged with excitement, "Zaremba? Zaremba, we have your wife! Don't hang up!"

"Say 'hello' to him," he instructed Cordelia, holding out the phone.

Cordelia shook her head. She wouldn't do it. They couldn't make her. Please let Darek think they were just trying to trick him.

"Wait a minute," said Military Cut into the telephone, and to Cordelia, "Ma'am say 'hello' nicely or we're going to have to continue as before."

Cordelia turned towards the door. It wasn't so much courage as an inability to stand the tension. She had an intense desire to get it over with. Blandface jerked her back, his hand over her mouth.

Hang up, Darek, she thought. Just hang up. *Please*, *hang up, please*. But he didn't. He appeared to be listening. Military Cut was telling him to meet them at – he pulled out the piece of paper and spelled the name –

'P.r.z.e.s.t.r.z.y.n.a.' Military Cut listened and gave Blandface a thumbs-up sign. Zaremba was to be at the station. Zaremba was to join them in front of the station; they would leave the station together quietly; his wife would accompany them to the waiting vehicle and be free to go. And then Military Cut turned the phone off and put it in his pocket. He took out his own phone, called a number, and arranged for a vehicle and agents to be waiting outside the station.

If only, thought Cordelia, someone would come. But no one came.

22

She should be thinking of plans, countermoves, something, anything, to keep the inevitable from happening. But she couldn't. Her mind was blank, as clear of ideas as a clean sheet of paper. It seemed hopeless. Sometimes she would begin to imagine a course of events, of possibilities, and then she would give it up, knowing it to be impossible, to be fantasy. She had used up her small capacity for resistance and now sank into a state in which apathy and tension combined to make her nearly catatonic.

Eventually, by the appearance of more construction and more frequent road crossings, she became aware that they must be getting closer to the town of Przestrzyna. She checked her watch. Half an hour more. Ten minutes more. The tension was almost unbearable. Darek, don't be there, she kept praying. But she knew he would be.

People were beginning to appear in the corridor with their luggage, ready to get off. This fact and its possible uses had just crossed her mind, when there was a knock on the compartment door, and a railway official entered, with a polite good-day and the usual air of weighty official duty. "Tickets please."

Cordelia sought automatically in her purse, pulled out her ticket, handed it over. The controller looked at it and handed it back, and all the while she was wondering – should I say 'save me from these men'? But surely the agents would simply pull out badges or something official-looking like that and tell the man to go about his business. But perhaps it would cause a delay? She wavered, the outward normality of the situation – three people in a railway carriage, being approached by a controller – and the reality of it – her violent subjection to foreign agents – seemed too surreal, too melodramatic to be believable. Without some impetus to action she didn't know how to begin; her heart rate increased again to a deafening pound and yet, as before, a number of deeply ingrained barriers paralyzed her: to speak or not to speak? The controller turned to the two agents. "Your tickets, please."

Blandface and Military Cut stared back nonplussed.

"Your tickets, please."

It wasn't just that they hadn't understood, Cordelia realized, they didn't have tickets.

"Teekets, please," the conductor was asking in English, "Teekets."

"They don't have any," she could say to the controller, in Polish, "they're intending to get off at this station without paying." But she couldn't do it, even against her captors.

The controller, however, had experience in reading expressions, even the expressions of foreigners. He raised his eyebrows and shook his head; he spoke into a cell phone and asked for reinforcements.

"You doan have teekets," he was saying to the agents, in heavy slow English. Ees not good. You pay big fine."

Cordelia could see the two agents tensing. The controller had moved between her and them.

"Give him a bribe," snapped Blandface to Military Cut. "Hurry up. We're almost there."

The controller drew himself up proudly. "I doan take. You are beeg problem."

The train was coming into the station; she reached for her crutch. The agents were reaching for something in their coats – badges or papers or something, she supposed, their guns, perhaps. The other guard arrived, he was opening the door. She was upright and scooting through it before he had time to enter. She was in the corridor. Behind her the agents rose in pursuit and cannoned into the first controller, while the second guard slammed the door on them and held it from the outside. Cordelia scrambled madly along the corridor, knocking into the other passengers, into their luggage, begging them to move, please, move out of the way. Her panic was such that they moved, everyone turning to see what was happening in the compartment behind them, where there seemed to be a brawl underway.

Here was the door at the end of the car. They were running alongside the platform. The train was stopping, it was not quite stopped. She could see the pavement passing still. If she jumped she would fall; if she hesitated, if she waited till the train stopped, they would catch her. She imagined their hands reaching for her; they were surely almost upon her. She pushed off with her crutch and fell onto the platform. She was up and hobbling as fast as she could. She would have seconds, perhaps, to find Darek and tell him to run – to run! He didn't seem to be in front of her – but maybe she couldn't see him. There were other passengers about, other people now, climbing down from other wagons. The agents had said he should meet them where? In front of the station – where was the front of the station? She was hurrying so frantically she couldn't take in her surroundings properly. The station building was to her left, but it seemed to be separated from the platform; she couldn't see the entrance to it.

She was hobbling as fast as she could, but it would never be fast enough. She couldn't draw breath quickly enough, couldn't make her legs and arms move. There was an underground passage – she would have to go down the stairs to reach the station.

Darek! She wanted to shout. Darek!

Hope and sharp disappointment mingled at his absence. But no, he was there, he was coming racing along the platform towards her, he was there and he had hold of her arm, was dragging her along with him.

She jerked away from him. "Run!" she begged him, "don't wait for me, please. Run! Because they're coming – they're on that train. They'll be here any moment. Run!"

Behind them a mass of people half-tumbled, half-exploded from the railway car onto the platform; Cordelia could make out Blandface and Military Cut brutally shaking off the two controllers and eluding the grasp of bystanders who tried to stop them, were reaching for their clothing, catching them off balance. Military Cut collided with a refreshments cart, sending soft drinks flying. Curses filled the air, and the owner of the cart joined the melee. But they were coming still, coming towards them. Flight was hopeless and yet Darek was helping her to run, she couldn't look back again. Any moment the agents would be upon them.

A group of young men was passing – a group of the same sort that had accosted her on the tram – Cordelia screamed to them: "Help! Help us! Those men – they're attacking us – stop them!"

The young men entered the fray with a will. Darek grabbed Cordelia up in his arms and ran with her. Behind her she saw the group close round Military Cut and Blandface, saw Blandface reach for his gun and then think better of it – saw the controllers arrive again – there were shouts of assault and an unpaid fine and shouts that were just curses.

She was being carried swiftly down a flight of steps. She had a confused idea of a multitude of faces, and of Blandface breaking free behind them. No, he had tripped, or someone had tripped him.

They were racing through an underground passage, emerging into the train station. Darek was barging through a door –

"No!" she exclaimed, "it's the women's."

They went through anyway. They were inside. Darek put her down and leaned against the door for just a second, taking in the white-tiled room. One of the cubicles opened and a woman emerged, giving Darek and Cordelia a curious but not indignant look. Darek moved briskly aside. She went out. The white-tiled lavatory appeared to be empty.

Behind them, the sound of running feet rang on the marble floor of the station hall. There was no time.

"That window," said Darek breathlessly. "Go through it, while I hold the door. Run, don't look back!"

"I can't," said Cordelia. She couldn't reach the handle, she couldn't open it, she couldn't get through it on her own; it was four feet off the ground.

He was there beside her, the window was open, she was being stuffed, almost hurled through it, landing on the ground in a heap; she was in a parking lot behind the station; she picked herself up and started to run, along the side of the building; then she stopped, not knowing which way to go. But Darek was beside her, helping her to move.

"This way!" he said, "the others – their car will be out front."

They crossed the parking lot at what speed Cordelia could manage, circled an elderly brick building, came to a street. A bus was just pulling away from a stop. Darek dropped Cordelia's arm and ran for the bus, banged on its side and hollered. The bus stopped with a lurch, and the rear door opened with a hiss.

They got on.

It was nearly full; Darek indicated a seat to Cordelia.

The homely nature of the gesture, of the location, of the archi-normalness of a ride on the local bus after the violent unreality of the past minutes almost sent her into hysterical laughter. But habit was strongest of all.

"No," she gasped, "We have to – buy tickets."

Darek gave her a look full of amazement – that she would think of such a thing at such a moment – but when she started, still panting heavily, in great gasping breaths, towards the front of the bus, he took the bill she had extracted from her purse, motioned her to the seat again and went to purchase tickets from the driver.

So, she thought, letting her head sink down on her crutch arm – it was as easy as that. And then, in turn – if I ever do that again it will kill me. I am not meant for this kind of thing. I'm not. And then again – are we safe yet?

They didn't speak on the bus. Cordelia sat and Darek stood beside her, hanging onto a strap. She was intensely aware of his presence beside her – that he was pulsing with excitement and anger and a sort of pleasure – but they thought their own thoughts. At every stop Cordelia expected to see the agents appear, to see them boarding the bus in a rush, to be upon them. She scanned the streets as the bus swayed noisily through the town but saw no one but perfectly ordinary Polish people, going about their business.

The bus left the station area, drove along streets lined with modern apartment buildings and then moved into the older part of town, where there was the architecture of the Austro-Hungarian empire and a lot of little shops. Stopping at every block, the bus lurched past an old market square, and came to a halt by the gate of a small park.

"Here," said Darek suddenly, "we'll get out here."

They descended and entered immediately into the park. It was situated on a slight rise and was cut off from the street on one side by a disintegrating brick wall. They passed through the gates and followed a path between bare-branched trees for fifty feet. There was no one about. The park was deserted.

"Now," said Darek and turned to Cordelia. His grip was fierce enough to allay any remaining doubts that it might truly have been he who had sent that message.

When he let her go, they walked on in silence; the path was wide and presently seemed to be circling. Beyond the edge of the park, at the far end, was a small Orthodox church, wooden and deserted, its parishioners long dispersed: a reminder of past lives disrupted by the arbitrary will of the authorities. They walked towards it, and the lightest of snows began to fall again, onto the onion spire of the church, the black branches, and the still green grass of the park.

There was a bench.

"Here," said Darek, "we'll sit here for a moment and catch up on each other's news."

He threw himself down on the bench and leaned back, in spite of the clinging black lace of icicle along the top board. Cordelia perched on the edge, turned towards him, waiting quietly.

"Tell me everything," he ordered after a moment's pause.

"Yes," she said, "but first – did you see? One was reaching for his gun at the station – do you really think they could get away with shooting someone at a train station?"

"I don't know. I doubt it – and I presume they doubted it too, since they didn't try. But I suppose they considered that if worse came to worse they'd call in their cohorts, and there would be enough of them to hold off the authorities until they made their get away. The others were coming in as we left, did you see?"

She shook her head.

"Five or six of them. We were lucky the crowd reacted the way it did. It might easily not have – there's never any telling with a crowd."

She nodded.

A casual observer might have considered that she presented a fair semblance of her usual prim and refined self, but in point of fact, her throat was so dry with the fear of the last hours that she had an intense desire to throw herself down and chew on the snow under the park trees.

"So tell me everything," he said again.

She didn't know where to begin. So she started with what she thought might be most important: that she had called his friend Zbyś and had asked him to call the Helsinki Foundation and the Civic Rights Ombudsman, and anyone else he could think of.

"Yes," said Darek, "I know you did, because I talked to him, just after I hung up with the agent. We'll have to call him again and let him know what's happening – he doesn't know about the two others – that is, I scarcely mentioned them, I was thinking of you and me at that junction, but they're the point now."

"What two others?"

"Nagib Hasan and Ali Mashrawi, the Syrians. They've got them too. We'd all be long out of the country by now, only the weather conditions have been so bad – there's been heavy fog – that they can't get the plane in to take us out. To think – a little vapor is all that stood between me and jail in a distant country."

"Ah." Cordelia's eyes widened. And then – "how did you escape?"

"Luck – the right circumstances. Just like at the station – but no, that wasn't all luck, you were great!"

Cordelia blushed.

He continued, "Anyway, to go back to how I escaped – we had hoods over our heads and we were handcuffed together and at first they tied our feet together too, but after the second day, they grew laxer and sometimes didn't bother with the feet – for me, anyway. I think perhaps they thought it was such a remote place and there were so many of them that we wouldn't have a chance to get away anyhow. And on the second day, too, they decided to give us food occasionally, so they took off our hoods and undid our handcuffs, one at a time, so we could eat. They'd just undone me, when someone drove up outside the house, the building – I have no idea where we were – we were carried in in the hoods and later, we were only in the one room. The windows were shuttered. My guess, from that one room, is that it was a communist-era building of some sort – peeling paint, shoddy workmanship, that sort of tell-tale signs. I think there had been a guard out front, but that he'd got cold and come in – some of them had come from Italy, I gathered. Anyway, someone drove up, probably by accident. From the agitation among the agents, I think it wasn't anyone who was supposed to be there. Someone said 'it's a whole carload,' and the person who had unlocked my handcuffs stepped away to see what was happening. At that point, I jumped up and crashed through the window. The shutters gave way – I thought they would. I just didn't know if I would find myself dropping three feet, three stories, or over a cliff."

He considered this fact for a second and his eyes met Cordelia's with a look of self-mockery.

"It was three feet. They weren't expecting it. It worked. Like I said, there was deep fog around and the ground dropped steeply. I ran and slid for what seemed like miles, not knowing where I was going, what I might fall into, unable to see. I don't know if I was pursued or not. They couldn't shoot at me because of whoever it was that had come, or even make a commotion chasing me, and they wouldn't likely have hit me or found me in the fog anyway. At least, as you see, no one did catch me. When I realized I wasn't being pursued I slowed to a walk, and I walked all night, not knowing where I was going. Perhaps I walked in circles, I don't know. This morning I came upon houses, a road; I got a ride into the next village. I found a fellow with a garage, and explained my situation – well, a version of it – and asked him if he could look me up on the internet – there's an article there where I'm test-driving an Audi from a year or two ago – fortunately, it has my photo. And so he did, and then he was very helpful. I'm to pay him later, etc. The point is – I borrowed a car from him."

Cordelia smiled, if a little wanly. Of course, just like that.

"I left it running to the side of the station." He shook his head, shrugged his shoulders. "I hope it doesn't get stolen. But I'm getting ahead of my story – I asked to use the garage guy's telephone, and I called you. So then, of course, I had to change my plans…That's why I left the engine on. I was waiting for you at the side of the station where I could see to the trains, but when I saw you come running down the platform alone I went to meet you and left the car. The diversion, the collision, was supposed to take place a little later – but your way worked fine."

"Oh," said Cordelia, rather blankly.

"How did they…What were you doing on the train with them? Did they trick you into going with them or threaten you or what?"

"No. I got on the train myself. They found me there. I don't know how. I suppose they had my cell phone traced. I suppose they came to Warsaw looking for me as soon as you disappeared."

"But what were you doing on the train then?" he asked, puzzled.

"I was coming to rescue you."

"You? To rescue me?" He could hardly have been more incredulous. To be stared at by Darek was worse than being stared at by the agents. She shifted away from him on the bench.

"You?" he added more softly, "who are afraid of everything, even your loving husband?"

Her fingers played nervously with her crutch handle.

"Yes, I went to this private investigator – Bzikowski?" She looked at him to see if he recognized the name.

"You went to Bzikowski," Darek repeated, his eyebrows lifted. "*Kurcze.*" And then: "Go on."

428

"And he found out where you were. So I set out. I didn't suppose I'd succeed, but I had to try." She felt suddenly very shy again.

He stared at her. "My female of the species," he said finally. And then, as she dropped her eyes under his gaze, "They didn't hurt you, did they?"

No, she thought, they threatened to throw me from the train, but that's all in a day's work by now. She shook her head. She wouldn't tell him about that at present. "They didn't behave like well brought-up people, but as you see, I'm whole."

"No, dammit," he said, looking her over. "You look terrible."

"So," she replied tartly, "do you."

They laughed a little together. The laughter of two refugees from disaster.

"You were skinny before, but now you look like a bird. And those circles under your eyes. Tsk." But this was said tenderly; he put a hand under her chin and looked at her, then he raised a hand to his own chin, which was covered in stubble. He also had various scratches on his head and hands, his pants' legs were wet and dirty and he looked, in spite of an extremely keyed-up alertness, tired. Cordelia realized that she had never seen him look the least bit tired before.

"Come," he said, rising, "we'll go get something to eat – I'm as empty as – I don't know what – "

"Those agents' heads?" she said with a scowl.

"You know, that's probably the harshest thing I've ever heard you say – I like it. Yes, that empty. We'll eat and then we'll discuss our plan of action."

Plan of action? Thought Cordelia, but I don't want any more action! I want to go home and go to bed for a

week and be safe. But she walked quietly, uncomplain-
ingly, at his side.

23

They came out of the park by the church, and found themselves, having traversed one or two cobbled streets, on a narrow, little-frequented street within the vicinity of the market square. Here there were many small restaurants; they skirted a heavy farm horse standing with a wagon of cabbages at the curb and entered a door. The warmth that wrapped them round came equally from a roaring fire in the hearth and from the kitchen. They sank into deep chairs at a dark oak table.

"I suppose," said Darek, "judging by the wagon and the odors, the menu will be all *kapuśniak*."

"That's fine," said Cordelia.

But the pretty young waitress who brought the menus informed them earnestly that indeed they had a choice: cabbage as *kapuśniak* or cabbage as *bigos* or cabbage as *pierogis* or cabbage as cabbage.

"Okay. All of that!" said Darek.

And then, seeing that Cordelia looked unenthused, she suggested – well, there was also *żurek* and maybe the cook would make cutlets.

"Yes. That too!" said Darek. And awhile later Cordelia watched the steam rise from their soup bowls as it was rising from the fat sides of the horse outside, and began to feel that perhaps she could eat again, since everything was all right, since Darek was safe...But were they safe? She wanted to ask, to be reassured, but her husband was eating with an intensity which indicated long abstinence, and she decided to wait.

They dined extensively, silently, and followed up the dinner courses with *szarlotka* and coffee.

It was after the coffee had been set down that Darek suddenly turned to Cordelia. "You do have money with you? Because I've just remembered, they took my wallet."

"Yes," she said, blushing, and apologetic, 'I took it from your account. I'm sorry – but I thought in the circumstances...I had to, you see, because I'd used up all my own savings."

He looked puzzled. "How did you do that?"

"To pay Bzikowski."

What Darek said of Bzikowski was not very polite.

"No," Cordelia said, "it was worth it – because otherwise I wouldn't have known – I mean, if you hadn't escaped...I would have thought forever..." She trailed off. She didn't like the way he was looking at her.

"Cordelia, you didn't believe that message they sent?"

She didn't want to answer, but he was insisting. "Did you?"

"Yes, at first." She stared at the table.

"I thought about it all the time," he said at last, in a low, ireful voice. "They told me what they'd written. I suppose it was just a little bit of gratuitous cruelty. Mostly I thought you wouldn't believe it. And then, sometimes, I suspected that you just might be that crazy."

"But," she said, growing even more flustered and apologetic, "when I heard the recording where you're supposed to be a terrorist – I didn't believe *that*."

"*What?*"

432

"D-didn't Zbyś tell you?" And then she realized that he didn't know about any of that, and she would have to tell him. But not about the last article in *Śmiećpospolity*. She couldn't tell him about that yet. He'd be so angry. She filled him in on the rest and he listened in attentive, concentrated silence. When she finished, he replied briskly:

"Now some of what the agents were saying makes sense. Obviously, I knew it had something to do with Hasan and Mashrawi, since we were all there together. I was fairly certain they weren't extremists in any shape or form, but I thought maybe they had unfortunate-seeming connections – and I was just involved because of our dealings. But now it's all clearer."

He dropped his voice, although the restaurant was empty.

"So listen. First things first: about the money – that's our account and our money. You obviously haven't realized you're my wife yet, but we'll work on that later. You don't trust me in the most elementary way – that also we have to leave for later."

Cordelia started to protest, but he cut her off. "No, there's no time now. I have to sleep. I'm going to sleep here for an hour. Then you must wake me up and we have to find where they're keeping the Syrians and we have to stop them from taking them out of the country. We've got a lot to do. Pay the bill so we'll be ready to leave." And with that, he moved his dishes aside, put his head down on his arms and was instantly asleep.

Cordelia ordered another cup of coffee and paid the bill and sat beside him, feeling small and bruised, and wishing he weren't displeased with her. She also found it odd to be sitting in a restaurant beside a man who was sleeping, but she would have guarded him like a snarling

433

dog had anyone suggested he should wake. Fortunately, there was no one to notice.

Outside the casement window the horse and wagon had moved on, and she saw only the wooden window frames and dragon downspout of the tenement building across the street. These were typical, homely Polish sights, as reassuring as the scents and crochet curtains of the little restaurant. And Darek was here beside her, a solid form, his arm six inches from hers. The evil that had erupted so incredibly into their lives seemed to fade a little. But Darek had said they had to stop the agents from taking the Syrians. How were they going to do that? And then again, she didn't want to do that. She wanted safety. She would tell Darek so when he woke – even if he disagreed, even if he were more angry yet, she would tell him that she didn't want to be further involved, and she didn't want him to be involved either.

She looked at her watch. It hurt to raise her wrist, Blandface had twisted it badly or maybe she had injured it going through the station window. Darek had been asleep for an hour. Should she wake him? The waitress came by and asked if she wanted anything more. She shook her head and the waitress, having been well tipped before, took herself off. But her voice had disturbed Darek. One moment he was sleeping and the next he was seemingly wide awake. He raised his head and called the waitress back:

"Excuse me *pani*, is there an internet café near here?"

Yes, she said, just off the market square, around the corner.

"So," he said to Cordelia, "let's get going." He rose, took their coats from the rack, was holding hers for her.

"Home, you mean?" she said, as she slid into the coat.

He didn't answer until they were out the door and in the street. It was dark by now and the light from buildings and street lamps came filtered through a layer of hanging fog from which the occasional snowflake fluttered down in zigzag paths.

"No. I mean we have to find where they're holding my two companions in misfortune and we have to summon everyone we can to the place and we have to stop them from being transported. And we may not have much time because I don't know how long the weather will stay bad. They were saying it was expected to clear tomorrow afternoon or the next day."

"It sounds," she said slowly, "very risky. What if they catch you instead?"

He shrugged and started walking with long strides in the direction of the internet café.

The point of her crutch slid awkwardly on the cobblestones as she hurried to keep up with him. He slowed for her.

"Are they your friends?" she asked tentatively.

"No, I hardly know them. Just business acquaintances."

"But you're willing to risk everything for them…?"

He grinned, his usual humor returning. "They haven't finished paying me."

She ignored his jest.

"Right now," she said carefully, stopping, so that he was forced to stop too, "you are comparatively safe. You are free and able to complain to various agencies and organizations; you can make it clear that you are innocent. You can try to trace the recording to its source, try to find out who passed it to the agents and pursue that person through the courts. Once there is enough publicity it is unlikely – you've said so yourself – that they will come back for you. But if they catch you now, they will whisk you away to some distant place and it may be that no one will ever hear from you again. They can not be held accountable." She paused to draw breath. "I want you to stay safe."

"All that you say is true," he replied, growing serious to match her seriousness, "but the Syrians are going to be shipped out. It is likely that *they* will never be heard of again. Basically, their lives may be at stake. I can't *not* do anything."

"I am very sorry for them," she said, "but you matter more to me than they do – and even if that were not the case, if I had no concern for you, I would think you could do more for them by seeking help. If you are safe you can make every effort to get justice for them. You can do everything for them that I would try to do for you – and you will do it better. If you are caught, you'll be in their situation yourself."

"I'm sorry, Cordelia," he said, "but I have to try to stop this. You could be a help to me, but if you prefer you can get away from it all at once."

"Please come with me." She had never asked him for anything before.

He raised his hands. "I can't. And I can't spend time talking. There are things that have to be done. There's no time to waste. So – we'll part here for now."

She stared at him disbelievingly.

"Cordelia," he said, "please…" But she turned away from him. "Don't go to Warsaw," he said to her averted face, "take the bus and go spend some days in Cracow. They won't look for you there. I've asked Zbyś to send a security company round to your family's house. I'll see you soon." He took a step towards her as if to kiss her goodbye, but she stepped back, not angrily – how could she be angry with him? She understood him – but because of the distance that had opened between them, because of her sense of powerlessness to stop what she saw as a disastrous course. 'Darek!' she wanted to cry. He looked at her for a long moment, an indecipherable expression on his face, and then turned away, was walking away.

And suddenly she remembered that she could stop him.

She said, very clearly: "But I have the money."

It stopped him in his tracks. He had none. There was nothing he could do without it.

"I'd forgotten," he said turning, and then, "how much do you have?"

She told him. His eyebrows went up.

"What were you planning to do?"

"I don't know. I wanted to be ready for anything."

"Yes, excellent. Take what you need and give me the rest."

She shook her head, her heart pounding. He stared at her incredulous.

"Cordelia, give it to me."

"No." Her voice was small, but her determination was plain.

He took a step towards her and it flashed across her mind that he could easily take the money from her, and that also, if he used physical force with her, it would be the end between them. The same thought obviously occurred to him, because he said, furiously, "Don't quake like that – you know I won't take it from you."

She backed another half-step away from him. "Please consider…" she began.

He interrupted her. "I can't believe you could be so callous," he snapped.

"Think of the possibilities," she tried again.

But he merely added, more coldly still, "I'm disappointed in you."

Cordelia was crushed but unyielding.

"I'd rather," she said, as tears began to drip, "you were disappointed than dead. You think you're indestructible, but you're not. If you really want to help those men, you won't do it like that."

A passerby gave them a curious glance and a shrug. A lover's quarrel, nothing new.

Behind Cordelia, a cement traffic pylon was blocking an alley. She sat down on it. Darek wavered, walked six rapid steps up the street, and then six steps back. He stood considering, and then he took a deep breath, and came towards her. He knelt beside her, wiped her tears away with his hand, and said, "I didn't mean what I said." He paused for a moment, while she waited tensely. But all he said was, "Could I at least have the wherewithal to buy cigarettes?"

She gave him the money and he jogged up the street to the light pouring out from a small grocery store and in a minute came strolling thoughtfully back, smoking. He sat down on an adjacent pylon and regarded her over the cigarette smoke.

"The CIA has taken thousands of people around the world. Like that fellow from Germany – you've probably heard of him – he was abducted because a certain CIA official, quote, 'had a hunch he was someone else.' He was lucky, he was eventually freed. Most aren't. You know what happens to them. God, Cordelia, they even take children and subject them to who knows what! These two fellows, they have wives, one I know has children – they may never see them again."

"I know all that!" said Cordelia, in pain.

"You know it and it doesn't matter?"

"Yes, yes it does – and I know too that Cheney talks about how the US will 'work through the dark side' and 'use any means available.' Any means available to the US! It is too large to fight by yourself! This isn't the CBA. These aren't Poles who, however unscrupulous, may still be accountable to someone, sometime. These people are completely lacking in morals and they are untouchable. You will just end up along with the others – in Afghanistan or who-knows-where and I will never see you again."

"And still, I have to do it. Please try to understand."

She did understand. She understood it in all its angles. She said, more quietly: "So many people have been abducted – you knew that, but did you ever feel called upon to do anything about it before?"

He flicked the ash off his cigarette. "Actually, yes, for several years now I have been making quite sizable contributions to various organizations working for the respect of such prisoners' rights."

That stopped her for a moment. 'Quite sizable' must really be a lot; he never said, in speaking of money, anything other than 'a bit' or 'a little.' When he said 'a bit' it meant half a million or some such sum. She turned this over in her mind, realizing with a pang that there were a great many things about him that she didn't know yet.

He added wryly, "I little thought it might have such personal application, but of course, when such things begin to happen, no one's safe."

His cigarette smoke mingled with the fog. Perched between the darkness of the alley and the dull light of the street lamps, he waited patiently for her to come round. Cordelia felt overwhelmed by the unreality of their situation, by her sense of terror, but she pulled herself together for another attempt to dissuade him.

"But," she argued, "you never felt the need to rush out – you, yourself – to save anyone physically before. Why go to such extreme lengths now, when it could be so dangerous?"

"Because I am personally involved and," he hesitated just slightly and then added, "it's a matter of honor."

Oh, she thought, that was really unfair.

There was a long pause in which everything held in the balance.

But there was nothing she could say after that. She had to give in. If he really thought that and she prevented him, he would lose his respect for her and would eventually cease to love her. She would rather he was alive and indifferent than that he was dead; but if he were alive and diminished in his own self-worth, because he had given up on what he considered a matter of honor? It wasn't possible.

"But if our roles were exchanged," she said finally, defeated. "You wouldn't try to keep me safe?"

He hesitated too long. "But I've already told you I need your help."

Yes, she thought, but at a certain point, at the point where things get dangerous, you will leave me behind. But she did not say this; she rose, reached under her coat and undid her money belt, handed it to him, and said quietly, "You'd better tell me what you want me to do then."

"Come," he said, with a look of relief and gratitude that wrung her heart.

"So," he said, as she followed him up the street towards the internet café. "The situation is this: there are a dozen of them – at least that's about the number of voices I could distinguish, I didn't see many of them…"

"Including Military Cut and Blandface, or without?"

"Who are they?"

"Military Cut is the guy who says 'ma'am' all the time…"

He smiled. "No one said 'ma'am' to me!"

"Oh…no, I suppose not. And Blandface is the nervous one with the foul vocabulary. He says 'shut up' all the time."

"Oh…no, I think that one's name is Bob. At least that's what he's called – they'll all be code names. He's the leader, I think."

"Go on, I interrupted."

"Yes, so there are quite a number of them – I think a dozen from their voices, I couldn't see them because of the hood – including M.C. and Blandface, and, as you noticed, they are all extremely nervous because things are not working out as expected. The plan, I believe – because I only heard scraps of talk – but, on the other hand, they talked about nothing else – was that they were to grab the three of us all on the same day. The two others were easy – they went to their apartments in Warsaw, some time in the very early hours of that morning we left the hotel, flashed badges, said 'police, come with us,' and the men went docilely, believingly, were shown into an unmarked delivery van where they were knocked to the floor, their clothes were cut off, they were dressed in grey track suits, handcuffed, draped in hoods, drugged, and driven here. No fuss, no one noticed. I was a little more difficult – they had been told, I'm afraid, that I probably wouldn't be caught that way. So they tracked us to the hotel – again, I imagine through the cell phone, which argues accomplices somewhere in the CBA, I suppose, or secret service; fixed the car to break down and expected to pick me up along the road. I'm not sure whether you were going to be picked up too, because they didn't want a witness, or whether you were to be left by the side of the road. Only their sabotage didn't work as quickly as expected and then we took the turn-off instead of staying on the main road. It was fortunate that it worked out the way it did – when they came up to me at the station they said if I came quietly they'd leave you. So I went. And they took me to the van and – well, good thing they realized their standard-size track suit wouldn't fit me before they starting snipping my clothes…I got better treatment than the Arabs did anyway."

His voice hardened and Cordelia glanced at him, but he was intent on his story.

"So we were taken to this place, somewhere in the wilderness near here, and the next morning a plane was supposed to land and we were to be put on it and shipped out. Everything was working like a charm up to that point. Only then the weather changed, and the plane couldn't get in to land. Not to mention they drove the van over a well head and so it's stuck with one wheel down the shaft and they didn't have in enough supplies for everyone and there's a problem with the heating in their hideout – that's why they let me keep my coat – otherwise I'd have been in bad shape when I escaped. Hasan and Mashrawi were taken in their pajamas and they're suffering. I begged blankets for them, but I just got gagged for my pains. In general though, I wasn't subjected to anything like the same humiliations and indignities they were – a racial thing, I think. I'm fair and don't match their idea of a Muslim terrorist, whatever they may have been told. The others do. Anyway, of the agents, only one speaks any Polish – very brokenly. Three were apparently here already in the country; the other fellows seem to have flown in especially for the operation. Now they're all feeling trapped and they want to get out as they know it's only a matter of time before a lot of people know that something's up. I think the change of government has them a bit thrown because they're not sure of the new quantities."

They had arrived at the internet café.

"What are we going to do here?"

"I'd like you to go in and find out where are the nearest airports; then make a list of all the tourist or other lodging facilities within walking distance of the village of Trawka. And mind you, I don't know how far I walked. I was traveling all night, and one would think a man might easily cover, say, twenty-five miles in that time. But it was dark, the terrain was very rough, and I may have walked, as I said before, in circles. I don't think it will be very close to the village, because they won't want to have been disturbed. On the other hand, I don't know how remote, either. So make a list of all the possibilities. Here," he reached into his coat and took out a pen and small memo pad and gave them to her. "I got these for you."

She looked at them. "You bought these when you went for cigarettes, didn't you?"

He realized his mistake and gave her a rueful smile. "Unlike my wife, I have great faith in my spouse."

"Yes, well, and what are you going to do?"

"I'm going – circumspectly – to get the car and then I'll be back. Don't look like that – really, I'll be back." He paused a moment, then added, "but just in case, here's some of the money back. If I don't return in say, four hours, then call Zbyś, tell him to contact the police, and you go yourself to Cracow, all right?"

443

She nodded and watched him jog to the end of the street and disappear. I may never see him again, she thought. She went into the café.

The interior was rather dark and there seemed to be a great many young men playing, from the sounds, war games on their computers.

Soon she was seated at a terminal. Once, she thought, as bullets appeared to ricochet from the computers on either side while the players jerked and moaned as if truly engaged in battle, I had a normal life. Once, in the very, very distant past – almost two months ago – I lived an exceedingly quiet and mouse-like existence. Those days are gone.

She set to work earnestly, looking first for airports. There were two within a reasonable distance of Przestrzyna; the next nearest was near Rzeszów. One, it appeared, the closer, had been shut down a month ago due to an ownership dispute after privatization. That was the one Bzikowski had mentioned. If she had gone looking for Darek there she would have been disappointed. The other was in operation, taking both cargo and passenger planes of some size but having a relatively short runway. Or so she read; she did not know what made a runway short, or if that was significant. Probably, she thought, making notes, it would influence the kind of aircraft that could land there.

Next she found a satellite picture of the area and had it printed, in multiple sheets, so that she had a large map of the area covering Przestrzyna, the village of Trawka, and the airports. Then she began to look for lodgings to let in the area.

The list was long. She discarded all those that were merely rooms in a farmhouse and marked down the addresses and phone numbers of those that appeared to be individual cabins or vacation houses. She also looked for any army bases, used or not, in the area. She did not find any listed, and the only thing that might have corresponded to such a facility on the satellite map was a curious cluster of buildings that did not have the appearance of farm buildings and was oddly located for an industrial site. It might also have been an old communist vacation centre, but, on closer inspection, it appeared to have a wall or fence around it, and Darek hadn't said anything about having to cross a fence during his escape.

She started with the village of Trawka. Darek, she thought, would not have walked in circles; he would have walked downhill, as he had mentioned to her that they would do on leaving the Jaguar that day. The village was on a rise. But he had come to a road first. There were three roads leading into the village. She had to look for constructions from which, by walking downhill most of the night, he could have come to one of these roads.

She didn't know how long it would take Darek to get the car. He would have to take the bus there, she supposed – or would he take a taxi? If he took a taxi, it wouldn't take long; he would drive back. It wouldn't be more than half an hour – forty-five minutes at the most. He had been gone an hour. He had said that if he didn't return in four hours she should call Zbyś. It wouldn't take four hours to get the car – she had realized that when he left. What was he doing? She pushed down her anxiety and went on with her task.

At length she had a long list of lodgings that she had located on the map and seemed like possibilities. Two hours had passed and Darek still hadn't returned. Well, she thought, if the abductors had him again then the sooner she had an idea where he was, the better. She turned to the young person seated next to her:

"Excuse me?"

"Aw, *prosze pani!*" said the young person in dismay, "*pani* distracted me; *pani* made me get killed."

You have no idea, thought Cordelia, no idea at all, but she apologized humbly and asked if he knew where she might find a pay phone. There wasn't a pay phone that worked in all of Przestrzyna he said — suddenly seeming to take note of her features and being stirred to helpfulness — but if she wanted to buy him a new phone card at the grocery store down the street, he would let her use his cell phone. She thanked him and rose to carry out his suggestion. His eyes swiveled, as if by magnetic force, back to his screen.

Cordelia stood on the step of the internet café with the stranger's cell phone and a list of telephone numbers. Darek had been gone for two and a half hours. It could not have taken that long to fetch the car. Her stomach began to knot again. I am not made for this, she thought, I'm not, I'm not. She breathed deep of the cold, damp air; she could hardly see the end of the street through the murky weather. Here and there some figure, well-bundled up, emerged between the snowflakes, but none of them came with Darek's firm step.

She called one number after another. Half the premises were still available for rent, and had not had occupiers yesterday. Several owners did not answer their phones, and several others said their places were occupied. So that made quite a few possibilities, she thought. Plus any houses or facilities there might be that were not on any lists. But she thought it less likely that the CIA would use those — how would they find such places unless they were government constructions?

Perhaps she should also call the journalist to whom she had spoken just before leaving Warsaw? Perhaps he had found something out, would know something useful? He had told her he would be making every effort to discover how the journalist from *Śmiećpospolity* had got hold of the original recording. And if he could do that, then he might be closer to finding who had made it. He didn't have time to tell her how he had traced the recording to the computer in a government office, and he didn't know who had used the computer, but he would continue his investigations. She had promised to keep him informed of her own adventures and had left him fired with enthusiasm. It seemed to her that contacting him would be a good thing to do – but she was unaccustomed to making such decisions. Would Darek think it was a good idea for her to be in touch with the media? Her last attempts in that direction had certainly gone awry. She trembled before the idea that she might make matters even worse than they were, and yet, it would shortly be nine-thirty, and after nine-thirty it would be improper to call. She hesitated a little longer, then took out the journalist's card and called his number.

When she had finished she went inside again, sat down beside the phone's owner, and in an apparent pause in his activities on the screen, managed to purchase the phone from him. She thought he sold it to her as much to stop her from distracting him as from the large sum of cash she offered. He took her money and then they both turned back to their respective screens.

She had better let her family know what was happening with her too as she was certainly not going to be back that evening. What were they all doing, she wondered? They would check the news, but she knew from checking internet sites that there wasn't anything there and that would be their only source. She would write an email to Antek. She had to summarize for him what had happened and that was a difficult task. She stared for a while at the blank screen and decided on brevity: "*I'm in Przestrzyna, with Darek. We are both safe. Darek was abducted by the CIA and escaped; I was also their prisoner for a while and I too escaped. You will think that I am delusional but I assure you this is not the case. We will be back tomorrow, I hope. Love, Cordelia.*" She sent the message.

After a time she checked her mail again and found a laconic reply, in Antek's characteristic combination of nervous pessimism, oddity, and common sense.

"*I noticed you didn't come back from town. At least you're with Darek. If there's anything to be done let me know and I'll try to do it. Good luck.*

P.S. The new technologies identify people by their retinas. I just thought I'd mention it in case you were considering plastic surgery. Plus, I've developed your wedding photos and they wouldn't match any more."

She logged off the computer and checked the clock on the wall. "Good luck." It was becoming increasingly apparent that their good luck might have run out. Three and a half hours had passed. By Darek's own assessment, if he didn't show up in another half hour it meant something had happened to him.

She had expected something of the sort when she'd tried to stop him in the street. Being right wasn't comforting though. She went back over their conversation as strange, vaguely-connected ideas passed through her mind and she watched the hands of the clock. She remembered a book on ballet showing a dance choreographed from a male and a female point of view. In the female point of view the ballerina is lifted in a white dress, in the arms of the male dancer; in the male

448

view, the ballerina clings to his leg while he strikes a pose of anguish and tries to get free. Did Darek see her that way, she wondered, even a little bit? He had assured her that if they could survive the next few days – if they could not fall into the hands of the CIA before the airplane took the agents away – then they would be safe. But he wasn't going to make any effort to stay safe and perhaps the necessity of appeasing her had weighed on him, like the ballerina in the choreography from the male point of view. She didn't like this image of herself. And yet if she hadn't been so worried she would have been angry. Why hadn't he come back?

There was nothing to do but wait. Three and three-quarter hours. Various bits of poetry and snatches of psalms passed through her mind, but she couldn't keep hold of any. The seconds just ticked by. Something must have happened to him.

24

If he wasn't back in eight minutes, she was to call Zbyś. There didn't seem any doubt now that he wasn't coming, but she waited out the last minutes with a sort of empty dread, realizing that she might never know what had happened to him.

If he had been killed, then, at the town hall, when the guns went off and she saw him fall, she would have regretted him deeply, mourned him, had great difficulty returning to her former life – but his memory would have faded; there would have been too little to hang onto. But now – if anything were to happen to him now – his absence would be with her forever; perhaps time would numb her pain but her grief would be unending, boundless; she would never get over it, never.

Four more minutes.

And then a car was pulling up outside the café windows, someone was emerging hurriedly. She didn't recognize him at first – he was wearing a ski cap and had changed his coat. Darek! Her heart leapt with wild relief. He was here, he had come, her life, her love! She rushed to the door and met him coming in.

"Quick!" he said.

She was as quick as she knew how. Three steps and they were at the car, he was opening the door, she was in; he was running around to the other side.

"Get down," he said, turning and pretending to fumble in the glove box.

She bent down below the dashboard, only taking in, with some remote corner of her mind, the unfamiliar plastic of the dashboard, the slight smell of cigarettes and upholstery soap.

A large vehicle, a Hummer with dark-tinted windows, drove slowly past but did not stop.

"Stay down," Darek said and they followed the Hummer at a distance, but when it turned right towards the old market square — they watched it maneuver the tight corner with difficulty — they turned left and drove away from it, through nearly empty streets. They drove past old tenement houses and shops with grilles covering their windows, until eventually, opposite a looming Catholic church with twin spires and baroque embellishments — just such a church as they had been married in, only two weeks ago — they turned into a short alleyway, emerged in the courtyard parking lot of an aging apartment building, and came to a stop again. Cordelia looked at Darek and swallowed, but he relieved her a little by smiling — a gay smile, a smile full of excited pleasure overlaying his high-wired tension. Some part of him was enjoying these disasters, she noticed with a bit of anguish.

"What's happening?" she asked.

"That's why I stopped — I thought we'd better fill each other in. Did you get a list of possible accommodations?"

She told him all that she had done, hoping she had done well.

"Hmm," he said appreciatively when she finished, "I always thought it was a pity you didn't come to work for me."

No, she thought, horrors. He was polite to his employees but he expected them to jump and read his mind.

"Being married to you is good, but being your boss would have been better," he teased.

She didn't smile back at him; she was too tense, too frightened.

"Hey," he said, "things are looking up."

"That's why we're hiding in a courtyard?"

"Well, I'll tell you about that. So – the first thing I did when I left you was to go to the police – "

"You did?!" she interrupted, furiously, "But I thought you said we couldn't go, because we couldn't be sure that faced with such a story the police wouldn't call someplace higher up, and someplace higher up might tell them to hand us over? Didn't you say that?"

"Er, ye-es. And it was true – that's why I didn't take you with me."

"But," said Cordelia – "oh" said Cordelia – and then she stopped and compressed her lips. It was useless. "Go on," she said instead.

"And I talked to the chief – who was everything one could want. Very correct, listened carefully, said that of course it was unthinkable that foreign agents should engage in illegal activities on Polish territory," Darek's eyes were smiling but his voice had taken on the rather ponderous inflections of a Polish police officer, "and that he would do everything he could to stop such activity should he have proof that it were really occurring. Nor, if he were aware of such activity, would any directives from above deter him from the prosecution of his official duty, etc., etc."

"Oh good!" cried Cordelia, "then he'll take care of it all! I'm so relieved."

"Well, but then – not so good," Darek continued in his own voice, "he said that he had to tell me that he had heard of me, read about me, seen me on the news, etc., and that he had an idea that I was a person who liked publicity – " Darek grinned, "and that it was crossing his mind that this might be just another publicity stunt, and if so, he didn't want to be involved, because he didn't think the last persons who got involved that way had come out of it so well."

"No," said Cordelia, "they didn't."

"Yes, I said, but they had been abusing the law and he would be upholding it – there was a world of difference. All very possible, he said, but he'd rather stay on the sidelines all the same, thank you."

"But there are these two men about to be shipped to torture in a foreign country!" exclaimed Cordelia.

"That's what I said too – as to that, he said, I hadn't brought him a scrap of evidence, but he was willing to make out a report, and if I had any further information I could call him."

"He won't try to find them?" Cordelia cried in dismay. "He won't do anything? How can he not do anything?"

Darek shook his head. "He said that even if he wanted to, he would be unable, because he's understaffed, there are gasoline allowances, and the resources of the station simply won't allow him to carry out investigations that he thinks likely to come to nothing. So I asked him if I found them myself would he send sufficient officers to prevent their leaving the airport?"

Cordelia bit back an objection and Darek went on.

"He said the airport was not his jurisdiction, but in that case he would do what he could...Well, I've paraphrased a lot, but that was the gist of our conversation. I'm quite encouraged. He's an okay guy. I think if we can find them, he'll come to the rescue. Or try to, at least, which is all we can hope for."

"Why doesn't the police chief just send someone to stake out the road to the airport? Then when they come along he can call for reinforcements."

"Because by then it will be too late. One policeman or even two or three won't be enough to stop them – that's why it's important to find them ahead of time. So when the coast is clear I'll get going."

You'll get going, thought Cordelia, noting the pronoun with part of her mind.

But all she said was: "Yes – but you haven't told me why we had to run from the internet café – were those the agents in that dark vehicle?"

"The Hummer. Yes. I think the station's closing so they've given up watching it – that's what they were doing before – and they're circling the city on the off-chance of spotting us. They won't keep that up long. I'll give them a while to go home because I don't want to meet them on the road, and I have an idea they're going to be stopping soon. I didn't think tailing them to their hideout would be possible, given the scarcity of traffic on the country roads – and other difficulties."

"How did you get the car if they were watching the station?"

"Well, so I walked from the police station to a gas station, to get some gas, then to the railway station – it's not far – and as I was approaching I saw that there was this Hummer there, just sitting, sitting, and the windows are dark-tinted. That would have seemed quite suspect to me in itself, but I'd heard them mentioning 'the Hummer' there where I was kept, so I retreated, found a supermarket selling winter clothes and bought these things – I bought you a new coat and hat too, to make you less recognizable – just in case, just until things settle down." He reached into the back seat for a dark down parka and cap – "Here they are…Put them on."

She changed her coat.

"Nothing will hide my limp – but tell me the rest."

"So, disguised as you see me now, I was going to walk right past the Hummer and get in this car – it was parked a little ways in front of them. And as I get close to the Hummer I can see that it's full of agents, so I bend down by the back tire, unscrew the cap on the vent, and jam it open with a small twig. Then I walked on and put the gas in my car – I'd left it running, you know, when I came to you on the platform, so it was on less than empty – and drove away. They didn't notice what I'd done – they were all looking at the station entrance, I suppose – they didn't recognize me as I walked past or as I worked on the car in front of them. Hah! They'll have a flat tire!" He laughed. A carefree laugh with a certain glee in it.

Cordelia stared at him in disbelief. "You're crazy!" she jerked out the words angrily, "Crazy! How can you do things like that? You risk everything – for nothing! For a joke!"

"I didn't risk everything – I knew I wouldn't get caught."

Cordelia bit off the words and turned her head away, leaning it against the window, anger against him boiling in her heart.

"Cordelia – " he said, after a moment.

"No! Don't Cordelia me! This is serious – and you don't take it seriously. You convinced me that you have to do all this because of those two men. But you won't be reasonable, you won't be careful, and you will end up just like them!"

"Cordelia –"

"I'm worried to death and you're laughing!"

He pulled her into his arms and she clung to him. But after a while, he said, into her hair, "I do take all this seriously – very. I deeply do not want anything to happen to my acquaintances and I'm going to do everything I can to prevent it. But at the same time – if I can't keep some sense of fun what's the point of living at all?"

You might not live at all, she thought, lots of people have died. She didn't say anything though. His natural high spirits were one of the things she loved in him – how could she want him to change? It was all so complicated and she was exhausted.

"I'll take you to a hotel now," he was saying, "I can feel how tired you are – I forget sometimes."

"No!" she said, pulling back to look him in the eye. "I'm going with you!"

"No!" he said firmly.

"Yes," she said, with an icy resolve that took him aback.

"But –"

"Yes, I know I might be an encumbrance," she said carefully, "I've thought of that. I've weighed the possibilities. Still – I think you will be safer with a ball and chain on your leg. And you've just proved it."

"You want to be my ball and chain?"

"I insist."

"But I'm not intending to do anything drastic; I'm going to try to find where they're at – if it can't be done from a safe distance it can't be done at all. You don't need to come with me."

"If there's no danger then there's no reason I shouldn't come."

He looked for a moment as if he were going to argue, then he tilted his head: "Fair enough," he said, after a pause. "We'll wait another half-hour and start our search."

She gave him a glance of relief and gratitude. "Oh," she said, "and I bought this." She handed him a cell phone. "I bought it from one of the game players at the internet café. I suppose I paid a ridiculous amount for it – but I thought it would be good to have one."

"Oh, very good! I was thinking we'd have to find someplace to buy one."

"Here, you keep it. You'll be faster if we need to call the police."

He took the phone, saying "the police – that reminds me. There was something puzzling. The police chief wanted to talk to you, and I told him you'd come in later and make a report….but from something he said I got the impression he disliked me because he thought I'd been mistreating you. Isn't that strange? I wonder where he got such an idea?"

"Ah," said Cordelia, any remaining ire vanishing in the rush of returning guilt. "Ah," she said again, turning her head away and leaning it against the window again.

"Ah?"

"Yes," she sighed unhappily.

"Hmmm," he answered, a long-drawn out, reflective sound. "Er?"

"Well, you might as well know," she said, resignedly, "While I was waiting for you at the café, I made print-outs of all the newspaper articles. I thought you'd want to see them." She handed over the ones about his being a terrorist. "These I've already told you about."

He took the sheets, turned the overhead light on, and read.

"Yes, it's as you told me."

"It's much worse even than before – when it was being implied that you were involved in corruption, isn't it?"

"I don't know," he said grimly, "this is so far-fetched I think it won't be much believed. The other, that was something everybody would believe easily because it's quite common and Poles tend to think anyone who has money must be dishonest anyway. But you said you got corrections or refutations in some papers?"

She handed him some others: "These are the articles that were printed after I talked to the journalists." She kept back the one from *Śmiećpospolity*.

"And you really remembered all this conversation we had?" he asked, as he read the first.

"Yes – you don't?"

He twitched an eyebrow. "Some things I remember. What we said about our finances, for instance. Other than that – only the general outlines."

She contemplated for a second the immense difference in their world views.

He went on reading.

"Very nice – well done," he said when he had finished. "I'd say you handled it extremely well." He was angry though, she could feel the vibrations of it in the car.

"I thought it would be better to tell it like it was, sort of," she said, taking a quick glance at his profile, "but it was very embarrassing and then…" She didn't finish her sentence, about how she knew she'd made a hash of it.

"Yes," he said, "I can imagine it must have been very difficult for you – I'm surprised you did it, actually. Surprised and impressed. You've all sorts of talents I knew nothing about."

"No – that's what's so awful. I tried to do something and it backfired entirely. I..."

"How so? With one meeting you persuaded a group of journalists to do the sort of thing I only managed to achieve by that whole hoopla at the town hall. I'd say your plan was beautifully economical in conception."

"In conception, maybe, but in consequence...well, there's this one –" she kept it between her fingers though, she didn't give it to him.

He waited a moment and then reached over and slid it out of her hand. She looked at him nervously, waited while he read. There was a moment of stunned silence.

"*Gawd!*"

She turned her face back to the window, her fingers twisting rather franticly in her hair.

"They made this up!"

"No, all the words are ours. It's just – out of context."

"*Jesus.*"

"I – I'm so sorry," she was stammering, "I thought if I told the journalists a little of our true conversation – that it would be better than having everyone think you were a terrorist – then this journalist got access to our real words – and because I had revealed some of the conversation before – that's what makes it so dreadful – they're able to say they're quoting me...so it's really my own fault."

"It is not your fault! It's journalism of the filthiest kind!"

She didn't turn back to look at him. "I'm so sorry. You wanted to go into politics – and I started your career like this."

He considered this for a long moment. Then he crumpled up the piece of paper and tossed it into the back of the car. "I'm not going to lose any sleep over it," he said, but his voice was forbidding.

When she didn't turn away from the window, he reached out and gently disentangled her hand from her hair. "Cordelia, my possible political career isn't the first thing on my mind right now. It's also never going to be the most important thing to me. And I doubt if such an obvious slander will be very damaging anyway – but you'd better act mighty happy whenever you're with me, okay?"

She turned and looked at him. "You're not angry?"

"At you? Let me show you how angry I'm not."

These might be her last memories of Darek, Cordelia thought, these embraces in a strange car, in a dark courtyard, with the snowflakes melting on the windscreen, and the light a dim yellow behind the rectangular windows of the tenement buildings. They were parked between a wooden staircase hanging crookedly against an outer wall and a row of metal garbage bins. Someone's laundry, hung on a balcony in the vain hope that the wind would dry it, was growing damper. Even by night Cordelia knew the building would be missing large chunks of stucco. It was a squalid location, a location from a previous century, but the inside of the car seemed like an isolated world, warm enough with the motor running occasionally, and cozy. I have been married two weeks, she thought; it is not enough, but I would have memories for a lifetime.

"It's time to go," said Darek, "the coast should be clear by now." He put his hand out to the ignition. "They should have had time to fix that tire and get back."

It was nearly midnight when the car nosed out of the courtyard, through the dark alley and into the light of streetlamps. It turned sedately from the alleyway onto the street and there was a popping sound, a crushing sound, and a distinct sideways lurch to the vehicle.

Darek pulled over to the curb.

"What is it? What's happened?" asked Cordelia.

"*You*," he said vigorously, "will say it's poetic justice, I suppose."

"And what will you say?" she asked in alarm.

"Oh, '*bugger*' I suppose – only you won't let me, will you?"

"No."

"So *dammit*, I'm left speechless." He was teasing her, but he grimaced as well. "We've got a flat tire. I must have run over a beer bottle." He was already sliding out of the car, "I just hope there's a spare and a jack." He went to look.

Cordelia twisted in her seat and watched him rapidly removing various items from the trunk. So there was a spare. So it was all right then.

She turned back to the street, which was nearly empty, only a very occasional car still passed, or the occasional pedestrian, of the kind that summoned up images of stray cats wandering the night. The church was there too, cold and closed-looking now. But perhaps there were candles still burning inside. The idea pleased her and so, to calm herself, she said a 'Hail Mary' and then went on:

"*Our Father who art in heaven/ Hallowed be thy name*"

461

She felt the car being jacked beneath her, and simultaneously, she became aware that someone was shouting somewhere nearby, the sound coming muffled as if through a wall.

"*Hallowed be thy name*"

"*Baaastard*!"

The word intersected her prayer with a jolt. She tried to concentrate on her devotions, but the shouted words became gradually louder, reached full-extent-of-the-lungs volume, and resolved themselves into a man's voice and a woman's voice, a marital or extra-marital quarrel, occurring somewhere in the building beside which they were parked.

Cordelia tried to shut it out. "*Give us this day our daily bread.*"

"*Did you bring any money home? Did you? And there's not a scrap of bread in the house!*"

"*Kurwa!*"

"*Forgive us our trespasses…*"

The participants were not sparing each other either insults or obscenities. Cordelia shuddered and resolutely finished the prayer. The battle continued. She wondered what Darek was thinking – if he remembered their disagreement that afternoon (but of course he did) – and if he wondered whether it was possible they might ever carry on in anything remotely approaching the manner of these combatants.

Something crashed inside the building. It appeared the pair was throwing things now. Please God they wouldn't start beating on one another.

Darek rose from the pavement beside the front wheel and opened her door. "Do you hear that?" He gestured with the tire iron.

She nodded. "Yes, I hope they don't get violent."

"I hope they kill each other at once and get it over with."

"Tsk."

"Yes, but you know, if I think someone is getting beat up I can't just ignore it. I'll have to go and try to stop it. So I'm warning you ahead of time – if I take off that's where I've gone."

New vistas of danger opened before her. He would go to separate a quarreling couple and get knifed or clubbed! "But your friends with the CIA…" she started to argue.

He stared at her for a second, and she backtracked.

"Okay. Never mind. You have to do it. Hopefully they'll stop."

He gave an uncertain and disgusted look up at the building, where the screeches still continued but no one seemed to be getting injured, and went back to changing the tire.

Cordelia rolled down the car window and leaned out. "Darek?"

"Hm?" He didn't look up.

"How will you get into the building?"

"Hopefully someone will open when I ring at the intercom. I can break the door if I have to."

"Wouldn't it be better to just push on the intercom button and say 'here's some bread,' or, alternatively, 'police'?"

"I won't know which apartment is theirs."

"Push on all the buttons and say 'police' to everyone."

"Cordelia," he said with approval, "you have unsuspected depths of depravity."

No, she thought, I just want to keep you safe and it sharpens my wits. But the noise above was decreasing, and then, with the hurling of a few last epithets, ceased entirely. Darek turned from where he was tightening a lug nut and looked up at the building.

"Do you think…" Cordelia began.

"That someone's dead? I hope so. People who behave like that are no loss, in my opinion."

"We were quarreling in the street," Cordelia reminded him, tentatively, because she didn't like to remember it, but partly out of incurable fair-mindedness and partly because it still bothered her, "just this afternoon."

"We were having a deeply moral discussion over means, that's hardly the same thing." Darek gave another twist to the tire iron.

Cordelia leaned her chin on the edge of the door and contemplated his profile. She adored his profile. "We were quarreling about money."

"That's what I said." He smiled at her, and after a second she smiled back, but somewhere a slight worry remained.

"When I think," he added, after a minute, "that I might have been sidetracked from trying to save some real victims! But I'm glad they've stopped. We've got to get on. I'm almost done here."

But you don't have to go around saving people, thought Cordelia. Then again, maybe he did, maybe it was part of who he was. But was it part of who she was? A faint memory stirred: Darek saying 'but you're always laying yourself out for others – your family, your dog – me. You just don't make any fanfare about it.' She had brushed off the thought then and she did so now. She had very large doubts about her capacity – physical or mental – to do any sort of saving, in whatever minor manner it might be construed. So had she really meant it about being a ball and chain? It didn't seem like a very appealing role. And yet – he might get hurt and she had to look out for him. It was all very complicated, and, as he said, the night was passing.

But he was putting away the punctured tire, throwing the tools with a clang of metal into the trunk, jumping into the car seat and starting the engine again. They made a rapid u-turn in front of the tall church and were driving through Przestrzyna and her mind instantly reverted to previous worries.

Having traversed the town, they took the highway into the woods and fog and unseen meadows, toward the village of Trawka.

They were passing along a road lined with small houses, each with its garden and outbuildings, and an occasional small store or workshop.

"That," said Darek, as they passed a garage, "is the establishment of my friendly garage-keeper. This was the only car he could lend, he said, and he's just brought it from Germany and doesn't know what its defects may be, if any. It's a BMW, I don't know if you noticed. It sounds to me like the timing is off or the valves are loose and it has one or two other defects, but for the moment it seems to be running all right – but it's not a very new car, far from it, and we'll have to hope for the best."

"It has gasoline?" worriedly asked Cordelia, whose knowledge of the inner workings of automobiles was nil but who had vivid memories of various outings with her father.

"It has gasoline."

"So," she said with relief, "according to the maps I found, there are three roads leading off the highway after the village. The first address we should check, I suppose, is the one taking off from the first road. It's about five miles from here."

"I think it was further than that," Darek said, "but I can't be sure."

"And anyway, once we get to these addresses, what will we do?" asked Cordelia.

"Absolutely nothing except phone the police. Do you really think I'd have brought you if I intended to do anything else?"

"Yes, but how will you know if it's the right address or not without knocking on the door?"

"There will be a large white van and a Hummer parked in the vicinity, I presume."

"Ah."

"Hopefully the van is still stuck. From the sounds of it, they weren't having any luck in their efforts to extract it. I think they were planning to take us all to the airport in the Hummer, but there isn't room for everyone, obviously, so that will make difficulties. It will mean at least two trips."

Cordelia was silent for a moment. "They must be very frightened, your acquaintances, I mean." She shuddered in compassion.

"I imagine they are. But at first they were tranquilized and most of the time they were gagged, so we didn't get to discuss our feelings."

"No."

"I've had lunch with them a number of times. The younger one, Nagib is his first name, is very religious. Not in any radical way, but – I had the sense that his faith was a matter of real importance to him. He's a very gentle fellow, tender-hearted, I think, and probably only in business because it's the family calling. The older fellow is about as Muslim as most Poles are Catholic – that is, very much so on the surface, if asked, but doesn't think about it most days of the week. I should think after an experience like this they'll both become jihadists."

"I wonder why you weren't tranquilized? Don't tell me you were better behaved."

He gave her a glance. "No, like I said, I think it was a matter of racial discrimination. At first they seemed to think I was Muslim as well and Iranian, of all things, can you believe it? With a name like Dariusz Zaremba! – "

"We-ell, it's not totally far-fetched when one thinks that Dariusz does come from Darius the Persian. But of course anyone familiar with Poland would know it's a common name here."

"They're not familiar with Poland, or Persia either. However, they were disillusioned – if not by my persuasive speech than by the physical evidence. Although I had to explain that to them too."

"But if they knew you weren't a Muslim – and they had been told that you were – then they must know that they've been fed misinformation."

"Yes – but you know, I don't think that matters to them. Certain of them, urged on by my enemy or enemies in the CBA or ex-governing party, had the idea of abducting us and they don't want to admit they made a mistake – maybe not even to themselves. It would make them look bad in their own eyes and incompetent in the eyes of their superiors – if they have superiors. No one really knows who supervises whom in the CIA. The others are just following orders."

"Are they really so incompetent?"

"They're not incompetent in violence. And I don't know if they're just naturally amoral or if that's the indoctrination they get at Foggy Bottom or whatever bottom they–"

"Tsk," said Cordelia, shocked, and with enough force to prevent him from finishing his sentence.

He gave her a look, half amused and half wry.

"You were saying before that..." she prompted primly.

He went on, "In everything else, yes, I think there are. At least, everything I've ever read about such organizations has filled me with the deepest conviction of their capacity to pursue their goals with the greatest ineffectiveness and collateral damage imaginable. Not to mention the morality of breaking the laws of other countries and ignoring the rights of individuals for the sake of their own country's – supposed – interests. The harm to the world at large from the example they set is incalculable, criminal."

She had no reply to make; given the circumstances, she was certainly not inclined to defend the agency.

They drove on and eventually turned off the highway and then turned again and drove uphill for a time.

The house of the first address they could see from the road; it had a small blue Skoda in front of it, no van, and lights in several un-shuttered windows. It was clearly not a place occupied by the CIA.

The second address required them to leave the road and take a lane between heavy underbrush. This was one of the rentals whose owners Cordelia had not been able to contact by phone.

"I don't think this will be it," said Darek, "it doesn't look like the brush has been disturbed for quite a while, and there are no tracks in the new snow."

"No," agreed Cordelia, "but if you get half a mile down the lane and meet the Hummer coming up it – what will you do?"

"Hmm," he said, turning down the lane, "good point. However, I am a demon at driving backward." He raised an eyebrow at her.

The branches closed over their heads and touched against the car sides; only the snow lightened the way a little.

"No, this can't be the address," Darek said, slowing almost to a stop after they had gone only a short ways, and at that moment, ahead of them, car lights flickered in the darkness, flickered and bounced on the uneven terrain.

Cordelia gasped as the car beneath her shot backwards and backwards, spun around and was whipping out onto the main road almost before she had time to catch her breath. They were driving away at speed and behind, in the distance, a car emerged onto the road and headed in the other direction.

"Well, I was right – I was pretty sure that wasn't a Hummer when I saw the lights," said Darek calmly, glancing in the rearview mirror and slowing.

"Then why did you back up like that?"

"Better safe than sorry or for the fun of it – you can take your pick of answer." He grinned at her.

She gave him a very darkling look. "You know what Alexander the Great's men said to him, as they begged him to turn back from his conquests?"

"No, what?"

"'O king, your great enterprise has defeated not only your enemies but your soldiers...The idea is worthy of your greatness, but for us it is too exalted.' I sympathize with his soldiers."

"Hmm. Do you know what Cleopatra said to Antony?"

"No, what?"

"O king, you're worthy of my greatness, but I prefer my soldiers."

"Tsk." But she couldn't help smiling a little.

"That's better."

"It's starting to clear," said Darek, as they came over the top of a rise, and in the slight moonlight, shining through the clouds, they could see the black outlines of windswept ridges, and below, a blanket of cotton wool pulled over the valley. They plunged into the cotton wool, and drove for a time with very little visibility, but after a time, there would be spaces where the fog was dissipating, trees would emerge and rocky hillsides.

The third address they ruled out from a distance, as being located in the open sweep of a plain; the fourth house, a small chalet, did indeed have shutters but was far too small – they continued down the list.

They had been driving for a long time by now, quite slowly often, because of the weather and the necessity of finding unmarked lanes in the dark. It was getting on in the early hours of the morning. They had left the main highway and taken a smaller, unpaved road through the woods. The gravel pinged lightly against the bottom of the car as they drove along at a good clip, searching for an address.

"Listen," said Darek, "do you hear that?"

"What?" said Cordelia in alarm, instantly all ears. "Is something the matter?"

The car began to coast, to slow.

"Could be…that's all we need." He began to swear softly. "Oh, there, the temperature warning light has come on. I said it was a junker!"

He pulled the car over to the side of the road, was out of the car almost as soon as it stopped and had the hood up.

Cordelia's view of him was blocked by the hood. She could only see his moving shape through the crack between the hood and the body of the car or when he moved off to the side.

She opened her door and stepped out; not because she could be of any help but only to stretch her legs after hours in the car. There seemed to be steam everywhere, or maybe smoke, mushrooming up from the car's engine. Even to her ignorance, the symptoms seemed dire.

She didn't say anything – what was there to say? The idea that they might, through no action of her own, be prevented from proceeding crossed her mind and only for a moment induced a sort of upsurging relief and was quickly replaced by conflict: she wanted Darek to be safe and she wanted him to succeed.

Darek was bent over something internal to the car. She looked about. They seemed to be in the vicinity of a small hamlet, where there were a number of tidy new houses. All the houses were dark; the inhabitants would be sound asleep at this hour of the night.

"Cordelia, are you wearing pantyhose?" asked Darek suddenly, out of the depths of the steam.

"No," she answered, startled. She never wore pantyhose under her trousers.

"Damn!" he replied.

She didn't dare to ask him why, she only felt a sense of deep culpability for being inappropriately dressed. She retreated towards the rear of the car.

"Cordelia?"

"Yes?"

"I'm going to leave you here for a moment, and then I'll be back."

"But where are you going?"

"To one of those houses. I need something."

"But they'll all be asleep."

"I sincerely hope so."

But why? she wanted to ask a dozen more things, but bit back the words. Hers not to question why.

He was already jogging away from her, down the road toward the houses. She was left alone in the blackness of the night with the still fuming engine. Above her, she could just make out the branches of spruce trees, reaching towards the road, darker even than the sky.

Darek had disappeared. She listened for a sound but there was none. Not a dog barked or a voice rang out. The houses beyond remained still and unlit. So Darek hadn't found anyone at home. She wished he would come back. Her eyes strained at the darkness. Perhaps there was some movement there among the trees, at the side of the road. Yes, definitely, something was moving there. She wished she were in the car. She was standing by the trunk, the door was six feet away, but she seemed paralyzed. Something detached itself from a tree branch and came floating from the sky towards her. She stepped back hastily in fright and it glided past her head. She had an impression of wings, feathers, and eyes and then it flapped once and was gone. An owl. She caught her breath. It was hooting now, a low drawn-out sound, somewhere in the woods beyond her sight. She hurried to the car and got in, sat blowing on her fingers to warm them until, with a lift of her heart, she saw Darek come trotting out of the darkness again.

He grinned and waved something at her. A pair of pantyhose.

She got out of the car again.

"To replace the fan belt," he explained, as he began to tie knots behind the light of the headlamps.

"But where did you get them?" she asked, a horrible suspicion entering her mind.

"The second house."

"I didn't see any lights come on."

"I stole them," he returned baldly, calmly.

"You didn't!" she gasped, horrified.

"Yes, I did," he carried on with his job, not looking at her, "but don't worry. I left an amply large sum in payment."

"You went into someone's house while the owners were sleeping, you searched through a drawer until you found pantyhose and you stole it??"

"No. They were hanging to dry in a bathroom. That's where pantyhose usually is, in my experience. I could reach them from the window." He shrugged, "There are a number of things in or about most households that would serve the purpose. I hoped to find something and I did."

"But you can't just go and burgle people's houses! You can't do that!"

She was so shocked and indignant that he paused for a moment, obviously torn between the sudden urge to fight back, to crush her with a biting rejoinder or a simple and vulgar command to get lost, and the more difficult tactic of persuasion. Cordelia saw the various emotions pass over his face and fell back a step, but her scowl of horrified disapproval did not diminish. If she had been less frail, less timid, the situation would have rapidly evolved into a flare-up of dramatic proportions; but he had grown protective of her even from himself.

"So," he said, leaning against the car for a moment, "which is more important – that we should be able to carry on looking for these fellows or that the inviolability of private property is maintained?"

"But couldn't you have knocked and asked?"

"I didn't think anyone would open to me at this hour of the night, and if I woke them the game would be up."

She bowed her head, stabbed the ground with the end of her crutch. He pursued his point: "So the question is this: would anyone, if asked, consider that her right not to lose a pair of old pantyhose, and to be willy-nilly recompensed at an exorbitant sum, was a matter of higher priority than the chance of saving two men from imprisonment, from torture, possibly even of saving their lives? Of course not. Is it something to which any right-minded person would submit for the greater good? Yes. So there you are. I've committed a highly ethical act in swiping this hose. Think of it as a sort of eminent domain." He held up the hose. "A large lady, by the looks of it," he said consideringly. "She had other pairs," he added. "Don't worry about that."

Cordelia turned away in disgust. She had to admit to herself that his argument sounded good, but she could hardly bear to look at him or his trophy. She didn't ask him how he had got the window open. He would have his ways and she supposed people didn't barricade their houses as carefully here as they did in Warsaw. She went to sit in the car.

"But," she said, taking up the argument when he came to join her in the car, "I suppose the people who authorize renditions think they're doing it for the greater good too."

"No. The principle is not the same. No one would agree to be tortured or deprived of all rights. That is, no

474

right-thinking person would consider that one group of people should be deprived – not of pantyhose – but of their humanity for the possible good to a larger group – you can see where *that* sort of a principle would lead – where it does lead. No one is safe – as we've seen ourselves."

She had nothing more to say.

"Well, one thing we know," he said, "this isn't the address, so let's hope my repair holds." He started the car again and watched as the temperature gage returned to normal. Then they continued on their way.

"So," he said, after they had driven for half an hour or so in complete silence, and had checked out two more addresses, also obviously not what they were looking for, "are you going to stay angry with me?" His voice held a trace of bitterness.

"I'm not angry with you," she returned slowly, "I don't like what you did – but I can see that your principle may be good. It *may* be, I say, I haven't thought about it enough yet. But what really afflicts me is that you take such risks without even giving a second thought to all the things that could go wrong. Suppose there was a burglar alarm, suppose – ."

He shrugged. "You worry too much."

She had no answer to make to that, because it was true. And she couldn't even point to any greater success that she had achieved by caution as opposed to his more venturesome attitude. And perhaps he really did weigh the risks before he acted; she couldn't truly say that she thought him reckless. Once again she had the uncomfortable feeling that she might be in the wrong.

"I'd like to think," he said, rather stiffly, as they drove along, "that you were with me in this."

"Maybe," she said, after a space of silent brooding, "it's like in *Erec et Enide*. Do you know it?"

"No," he said cautiously, obviously not sure where she was heading but willing to listen, "It's one of those medieval romances, isn't it?"

"Yes. Erec is a knight at King Arthur's court but when he marries Enide he submits to her too far and stops doing knightly things, and so he begins to feel a bit, well, emasculated maybe, or as if he were failing in his duties. So they set off together on horseback, the two of them, into the wild, and have all sorts of adventures in which Erec has to slay monsters and overcome evil knights, and so on, and Enide is not allowed to say a word."

"I suppose the book is on the feminists' black list."

"I don't know. Maybe. The point is she's supposed to learn to have trust in his leadership."

"Dingbat, that Erec...Ah! Oh, I see. You think I'm treating you that way?"

"No. I didn't mean that..." She stopped, confused and embarrassed.

"I suppose it ends tragically? Erec doesn't listen to Enide and comes badly acropper?"

"No, it ends happily." She blushed. It ended voluptuously. "Leadership was the wrong word. She has to trust his abilities."

"There you are then."

"Yes."

"Oh – oh, good. You had me worried for a moment."

Harmony restored, they continued their search.

"This had better be it," said Darek, rather grimly, two hours later, and Cordelia, whom this last interval spent with Darek, without mishap or alarm, had calmed, now began to have qualms again. Suppose she had somehow missed the one correct address? Would he blame her? Would he think she had withheld it on purpose? Yes, she guessed, as some level he would always doubt her.

They wasted a lot of time searching for the address; they drove back to Przestrzyna for more gasoline; they studied the maps; they returned to the countryside; this address was not it either.

They sat in the car, in the midst of what would doubtless, on a summer's day, be a lovely setting – a low hillside with meadows and scattered trees; now dark except for the dim moonlight. The rental house was entirely dark and there were no vehicles in the vicinity, nor any particular sign of habitation.

"This isn't it," said Darek. "There's no one here, and there's not enough slope to the hill anyway."

"No," said Cordelia. "What do we do now?"

"We can stake out the airport – but it gets more difficult. They won't bring the prisoners until the plane has landed – at that point, there won't be time for the police to arrive, even if summoned."

"But we can't be certain which airport they will use."

"No, we'll just have to assume they'll use the nearest that's open. If they don't – then it's out of our hands. It may be anyway – we haven't a lot of time left." He swore, comprehensively and vehemently.

Cordelia hesitated, then she reached for the print-outs again: "There are these buildings here – I don't know what they are – they look to me as if they could possibly be some sort of vacation centre or maybe barracks."

Darek looked.

She pointed with a finger, "but there's a wall or a fence with a wide foundation, see – at least I take this fine line here for such – and you didn't come to a fence, did you?"

He shook his head. "No."

"So I'd ruled it out. But if you had leapt out of the window of this building, say, or this one, you could have run downhill, but not directly downhill, to the side a little, then you would have come to this area here, where it looks like the fence has been removed. It would be a slim chance, of course, that you would come across the opening, but…maybe it could have happened that way. It doesn't seem very likely, really, but since we don't know where else to look…" She glanced at him uncertainly, and he nodded.

"Then around this way to the road – it's quite a distance though…If you had gone this way, you would have come to the road here, and it would have been close, only a little ways. But the other way is far. And if it's here, I don't see how we could get close enough to see anything without their knowing that we were snooping around."

"Yes. Let's go though. There's no time – no time." She heard the strain in his voice.

25

The forerunners of day hung in the night air.

"It's definitely cleared," said Darek. "I don't know how long it will take for them to make the airport arrangements, but they won't linger a moment more than necessary. For one thing, they could get socked in again within hours. But they'll have to wait for the plane to arrive from wherever it's coming from."

The telephone rang in his pocket; he pulled it out and handed it to her to read.

"It's a text message from this journalist I told you about," she said, "he's asking for information. He says he's come to Przestrzyna with a journalist colleague and a camera person."

"Good," said Darek, "very good. Tell him to go to the airport and await developments there. Even if we can't find the agents in time to summon the police, having someone witness the departure from the airport will be better than nothing. Tell him to stake out the road – that's the only place he'll be able to get close – and look for a Hummer or a white van. But I think it'll be the Hummer. If he sees either, he should call the police and ask them to come in full force." His fingers tapped impatiently, nervously, on the steering wheel. "They won't come though, or if they do it'll be too late."

She called the journalist, spoke to him, and then relayed the response: "He says he'll go there just in case."

"Only there's no 'just in case' – they will be going out – it only remains to be seen whether they get away without anyone seeing them or not. At the moment, it looks like the chances are on their side. The journalists won't be allowed near enough to get any sort of film of anyone boarding." His feelings found expression again in a stream of bad language and he reached for his cigarettes. Cordelia had never seen him smoking while driving and the sight was not reassuring.

"But I don't see how we can get near enough to see anything, anyway," she said again tentatively, "perhaps we should just go on to the airport."

"We won't get the police to come beforehand without a reason. The airport will be too late. The police will arrive in time to see a Gulfstream jet disappearing into the clouds."

"A Gulfstream?"

"It's the kind of plane that's ordinarily used for these expeditions; they're leased from various companies, generally companies set up specifically for the purpose; they also use the Spanish CASA C-212 jets because they can take off on short runways."

"Ah," said Cordelia, "that's what it said about the airport in Holubek. That it had a short runway...You seem to know a lot about all this?"

"It's the sort of crime that interests me – even before I became a target for the Anti-Corruption Bureau. The activities of ordinary criminals pale in comparison, if one considers the damage to society and the rule of law."

All that was true, of course, thought Cordelia, but she had heard him talking this way before and she did not find it reassuring. And yet Mr. Hasan and Mr. Mashrawi were somewhere near presumably: they had already been taken into that area where there was no longer any law or boundary. Cordelia shivered; she could, actually, spare them a moment of compassion from her other worries.

"I should take you back to town now, but there's no time."

"No, there's no time."

His foot went down on the accelerator; his language descended the ladder of profanity. "Will you mind waiting in the car while I make a reconnaissance on foot?"

Yes, thought Cordelia, I will mind horribly. "No," she answered.

The turn-off was difficult to locate; there were many slight turn-offs along the road, some were forest lanes, some farm lanes, each had to be examined, if only cursorily. They drew up on the side of a mild slope, entirely wooded on one side and half upland plain on the other, and weren't sure if they had the right place. To the left a lane led straight between an alley of thick-trunked trees and dense brush. Were the two men waiting, gagged and blindfolded, at the end of that alley? Or were they somewhere else entirely?

"This lane goes very straight, like in the satellite picture," said Cordelia.

"Yes." He pulled the car a little further off the road. "And it also looks recently traveled by some heavy vehicle – look at those ruts. And by a smaller vehicle with a wide wheel base – that could be the Hummer. Or it could be a farm tractor of some sort, who knows? But I have a feeling this might be it. The questions are if or where they will have set a guard and whether we've read the photo right about the fence."

481

"In Poland, fences always have holes in them, somewhere," Cordelia offered, wondering if she was suggesting his path to death.

He smiled. "True. So I'll try not to be gone long – I've pulled far enough over so the car won't be seen from below, but if any suspect vehicle comes up that alley, then just duck and stay out of sight. The airport is in that direction, down the hill, so they won't come this way. If they do, I think it extremely unlikely that they would associate the car with us – if no one is visible it will seem as if the driver has just – well, stopped for the reasons people do along the road here. I very much doubt, though, that they would come to investigate on their way to the airport. You'll be all right."

"Okay."

"You know how to start the engine if you get cold? It's an automatic transmission."

"Yes."

He was sliding from the car without a backward look, jogging down the hill. She watched him for as long as she could, his figure appearing at intervals through the breaks in the brush, between the trees, until distance, the dimness, or a slight bend in the alley took him out of sight.

She waited. It was getting light, no doubt about it. Far in the east the morning sun crested a ridge, dodged a bank of clouds, and began to shine upon the world. The grey shadows began to lift from the rusty long grass of the meadows and from the snow in crevices of tumbled rock. Her perspectives grew longer.

They had not agreed what she would do if he did not come back, or how long she should wait. He had the cell phone. If he did not come back, she decided, she would have two options: to hitchhike back to Przestrzyna, or to set off after him. Neither would be of any use in saving him.

She grew cold and periodically she leaned across the driver's seat, switched on the ignition, and started the car. When the heater had somewhat warmed her, she would turn it off again.

And so time passed. 'They also serve who only sit and wait.' She tried to wile away the time by thinking of the future, a future in which they didn't have to worry about the agents of secret government bodies, a future in which there was no likelihood of violence but only the usual tasks of daily life. She didn't believe in that future anymore; her imaginings of an ordinary life in Warsaw had all the qualities of a fantasy and she couldn't keep it up.

Time was passing; it was getting on for day and the air was clear. He should have come back by now. Strain her eyes as she might, she couldn't see anything beyond the beginning of the alley. Perhaps if she got out of the car, and walked just a ways down the hill, she could see beyond the trees, could see something, anything. Perhaps she would catch a glimpse of the white van and know they had caught him and there was no hope left.

She took the key from the ignition, stepped out into the cold air and locked the car. Then she set off, struggling through the scraping branches of alder brush and young acacia trees to reach the edge of the meadow beyond. She concentrated only on moving ahead. Her muscles quickly grew weary, but she hardly noticed. The cold air cleared her head; she could endure a little longer.

She had come a ways from the car, and still she could see nothing but the woods, the grass and the snow. It would be pointless to go further. She couldn't see anything, not a structure or a vehicle, or a sign of life in the distance. Something, she was sure, had happened to Darek, but she had no idea what to do next.

Standing thus in indecision, she shivered so violently that she dropped her crutch, and as she bent for it, she heard voices, carrying to her clearly across the cold upland air. She froze, while her heart pounded in her ears. The voices were speaking English. American English.

"This is a wild goose chase we've been sent on."

"He said he saw something move."

Cordelia couldn't see anyone; she wanted to run, but instinct told her that she would be less visible lower down. She let her legs slide out from under her so that she was lying in the snow and grass.

"We're sitting ducks out here," said one voice tensely, "Someone could be taking aim at us from any side."

"This isn't a war zone," said the other, equally jittery-sounding.

A crow squawked somewhere, loud and raucous in the frosty air.

"What was that?" The voice was alarmed.

"I dunno. Why don't you go search around there then? Or are you chicken?"

"Hell, Garver, you like those poultry images. I'm not searching."

"Let's go back. Bob says the plane's coming – we'll be gone within the hour anyway."

They didn't speak anymore, but she heard the sound of their movement. They were going away.

If they came this way they would see her, Cordelia realized; in her dark coat against the white hillside, she would stand out like a fly in milk, and if they went up the hill, then they would see her if they turned around and looked back. They were nervous; they would certainly look behind them.

She lay very still, hoping that from a distance, if she were visible, she would only resemble a rock or a dark piece of ground. She wasn't large.

She lay for what was perhaps minutes but seemed like a long time in the snow on the hill. Finally, there was no sound, stretch her ears as she might, and when she dared to lift her head, she could see nothing. She rose and made her way, as quickly as she could – expecting every moment to hear a shout, the thudding feet of pursuers – back towards the car.

The highway was near; she stopped to catch her breath and look behind her.

So maybe Darek was back there somewhere, maybe he was caught. What was the point of going on? She didn't know what she would do when she did reach the car. She was wet and cold and exhausted; she thought fleetingly of lying down in the snow and dying. Darek had the telephone; there was no one she could call. Perhaps if another car came by she could stop it and ask to telephone the police. But the roads were deserted at this hour of the morning.

She looked behind at the hill, where the agents were surely keeping the two prisoners – and maybe Darek? – and she saw the faintest stirring of movement. She stared at it; she couldn't be sure, but she thought it was a vehicle. It disappeared. She continued staring until her vision began to blur. And yet something was moving there. Something in the far distance, glimpsed now and then, between the breaks in the vegetation. She strained her eyes towards it. It wasn't a person, it was too large. A vehicle.

She began to hurry toward the BMW. If the coming vehicle were the Hummer, it would shortly come out on the alley. If it did, she might be seen here through the brush.

Her muscles wouldn't move; they wouldn't carry her on; she was wading through sand, every motion hampered; she would never make it; she couldn't draw breath.

She would do better to lie down, behind the largest clump of brush and hide, try to lie still.

They would get away. And Darek hadn't returned.

She watched the vehicle coming...It was slowed by the potholes in the road; she could see it bouncing from side to side. It was too large, too wide and tall for an ordinary passenger car. It was the Hummer.

She should get down but she couldn't tear her eyes away from the vehicle. They would have the two men inside. The prisoners would be shipped away, there was nothing she could do to prevent it, she could only stand there, helpless as the time she had watched her mother on the railroad tracks.

The Hummer was getting nearer. She could see it clearly now.

Suppose Darek were inside the vehicle? Suppose they had found him spying and captured him again? Suppose he were inside?

The Hummer was closer, much closer, in a minute it would be out on the highway and away. She had split-second fantasies of running towards it, of halting it by superhuman force – but how? She couldn't run and even if she could, she couldn't stop them. Was he in the Hummer or not? Oh please, Darek, don't be in there, she begged some unknown power, please, please, please.

If only she could drive, she thought in agony, she could chase after them in the car, she could…what? She took a panting breath. It was no use. There was nothing she could do.

She had again the wild image of hurling herself in front of the vehicle; but what would that do? She was hallucinating because of her fatigue. It was the car she should drive down in front of them.

She didn't know how the idea came, but there it was. She had never driven a car before but she knew the principles.

If she could only reach the car. She looked behind. Yes, she could see the Hummer more clearly now, definitely a moving object now appearing now disappearing amongst the trees. She was scrambling up the hillside to the car. She had another fifty feet, another twenty, she was there, she was dropping her crutch, digging in her pocket for the key; her hand was shaking so badly she couldn't fit the key, she scratched the paint, but the key went in, she was in the car. She was fitting the key in the ignition with the same clumsy jabs.

The key turned in the ignition, but in her nervousness she turned it too far and there was a shriek of metal on metal and then silence as she accidentally turned the key back too far and the engine died. She jerked her hand away; she must be calm, she told herself, calm and do it carefully. The Hummer was nearer. It was more than halfway up the alley. There was no time but she had to be careful. She tried again, gradually turning the key in the switch. The car vibrated beneath her, it was running.

Now there was the parking brake. She had seen Darek pull and release such a brake a hundred times. She pulled it up but it wouldn't release – she jerked on it in anguish, but it still wouldn't budge. No, she thought, she wouldn't be able to do it. The Hummer was coming. She had seconds only. There was a button in the top of the brake handle. That must be for something. She pushed it in as she pulled the brake up and the brake released, but there was no time for triumph. She reached for the gear selector and moved it over into drive. The car began to roll down the hill. She grasped the steering wheel with her good hand. She had never driven a car before, never even steered one, but she couldn't get it wrong. She let the car coast for a minute, feeling it respond as she moved the steering wheel so that it came out onto the highway and began to gather speed. She dropped the wheel to pull the brake; the car slowed. She let up and the car continued. She was coming to the curve, where she had to turn into the alley. She couldn't make a mistake, she thought in panic, she couldn't, Darek's life might depend on it or maybe it was only the lives of the other two men, but she couldn't make a mistake. She would surely make a mistake. Now, now, she had to turn it.

She took the curve too fast, and the car headed in an uncontrolled arc for the bushes. She jerked the steering wheel back and the car slashed through tearing branches on the other side; another jerk and it rocked back onto the alley; the Hummer was just ahead, fifty feet ahead; she didn't look to see if it were slowing or not, she moved her foot to the gas pedal, straightened the steering wheel and pushed down on the gas. The car shot forward; the Hummer made a last second effort to swerve out of the way but was prevented from escaping by the brush and trees. She steered straight for it.

There was a terrific jolt, a screaming rending of metal, the punch of the air bag, and a spray of broken glass.

The air bag prevented her from being thrown into the windshield, but the impact left her stunned. There were a few split seconds of confusion, where she wasn't sure what had happened or what would happen next, when she didn't know if she were dead or hurt or quite all right. And then, too, a split second of triumph – she had stopped the Hummer.

But these were thoughts and feelings of fractions of seconds only; forms, masked and faceless forms were emerging from the Hummer in all directions, running towards her, screaming obscenities and directions. Someone was pulling on the driver's side car door but it wouldn't open; someone was shouting: "It's Zaremba's wife!"

Someone was breaking out the driver's side window as she cowered away from the blow; the car was surrounded. Hands were reaching for her through the window, grasping at her clothing. She tried to recoil, but there was nowhere to go, she was being jerked, through broken glass, through the window. She heard her jacket ripping, felt her leg twisting, and then she was being set on the ground, only she couldn't stand and started to fall. She was jerked upright and faced a semi-circle of masked figures.

Their language appeared to consist entirely of obscenities. The words they applied to her plumbed the depths of vulgarity but she hardly noticed. She had not expected them to be pleased. She was frightened nearly to death.

Finally, one sentence of clarity was spoken: "What are we going to do with her?"

"Leave that for now!" someone commanded. It was Blandface, she recognized the edgy voice. "Move the car out of the way. Come on – get it out of the way. See if the Hummer runs." More obscenities.

She was pulled into the icy slush at the side of the road. Her arm was twisted behind her back, and she was off balance and had to lean on her captor for support as her crutch had stayed in the car. She struggled to right herself, to stand upright, but a jerk forced her into immobility. She was still dazed; she couldn't speak for the pounding of her heart.

"Ma'am, you're nothing but trouble," snapped the voice of her captor, taut with nerves. It was Military Cut then. "We should've thrown you off the train, for sure."

Four or five figures were hurriedly struggling with the BMW; prying with a tire iron at the metal entangled in the other vehicle; heaving it backwards; but there was a problem, the thick brush on either side of the alley here prevented them from pushing it to the side; they were obliged to push it a long way backward, up the alley, through a number of potholes, before they could get it into the ditch. From the amount of swearing, it did not seem to be an easy task.

And then a thought struck her – if Darek were caught too, the owner of the BMW wouldn't get paid for his vehicle – and she had deliberately wrecked it. This thought did not overpower the fears for her own safety or for Darek's, but it added a sort of ghastly guiltiness to her mental attitude.

Blandface left the others pushing and came to stand talking to another man. They were at some distance, but Cordelia could hear the two as they put their heads together.

"We could leave her in the car – make it look like an accident."

"We don't have clearance for that. And there're too many of us here. That's not an option now."

Now. Thought Cordelia, as these words registered. Did they mean that killing her wasn't an option any more, or only not at this moment? But she should be glad, she thought, that she wasn't to be murdered at once. She didn't feel glad, only burdened by the wait.

A final push and the BMW rolled the last little way. It struck a rock and stopped, but it was out of the way.

The road was clear. So much for her plans of stopping them, so easily overturned, 'so quickly bright things come to confusion.' The words came unbidden to her mind. There had been many bright things lately, with Darek – all come to nothing.

"Let's go!" commanded one of the masks, and the men were surging back towards the car.

"What do I do with her?" asked her captor.

"Can't leave her now. She has to come. Put her in."

Military Cut began to half drag, half push her towards the car.

"The police are coming," said Cordelia, loudly.

That stopped them all in their tracks.

"What do you mean?" Blandface was snapping at her.

"They know what you're doing and they're on their way. You won't get away with it."

"Yes, we will," he barked at her and then turned away as he was approached by another agent.

"Look," said someone, "I found these in the car." He had the satellite print-outs in his hand and he showed them to the other man.

More obscenities. Couldn't they speak normally? thought Cordelia irrelevantly.

The men were obviously uncertain what to make of it all. But that they were, as Darek had said, exceedingly nervous, was clear.

"Okay. So put her in the car, I said. She's coming with us," Blandface ordered again after a brief pause. "Come on, come on, the plane is waiting."

The plane was waiting, thought Cordelia, as she was dragged to the car. Every muscle cringed. She was lifted and dumped into the cargo compartment, face down; it was Military Cut who knelt beside her, twisting her arm. She struggled, which was to no avail. So she squirmed, which worked better, and as the Hummer began to move, began to bounce and jolt in the bumpy road, her captor relaxed his hold and she managed to wiggle herself into a semi-recumbent position, where she could at least look around. The vehicle seemed to be full to overflowing with men. She saw only the backs of their hooded heads; she had a vague image of the Ku Klux Klan. But Darek wasn't there, she was sure of it – she had a wild feeling of relief – he wasn't there…they hadn't caught him – unless they were intending to bring him on the next trip? Because there was only one prisoner – she recognized him, he was sitting right in front of her, flanked on either side by a black hood, but his was gray, a gray hood, she couldn't see the front, but she knew from what Darek had said that it would be without eyeholes.

Darek, she thought, oh. If she had only stayed quietly in the car, none of this would have happened. She wouldn't be here now. And where would they take her and what would they do with her?

Perhaps, if she were lucky, they would just drop her out on the tarmac, at the airport, when they were ready to leave? Or would they take her to a jail in some distant country? Or simply dispose of her somewhere? Her mind raced over various possibilities – suppose they just opened the airplane door, someplace high over a body of water or a forest, and pushed her out? Oh, why had she thought she could stop them?

And where was Darek?

They had turned onto the highway, were cruising fast to somewhere; they had turned in the direction Darek had said they would, so presumably they were going to the airport.

"So what are we going to do with her?" someone was asking.

"We'll put her on then you go back for the others, as planned," Blandface decreed. "Better gag her."

"With what?"

More obscenities.

"Rip up a shirt."

No one seemed eager to sacrifice his shirt, however. The hoods stopped bouncing about in their seats and sat immobile.

"She says the police know," said someone.

More obscenities.

"I'll get on it," said Blandface, and then, another command – "somebody put earmuffs on her. Earmuffs, a gag, handcuffs – look sharp."

"We haven't got any more," said someone.

More obscenities.

Through the window Cordelia caught occasional glimpses of trees – fir boughs and the occasional oak branch with brown leaves still hanging – or sometimes the side of a hill, bare and windswept with rocks among the grass. They were blurred; the Hummer was traveling at an unsafe speed, a speed that had more to do with the nerves of the driver than with necessity.

Ideas tumbled one after another through her mind: was Darek free or captured? Had he called the police? Would the journalist make it to the airport on time? Would the police? Where would they take her? Would she ever see Darek again? Was the man in front as frightened as she was? Would his wife wonder, always, what had happened to him, as she had wondered about Darek, and not know? Her family; her brother Hal in the United States, careful and conventional, what would he think or do? The car she'd wrecked; the injustice of it all. And then, just numbness again. There was nothing to do but try to still the exhausting pounding of her heart.

She tried to remember from the satellite maps the route the car would have to take to get to the further airport. She waited for the turning, unable to measure time, but knowing that they would come to an intersection and then they would have to turn right or left. If they turned left, it meant they were going to the nearer airport, the one that was closed, the one she and Darek had ruled out, or further, on to the airport at Rzeszów. If they turned left, it meant that she and the prisoner were beyond the reach of all help and they could give themselves up for lost. The car was braking hard; please, she thought, turn right. Turn right, turn right, turn right. With a swing that nearly unseated the passengers and a squeal of tires, the car turned left. The last little bit of hope, cherished somewhere at the bottom of her heart, whimpered and died. She felt only numb. The Hummer accelerated rapidly away from the intersection.

"You're going the wrong way," someone said.

Obscenities.

"Look at the map," someone said.

"I don't need to look at the map," said Blandface.

"*I'll* look at the map," someone said.

494

"Fine," shouted Blandface, braking sharply and jerking the vehicle around in a u-turn, so that the passengers hastily snatched for handholds again, "You tell me where to go, if you're so smart. I bet we end up in Russia."

"Poland does not border Russia," said the same someone, a tense voice, full of controlled irritation, and, Cordelia recognized, fear.

"Yes, it does, it borders Ukraine," Blandface was shouting back.

"That's not Russia."

"Same diff."

"Not really."

"*Shut up*, would you?"

There was silence then, only the rustling of what Cordelia guessed was the map.

Perhaps, thought Cordelia, these were perfectly normal-seeming men in the usual course of their lives; perhaps they went home to wives and children; to tidy homes in leafy suburbs, maybe they took their sons to football games, went to church on Sundays, and maybe they even read books. Maybe some of them were brainwashed into thinking they were performing a patriotic duty and maybe some were criminals by nature who had found a niche in a government job. They were all equally dangerous.

They traveled for a time in silence.

She didn't know how to calculate the time; it seemed that they had been traveling for quite a while, but that might only be her fright, she recognized, making every second seem longer. But no, it had been a time, because it seemed they were approaching their destination.

"See, just like I said," the righteous voice grumbled, but he got no answer.

They were coming to the airport, she knew from the murmurs among the agents.

"There!" someone was crying joyously, "it's come! The plane's here! That CASA – that's for us."

A cheer went up among the passengers.

And then, through the cheers, Blandface's voice telling Military Cut, again, to do something about Zaremba's wife.

"Here," someone said, "I've taken these off the Arab guy's legs." A pair of handcuffs was passed to the back.

The Arab guy was worse off than she was, thought Cordelia, as her arms were jerked about and the handcuffs were snapped on her wrists. At least she could still see – and then something, some cloth was being draped over her head and suddenly the world was gone. She had a moment of panic, of suffocation, and then she calmed herself. The only thing she could do, anymore, was not to panic – and she was very, very close.

And then the vehicle was slowing, was driving more cautiously, was stopping. She heard the agents jump from the vehicle, felt the air beat with their movement, the car doors opening. And then the back door of the Hummer was opening, she felt the cold air, and she was being jerked out of the vehicle, set unsteadily upon her feet, being pulled and hustled somewhere, into the dark. She tried to struggle, lost her feet, and was being pulled upright. She screamed for help, knowing there would be no one to help, but doing it anyway, because some little piece of spirit told her to resist. Her voice was miniscule in the vastness of the space around her, the shriek of a mouse in the jaws of a cat. Someone was clamping a hand over her mouth, over her nose, over the cloth, and she couldn't breathe; she jerked her head to find air.

"Shut up! Nobody's going to hear you anyway," someone shouted in her ear.

She was being dragged along. Her feet struck something and she was being half lifted, half forced up a small stairway. An airplane stairs, she knew the feel of the metal, the short steps, beneath her feet. Then there was a solid platform and she was being shoved backwards and found herself sitting.

"Sit there, and don't move!" Someone ordered. She could hardly do otherwise, being handcuffed to the seat. She tried to catch her breath, and then, when she had, jerked her head repeatedly and the piece of cloth that had covered it – someone's jacket – fell off. She was, as she had surmised, inside an airplane, a largish one, which seemed to be lacking the usual number of seats. The agents were busy with their other prisoner. She turned her head and looked out the window. There was the Hummer, with one of the agents still standing beside it, and then dark fir trees on all sides, cut through by a long stretch of light-colored runway, glistening with ice and snow along the edges, and far in the distance, what looked like a control tower and a very small terminal, or perhaps only an airport headquarters.

It seemed unreal. It couldn't be happening. She looked across at the other prisoner, who had been handcuffed to his seat, too. As she watched, he bent his head to his knees and moaned a little. She felt for him, but there was nothing she could do. She turned back to the window. The Hummer was leaving, racing across the tarmac and away. It was going back for the other prisoner and the other agents, she knew. Please don't let Darek be among them, please, please, please.

She tried to calculate the time it would take them to go and come back. She didn't think it had taken more than fifteen or twenty minutes to come. That meant a half hour to forty minutes at the most, if she was right. Of course, it was always possible that in her present mental state her sense of time was quite distorted. She tried counting seconds, but she became confused and gave it up. They would come when they came; there was nothing she could do anyway.

"We have to leave," someone, the pilot presumably, was saying firmly at the front of the plane, beyond a barrier. "The weather's not going to hold much longer. And we've got the slot at the other airport to think about. We can't wait. You were late."

"They're coming. They're on their way," she recognized Blandface's voice, reassuring the other man. "I'm in contact with them. They'll be here in ten minutes."

"Ten minutes, okay, ten minutes, it's not so bad," said another voice, a calmer voice, a slow American drawl. Another pilot, she supposed, the co-pilot.

There was silence in front for a while and then the voice of the co-pilot saying to Blandface, "How did you enjoy Poland? I hear you've been waiting for some days."

"Poland sucks."

"That bad? I suppose the climate's not great. Well, you'll be in warmer parts in just a few hours. They've got great shrimp cocktails at the Vizir Hotel. Pool's Olympic size, too."

"Can't wait."

"So that's the two of us then," said the pilot.

The minutes passed. After a time they started the engines. Cordelia could hear the whine, the vibration. Then she could feel the plane moving. It was infinitesimal, but definite. She realized that the prisoner felt it too, as he shifted in his chair. She thought she might be sick. Maybe, she tried to calm herself, they would take off without Darek – maybe it was good. But after a minute the engines shut off again.

"They're late," said the pilot. "Where are they? They should be here."

"I've just talked to them, they're a mile away."

Half a minute passed, a minute. And then there was a cry, "they're here." And then, in an entirely different tone, a tone of dismay and anger: "what the…"

She looked out the window. Far down the tarmac, off to the side, by the airport terminal, there appeared to be a crowd of vehicles. Perhaps they were simply the cars of employees or even of passengers, although she didn't see any other planes in sight. She strained her eyes. She might be mistaken but she thought – with an increase of dread – that it was the Hummer and a number of vans and some smaller cars.

Then from the agitated comments among the agents, she concluded that she must be seeing correctly, that it was their returning vehicle. And the others? There appeared to be a problem.

The leader's cell phone was ringing. He was holding it up to his ear, listening intently.

"Hang on," he said sharply, after a moment, "I have to call our contact. Hang on, and we'll get it straightened out."

"Those are police vans," said the co-pilot, no longer drawling.

And then the pilot, sharply: "We're leaving. We were late as is."

"Hold on!" said Blandface. "I'm talking…" and then he was speaking into his cell phone, explaining to someone that there was a problem, that some police vans had showed up – no not the border guards, the police, the local police! – that they had stopped his agents, that they were asking about the prisoner, that they were demanding the return of all the agents and the prisoner on the plane…

The plane's engines started up.

No, thought Cordelia.

The plane was beginning, again, to move.

Blandface was arguing with whomever he had on the phone, "yes – but…yes, but you said…." And then he was shouting, "I don't care if the whole country thinks Zaremba's innocent and I don't care if you've got people of all types crawling all over you, I've got two Muslims here, suspected of serious – what do you mean, they're not? What do you mean, yellowcake meant something to eat? I knew that? *I* knew it? How can you say that? What do you mean, too hot to handle? You what???!!! Abort the mission at this stage?!!! Let them go???" The obscenities that followed, loudly into the phone, were chorused sotto voce by the other agents.

The plane was beginning to roll at a brisk pace.

"Are we leaving the others?" someone said, twisting in his seat. The other agents were crowded around the windows.

Blandface seemed to become aware that the plane was moving.

"Stop the plane!" he yelled. "If you ever expect to work for us again, stop now."

"I don't," shouted the pilot, "This was supposed to be easy money. I don't want to end up in a Polish jail."

"They have no business being here. We were assured there would be no problem."

"Well, looks to me like you've got a problem. Those people make a move and we're outta here, I don't care who gets left behind. I've got my clearance."

The plane ceased to pick up speed, but its movement had brought it slightly closer to the terminal. Cordelia could see a small crowd of people, but she couldn't make out any figures, she couldn't tell if Darek was there or if the agents still had their face masks on; she could see the police vans clearly and the Hummer and another vehicle, a white one with markings, that looked like one of the cars that had showed up at the villa that day when the journalists were asking her about the recording.

The leader's cell phone was ringing again. He was listening.

"No," he said, "We're not stopping. He has no jurisdiction to stop the plane. You come. His wife stays until you come. Then I'll let her go."

'His wife,' thought Cordelia, Darek was there then.

"Tell the police chief that we have clearance at the highest level and that he is seriously jeopardizing his career."

He listened again. Then he said, "No, I'm not letting him go. And then, to the pilot, "Carry on. Slowly – give them time to change their minds."

"Yes, sir," the pilot was all willingness.

Blandface was talking, shouting into the phone again, this time, Cordelia surmised, to his contact in Warsaw. "We've got a situation here. And it looks like there are journalists too. So you need to tell them to back off! Just call them and tell them to back off. I'm telling you, just tell them to back off!" And then, apparently, the phone went dead, because he was shouting, "hello, hello?" into it. Then he threw it across the airplane. It struck the wall and fell apart.

The airplane had been taxiing faster.

"All right," he shouted to the pilots, "we take off. Go. Go, go, go."

The airplane continued to taxi for a moment, and then there seemed to be a change of heart amongst the pilots. The plane began to slow.

"What is it? Why aren't we taking off?" shouted Blandface.

"We were just hired to fly an airplane, mister. If you have problems with the police you'd better disembark," the co-pilot drawled. "It's really not our affair. There's someone filming there and they've got our airplane number. We don't want problems."

Blandface's answer was obscene.

"So put the lady off and the guy, like they say. Then we'll go."

Someone had another telephone out, was handing it to Blandface. "Arrange an exchange."

Blandface hesitated a moment and then took the phone. He was obviously speaking to his agents. "All right. Tell them that you'll come and the Arab guy and Zaremba's wife will get off....We'll be on the tarmac. When you're half way across we'll let them go."

Someone was undoing her handcuffs. Someone was taking the hood off the other prisoner. A youngish man, Cordelia saw, with terrified eyes. She supposed she looked the same. He was still gagged. They undid the gag, pulled him to his feet. She was being pulled to hers, shoved towards the entrance. There was a short wait, while the stairs were let down. Down the stairs, no one holding her now. The Syrian man followed.

"Go on," said Blandface, "keep walking." They started across the pavement, in the wind, both hobbling, Cordelia because she was crippled and the other prisoner, no doubt, from ill treatment. They didn't look at one another, but at one point they stumbled into each other and thereafter they supported one another, like a strange

Siamese twin as they made their slow progress down the runway. There was a crowd waiting at the other end, in a sort of shimmer of late autumn light that was occasionally intersected by flecks of snow. They moved onwards, and at some point, a number of still hooded figures left the group and came tearing towards them. Cordelia and the Syrian flinched at their onset, but they swept past, and ran on to the plane. Behind her, Cordelia could hear the roar of its engines again. And then the crowd of people began to have faces and Darek was running towards her. She left her companion, and went to meet her husband. He stopped short in front of her.

Once, she thought, she had seen him look like that. The time he had gone out on the ledge of the sixth-floor window, and then realized he was afraid of heights. That time too, he had been so white in the face.

"Cordelia," he croaked.

"I wrecked the car," she said.

And then there were a great many people about and they were all asking questions. She dropped her eyes, and looked at the pavement, because that's what she always did when there were people about, but she realized vaguely that most of them were large and wearing uniforms, that they were policemen, and vaguely she realized that the two Syrians were standing together, looking haggard, hollow-eyed, and as if they had never known the iniquity of the world before. Then there was a face she remembered from some distant point in the past, only she didn't quite know from where. The face was attached to hands, and the hands were holding a recording device. Someone was filming too. Now she remembered: her journalist acquaintance.

Behind them, the airplane took off into the clouds. The Hummer stood abandoned to one side.

"So you came," she said to the journalist, because he was standing in front of her and some comment seemed required.

"Yes, *Pani* Zaremba, I'm your fervent admirer –"

Why? she wondered: oh yes, because he got a story, what a business.

"*Pani* Zaremba, could you tell…"

He was cut off by a police officer, a man whose assumption of authority told her he was probably the chief. The journalist was being shooed away, was being promised that he could ask questions later.

She didn't follow the conversation of all these people; there were too many bodies about and too much talking. Darek was holding her arm, holding her upright; she turned her head to him.

"Did they catch you?" she whispered.

He bent his head to hear her over the talking around them.

"Did they catch you?" she tried again, only her throat was so dry it was hard to talk.

"No," he said, "Did you think they had?"

She shrugged. "I didn't know. You weren't there. You wanted them stopped."

"You drove the car down to stop them." It was a statement, not a question.

She nodded.

"When I saw the car," he said, "I suspected what had happened. Only I didn't know what they'd done with you." And then, after a pause, "the hideout wasn't where we thought at all, but further on, amongst the trees. It took me a long time to find, it's kilometers round –"

She nodded.

He was continuing: "When I got close I saw them taking Nagib out. I couldn't get back then because a couple of the agents who stayed were in the yard and they'd have seen me, so I had to wait. I called the police, and by the time they came past, I'd got back to the road, so they picked me up. By that time I'd seen the crashed car and you were nowhere about. A moment after I got in the police van, the Hummer came over the hill on its second run. So we followed them on to the airport and stopped them here."

She nodded. So it was all explained, but she didn't really care. She wanted to go away someplace, far away, and be alone. She noticed the police had formed a semi-circle, were listening to their conversation. The two other prisoners waited together to one side, forgotten and shivering.

She waved an arm at them, an arm she could hardly lift. "They'll be cold."

Suddenly they were all being bundled towards the police cars, towards the vans, the cameraman pursuing.

A police officer was saying something to her, very politely, about a statement but it didn't quite register.

"Yes," she admitted in her strained voice, "I wrecked the car. I wanted to stop them but it didn't work."

"It did actually," said Darek, "if you hadn't stalled them, the police would never have arrived on time. It was a matter of minutes."

"That's true," corroborated the police officer. "That's absolutely true."

Shivering, she got into the police car and sat beside Darek. The rest became a blur.

26

Cordelia came to slowly. She was in bed, she realized, and Darek was sitting in a chair beside her. It was an unfamiliar bed in an unfamiliar room. Beyond the open curtains the windows gave onto onion spires that she had seen sometime in the not-too-distant past: a hotel room, she remembered. It was strange yet to wake beside her husband – strange, but very nice and reassuring. She had a feeling that she had woken before, maybe more than once.

"Cordelia? Breakfast is here," said Darek softly.

"Good," she murmured, and went back to sleep.

It was some time later, perhaps much later, when she opened her eyes again. Darek was still sitting beside her. He was watching her with an intent look.

"Hi," he said, "I'm glad you've finally woken."

"Oh, yes," she said, trying to arrange her thoughts, "you said breakfast was here."

"That was six hours ago."

She lifted her head. "But it's dark out," she said, puzzled. She dropped back down into bed. She was incredibly weary and all her muscles hurt, all over her body. She put a hand to her head. The previous day came back: the CIA and – she gasped and reached out her hand to grasp Darek's shirt.

"Did you pay for the car I wrecked?"

"Not yet, but I will." His voice was patient.

"Did I ask you that before?"

"About ten times."

"I'm sorry. I can't seem to think straight, so many things have happened."

She lay still for a moment, while the room and everything in it came into focus and the normal world reasserted itself. She felt as she imagined a shipwreck survivor must feel when he wakes on the island, after the storm.

Her fingers were still clutched on Darek's shirt. She felt the hardness of his arm under her touch. How different male flesh was than her own, she thought, irrelevantly, and how unyielding. And how oddly he was looking at her.

"What's wrong?" she asked weakly, alarm beginning to ring somewhere, and the feeling, too, that she wouldn't be able to respond, that she had no energy left. "Why do you look like that?"

"I was worried about you."

"About me?"

"It's evening. You've been asleep for over twenty-four hours."

"Oh," she said, struggling to rise.

"No," he said, "stay still, you can sleep another twenty-four if you want."

"I'm keeping you from doing something, I'm sure."

"No."

"Have you've been sitting here for long?"

"All day."

She thought about that for a moment. "Why?" she asked at last.

"Because I nearly lost you and I can't quite get over it."

"So you're not still angry?"

"Angry? When was I angry?"

"Well, not angry exactly – but disappointed. When I didn't want you to look for those two. You said I was callous and that you were disappointed. I know you said you didn't mean it, but I thought," she took her hand off his shirt and began to twist her hair, "some little piece of resentment stayed. It didn't just go entirely away. You're not still disappointed in me?"

"What do you think? You've been heroic. You saved two men."

"I never thought about them."

"You didn't?"

"No. Only about you. That's not heroic."

"Jesus. It'll do."

"Oh," she said, relieved, "everything's all right then."

"It's very all right."

"So – is there still any of that breakfast?"

He smiled, "I'll order dinner if you like."

And some time later, after she had eaten a small meal, sybaritically, in bed – "I can't eat in bed," she had said, shocked, when he suggested it, "I never have," and he had replied, "One more new thing and you're exhausted, but this one's not as difficult as some have been lately," – he brought her the newspapers to read.

"Do I want to?" she said, as he took her dinner tray and handed them to her, neatly folded, "It's not bad, is it?"

"No, your journalist friend –"

"He's not my friend," interposed Cordelia, blushing slightly.

"Well, your very professional contact then – knows how to repay a debt. He's done you proud and I don't come out so badly either. He's written it up like an airport thriller."

"Hm, 'thrilling' is not exactly the word I would have used, somehow," said Cordelia dryly as she took the papers.

"Ah, come on, it was fun – or, okay, not fun – exciting."

"Bring back my dinner tray, please, so I can throw something at you," she said, sinking wearily back against the pillows and beginning to read. Yes, the articles put her and Darek in a very good light, first as victims and then as heroes. That was a relief, at least.

"What will happen now?" she asked when she'd finished, "What are the Syrians doing? I suppose they'll never want to see Poland again."

"They've gone back to Warsaw. They're extremely shaken of course, but I have to give it to them – they aren't as full of the desire for revenge as I am. I think the fact that the Polish police came to their rescue is an ameliorating feature for them. They're planning to bring charges in a Polish court."

"Against whom? They won't know who did it – the agents can't be traced. And even if they could, they won't be extradited. Look at the case where those agents kidnapped the fellow in Italy."

"No, they probably can't. It may be possible, however, to find who made the original recording, doctored it, and passed it on to the agents. This journalist traced it to a government office, for instance, and the journalist from *Śmiećpospolity* knows something, or knows one link in the chain; I think it's only a matter of time before a lot of other people have the information as well.

From what you overheard on the plane, that's probably why the CIA's high-level contact backed out. It may be possible to find out who he is – or they are. What I'm saying is it may be possible to catch the Poles who are guilty – but not the Americans."

"That's not very fair."

"No."

"Will you join in making charges?"

"Yes, I think it's important. Unless you don't want to? But whatever we decide to do, if Hasan and Mashrawi press charges, I'm afraid you'll be involved as a witness, whether you like it or not."

She considered for a while, and then answered slowly, "I don't think revenge is a moral attitude. But perhaps the perpetrators shouldn't be allowed to get away with it because they might do it – or something similar – to someone else. What do you think?"

"Yes, that's what I feel too – the latter bit, that is. Although actually, once again, I'm afraid, it's the bad publicity that will be the greatest deterrent, not the court case. I think the most useful thing, for the bigger picture, would be to work towards an investigation into who allowed the CIA to use Poland for its illegal purposes in the first place."

"Yes."

But it was such a dull 'yes' that he took the papers from her hands, and said, "Never mind. It's not really your sort of thing. I won't involve you any more than I can help. It'll just be a little hobby of mine – I dare say it'll keep me interested for years."

"The early hobby horse of your political career."

"Speaking of which, these latest newspaper reports are very flattering, aren't they? I should think they'll probably override any harm from that bit in

Śmiećpospolity." His eyes were alight and his voice full of enthusiasm. "Life's been rivetingly full of ups and downs lately. There hasn't been a dull moment since I met you."

Cordelia put out her hand to him, "I would love a dull moment."

"Oh *kochanie*," he said, kissing her hand and making an attempt at seriousness, "Such a tall order but I'll do my best."

"Thank you," said Cordelia. She couldn't begin to keep up with him. "I do *so* desire to be bored, but right now I'm going back to sleep."

And three days later, after they had answered a great many questions at the police station and filled out long reports and given endless interviews to various branches of the media, it was time to return home.

So when the BMW had been towed from its ditch, and the Jaguar had been recuperated from the hillside and had been found to be miraculously not much damaged, and when the garage-owner in Trawka had been sufficiently well compensated for his vehicle and generosity that he had been left feeling that for him personally renditions were the best thing in the world, they took the road for Warsaw again.

Cordelia was still limp but beginning to feel as if someday she might be human again. It was lovely, she thought, to sit in the Jaguar, to be driven through the countryside on an unexpectedly bright late-autumn day and to have for a space of time no responsibilities, no questions, no need to think. It seemed unlikely that life was going to be completely smooth and uneventful any time in the near future; she had made her peace with the fact – she would simply treasure these respites the more.

As if reading her thoughts, Darek said, "Does this count as a dull moment?"

"It'll do fine."

There was a long pause and then he said abruptly: "I don't need to go into politics."

She looked at him in surprise. "You mean you could just go on with your development business? But you said you were bored with making money."

"Yes, well, I don't need to work actually. I could retire. We could do...other things." He thought for a while, obviously finding 'other things' rather hard to imagine. "Travel, for instance."

"Travel's nice. But you've been to many places already, and so have I. Besides, you like Poland best."

"Well, we could...I don't know, what do people do? We could go to concerts. Maybe I'd learn the difference between what's-his-name and those other what's-their-names. Maybe I'd learn to like opera."

"And maybe not," she suggested. He was completely unmusical. The one time he'd taken her to a concert – solely for her sake, she'd realized later – she'd been aware of his knee jiggling in restlessness beside her the whole time.

He grinned now, beside her in the car, knowing what she was thinking. "Okay, so not concerts. How about plays?"

"No, I can't really see you waiting for Godot."

"No, I can't either. Or not often, anyway. But you say you've changed – maybe I could change."

He couldn't be serious, whatever he might be saying. "Or maybe," she said, "you should forget about what you think I might like and just do what you'd be really good at. I think you'd make a great politician."

"Well, I'd really like to try it. I admit I'm full of plans and ideas. But it occurs to me that I made the decision rather unilaterally. "

"No, you did ask me."

"Yes, and you were generous enough to agree, but," he grimaced, "I wouldn't have taken no for an answer – I'd have badgered you round – so the asking hardly counts."

Her spirits had risen with the altitude, with the sparkling autumn sunlight around them, with the glinting light on hill and crag and valley. They would go home and she would live with her love.

"Because," Darek was continuing seriously, "listen, Cordelia, what you were saying before – that you did it all for me – I'm very moved, but – I don't want any more sacrifices from you. I feel, in justice, that you've made enough. When I asked you to marry me – when I asked it that second time – I really thought I could make your life better. Don't misunderstand me – I don't mean it was altruism, I certainly expected to get quite a bit of pleasure out of the arrangement as well, but I – I thought for you it would be…I wanted to make everything good for you, and instead…" The fact that he was fumbling for words, he who could be so glib, startled and touched her.

"I've never been happier in my life," she said with great firmness.

He glanced at her, smiled, said teasingly, "You look like something the cat dragged in, you can't be happy."

It was a sign of her new self-confidence that this unflattering appraisal did not in any way set her wondering about his affection.

"But I am. These have been the best two months of my life."

"Bar one or two small incidents," he added wryly.

She shrugged, and added slowly, "You know, since I've met you it has often seemed to me that I was like a non-swimmer on a ship who's told 'there's the land' and is tossed into the sea a mile from shore. But since our adventures seemed to have ended all right, I don't think they were really such a bad thing for me. I did make it to land and I feel like whatever happens in the future will be less than this, or at least, not worse. It's given me a certain – well, not courage – that's much too strong a word and I never had any –" She paid no attention to his sound of dissent, but continued, "I've gained a sense that I can survive, I guess. I feel I can take on so much more than I once believed possible. Even your politics and all that. I'm more ready now. Maybe I can even help."

"You're starting to trust yourself." It was a statement, not a question. He added, after a moment, "and consequently, me. God knows why."

"Oh," she said, not telling him the real reason, not saying, 'because your white face convinced me you love me,' but instead, "because you always come out all right, don't you?"

"Thanks recently to you…So we'll be partners then in this too?"

"Well – a little bit anyway."

"Excellent!"

The car soared up the hill and her heart soared with it.

THE END

QUOTES (PART 1)

(Translations mine, except for the statement of the Helsinki Committee)

Ch. 1: 'Then escorted...': Col. Eugeniusz Gardas in an interview with Violetta Ozminskowska, *'Uziemniony'*, *Newsweek Polska, 11/11/2007*

'But what is...': Adam Michnik, *'Pełzający zamach stanu'*, *Gazeta Wyborcza*, 7/30/2007, extended version of an article that appeared in *El Pais*.

Ch. 3: 'The rash and...': statement of the Helsinki Committee in Poland, 15/3/2007

'Since the...': Marek Safjan quoted in Aleksandra Pawlicka, *'Tyle państwa że strach'*, *Przekrój*

'Persons defending...'Jarosław Kaczyński quoted in *'Premier: Osoby broniące doktora G. bronią elit i grup interesów'*, *Gazeta.pl Wiadomości*, 7/5/2007

Ch. 4: 'Please believe...': Janusz Kaczmarek in an interview with Jacek Żakowski, *'Diabeł i ja' Polityka*, No. 34, 25/8/2007

'A politician...': Andrzej Lepper, PAP, 17/5/2004

'They are gangsters...': Janusz Piechociński in an interview with Krystyna Naszkowska *'Kaczyński chciał zagryźć Leppera'*, *gazeta.pl*, 14/7/2007

Ch. 5: 'The Kaczyński brothers...': Artur Zawisza quoted in WZ, *'PiS idzie na wojnę z Platforma i Agorą'*, *Gazeta Wyborcza*, 3/18/2006

'The Kaczyńskis...': Kazimierz Kutz in an interview with Przemysław Szubartowicz, *'Bunt zmiecie Kaczyńskich'*, *Przegląd*, No. 23 (335), 7/6/2006

'Poland is...': Irena Kamińska, *'Jestem sędzią Rzeczpospolitej Polskiej' polityka.pl*, 4/9/2007

Ch. 6: '...the functioning...': Marek Safjan in op. cit.

Ch. 7: 'As far as...': Michnik, op. cit.

Ch. 8: 'Both these parties...': Michnik, op. cit.

Ch. 9: '...the situation...': Andrzej Zoll, *'Czy Polska jest państwem prawa?'*, text of a lecture given at the Polish Academy of Learning on 24/6/2006

Ch. 10: 'The CBA...': Beata Sawicka in an interview with Violetta Ozminkowski, *'Kuszenie Beaty'*, *Newsweek Polska*, 18/11/2007

Ch. 12: 'In the last...': Michnik, op. cit.

'Some former...': *'Metamorfozy Kamińskiego'*, AST, PŚ, GIN, *Newsweek Polska*, 11/11/2007

OTHER SOURCES/NOTES

Ch. 4: summary of Col. Gardas's tribulations based on the article in *Newsweek Polska*, 11/11/2007

Ch. 5: Minister of Justice's statement quoted on *TVN24.pl*, 6/9/2007

Ch. 8: summary of Mr.Kluska's tribulations based on *'Roman Kluska ujawnia nowe fakty o akcji fiskusa skierowanej w jego osobę'* on *Bankier.pl*, 8/6/2004

Ch. 8: Władysław Bartoszewski: 'If PiS is able to govern alone in Poland, as they are striving to do, then my wife and I will leave the country as political emigrants. My wife is 80 years old, I am 85, we want to die in a democracy.'

An interview with Jerzy Kuczkiewicz for *Le Soir*, 19/10/07 – ergo, in fact spoken some weeks after the events of the story.
Ch. 12: on Glock guns and the CBA…see Grzegorz Praczyk, '*CBA: 40 tysięcy złotych za dwa milimetry*', *Polska Dziennik Zachodni*, 19/10/2007

QUOTES and SOURCES (PART 2)

- "*A lot of what needs to be done here will have to be done quietly, without any discussion, using sources and methods that are available to our intelligence agencies, if we're going to be successful. That's the world these folks operate in. And so it's going to be vital for us to use any means at our disposal, basically, to achieve our objective.*" – Dick Cheney, quoted by Jane Mayers, 'Annals of Justice, Outsourcing Terror, The Secret History of America's 'Extraordinary Rendition' Program,' *The New Yorker*, Feb. 14, 2005l

- '*Between the end of 2001 and the end of 2005, flights involving aircraft directly or indirectly operated by the CIA stopped over at European airports more than one thousand times.*' – 'Working Document No. 8 of the European Parliament 2004-2009 Temporary Committee on the alleged use of European countries by the CIA for the transport and illegal detention of prisoners,' November 16, 2006

- "*They picked up the wrong people, who had no information. In many, many cases there was only some vague association* [with terrorism]" – CIA officer quoted by Dana Priest, 'Wrongful Imprisonment: Anatomy of a CIA Mistake,' *The Washington Post*, Dec. 4, 2005.

- '*To carry out its mission, the CTC relies on its Rendition Group, made up of case officers, paramilitaries, analysts and psychologists. Their job is to figure out how to snatch someone off a city street, or a remote hillside, or a secluded corner of an airport where local authorities wait….Members of the Rendition Group follow a simple but standard procedure: Dressed head to toe in black, including masks, they blindfold and cut the clothes off their new captives…Their destinations: either a detention facility operated by cooperative countries in the Middle East and Central Asia, including Afghanistan, or one of the CIA's own covert prisons -- referred to in classified documents as "black sites," which at various times have been operated in eight countries, including several in Eastern Europe*" – Dana Priest, *Ibid.*

- "*…the two countries did host secret detention centres under a special CIA programme established by the American administration in the aftermath of 11 September 2001 to "kill, capture and detain" terrorist suspects deemed to be of "high value". Our findings are further corroborated by flight data of which Poland, in particular, claims to be unaware…*" – Dick Marty, rapporteur for the Council of Europe, 'Secret detentions and illegal transfers of detainees involving Council of Europe member states: second report,' for the Council of Europe Committee on Legal Affairs and Human Rights, 7 June 2007

- "*… the "global spider's web" – the image I used to describe the system of secret detentions and detainee transfers spun out around the world by the US Government and its allies.*" – Dick Marty, rapporteur for the Council of Europe, *Ibid.*

-*"D was like our default option: Detain. Like if we pick up some guy in a raid where we also got one of the HVTs [High Value Detainees]... and maybe we've got nothing on this guy, but obviously we're still gonna hold him."* – source quoted by Dick Marty, rapporteur for the Council of Europe, *Ibid.*

-*'According to our sources, the CIA simply could not embark upon sensitive covert action to dismantle terrorist networks and kill, capture or detain their members overseas without the express knowledge and approval of key US allies – particularly European allies.'* – Dick Marty, rapporteur for the Council of Europe, *Ibid.*

- *'....Poland, where the most important of the C.I.A.'s black sites had been established...*

Poland was picked because there were no local cultural and religious ties to Al Qaeda... Most important, Polish intelligence officials were eager to cooperate. "Poland is the 51st state," one former C.I.A. official recalls James L. Pavitt, then director of the agency's clandestine service, declaring. "Americans have no idea."' – Scott Shane, 'Inside a 9/ll Mastermind's Interrogation,' *The New York Times,* June 22, 2008

- *"Unlike the military's prison for terrorist suspects at Guantanamo Bay...there is no tribunal or judge to check the evidence against those picked up by the CIA. The same bureaucracy that decides to capture and transfer a suspect for interrogation-- a process called "rendition" -- is also responsible for policing itself for errors. ...With operations officers and analysts sitting side by side, the idea was to act on tips and leads with dramatic speed.'* – Dana Priest, *The Washington Post,* December 4, 2005

- *"We conclude that, given the clear differences in definition, the UK can no longer rely on US assurances that it does not use torture, and we recommend that the Government does not rely on such assurances in the future.""* – Statewatch's Observatory: 'Report from the UK House of Commons foreign Affairs Committee: Human Rights Annual Report 2007'

- On the use of children and family members as hostages and for leverage see, amongst other places: Statewatch: 'Off the Record, US Responsibility for Enforced Disappearances' which cites also: 'Statement of Ali Khan,' Apr. 16, 2007, and Olga Craig, 'CIA Holds Young Sons of Captured al-Qaeda Chief,' *Sunday Telegraph* (U.K.), March 9, 2003.